- The
Black Mausoleum

Stephen Deas

GOLLANCZ

LONDON

Copyright © Stephen Deas 2012
Map copyright © Dave Senior 2009

The right of Stephen Deas to be identified as the author
of this work has been asserted by him in accordance with
the Copyright, Designs and Patents Act 1988.

First published in Great Britain in 2012 by Gollancz
An imprint of the Orion Publishing Group
Orion House, 5 Upper St Martin's Lane,
London WC2H 9EA
An Hachette UK Company

A CIP catalogue record for this book
is available from the British Library

ISBN 978 0 575 10048 0 (Cased)
ISBN 978 0 575 10049 7 (Trade Paperback)

1 3 5 7 9 10 8 6 4 2

Typeset by Deltatype Ltd, Birkenhead, Merseyside

Printed and bound by CPI Group (UK) Ltd, Croydon, CRO 4YY

The Orion Publishing Group's policy is to use papers
that are natural, renewable and recyclable products and
made from wood grown in sustainable forests. The logging
and manufacturing processes are expected to conform to
the environmental regulations of the country of origin.

www.stephendeas.com
www.orionbooks.co.uk

True courage is not the brutal force of vulgar heroes,
but the firm resolve of virtue and reason.

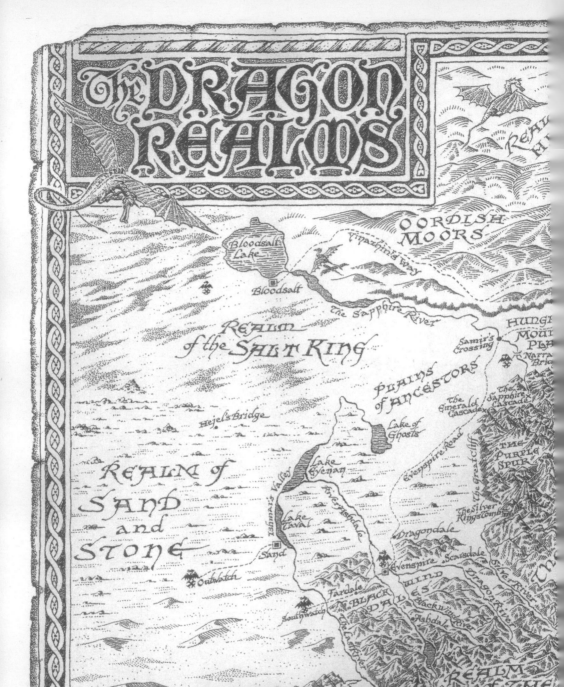

THE DRAGON REALMS

OORDISH MOORS

REALM HI

Bloodsalt Lake

Yinazhin's Way

Bloodsalt

The Sapphire River

REALM of the SALT KING

Samir's Crossing

HUNGI
MOUT
PLA
Natta
Bri

PLAINS of ANCESTORS

The Emerald Cascade

The Sapphire Cascade

Hejel's Bridge

Lake of Ghosts

THE PURPLE SPUR

REALM of SAND and STONE

Lake Cyenan

Ravenspire Road

The Silver Kingstomb

Lake Taval

Dragondale

River Ashgha

Sand

Ravenspire

Scarsdale

Silver River

Outwatch

Dragon River

Fardale

THE BLACK

Blackwind River

Southwatch

The Last River

WIND

DALES

Ashdale

REALM of THE

THE

WORTH

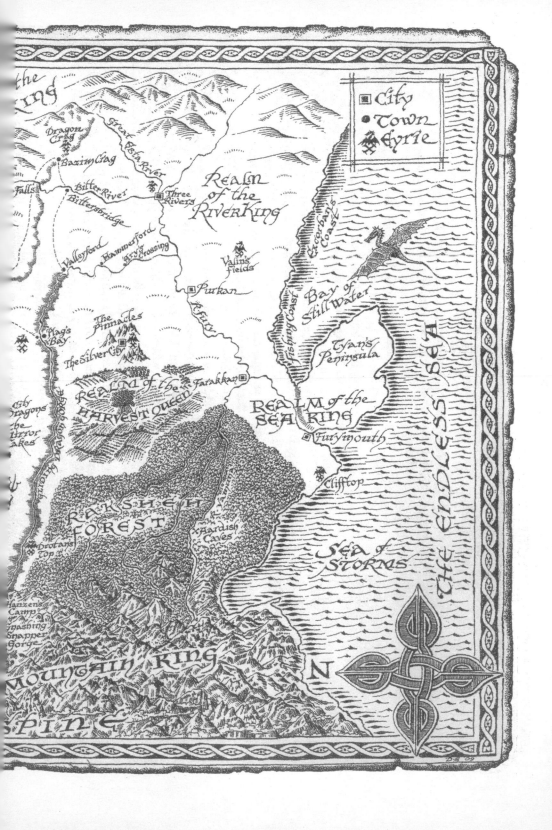

City
Town
Eyrie

the
...KING
Dragon Crag
Bazim Crag
Falls
Bitter River
Bittersbridge
Great Esta River
Valleyford
Hammerford
Fryk Crossing
Three Rivers
Realm of the RIVERKING
Valin's Fields
Purkan

Escorban's Coast
Fishing Coast
Bay of Stillwater
Tyan's Peninsula

Flag's Bay
City Dragons the Mirror Lakes
The Pinnacles
The Silver City
REALM of the HARVEST QUEEN
Farakhan
REALM OF THE SEA KING
Furymouth
Clifftop

Smashing Dragon Strand

RAKSHEH FOREST
Drotan's Top
Haardish Caves

THE ENDLESS SEA

SEA OF STORMS

Hanzen's Camp
Smashing Snapper Gorge
MOUNTAIN KING
SPINE

N

The Silver City

I

Kataros

Twenty-three days before the Black Mausoleum

He wasn't stupid. Kataros had seen the way he looked at her, right from the start. Her jailer. She was a woman in a prison cell, frail and fragile, and he was the man charged with keeping her, a brute, massive and scarred with one crippled hand. In stories that went one of two ways. Either he'd fall in love with her, or he'd try to rape her and she'd get the better of him. Either way, in stories, fate always found a way to save the frail and fragile woman.

Actually no. In the childish stories she remembered the frail and fragile woman never saved herself. In those stories she stayed exactly where she was until some gallant rider on the back of a dragon tore open the door to her cell with his bare hands and whisked her away to a happy-ever-after. But in this story that wasn't going to happen, which left her back where she started. He was interested. He didn't take much trouble to hide it either. He wasn't ugly, at least not on the outside, despite the scars. He was an Adamantine Man, though, and so her story wasn't going to end in love.

There weren't many cells down here. As far as Kataros could tell, there hadn't been any at all until recently. Whatever this place was it had served some other purpose, something more benign, probably until the Adamantine Palace had burned. There were patterns on the floor, tiles, half buried now under a layer of filth. Ornate murals and faux arches decorated the walls. They were all over the place those arches, in almost every room she'd seen as they dragged her here. At the far end, towards the door that was the only way out, hangings lined the walls, intricate pictures of Vishmir and the first Valmeyan duelling in the skies; of the body of the Silver King, carried towards his tomb by men in masks and veils; of Narammed holding the Adamantine Spear, bowing down so he looked almost as though he was worshipping it – she could understand that, knowing now what it did.

Yes, it had been a genteel room once, quiet and out of the way and meant for reflection until someone had slammed in a few crude rows of iron bars and called it a prison.

There was no privacy. The prisoner in the cell next to hers had stared the first time she'd had to squat in a corner. The Adamantine Man, at least, had looked away.

She steeled herself to wait until the gentle sunshine glow of the walls and of the ceiling faded to starlit night. Not that waiting was difficult. She hadn't been fed since she'd arrived and so hadn't eaten for most of a week, and a few more hours would make no difference. The man in the cell next to her had been here longer. He'd been little more than a skeleton when she'd arrived. These days he hardly ever moved. He was dying, slowly but surely.

There weren't any others, just the two of them and three more empty cells. Their floors were like hers, covered in filth crusted dry with time, yet the air in the prison smelled fresh and cool. That was the magic of the Pinnacles at work, the magic of the Silver King who'd come from nowhere and tamed the dragons, who'd built the world that every last one of them had come to know and then been torn down by jealous men.

Kataros spared a glance for the other man. His name was Siff, but she thought of him as something else. The Adamantine Man called him Rat, and she could see that too. He'd talked a lot when they'd first thrown her in the cell beside him; mostly he'd talked about all the things he'd like her to do for him, or the things he'd like to do to her if only he had the chance. That had been before starvation had turned its final bend and the lechery and the leering had given way to ranting and raving. Once, as the madness took him, he'd let slip his name.

He'd told her a lot of other things too, as he slipped away, more than enough to make her wish she'd heard them when he was lucid. He'd come out of the Raksheh. He'd crossed the whole

Realm of the Harvest Queen and yet the dragons hadn't eaten him. You had to admire anyone who could do that yet here he was at death's door, starving. A week or a day or somewhere in between, was all he had left.

She let him go and turned her eyes back to the Adamantine Man. He was watching her. There was no pretence about it – today he was simply staring. Something had changed, had it? Most likely the man who called himself King of the Pinnacles had decided there would be no reprieve. Hyrkallan, that was his name. She'd heard of him before she'd come here, but she hadn't understood his hate for her kind until it was too late. There would be no change to his law, no clemency for any who called themselves *alchemist*, no matter what they might bring. And what *did* she bring? A hope that was no hope at all. An impossible idea. Another mouth for a starving court to feed.

She looked at the Adamantine Man as he stared at her. She bit her tongue until she tasted blood. 'Hey.'

He didn't move.

'Hey!' Half the Adamantine Men she'd ever met thought that the War of the Two Speakers had made them into gods. The other half were mad, as if there was much difference. Some managed to keep some seed of civilisation inside them, but most of the ones she'd seen were violent drunkards, brutes, rapists who thought they had a right to anything and everything. *We are swords. We sate ourselves in flesh as the need comes upon us and then we move on*, that was their creed and they were proud of it. Sometimes they killed dragons like they were supposed to, but usually when they tried that they just died.

This one still didn't answer. His eyes didn't flicker. He was making it hard for her, harder than it already was. The blood in her mouth sharpened her mind. She could see the knowledge in his eye. They both knew what was coming.

'Hey.' She made her voice softer this time. He moved a little now, tilted his chin slightly and looked at her some more, silent as the still air. She forced herself to get up and walk towards him until she was almost against the bars. If he'd wanted to, he could have reached through and touched her.

For a long time they looked at each other.

'I'm hungry,' she said. Each day he brought them water. Water, water, always water, the one thing the Pinnacles never lacked. He never brought food. He never ate in front of them either, but she could smell it on his breath. Food. The answer was in his eyes. *Everyone is hungry.*

'Are you going to ask me to be gentle?' he asked.

2

Skjorl

Eight months before the Black Mausoleum

Bloodsalt. There used to be a city here. Skjorl had never seen it in its glory and never would because it had been gone for more than a year. Burned. Flattened. Crushed. The alchemists said it had been the first city to fall when the dragons had broken loose, the first place they'd gone after shattering the tower at Outwatch. The first and now the furthest from the few companies of Adamantine Men who still survived. Skjorl watched the sun set behind it. There was nothing left, nothing but ash and sand and salt and ruin. The dragons had dammed the river. Changed its course. Whatever they hadn't burned, whoever had stayed hidden, had been left to parch in the relentless sun. The more foolish probably tried to drink from the lake; they would have been the ones to die first, for the waters of Bloodsalt had earned their name. As for the rest, the last survivors? Skjorl had walked past their bones, scattered along the Sapphire valley.

Now he lay on the top of a low hill, squeezed between two rocks and hidden beneath a thorn bush, itself old and dead and dried. The river had found its way through the dragon dam in time, but not until everyone here was long dead. Nonetheless he kept absolutely still. There were still things alive at Bloodsalt. There were dragons.

His fingers tightened around the haft of his axe, closer to him and cared for with more tenderness than any lover. He squinted. Two adults. The same two adults he'd seen every day for more than a week now as he and what was left of his company of men eased their way along the Sapphire valley towards the lake and the ruins of the old city. Two adults and perhaps a score of hatchlings. More dragons than any of them had seen in the year since the Adamantine Palace burned.

The Adamantine Men had done their duty when the dragons first awoke. To eyrie after eyrie the word had come before the dragons did. Quietly and without fuss, the alchemists had slipped poison into the potions they fed to adults and hatchlings alike. Quietly and without fuss, the dragons had burned from the inside and died; and while they were burning, the Adamantine Men had taken their hammers and their axes. They'd marched into the hatcheries and the egg rooms and they'd done what needed to be done. In some places there had been fighting between the Adamantine Men and soldiers loyal to an eyrie master or the dragon-king or -queen who owned him. Always fights that the Adamantine Men won. Across the realms eggs had been smashed, dragons poisoned.

Except here. Here and Outwatch. Had Bloodsalt had any warning? They'd had seconds at Outwatch. Seconds, and that had still very nearly been enough.

'Any kills, boss?' whispered a voice in the thorns beside him. 'I don't see any kills.'

'No.' Skjorl shook his head. There was nothing to eat near Bloodsalt for anything larger than a sand lizard, much less a dragon. The adults probably flew up into the Oordish Moors to feed, hundreds of miles away, but they always came back. The hatchlings? He didn't know if they'd go so far. He was hoping not, otherwise they were all wasting their time.

'Bollocks.' The thorns rustled angrily. Skjorl stayed silent. No kills meant nothing to poison. Until there was something to poison, they'd stay where they were, hiding in the dust and the salt, drinking brackish water, eating their own boots and being bitten to death by sandflies. He could live with that if it meant taking down a dragon. Skjorl had his own cask of dragon poison, more than enough for a full-grown adult. He had his axe too, in case they got as far as the eggs. Yes, he could wait right enough.

They'd had a hatchling in a cave at Outwatch. A rogue the mad queen had made. The old greybeard who ran the eyrie had let slip what it was and that had been good enough for Skjorl, good enough to kit up in dragon-scale armour, dismantle a scorpion and carry it down to the caves. The dragon had strained at its chains and spat fire at them, but those chains had held. They'd carried the scorpion in pieces to the far end of its cave, to the hole in the cliff face where the sunlight and the air poured in. They'd carefully built it back together while the hatchling had watched them like a hawk. Somehow the first shot had missed. Then Skjorl had looked outside and he'd seen the white horror gliding through the sky towards them. Riderless. Coming home. The greybeard eyrie master had seized the scorpion for himself then. Skjorl hadn't waited. He'd run, shoving his men out in front of him, last one out slamming the door as he went. Didn't pause to see what became of the eyrie master. Death walked beside every Adamantine Man. When it came it came quick and you went one of two ways, crispy or crunchy. They'd run and run, all through the tunnels under Outwatch as the citadel came smashing down. They'd taken their hammers and their axes. Eggs smashed. Hatchlings murdered, the little ones butchered, the bigger ones fed poison. He'd taken servants, slaves and Scales, and battered them and strapped skins of poison to them, then thrown them to the howling monsters to be devoured. They'd have been dead anyway if he hadn't. And amid the screaming and the blood and the fire that came after, an unexpected smile had stretched across his face. The dragons had awoken. The end of the world had begun. It was what he'd been made for.

The same smile was still there. Crispy. The greybeard eyrie master had gone the crispy way. For ordinary men there was a third way too, the starving-to-death-under-the-ground way; that was something that would never happen to him, but he didn't mind a bit of waiting, not if there was a reason for it. In Outwatch he'd waited them out and they'd left. Left him and his company, what remained of them, stranded in the middle of the desert, a hundred miles from anywhere, surrounded by ash and ruin. It had been a lot like this.

The sun slipped below the horizon and darkness wrapped the salt plains. Skjorl eased himself out from under his thorn bush and crept back down the hill and into the tumble of rocks where the other Adamantine Men were waiting, still and quiet. There were seven of them left, a poor shadow of the fifty-odd who had left the Purple Spur three months ago. There was Jex, who'd been with him in Outwatch and ever since. Vish too. Jasaan he'd picked up on his way south, in what was left of Sand after the dragons had finished with it. Kasern, Relk and Marran, they'd come later when he'd trekked his way from Sand all through the dead Blackwind Dales as far as the Silver River and finally found what passed for the remains of civilisation, hiding out in the caves and chasms that reached from one side of the Spur to the other. Jex and Vish, they were his squad. They'd spent the best part of a year together, struggling every day not to be dead. The rest were all Adamantine Men, and three months creeping beside the waters of the Sapphire had told him everything he needed to know. They were alive while everyone else wasn't. They were survivors then. The best.

'Stay alive?' Vish tossed over a skin half full of water from the river. It tasted warm and foul. Everything out here was too hot. Skjorl drank, though. The taste was something he'd come to know. The bitterness and nausea and blood-iron tang of the powders the alchemists had given them. Mix with water and drink at least once a day so the dragons don't find you. Skjorl had no idea what that meant or how it worked, but it was true that dragons usually had a way of knowing where you were, no matter how well you hid. They'd found that out the hard way crossing the Blackwind Dales.

He tossed the skin to Jex. It was also true that on their trip up the Sapphire valley the dragons had seemed not to notice them. Maybe they'd been lucky, although seven left from more than half a hundred was an odd kind of luck. But he took his potion, however bad it tasted, and he'd keep taking it. Given how many of them were left, there wasn't much chance they'd be running out any time soon.

'Waiting, is it?'

Skjorl nodded. Waiting. Three months it had taken them to get this far. Soon enough they'd be done and then maybe they'd spend three months getting back home again, and if that's how it was, that's how it was.

Jex tipped the skin and poured water into his mouth. He tossed it back towards Vish but Kasern snatched it out of the air. He picked up another one and held them out in one hand, dangling them next to each other. 'What's that then?'

Relk shook his head and turned away. Jex and Vish were laughing.

'Tits,' Marran spat. 'That's what that is. I could murder for a good pair of tits.'

'That's not just any tits.' Jex rubbed his crotch and nudged Skjorl. 'That woman from Scarsdale, she had tits like that, eh? Old and saggy and wrinkled and yet oddly firm.' He chuckled to himself.

'More like two giant balls in a giant ball sack, they were.' Vish wrinkled his nose.

'Didn't see you minding at the time.'

'Didn't see anyone minding at the time,' grunted Skjorl. Four months it had been when they'd reached Scarsdale. Four months from Outwatch. Past Sand, black and smashed to bits. Past Evenspire, which just wasn't there any more except the Palace of Paths, so big and so massive that even dragons couldn't knock it flat. Four months and mostly all they'd seen were blackened corpses. Everything in the Blackwind Dales was dead even before the dragons. And then they'd got to Scarsdale. Twelve people they'd found there, hiding in the copper mines, creeping out at night for water from the Dragon River, eating fish and fresh-water crabs and whatever roots and leaves they could find.

'Shit-eaters, all of you,' grumbled Jasaan. 'And what about the other one? You remember her?'

This again. Skjorl tensed.

'Sweet Vishmir but she was ripe. If she was here now …' Vish leered.

'If she was here now you'd tie her up and show her your adamantine cock.' Jex licked his lips.

'Damn right.'

'Not before I showed her mine. Except I wouldn't be needing any rope. She'd be begging for it.'

Skjorl punched Jex in the arm. 'Old soldiers first, boy.' He scowled. 'Marran, put them away. We've none of us had a woman for months. My balls are full to bursting.'

'Any more of this and I'm going to start wanting to fuck the sandflies!'

'Lai's dick!' Jasaan waved his arms. His voice rose over the others. 'You ...' He had words to say. Anyone could see that, but they were old words and had been said before, and no one else gave a shit about Scarsdale and all the things that had happened there, no one except Jasaan. 'You're—' But by then Skjorl had slipped like an eel round behind him and clamped a hand firmly over his mouth.

'Shhh,' he whispered in Jasaan's ear. 'These lovely potions don't make a dragon deaf, so keep your voice *down*. You got something to say to me, you say it. But quiet like.'

Jasaan glared. He shook his head.

'No, I thought not.'

The soldiers fell quiet then, sitting still and alert as the sun sank and the sky darkened. They'd become night people in the last year and a half. The dragons flew in daylight and slept – or whatever it was they did – at night, and so the Adamantine Men had learned to be otherwise. At night they moved. Never too far though, never so far that they couldn't be sure of shelter come the dawn. Sometimes that meant they travelled for hours, found nothing and went back to where they'd been the night before. On the worst part of their trip up the Sapphire valley they'd spent six nights in the same cave. And that had been trouble too. The longer you stayed in a place, the more signs you left. Dragons were good at spotting signs.

Back then they'd numbered more than twenty-five. Now they were seven. Seven was a lot easier to hide. The way back would be quicker than the way here. A month, Skjorl thought. Not three. He crossed his fingers and hugged his axe and thought a little prayer to the Great Flame.

'Fucking dragons,' spat Marran.

Skjorl closed his eyes. 'Easy, lads,' he murmured. 'They'll go hunting sometime. We just wait here until they do.' He stretched. 'Then we slip in, slow and easy and do what Adamantine Men were born to do. We kill dragons.' He grinned and let out a little growl. 'A month from now we'll be back near the Spur and Jex can stop making love-eyes at the sandflies.'

'Yeah.' Vish laughed. 'He can make them at the snappers instead.'

'Snapper wants a piece of me, it'll be a sharp one.' Relk gripped his spear.

'Yeah, but Jex's got a spear that's every bit as hard, just not quite as sharp.' A low rumble of laughter rippled among the men. Skjorl looked about. Jasaan was gone, moved off a little while back after Skjorl had told him to shut up. It was dark now, desert dark with clear air and a bright moon and a thousand stars. Still, he wasn't about to get up and look for him. Man wanted to be on his own, that was his privilege, especially at night when there weren't dragons overhead. He grinned to himself. Jasaan was probably thinking about sandflies too. Or of the woman from Scarsdale. Not the old one, but the young one. The one with the soft skin and the hair like fur. How grateful she'd been for an Adamantine Man.

Sometimes men did terrible things, Skjorl had come to realise. When they knew there was no one to hold them to account, yes, sometimes men did terrible things. And sometimes they enjoyed them more than was right. And that was just the way of the world.

He sniffed, looked up, heard the slightest noise and was on his feet in a moment, sword half drawn. But it was only Jasaan. He cocked his head. 'Feeling better? No harm meant. I know how it is.'

Jasaan shrugged. There was hate in those eyes. Skjorl didn't even need to see it any more, he'd seen it so much. But Jasaan was a weak one. Too bothered with staying alive. He looked away and spat. Jasaan tipped his head back towards the quiet rustling waters of the Sapphire. 'Went for a little walk. Know what I found? I found a tunnel half filled with water. Want to know where it goes?' He pointed straight towards the distant remains of Bloodsalt and to the dragons that stood between them. 'That's where. Right into the city.'

3

Kataros

Men did terrible things. The Adamantine Men were finding that out for themselves, but alchemists remembered that it had been like this before. An almost forgotten time, lost under dust and layers of brittle parchment, a time before Narammed, before the speakers, before the Empire of the Blood-Mages, before the Silver King. Before all that, when there had still been dragons and there had still been men, and in that time, men had done terrible things. They'd done them to survive.

The Adamantine Man got up from his stool. Kataros watched him. His movements were slow and weary as though everything was inevitable.

'Hungry?' He shrugged and showed Kataros his keys. He had one for each of them, for her and the half-dead Rat. He opened Rat's cell and poked him. Rat groaned. The Adamantine Man shrugged again. 'Well he's not dead yet, but you can eat him if you want. I won't stop you.'

Kataros shuddered. They'd come to that under the Purple Spur too, eating the dead to survive. Sooner or later they'd come to that here as well, although it was something that no alchemist would ever do. Blood was power. Blood was magic and not to be tainted.

The Adamantine Man closed Rat's cell and locked it again. He moved slowly as though he had all time in the world. No one would come down here for hours, not until the walls and ceilings of the Pinnacles started to shine to declare to them all that outside, in the realms now ruled by the dragons, the sun had risen once more. Kataros looked at his crippled left hand. Half of it was little more than lashed up flesh and bone. It was an old injury, long healed. Two of his fingers were useless stumps.

'Take your time, woman.'

Time? The Adamantine Man might have had as much of it as he wanted, but not her, nor Rat either. 'So what did you do?' she asked.

'Do?' He laughed and fumbled for the keys again and slid one into her lock. 'What did *I* do?'

'Shouldn't you be out there. Getting eaten and killing dragons.'

'Oh I've killed dragons.' He chuckled to himself as he turned the key and eased open her door. He looked her up and down, his eyes lingering between her legs. Kataros took a step away. The corners of his mouth curled into a grin. 'You're going to rot and starve here like him.' He glanced at Rat. 'I could snap your neck if you like. Make it quick. Or … we could do something else.'

She took another step back and shook her head. The Adamantine Man took a step as well, backing her against the far wall of the cell.

'No?' He rubbed his crotch. 'So how hungry are you?'

She shook her head again and cringed away, biting her tongue to keep the taste of iron in her mouth. Blood, that was the key. Blood would set her free.

When the Adamantine Man moved, he moved fast. He closed the distance between them in two quick steps and then he had his good hand around her throat, almost lifting her off her feet, crushing her against the wall. The other hand, the crippled one, groped at her. He was strong. She flinched, struggling, but he had her fast, pinning her with the weight of his body. She could see the faint scars on his face clearly now, lines of pale skin. Knife cuts, not the kind of wound you got from fighting dragons.

'I'll kiss you,' she stammered. There. Plant the idea.

He threw back his head. 'Yes, witch. You will.'

There was no need to feign her fear or her revulsion. She tried to shake her head. His free hand was working on his belt. His breathing was heavy, his heart beating faster.

'Your sort brought this on us all,' he grunted, forcing her down. 'You deserve everything you get. You did this. You killed us all.

Now since you're so hungry, you can eat. If you're not a good little witch, I *will* snap your neck after I have you.'

A little thought came. *Let him. Do it his way. Do what he wants. It'll be easier. It'll be more certain.* The thought came and then it went and she was damned if any man, Adamantine or otherwise, was ever going to force her to anything, not now, not ever again. As his fingers gripped tight in her hair, she spat into her palms, tasted the iron, and then raked her nails down the outside of his thigh hard enough to draw blood, *his* blood, as hard as she could. She slapped the palm of her hand against the wound and held it tight, two droplets of blood mixing together. *Please please please be quick . . .*

He snarled, pulled her up and threw her away.

'You don't like it rough?' Her voice sounded frail and thin to her, desperately fragile.

'I'll show you rough, witch.' He came at her, trousers round his ankles. She closed her eyes and reached out for the blood she'd smeared over him. Her blood and his. Such a tiny, tiny link. Nothing. *Almost* nothing.

'Kiss me,' she quivered.

Fingers locked around her chin. For one fleeting moment the Adamantine Man looked confused. She put a hand around his neck and pulled him closer, pressed her mouth to his and wormed her tongue between his lips. His hands ran over her as she licked her blood into his mouth.

'Now you're going to bleed, witch!' He tore himself away and towered over her, a rampant animal thing.

'I already did,' she murmured. 'And because of that, you will never touch me again.' She felt it now, her blood inside him. As he reached for her with his huge hands, so she reached for him inside her head, following the path of blood.

'Stop!'

It was a whispered word inside her cell, barely rippling the air, but inside the Adamantine Man's head it was a command to shake mountains. She knew this was so because she'd felt it herself once, when her own master had done the same to her, when he'd bound her to him and elevated her from a Scales, a failure, to be an alchemist again. The binding was a price that she'd learned only after it was too late.

His eyes rolled back. Most men would have fainted; this one reeled but stayed on his feet. Very slowly his eyes found her face again. He lunged towards her and then paused.

'No,' she whispered. Now she had him, she wanted to laugh, laugh at how stupid he looked with his trousers round his ankles. She wanted to laugh to take away the scream that was clenched inside her.

'What have you done to me, witch?' he snarled.

'Dress yourself.' Reaching through the blood was an effort, but for now she barely noticed. Later she would have to conserve her strength and her touch would be more gentle.

He did as he was told, trembling now, fearful. She smiled. Even an Adamantine Man would crack in the end.

'What have you done?' he asked again.

Her eyes glittered. She bared her teeth. 'Now you know how it feels to be weak and helpless.' It was hard not to make him take a knife to himself, right there and then, hard not to remember another time, another place, a desert canyon, a rushing river, the river men all over her, the roar of the dust they'd given her in her head and then another roar, of fire and dragons, everywhere dragons …

No. She shook herself. Maybe later, when they were in the Raksheh and she'd found what she was looking for, maybe then, but for now she needed him. 'You're going to help me,' she said shortly. 'You're going to take me out of here. You're going to take me to the Yamuna River, to the Raksheh and then to the Aardish Caves. You're going to help me find the Black Mausoleum. You want to. For you this shall become the most important thing in the world. For all of us. If anyone gets in our way or tries to stop us, no matter who or what they are, you are not going to let them.'

She watched him closely, watched his slack face as her words reached through from her blood, mingling her desires with his. The Adamantine Man went out of her cell. He stood, uncertain, as she followed and closed the door behind her. She was free.

He looked puzzled. 'How?' he asked.

'With whatever means you have; but you will fight to the death before you let anyone take me back here.'

'They'll kill us both.'

'Then find a way so they don't!' She nodded towards Rat in the other cell. 'And he has to come too.'

4

Skjorl

Eight months before the Black Mausoleum

Bloodsalt. Stuffed away in the corner of the realms with nothing much around it except salt flats and desert. Blisteringly hot days, cold nights, no food, no nothing. A man came out here, he might wonder why anyone had ever built a city in such a desolate place. Might wonder, that was, until he tripped over his first nugget of gold just sitting there at the edge of the Sapphire. It had meant something once, gold. Fat lot of use to anybody now.

Adamantine Men had had no use for gold, even back then. The old Bloodsalt, the alive one filled with people, had had no use for the Guard, but it turned out that Vish had been there once, back in Hyram's time, when the new speaker had flown in with his grand master alchemist and taken a few of his Adamantine Men with him to show off. Vish had seen the city and that was why he was here, and because Vish was in Skjorl's company, that was why Skjorl was here too.

'Fucking hole at the end of the earth, if you ask me,' grunted Vish. 'Don't know why old shaky even brought us out here.'

Hyram and his alchemist were both dead now, so no one was ever going to find out. Not that any of the Adamantine Men cared. The waking of the dragons had changed everything, and now nothing mattered except food and water and watching the sky.

They moved along the slabs of rock and the loose shingle beside the Sapphire. The whispering of the water drowned their footfalls. They had an easy stealth to them, one that came with years of practice. Quiet was easy. Quiet came with careful, and a man who wasn't careful, well, out here he was dead.

'Here.' Jasaan held up his hand for them to stop. He pointed. The river drifted on towards Bloodsalt Lake, an inland sea almost as wide as a whole realm and yet never so deep that a man standing upright on its bed wouldn't still be breathing air. Where Jasaan was pointing, in the shadows of the far bank, a low stone building butted up against the river. Skjorl climbed a little higher and then he could see a line of something in the levelled sands, running from the water and straight into the heart of the city. Or where its heart had been, before the dragons had eaten it.

'So there's a tunnel that goes from here into the city.' Skjorl scratched his head as he eased back down to his men. 'What's that for?'

'Takes water from the river into the city cisterns,' said Vish.

Jasaan shrugged. 'I had a look. It's about knee deep. We could walk through it.'

'You mean it's like a canal?'

'Suppose.'

'With a roof on it? Why put a roof on a canal?' Not that it mattered. What use it was right now, that was what mattered.

Vish sniffed. 'Goes straight to the city cisterns. I saw them when I came with the Speaker. They're huge. And they're cool and damp.'

He nodded and Skjorl nodded back. Dragons liked to leave their eggs somewhere like that. Out here in the desert there simply wasn't anywhere. Or at least so Skjorl had thought.

'Worth a look then.' He shrugged. The hard part with dragons wasn't finding them. Man wanted to kill a dragon, he needed to be bloody sure the dragon had no idea he was there. Slip in, poison their kill, slip away and never be seen. Smashing eggs came after, when the dragons that had laid them were dead. If you ever got that far.

On the other hand, tunnels and water could mean people. Not that anyone was still alive out here, but he supposed he ought to at least look like he'd been told.

No. Not *people*. Alchemists. If it was just people, well there were people everywhere. Like cockroaches. Hiding under every stone and in every cave until a dragon sniffed them out. Just hungry mouths to feed; the last thing the Purple Spur needed was more of *them*. No, it was alchemists he'd been sent out here to find. Bloody waste of time.

'If there's eggs there, we don't touch them unless I say,' he growled. 'And that means we keep away from them.' In case one hatched while they were there but he didn't need to come out and say it, not to men like these. 'We look in case there's people. Then we take the adults. Eggs last.'

'People?' Jex laughed and shook his head. 'There's no people here.' And Skjorl reckoned he was right.

First thing was crossing the water though, easier said than done. The Sapphire might have been sluggish down this close to the lake, but it was wide and too deep for a man to wade. Jex went first since he could swim. He took a rope. The rest of them stripped, floating the things that had to stay dry on their shields and hauling themselves on Jex's rope. It took a while. Skjorl checked the moon. A third of the night gone, but that wasn't too bad. The covered canal would be a perfect place to spend the day if they could get into it.

The entrance was in the riverbank. A channel nearly a dozen strides wide had been cut into it. Shallow, just like Jasaan had said, but the channel narrowed inside and grew deeper until they were waist-deep in warm stagnant water. The moonlight quickly faded to nothing. The darkness inside was almost absolute.

'It's not flowing,' muttered Jex. 'Must be blocked somewhere. Can't spend the day here, not in this shit.'

Skjorl frowned. Had to agree with that. Man couldn't be standing upright when he was supposed to be resting.

'We could make little beds out of our shields and float on them maybe?'

'Daft bugger.' Skjorl scratched his head. 'Push on for now.' They had a place to shelter not far away if they crossed back to the other side. Less than half the night gone. Still safe to press forward.

'Ouch.'

At the front Jasaan stopped. Skjórl couldn't see his hand in front of his face, it was that dark. Some fifty yards behind them, the tunnel entrance was just a patch of black not quite as black as the rest.

'What is it?'

'Gate. Bars. Hold on.'

Skjorl stood his ground, stock still. He'd been in tunnels this dark before, plenty of times. Darkness didn't bother him, but other things did. Things *lived* in tunnels and dead ends made his skin crawl.

'Some sort of grille. Kasern, you still behind me? Give me a hand.'

Down in the mines of Scarsdale, for example. Plenty of tunnels there, and plenty of dead ends too. For once he'd been the hunter, sword in hand, already stained with blood. In Sand they'd explored the passages under the monastery. Plenty of tunnels there too. They'd found scholars and Adamantine Men and a friendly place for a day or two before they'd moved on, underneath the hell that the dragons had made above.

And before that there had been Outwatch, where they'd thought they were safe under the ground. Dragons were huge and the caves were narrow. Safe, as long as you were deep enough to escape their fire. He didn't know what had happened after he'd fled the room and left the greybeard to his scorpion, but the old fool hadn't killed the hatchling like he was supposed to and then someone had smashed down the door and the little bastard had come after them. Thin and wiry, all teeth and claws and flames, and whatever they'd thought about being safe, they'd found they were wrong. Alchemists knew better now. Jex and Vish knew better too. They were the ones who'd lived to talk about it, and the caves under the Purple Spur had grown a lot more big heavy doors after they'd embraced Skjorl and his men.

'Got it.'

Metal grated on metal, the sort of sound that carried much too far inside a cave. Skjorl winced. He had to remind himself: this time the dragons were on the outside. 'What is it?'

'Metal gate. Keeps animals out.'

Keeps animals out? Worth remembering for the way back then. 'Keep a hatchling out?'

'Don't know. Might. Might not.'

There wasn't much for it but to press on. 'Another hour,' Skjorl growled. 'We find a place we can stop for the day by then or we turn back.' He heard Jex and Relk groan. Knew how they felt – tracking back always felt like a waste, but that was how you stayed alive when there were dragons to be stalked. Impatience, that was the killer, always was. One thing you could always do, one way you'd always win against a dragon, was wait it out. Even if it knew you were there, if you waited it out, eventually it would go away. They got bored. 'I'll just mention Samir's Crossing and wait for you lot to shut up,' he growled. Half the men they'd lost, they'd lost at Samir's Crossing.

They sloshed on through the dark, slowly and carefully, wary of rubbish and rubble under the water. Didn't dare light a torch even if they could, in case there were holes in the roof. One gleam, one glimmer, one flash of light in the wrong place, that would be the end of them all. For all Skjorl knew, there were hatchlings right outside.

'Who builds a covered canal anyway?' he muttered under his breath.

'Means we can keep on going through the day though. Get this over with,' murmured Vish, and Skjorl hadn't thought of that. So set in their routine of sleeping through the day and walking at night, he never stopped to think about the *why* of it any more. Dragons didn't see so well in the dark. Mostly they didn't fly at night, so that's when you walked. In the day they had eyes like eagles. A man wanted to stay alive, he walked at night and he hid when the sun came up. Always.

He was on the brink of turning them all around and marching back to find a place where they could do just that when Vish stopped again. The roof had fallen in. Skjorl could see the stars in the sky and his hand in front of his face again. For maybe twenty, thirty yards the tunnel was crushed into a jumble and tumble of bricks and broken stone.

'Hold.' He clambered up, slow and careful and silent. The moon was gone now; it was later than he'd thought. Eyes peeled, peering into the starlight. Not that he had much chance of telling the difference between a resting dragon and yet another sand-swept boulder, but still, you had to try.

Nothing. He skirted the rubble and the canal went on, roof intact once more. He could almost see it: some dragon had come here, chasing after some whim of its own, and stood on a ridge of stone that turned out not as solid as it had looked. Or maybe it had been done on purpose. Maybe the dragons that destroyed Bloodsalt had come here. Crushed the veins that fed the blood-water to the city after they'd smashed and burned it to ashes, in case their dam didn't work. That was a thing you learned about dragons, if you watched them. Yes, they got bored, but until they did, they were nothing if not thorough.

Down where there was a roof again the canal bed was dry and covered in patches of old dead prickle-grass. The air smelled different. Old dry earth-dust, fine as flour, the sort to fill your nose and your throat and make you choke. No water here, not for a long time. Likely as not the cisterns were dry and empty then; but if the tunnel went on long enough to keep them out of sight, they had a place to hide in the day. He crept back.

'Get your scarves on, nice and wet.' He sniffed. 'What's the water in here like?' Hadn't thought to taste it.

'Tastes like shit,' muttered Jex.

'Tastes like blood,' said someone else. 'Salt and iron.'

'Leave it then.' He paused. Tried to think about how much water they were carrying. Not something he'd had to worry much about while they'd been following the river, but away from it, even out of the sun, desert heat was quick and deadly to a man who didn't have water. Found that one out the hard way, fleeing the ruins of Outwatch when the dragons had finally left them alone.

They had enough, though. Good for a day or two before they'd have to turn back. Time to get to the city and take a good look to know that no one was still alive. Maybe the dragons would be kind and bring back a kill. He wondered for a bit if maybe he should send the others away. Bring water from the river. Hide up here at night, right up and close, just him and his axe.

They walked on through the old canal, holding on to one

another in the darkness. Skjorl took the front. His company, his job, feeling his way with his feet. Here and there pushing a loose stone out of the way so no one would trip and stumble and make a noise. For the most part, the canal bed was flat and smooth and sandy. Easy going until he took a step and there suddenly wasn't anything under his foot. He had just enough balance to let himself go and sit down hard, both feet dangling over an invisible edge. 'Well that'll be the cisterns then,' he whispered, as much to himself as anyone. 'Oi! Vish . . .'

Shit. He remembered where he was just a little too late. Sitting on the edge of some underground place where sound would carry like water over an oilcloth. No idea how far below him the floor was, or whether there even was one, or how big the space in front of him might be. For all he knew, there could be a clutch of dragon eggs right beside him.

He felt movement. 'Boss?' Vish. Short for Vishmir, the same name as probably half the soldiers in the Adamantine Guard, but it always got shortened to Vish. Back before the war every legion had had half a dozen of them or more. He'd had Tall Vish, Loud Vish, Fat Vish, Blue Vish and Vish the Hands. Tall Vish and Blue Vish had died when the dragons smashed the Adamantine Palace. Loud Vish had gone at Outwatch, done by the hatchling that had hunted them through the tunnels. Fat Vish, well he'd just vanished somewhere in the northern Blackwind Dales. Dead, or else maybe he went back to throw in his lot with the survivors at Sand. Bad choice, but it probably hadn't seemed so bad at the time.

Vish the Hands had died at Scarsdale. No doubt about that one, since he'd died with Skjorl's stabbing sword through his guts. Now they had just the one Vish left. Quiet Vish he'd been once, but there was no need for that now. He was the last one and just Vish would do. Skjorl had come to think of him as their lucky charm.

'Boss?'

Skjorl shook himself. He pulled Vish down to whisper into his ear. 'You ever come and see these cisterns when you were here?'

'Nothing much else to do.'

'That where we are?'

'Canal empties right into it.'

'How far down is it?'

'It was full of water, boss. I got no idea.'

'Get a rope.' The air still smelled dry. If there had been water here once, it was long gone, same as in the tunnel. They tied a rope in a harness around him and lowered him slowly. He still couldn't see a thing but he felt at the wall as he went. Old dry brick or stone. Big slabs with sandy mortar between them. Crumbs of it fell away under his fingers, hissing down the walls. Too small and quiet to gauge any depth. No sound of hitting water, though. No water meant no people. Maybe no eggs too.

Meant this was a waste of time.

His feet touched something hard that crunched under his weight and then he was on solid ground. He climbed out of the harness and gave a few tugs on the rope, sending it back up. They'd wait for his call now. He felt in his knapsack for the alchemists' firebox, wrapped in an oiled piece of rabbit skin to keep it dry. A big handle on the top to hold once it was lit, a little winder to start it burning. Not like the cold smokeless lamps the alchemists made for living under the Purple Spur, this was more the sort of lamp Skjorl understood, with a wick and a warped glass screen and sweet-smelling oil.

He had it in his hand, ready to light. Instinct stopped him. Lighting a lamp in a place like this was like crossing a rising river. Once done, there was no return. He'd get to see whatever was in this chamber, but whatever was here, it would get to see him right back.

Then again it was that or stand here doing nothing.

He wound the handle. A small flare plumed between his hands. Dimmed again to almost nothing and then the wick caught and the light rose once more. There was a dragon egg right next to him. Tall as he was and as wide as a barrel. Under his feet were brittle pieces of shell. Dry, thank Vishmir. Whatever had hatched, it was weeks ago.

The fire in his hands grew stronger. He looked around. Deep shadows everywhere. Didn't hear anything except his own slow breaths. But there were eggs everywhere. The most he'd ever seen in one place. At Outwatch, one of the biggest eyries in the realms, they'd had eighty-six. He'd counted them as his company had smashed them. This – this was something new.

He thought for a bit. They couldn't go on, not with this here. They'd have to go back, all the way to the river where there was water, and they didn't have time for that, not before the sun came up. So they'd be in the tunnel, quiet as mice for the whole day, praying to the Great Flame. They could do that. Or they could set to work and do what Adamantine Men were meant to do. Kill dragons.

'Jex! Vish! Jasaan! Hammers and axes.' He set the firebox down and swung his own axe off his back. His lady, his lover, and in his hands she felt warm and strong. 'I serve the speaker,' he muttered under his breath as he lifted her. 'The Guard obeys orders. From birth to death. Nothing more, nothing less.' *Go to Bloodsalt. Look for survivors. Smash eggs. Kill dragons.* Nothing about coming back again. He brought the axe down on the nearest shell. The brittle outside split and shattered, and the axe bit down into the lifeless hatchling within. He struck again and then a third time, until he'd hacked the hatchling's head from its body. The next one was the same. They'd all be like that. Hatchlings, all grown and ready to break out of their eggs, just sitting inside their shells, quiet and still, waiting for the spark of life.

Jex was down. No questions; he just got his axe out and got on with it. The quicker the better. Needed to be done before daylight. Dragons mostly left their eggs alone, but you could never be sure. Vishmir's cock! There were hundreds of them! You could see that, now Jex had laid his own firebox down and lit a few rags and tossed them in a circle around him. The cisterns were huge. One vast empty space held by a forest of columns. Skjorl could just about make out the vaulted roof made of hundreds of little domes. Couldn't see the far walls though.

He paused for a moment. There had to be another way in. A dragon had come down here to lay, so there *had* to be another way in. A big one. Somewhere or other they must have brought the roof down.

'Vish. When you were here – how big was this place?'

Vish shrugged. 'Huge. They took us on a boat that way.' He pointed. Skjorl's best guess was he was pointing towards Bloodsalt Lake. 'Didn't see all of it either.'

'Where did you get in.'

'Up there.' Except *up there* was nothing but shadows. 'There's a passage that used to lead into the old fort in the middle of the city.'

'Any other ways?'

Vish shrugged. 'Lots, I expect. The cisterns run all over the city. No one builds upwards here. No tall towers. Nowhere to get the stone, apparently. They all dig down. Every house has its own cellar. Helps keep it nice and cool. A lot of them have tunnels that lead to the cisterns, if they haven't all caved in.'

Skjorl got on with smashing eggs. Tunnels were good. A man could hide in a tunnel. As long as there were no hatchlings in it.

'Skjorl! Movement!' The shout came from Jasaan, almost down the rope, ripping over the sounds of the axes. He was pointing. At the edge of their light an egg had toppled over.

For a faint moment Skjorl froze. Movement meant ...

Jex and Vish were already running and Skjorl ran too, axes held high. The egg rolled again. Cracked. Jex was a dozen paces away, Skjorl much the same.

The end fell off the egg. A nose, a head, two eyes, closed and blind. A neck. Skjorl hurled himself across the last few yards. Brought the axe down. Didn't hesitate. Dragons didn't give second chances.

The dragon opened its eyes. Looked right at him almost like it had seen him once before. And then the eyes closed again and fell back, its neck cleaved apart. Jex and Vish looked at him and Skjorl looked back. They were all breathing hard but they froze for a moment anyway. Listening.

Jasaan reached them. 'Wha—' A hand over his mouth from Vish.

They stood in silence.

'What?' hissed Jasaan.

Skjorl shook his head. He looked at Jasaan. 'Get in the harness and get out. Jex, you first. Then Vish, then Jasaan, then me. If we're lucky, we got it quick enough. If we're not, the adults felt it die and we're done for if we stay here.'

'What?' If Jasaan could have furrowed his brow any further, his eyebrows were going to touch his nose.

'They didn't teach you much at Sand then, eh? Its eyes opened. It saw us. Maybe we got it fast enough the big ones didn't get a warning; maybe we didn't. Get on with it. Quick. Smash what you can while you're waiting and then let's get out of here.' Making Jasaan the last man out ahead of him again. Turning into a habit, that was. As if there wasn't already enough trouble between them.

He watched Jex get into the harness. Watched Kasern and Relk and Marran haul him up. For a moment he paused from hacking at an egg. He leaned against one of the pillars that held up the roof.

And felt a tremor through the stone. And then another and then another and another. Footsteps. Dragon-sized. *Shit!*

'Dragon!' he roared. Jex was at the top. They were getting him out of the harness. Vish had shouldered his axe, waiting for it to come back down.

The ground shook. Skjorl felt it through his feet this time. A different kind of shudder. A second dragon. There was one up above them somewhere and now there was one down in the cist—

'Lights out! Now! Then run!' He fumbled for his own firebox, snuffing the wick with his fingers and never mind how much that hurt. The last he saw was the harness, coming back down for Vish. The whole floor was shaking now. He could taste dust in the air.

Sounds of something smashing, of stones shattered and falling. Where the covered canal had fed into the wall, where Jex and Relk and the others had been only a moment ago, Skjorl saw a patch of darkness that wasn't quite black. Stars. He was seeing stars. He was seeing the sky.

Then something blotted them out. Filled the hole. And as he looked away, the fire started.

5

Kataros

Twenty-three days before the Black Mausoleum

'He can't walk.' The Adamantine Man was looking down at Rat, his face saying loudly that he couldn't care less.

'Then you have to carry him.'

'What's the point? He'll be dead in a few days.' He did what he was told, though: he picked the outsider up and slung him over his shoulder. Rat groaned.

'No. You're going to keep him alive just like you're going to keep me alive. We need him.'

'To do what?'

Kataros ignored him. He was obedient – that was all that mattered – and she'd never said anything about not asking questions. 'How do we get out of here without being caught?' The Adamantine Man shrugged. 'You don't *know*?'

'No.'

She thought about that for a few seconds. While she thought, the Adamantine Man stood in the middle of the cell with Rat over his back. He didn't do anything; he just stood there, waiting. 'We'll have to find someone who does, then,' she snapped at him. *Think. Think!* The Pinnacles were surrounded by dragons. Back in the days of the speakers, when Queen Zafir had lived here, people had landed them on the tops of the peaks, but there were other ways in. There were passages and tunnels down to the ruin of the Silver City – Kataros knew that because that was how they'd brought her here in the first place.

She'd have to find someone else, someone who knew the ways. She'd have to make another blood-bond. Some of the alchemists under the Purple Spur had quietly been getting a lot of practice at that. There, like here, you survived as best you could. Every day you ate, someone else didn't. But not her. If she bound someone else, she might have to let this one go. There'd be consequences to that.

The Adamantine Man sniffed. 'Actually, I do know a way,' he said. 'As long as it's dark. Up and out the side.'

'Up?'

'Yes.'

'You want me to climb down the side of the mountain? They're sheer cliffs out there! And how are you going to carry *him*?'

He was shaking his head. 'No climbing. It's easier than that.' He frowned. 'It's like flying, I suppose. But not on the back of a dragon.'

She reached through the blood-bond, looking for the trick, for the deception, for the twisting of her demand, but there was nothing. He believed what he was saying.

'It's supposed to be a way down to the Silver City.'

'*Supposed* to be? You mean you don't know?'

He shrugged. 'I know what I've heard, and what I've heard is there's a way. You fly like a bird. I've not done it, but I've heard how.'

She looked a second time. He still meant every word.

'Once you leave, you can't come back. So they don't guard it,' he said.

'Show me.' Like a bird? Was that possible? How did a man grow wings?

'Do you know what it's like in the Silver City?'

'No.' She shook her head and she didn't care. They'd go where they had to, and that was that.

'You're an alchemist. Do you know how to make a potion so a dragon doesn't know where you are?'

'Yes. What of it?'

'Got any on you?'

She looked down at herself. A robe, torn and dirty, and that was it. 'Don't be stupid.'

'Well, since there's dragons down there, we'll most likely die then.'

6

Skjorl

Eight months before the Black Mausoleum

After the darkness, the brilliance of the flames pouring from the mouth of the canal was blinding. Skjorl couldn't look. Couldn't think. Was just thankful he could see again, could see where his feet were landing. Could run. That was all that mattered. Getting away. Everything else came later, if it came at all, with the dazed knowing that you were still alive.

The mouth of the canal was about the size of a dragon's head. The rest wouldn't fit. It would have to smash its way in. He had time. Time to get away.

Jex had been up there. Relk, Marran, Kasern. All dead. A snap of fate's fingers and gone, just like that.

A storm of warm air tore at his clothes. The dragon was too far away to hurt him. Yet. He tried to think about where each foot was going, in between the chaos of broken stones and dragon eggs. Just that. Nothing else.

Then he saw the second one. Down in the cisterns. A huge wriggling shape, a shadow in the distant haze, weaving between the columns. Saw a flicker of it, hundreds of yards away, coming towards him before the fire from the first dragon stopped, plunging them all back into darkness. Jasaan and Vish? He had no idea where they were, whether they were alive.

He kept moving. The alchemists said that dragons talked in your head sometimes, but he'd never had that. Kill, eat, burn, that's all a dragon was.

The ground shook again, now with the crash of tumbling stone. That was the dragon worming its way towards him, given up on not smashing down the columns that held the cisterns together.

A mad grin swept across his face. Maybe they'd all end up buried alive. Entombed together. A fitting end for an Adamantine Man.

His foot caught on something. Hurled forward, he curled up before he even hit the ground, rolled and let his armour take the impact. First thing he did when he was back on his feet was check the pouches of dragon poison wrapped around him. Instinct, that was. There wasn't much else you could do about a dragon except be eaten, and there wasn't much point in that unless you were going to take the monster with you. All burn together, him from the outside, the dragon from within. What else was the point?

Thing was to get to an edge, a wall, somewhere that would give shelter when the roof came down. Then hunker down and pray.

Shudders rippled through the ground. More tumbling stones and the cisterns lit up with fire again. He didn't look back, took what he could get and sprinted. There was no running from dragons, but that didn't stop a man wanting to try, not when there was one right behind you.

A deeper rumble shook the earth. The dragon behind him roared. The stones answered. A huge hand of air plucked Skjorl off his feet and threw him across the floor, bouncing between dragon eggs. He thumped into a step and cracked his head hard enough to make the world waver, even through his helmet. He blinked hard. Everything went dark again. The fire had stopped. The air was ripe with dust, rich with the smell of falling masonry and the rumble of tumbling stone.

He sniffed. Fresh air from outside too. Sand. The smell of sand and salt.

He smiled, but that wasn't enough so he laughed, and even then he needed more. 'You stupid dragon,' he roared. 'You actually did it. Vishmir's cock!' He stood up, filled with being alive. Filled with what felt like victory. Took a few steps back towards where the dragon had been before he stopped himself. Still couldn't see a thing.

There was the other one. Somewhere.

Ought to slip off. Tiptoe between the eggs and hope another

one didn't hatch. Ought to. Really, really ought to. That's what a man with an ounce of sense would do.

'Vish? Skjorl?'

Jasaan? He tried to make out where the call had come from. He counted to ten and when there wasn't a raging dragon coming after him he reached for his firebox. Mad. *What am I doing?* But by the time he'd asked himself that, the firebox was lit. Didn't help much. All he could see was a thick mist of dust.

'Skjorl?' Jasaan's voice was laced with pain.

'Jasaan?' Took a couple of steps. Stopped. *Somewhere* out there was still a dragon. Maybe more than one. Maybe the hatchlings too.

'Jasaan?' A second voice.

'Vish?'

'Yep. Still alive. Skjorl?'

'Still got all my bits.' Friendly voices in the dark gave him strength. 'Can you see anything?'

'I can see you.'

'The roof caved in.' Jasaan's voice was strained but he wasn't gasping.

'And the dragon?'

'It's not moving.'

'You can *see* it?' He couldn't make out any other light.

There was a pause. 'It's close. And I'm hurt.'

Skjorl frowned at that. Adamantine Men were never hurt. They kept going or they fell over and crawled off to die, and if that was what they were going to do, they did it on their own without bothering anyone about it. The creed of the Guard had no room for the sick or the injured, no time or space for helping the wounded. You stopped to help someone when there was a dragon about, you both wound up dead. That simple. 'Where are you?'

'Over here.'

'What about the dragon. It moving?'

'I think it's stuck.'

What Skjorl should be doing, he decided, was leaving. What Jasaan ought to be doing, unless he had two broken legs and two broken arms, was crawling over to wherever that dragon was and tipping poison down its throat.

No. *His* company. So that was what *he* ought to be doing.

Crap.

'Vish! You keep going. See if you can find another way out of here.'

'Bollocks! *You* do that. I got me a dragon to slay.'

'Where's the other one?'

'Can't see.'

'You keep away from that tunnel.'

'You think I'm an idiot, boss?'

Skjorl growled. He started to move as quickly as he could through the haze of dust and the litter of rubble. Off towards Jasaan. By the time he got there, he could see the pile of fallen stone where the dragon had to be.

The floor shuddered again. The other dragon, the one that had burned Jex and Kasern and the others. It was somewhere behind the cave-in now. Or could be a third. No way to tell.

Jasaan was standing up, leaning against the broken stub of one of the pillars. He had one foot held off the ground. Ankle. Skjorl could see that straight away. Couldn't walk. Could hop though.

'You're alive then.'

Jasaan nodded.

'That way.' Skjorl pointed back the way he'd come. 'Look for a way out.' Maybe there wasn't one, but it was that or climb past the collapsed roof, over the top of one dragon and straight into the path of another.

'Don't know why you're standing around gossiping. Got nothing better to do?' Vish trotted past them both.

'I can't, Skjorl.' There was that pain in Jasaan's voice again. 'I can hardly move.'

'You just wait here then.' Skjorl took a moment and then followed Vish. Through the settling dust he could see the edges of the collapse. It was huge. Some building or other had sat on top of the cisterns and the whole thing had come down. Great slabs of cracked brickwork, of tiled floor covered in mosaics. Stone pillars and old scorched beams that still smelled of ash.

Another rumble, a reminder that there was a second dragon around here somewhere.

'Hey! Dragon! Are you already dead under there?' Vish had his axe out, his own faithful mistress.

'Still plenty of eggs to end if it is.' Skjorl stared at the rubble. Looked up. He could feel a breeze. There was a way out here if they wanted it.

'Ah. There you are. Tyan's fury – if only I had a spear!'

The dragon was buried from the neck down. It's eyes were very slightly open, but it didn't move. Skjorl's first thought was that it was dead, but then he saw it blink.

'Spear through the eye,' muttered Vish as Skjorl stood beside him. 'That would do it. Right in deep.'

The head shifted slightly. Turned a fraction towards them. Despite himself, Skjorl froze for an instant. He had a dragon, right in front of him. A woken adult dragon. He took another moment to savour not being dead.

'Poison. We have to poison it.' There was always leaving it alone. Letting it starve until it burned from the inside. But no, couldn't do that. Couldn't leave a monster alive if he could leave it dead. Always the chance that some other dragon would dig it free.

The dragon's lips curled back, letting them see its teeth. Vish weighed his axe. As he climbed close, it tried to snap at him, but it couldn't turn its head far enough to reach, not with the stones crushing its neck. It sent a weak blast of fire at Skjorl, forcing him to shelter behind a shattered column, but then Vish was round behind it, and when it tried to reach him, Skjorl dashed up the rubble, and then they were both where it couldn't touch them, halfway up and round the back of its head. It shuddered and closed its eyes and lay still.

From the far side of the collapse, stone smashed against stone. Skjorl set to work on one side, Vish on the other. Killing the dragon with their axes was hard, like chopping at stone, but the monster never made a sound. Its eyes opened towards the end, looking at them as they finally hacked their way through its scales to the sinew and bone beneath, and then slowly closed again.

Skjorl stopped, panting from the effort. Vish kept chopping away until Skjorl raised a hand.

'Enough. It's dead. Let's go.'

Vish grinned back at him like a madman. 'We killed a dragon, Skjorl! We killed a dragon! With our axes! We killed a dragon and we're walking away.'

'And we've got eggs to finish. And there's still the other one.' The ground shook. 'Can't expect those stones to stop it for ever.' The Night Watchman had killed more then ten on the night the Adamantine Palace had burned, but he'd had the Speaker's Spear and the dragons still got him in the end. He and Vish, they'd killed an adult and they'd done it with steel and their bare hands. Not much chance they'd get back to the Purple Spur to brag about it, but Vish deserved his smile. They both did.

A stone the size of a child hit Vish square in the back with the force of a charging horse, arcing down from the top of the collapse. Vish sailed through the air like a thrown-away doll, arms and legs limp and loose. He landed like a sack of turnips. Skjorl stared in disbelief. Then jumped away and looked behind him. Just a pale white haze of dust and sand in the air lit up by his firebox. Beyond that: darkness. He could hear, though. Stones moving.

Vish!

He snuffed the firebox and dived sideways. Kept rolling until something stopped him. He felt the air tear as another stone hurtled past him in the dark, heard it bounce and smash. He knew what came next. Had enough time to curl up tight, cover his hands and his face, put his back to the rubble and let his shield take the worst as the fire came. The air roared. The wind almost toppled him. He put a hand out to balance himself and felt the heat burn at his palm where there was no dragonscale, only soft leather.

It was coming from the smashed-in hole in the cistern roof.

The next stone caught his outstretched hand. He felt the shock more than the pain. Screamed as he saw the boulder fly off amid the flames.

The fire wasn't stopping. It was getting him, slowly, finding its way through his armour. He jumped back to his feet and ran, let the dragon's flames light his way, weaving from side to side. Another rock whizzed past him, missed his head by a yard. The fire was weak by the time it reached him now. Weak enough that the few gaps and cracks between the dragonscale he wore would hold. The joints in his armour might be black and brittle by the end, but he'd be alive.

The next boulder didn't reach him. It hit the ground and bounded past, shattering a cluster of eggs. Lifeless hatchling bodies flopped out across the cistern floor. When the fire stopped, Skjorl eased his way sideways, getting as far as he could from where the dragon had last seen him.

'Jasaan?' he had no idea where Jasaan was.

Vish was dead. Should have been the other way round. Jasaan deserved a touch of dragon's fire. But Vish deserved his glory too. There'd be songs. Vish the dragon-killer. He eased his way through the darkness. Wondered for a bit if maybe Vish wasn't dead after all, but he'd seen the stone hit, seen Vish's head snap back and then forward, seen his body fly through the air and slide across the ground and then lie still.

Had to look though. Had to be sure. Didn't he?

Stupid. He took a deep breath. Adamantine Men didn't stop for their wounded. Didn't matter who they were, that was the way of it. Going back got you killed.

'Skjorl?' Jasaan, closer than he'd thought.

'Jasaan?'

'The other dragon. I can see it. It can't get through the rubble.'

Now he stopped to listen, he could hear it tearing at the stones. 'Can you swing an axe on your knees, Jasaan? If you can, you're still useful. You can kill eggs. If you can't, you might as well be dead.' Harsh, but Vish and Jex had been his friends. Couldn't say that about Jasaan, not after Scarsdale.

There was a pause. When Jasaan answered, it was with a sullen edge. 'Yes, Skjorl. I can still do that.'

'Then you do it. I'm getting Vish's poison.'

There. A good enough excuse.

7

Kataros

Twenty-three days before the Black Mausoleum

'What have you done to me?' He asked the same question over and over as he led her out of her tiny makeshift prison and into a maze of stairs and passages that bewildered her. She almost told him to shut up, but the blood-bound could be tricky. Too many different orders and he might freeze in confusion. The alchemist who'd bound her had only ever used the bond once, when he'd first made it. *You will be unswervingly loyal to my desires.* That was it and then nothing more, not in a year and a half of service. Most of the time she forgot it was even there. He'd been a kind enough man who'd never asked for much, whose greatest desire had been for her to grow into the power that he was offering her. She hadn't needed any help with *that*.

He'd shown her, after he'd bound her, how it was done, but he'd never told her what to do with it. He'd encouraged her, now and then, to bind others, but she never did, even though she knew that most alchemists had several blood-bound serving them. They did it for their protection they said, for the greater good, and in the squalor and hunger under the Purple Spur Kataros quite understood, yet every time she heard them, she remembered that they'd bound their Scales too, not long ago, and so they would have bound her if the Adamantine Palace hadn't burned and more than half the alchemists of the realms been slaughtered.

'You're going to help me,' she told him after she'd lost count of how many times he'd asked. 'You're going to help me save the realms.'

'How are we going to do that?'

She didn't answer, and the truth was that she didn't exactly know. All she knew was what the near-corpse that the Adamantine Man was carrying had told her two nights before.

'It's going to get dark,' he said a while later. The halls and vaults of the Pinnacles glowed from above like a softly starlit night, a legacy of the Silver King, who'd brought order to the broken world and who'd first subdued the monsters. Half monster himself, half living god, adept with magics that no one before or since could even understand, almost everything here bore his mark. The Pinnacles had been his home for more than a hundred years, until the blood-mages had found a way to kill him.

The Adamantine Man took her into later tunnels, ones carved by men. The twilight faded and the darkness grew. When she could barely see him any more, he stopped. 'There are lamps by your feet. Get yourself one. You can get one for me too.'

In an alcove beside her she felt the familiar shapes, the cold glass tubes of alchemical lamps. She hadn't expected that, not here in the Pinnacles, where to be an alchemist, it had turned out, was to be an avatar of evil. 'There are—'

'Your lot made them. Yes.'

'Don't you—'

'Believe that everything touched by an alchemist is cursed?' The Adamantine Man snorted. 'I was in Outwatch when the terror started. Then Sand. Evenspire, or what was left of it. Scarsdale. Got to the Purple Spur eventually. Spent more time there than I have here. I know what your kind are. You failed, that's all. You're no better and no worse than any of the rest of us. Not that that's saying very much.'

Kataros picked up a lamp. She turned it upside down, shook it and waited until the glow started. Then she handed it to the Adamantine Man and got another. 'Won't someone see the lights?'

'No one comes here these days.' He settled Siff over his shoulders and started on down the tunnel. The walls were different now. The light showed that they were rough, hacked out with picks and shovels and never finished. Utterly unlike the exquisite carved archways, the murals and the mosaics she'd seen elsewhere.

'Why?'

He stopped. 'This leads to the lowest girdle of the scorpion caverns. Used to be hundreds of them here. They're all ruined now. The poison ran out and then the bolts. Not much point sticking yourself somewhere you can be burned by a dragon when you haven't got anything you can shoot back.'

The tunnel went on, rough and uneven until it stopped at a fissure that ran up and down. Kataros couldn't see how far it went either way, for the alchemical lamps produced little light. She crouched, searching for a pebble to drop, but the ground was smooth and there weren't any. The Adamantine Man shifted Rat into a more comfortable position across his shoulders and started to climb. There were rungs bolted into the rock.

'Why are we going up, not down?'

'There's tunnels down below. Guarded and watched well. There's barricades and bolted doors and the speaker's riders down there, watching out against the ferals. No way out without a fight – not for one like you. This way's better. Gets us to the surface. No one goes out this way and you can't get back up again, so there's no one watching.' He chuckled to himself. 'You run into anyone up the top here, wave your arms at them and make ghost noises, that'll probably work. Hyrkallan's lot, they're like little girls. The ones who've been here even longer are no better. All spooked. Most likely they really do believe that you lot made all this happen like he says. Demons. So make like one. Easier than having a fight. If they come back with any soldiers, we'll be gone by then.'

She didn't know what to say to that, so she climbed after him in silence, up the slit in the rock, its sides worn smooth by water from another time. In places it was so narrow that Siff scraped against the far wall; from side to side, it spread out further than her lamp could reach.

'What is this place?' She couldn't help but wonder that. She'd been wondering that from the moment she'd come inside the Pinnacles and seen what it was really like. Even in chains she'd stared, lost in awe.

'There's shafts up and down like this all over,' he said. 'It's like one of them cheeses we used to get from up on the moors.'

He reached an opening and levered himself out. Kataros felt his tension as he crouched, ready to drop Siff in an instant, but there was only darkness and silence to greet them.

'Right. Quick now.' He started to run, lumbering off. She followed, keeping close behind. Her heart beat faster, excitement and expectation bubbling together as if she was brewing some potion. *Almost out. Almost out.*

He turned a corner and light – a patch of slightly lighter darkness anyway – loomed ahead. The scorpion caves. Vishmir and the first Valmeyan had fought here in the War of Thorns. Afterwards, Prince Lai had built the scorpions. They were supposed to defend the Silver City, but it seemed to Kataros that they did the opposite. History said that when the scorpions fired, the Silver City burned. If you looked hard now, she supposed you might see it burning still.

She saw stars.

Almost out!

The Adamantine Man slowed as they reached the lip of the cave. He stopped a good ten feet short, lowered Siff to the floor and peered around him, looking for something. Kataros stared out of the sheer side of the Fortress of Watchfulness, down over the Silver City, which wasn't still burning after all. They were high. She had no chance of climbing down, not from all the way up here.

'How far up are we?'

'Don't know. A few hundred feet over the plains.'

'And we fly like a bird?' She'd supposed there might be a rope, or some sort of lift or crane, but there was nothing. 'You bastard,' she hissed, and reached through the blood-bond, ready to claw his mind apart. 'What do we do? Flap our arms and pretend they're wings?'

The Adamantine Man stopped. His hands fell limp. He looked almost surprised. 'Yes,' he said.

She almost killed him there and then, almost let the blood inside his brain boil and rupture every vessel. She could have stood there and watched him bleed from his eyes and his nose and his mouth, from his fingers and his toes and every place in between, and she wouldn't have been sorry. But however hard she peered through the blood-bond, she saw no deceit. They were going to fly. He truly believed that.

'How?'

He went back to peering around the cave. After a minute or two he stopped. 'With these.'

It took a moment for Kataros to understand what she was seeing, simply because the lamps didn't make enough light.

She was seeing wings. Dragon wings. Lashed together and with a harness between them.

8

Skjorl

He found Vish easy enough. No doubt about how dead he was. His neck was broken, the back of his head was smashed in and he was lying in a pool of blood that was bigger than he was. The axe and shield on his back had been shattered. Skjorl stood for a moment. There wasn't anything special to say. Adamantine Men weren't long on rituals or on sentiment. When you fought dragons, you did what needed to be done, nothing more, nothing less. You did it fast and you did it without hesitation. Most of the time you died anyway.

He took Vish's potions, his poisons, his firebox, the alchemist herbs that stopped the dragons from finding them and left the rest. The shield and the armour were useless and he already had an axe.

The other dragon had left, judging by the quiet, but it wouldn't be gone for long. Looking for another way in, most likely. Back soon enough, one way or the other. He wondered if any of the others up top had survived. Didn't seem likely. Which left him and Jasaan. Jasaan the cripple. Jasaan and his principles. Easier to leave him behind.

He was starting to notice that his hand hurt. He took a last look at Vish. Quiet Vish.

Wouldn't have left you behind, would I?

No. He didn't suppose he would, and what was good for one was good for another. That was the way it was. And then there were all these eggs, which could hatch any time, and the small matter of not being able to use his own axe properly with only one good hand. Couldn't see how bad it was, but there was no getting around that it was bad. Bad enough it wouldn't be all fine again in a few days.

He'd have to give his axe a name, he thought. Call her Vish maybe, but Vish was a man's name and his axe was more his lady, his lover. Dragon-bane? He cringed at that. She deserved better.

'You walk?' he asked when got back to Jasaan. Jasaan shook his head.

'Ankle's done. I can hop.'

'Not down here with no light. You can crawl, right?'

'I can crawl.'

They shuffled along in the darkness, quiet as they could, Jasaan on his hands and knees, Skjorl inching his way beside him until they reached one of the cistern walls. Here and there they passed more eggs. With a bit of care, Skjorl could still swing his axe with one hand to smash them. It took Jasaan to cut off the unborn hatchlings' heads. Skjorl tried but he couldn't find a way to make his buggered hand work and he just made a mess. Quicker to prop Jasaan up to finish the job.

He didn't know how long they'd been going when they finished the eggs. Long enough he wanted to sit down. Back where the roof had collapsed there was sunlight filtering down through the hole, giving a dim light so he could finally see. The dust had mostly settled except where the two of them kicked it up again. He put his back to a stone and rummaged in his pack for something to eat.

'It just needs a hatchling small enough to squeeze through one of those tunnels and we're finished,' said Jasaan. Skjorl shrugged. Obvious really. Wasn't sure why it needed to be said.

'We're finished anyway,' he muttered. 'Look at us.' No place among the Adamantine Men for cripples.

'We'll heal.'

Skjorl took a deep breath and sighed. He passed Jasaan some of Vish's herbs to mix with his water and took some himself. Something to numb the pain. 'Sun's up. We've smashed a good few eggs but not all of them. There's others somewhere. As soon as one hatches, it'll be small enough to come after us. We could barely face an angry old crone, never mind a dragon.'

Jasaan offered some of his bread. Brothers together. Sharing everything. Live together, die together. Old traditions like that stuck with you, even in places like this. 'We did what we were asked to do.'

Skjorl shook his head and took his own bread instead. 'Some of it. There's no one left at Bloodsalt, but we won't be getting back to tell anyone that. And there's still dragons. We didn't kill the dragons.'

'We killed one of them.'

'Vish and I killed it.' Skjorl stood up. He was tired enough to drop and he had nothing he wanted to say. 'I'm going to look around for a bit. Get some rest. When it's dark we'll see if we can find another way out.' Which didn't make any sense — no point spending the day hiding somewhere when the dragons already knew where you were — but Jasaan didn't argue, and Skjorl left him sitting there, busy trying to make some sort of splint for his ankle. He walked on through the cisterns. Not really looking for a way out because he wasn't expecting to find one, but just to be on his own.

After a bit he walked back to where the roof had come in, to where there was some light, and looked at his hand. Tried to take his gauntlet off, but that hurt too much, so he was left with poking and prodding. Half pulverised. Two fingers shattered, a third one broken. At least the burns on his palm weren't too bad.

He stopped there, in a ray of sunlight, and listened. If the second dragon was anywhere nearby, there was no sign of it. No sounds, no tremors in the earth. It was almost a disappointment. Being eaten would have been easy, the quick way out, but when that didn't happen he looked at the rubble instead. A man with two good hands and two good feet could climb that. Scramble straight up. Simple. Might not be any holes big enough for a dragon to get through, but a man, now he wouldn't have any trouble at all.

Dragons had good eyes in the daylight. Could spot a man moving through the desert from a mile away. Couldn't pretend the temptation wasn't there, though — just start climbing. Never mind that he'd be leaving Jasaan behind. Never mind the noise it might make. Never mind being seen, just get up and go, and keep on going until claws and teeth closed around him.

Something scraped on the ground behind him. He spun around, fumbling for his axe, ready for a hatchling, but it was Jasaan.

'I thought that too. Could be the only way out.'

'Could be.'

'When it gets dark, then?'

'If the dragon doesn't come back.' Which it would. It knew they were there and it knew what they'd done.

'Perhaps we should look for another.'

'You go do that then.' The adult was away. Hunting. Had to be. The young ones, they could be anywhere, but the big one would come back in the evening. It would tear its way in and then they'd die.

No. No, by the great Flame, that *wasn't* going to happen. If he was going to die, it was going to be *his* way. 'Come on.'

'What?'

'Come on!' He started to climb up the rubble.

'What are you doing?'

'We stay here, we die. So we don't stay here. We get out before the big one comes back again. We get as far as we can. We hide up in the afternoon. As soon as it's dark, we press on. It'll look for us here but we'll be somewhere else. Not up the Sapphire valley. We head up towards the moors. Until we can kill dragons again. Then we come back and we finish what we came here for.'

Jasaan was shaking his head. 'There's hatchlings. They'll see you.'

'Us, Jasaan. If they see anything, they'll see *us*. And maybe they will and maybe they won't, but I'm not waiting down here to die, and you're coming with me.' Jasaan would slow him down, but in truth, neither of them was much use in a fight any more.

'No! Skjorl, stay here. Wait until night! There might be another way. There might be other tunnels somewhere.'

He was halfway up the pile of broken stone already. Didn't bother to look back or even to shake his head. True, there might be another way out of the cisterns, but he didn't care. There weren't any tunnels for people to hide in, not in a place like this.

No catacombs like in Sand, no endless caves like there were under the Purple Spur. Just desert. Hot, harsh and much too bright. No, and Jasaan wouldn't stay down here on his own either. Skjorl reached the top and waited, squinting against the fierce daylight. The cisterns had been built underneath some sort of palace, not that there was much left of it now. Dragons had taken their time over destroying it. Burned it from the outside and then smashed it down with tail and claw and trampled it and burned it again. Same as they'd done to Outwatch all those months ago. Pieces of carved masonry lay heaped about, broken statues, fragments of walls and floors covered in patterns of tiny coloured tiles. That sort of thing. All the pointless finery that had once surrounded the great lords of the realms. Looking at it now made him want to laugh. The sun was high in the sky, blistering hot. He took a swig of water from his skin. That was all he needed. The sun on his back, a splash of water and something to fight. None of this pointless pride.

A stone head stared at him sideways from the rubble, its body lost amid the tumbled stones. There was something familiar about it. When Skjorl turned and stared back, he recognised it. Speaker Hyram. The last one to serve out his years. The speaker under whom this had started. One dragon gone missing, that was all, the white he'd seen at Outwatch. One dragon and the realms were all but destroyed. Speaker Zafir had followed him. Easy on the eye, that one. Then Speaker Jehal, the one they called the Viper. Now Skjorl served Jehal's queen, Lystra. Or at least he had when he'd left the Purple Spur. For all he knew she might be dead by now too, another speaker raised in her place. Speakers came and speakers went. He shook his head at Hyram's still face. 'What does it matter now? What do any of you matter?'

Jasaan climbed up beside him. Skjorl turned. 'See. No one's eaten me yet.'

'Are they still here? Maybe they all flew off?'

'Haven't looked.' He pointed to the head of Speaker Hyram. 'Been talking to our old friend here.'

Jasaan looked sideways too. 'I remember him.'

'Don't we all. The shaking speaker.'

'Who buggered his pot boys and then murdered them and threw their bodies in the Mirror Lakes.'

Skjorl frowned. 'Don't think anyone ever knew more than they kept going missing.' Maybe Hyram hadn't amounted to very much as a speaker, but he'd been a mighty sight better than what had followed. Besides, it never did any good to speak ill of the dead.

'Relk always said he knew who it was who'd done away with the bodies. One of us. Different company but still one of us. Wrapped them in sheets and weighted them with stones and then tossed them into the middle of the lake.'

Skjorl had to smile at that. 'Relk reckoned he knew a soldier who'd shared Queen Shezira's bed, that the Night Watchman himself shared Speaker Zafir's and that there was a blood-mage living under the Glass Cathedral masquerading as a surgeon. Never actually saw any of it himself, mind. Always someone else.' He glanced up at the sky, screwed up his eyes and looked away. After the blackness of the cistern everything out here was too bright.

'There was a body went out to the lakes the night Hyram died. No one saw who it was. Wasn't a boy, though. Was a woman from the weight of it. Some assassin with a knife for Speaker Zafir, hiding in her rooms in the Tower of Air. Was King Jehal's riders – prince he was then – who took it away. Already wrapped up. Asked about a bit the next day and tracked where they'd gone with it. Out to the lakes in a boat. Don't know who it was. They said there'd been a fight, but I reckon they were full of crap. No blood. Not on them, not on their swords, not on anything, not even the smell of it in the air.' He sniffed. 'Me, I reckon we're better off without the lot of them. Speakers, riders, kings, queens, princes, any of them.'

Skjorl stiffened. Treason talk that was, even out here. 'We serve the speaker, Jasaan, whoever that might be,' he growled. 'Orders. The Guard obeys orders. From birth to death. Nothing more, nothing less.'

'And who do the speakers serve, Skjorl? Themselves?'

'They serve the realms, Jasaan. Any more talk like that and you'll hang.'

Jasaan looked as him as though he was mad and then burst out laughing. 'We're in the middle of a lifeless burned-out city in the middle of a desert. There's probably not a single other person alive for a hundred miles in any direction. I can't walk, you can't hold your axe and there are dragons everywhere; they know we're here and are probably hunting us, and you think I should be worried about getting hanged if we ever make it back? Vishmir's cock!'

'I'll hang you here and now if I have to, soldier.' Didn't expect to mean it, but he did. *From birth to death.* The most solemn oath in the realms. An Adamantine Man who didn't believe in that, who didn't believe in all the things that made them what they were, well, they didn't deserve to live.

'No, you won't, Skjorl. Don't be a dick.'

'This is still my company, Jasaan. You going to hop on your own all the way back to the Spur?'

'You're as crippled as I am.'

'I can walk, Jasaan. Big difference.'

Jasaan raised a hand in submission. 'Your way, boss. From birth to death. I always served as I was asked. I'm here, aren't I? Out in the middle of this shit?'

Skjorl let his anger fade. 'That you are.' Maybe Jasaan didn't deserve it. And three hands would be better than one on the way back, however far they got before a dragon ate them. And he was right, wasn't he? They were both as crippled as each other now. Two would be better than one. Just as long as they carefully kept on not talking about Scarsdale.

They stayed in the narrowest streets on their way out of the city. Once his eyes finally got used to the desert sunlight, Skjorl climbed up to the top of the smashed remains of something that might have been an old temple to the Great Flame. He searched the skies and the distant sands and salt flats and the waters of Bloodsalt Lake for anything that looked like a dragon, big or small. Past the city's bones was a yellow-white flatness, boiling and shimmering in the late-morning heat, and then the deep deep blue of the sky. If there were dragons out there, he couldn't see them. In the haze he wasn't sure he ever would.

They hobbled on, pitifully slow and sweating fit to drown.

Skjorl saw a lizard the size of his hand once, basking on a stone. Nothing else moved. When they stopped to rest and drink, he emptied his water skin without even noticing.

'Keep on like this and we'll die from the heat, never mind any dragons,' muttered Jasaan.

Skjorl nodded. 'We'll stay here then.' Probably they were far enough from where they'd killed the dragon. He looked about and picked a house still in one piece, made out of baked mud or some such and washed in white. One room, low roof. A few old blankets rolled up in a corner. Not much else. Whoever had lived here, they were long gone. Dead somewhere. Burned by dragons or maybe eaten. Or killed by the desert heat somewhere between the city and the place a hundred miles away where the dragons had blocked up the Sapphire. They'd found plenty enough old bones along the river's course. Skeletons. Skulls. Whole families sometimes. People died. Skjorl knew that better than most, but when you took a step and heard a crack and looked down to find you'd just snapped the sun-bleached bones of a child … Well, made you stop and think for a moment it did.

'Jasaan …'

But he was already asleep.

9

Kataros

Twenty-three days before the Black Mausoleum

Prince Lai's wings. She'd heard of them but she'd never met someone who'd seen a pair. The legendary prince had made them during the War of Thorns when the first Valmeyan had him trapped in the Pinnacles. The story went that he'd launched himself off the top of the Fortress of Watchfulness in the middle of the night and flown all the way to Furymouth, hundreds of miles to the south, to warn his brother Vishmir. After the war he made more, and across the realms there were said to be maybe a dozen pairs. If that was true then most of them were right here.

The Adamantine Man dragged a pair to the edge of the cave, first one wing and then another. Each was enormous, three or four times the size of a man, a fraction of a true dragon's wing but huge nonetheless. He bolted them together. 'Sit in the harness,' he told her. 'Left arm down to turn left. Right arm down to turn right. Both arms down when you're about to land. Come on.'

She stared at him. 'Come on?'

'Yes.' He pointed to the wings and then moved towards her, as if to help her buckle herself in. She hissed and recoiled.

'You don't touch me!' She reached into him through the blood-bond but he was still held tight. He meant her no harm, not now.

He shrugged. 'Suit yourself. You go first. I'll come after. I'll be heavier, so I'll pass you. Try and go where I go.'

She stared at him a while longer, then at the wings. Yes, she'd heard of Prince Lai's wings, like every alchemist who studied the history of the War of Thorns back at the Palace of Alchemy. She'd seen pictures. It had never occurred to her that they were actually real, that they were anything more than a nice story.

'Can we really fly all the way to Furymouth?' The Raksheh was closer.

The Adamantine Man laughed. 'That old story? These aren't going to get you much further than the Silver City down there, and even if they could take us further, there's no shelter on the plains. Sun comes up, dragons start to move. Then you die. You want to get to the Raksheh, we go the long way. Up the Yamuna. Not so many dragons up there.'

Kataros took another long look at the wings, taut dragon skin stretched over old dragon bones. When dragons died, they burned from the inside. They didn't leave much behind, just their scales and wings. The scales became armour for dragon-riders and for the Adamantine Men. Wing bones were used for all sorts of things – bows, mostly, but potions too. The skin from the wings was the most prized thing of all, softer and more flexible than the scales and still impervious to flames. Princes and lords lined their armour with it. Prince Lai had made his wings after the war, sitting in the Adamantine Palace with Vishmir the Magnificent, the first and only Emperor of the Nine Realms. After the War of Thorns there had been more dead dragons around than usual, so maybe that was why he'd done it.

The Adamantine Man cleared his throat behind her. 'Longer it takes before we're down, the less time we have before sunrise. When that happens we need to be somewhere safe. There's nests in the Silver City.'

She looked at the moon. The night was young. 'There are still people down there in the city. Will they help us?'

'The ferals?' The Adamantine Man laughed. 'Don't think they come up to the surface much, even at night. But still, got to get their food from somewhere. Help us though?' He shook his head and patted the axe slung over his back. 'Ferals find us, it'll be time for my lady to get to work. We get to the city, you stay close. We go down. Underground. Find a place to hide from the dragons, that's the first thing. Then we look for the tunnels. There's ways as far as the Fury. After that?' He shrugged.

Kataros stared at the wings. If she got ripped to pieces by feral men or eaten by dragons, that wasn't any worse than being raped and strangled in a dingy cell. And at least she'd be trying to *do* something. She took a deep breath and started to strap herself into the harness. It was simple enough, similar to a dragon harness, the sort of thing a rider would have designed. All buckled in, she tried to drag the wings towards the mouth of the cave, but they were so heavy she could barely move them.

'Let me help.' He lifted them up, resting them across his shoulders. Kataros walked towards the edge and then stopped. The sky was clear and she could see the shapes of the Silver City hundreds of feet below her. And she was going to jump? Madness! She shrank away and stepped back straight into the solid bulk of the Adamantine Man behind her. 'Get away from me!'

'Sorry about this.'

The next thing she felt was his hand in her back, hurling her forward. She screamed as her feet struggled to push against him, reached through the blood-bond, found him there, grasped the first part of him that came to hand and twisted and tore. The pushing stopped and he let go. Her feet teetered on the brink of the cave.

The wings collapsed on top of her, forcing her down and pitching her forward. She grabbed at them, but they were much too big and much too heavy and she was already too close to the edge. They toppled forward and tipped out into the void, and Kataros went with them.

10

Skjorl

Eight months before the Black Mausoleum

They waited for the evening and for the heat to fade. If the dragons were still in Bloodsalt, Skjorl didn't bother to look. Best chance of staying alive was to stay out of sight. He searched around the house for anything useful, but under the dirt and dust were only the blankets, an old table and a couple of stools. After that he had a good look at his hand. Took some Dreamleaf to take the edge off the pain and did his best to splint it up. Wasn't ever going to work right again, that was for sure, but maybe he'd still be able to wield his axe one day, that was what mattered.

Dragon-blooded. He picked up his axe and held her. He could call her Dragon-blooded, after the stains on her steel. Better than Dragonslayer.

After that he had a look at Jasaan. Hard to tell whether the ankle was broken or badly sprained, but it was swollen up like a severed head. He put a splint on that as well. Stools turned out useful for something after all.

When it was properly dark again they crept out, back towards the water of the Sapphire. They found the covered canal and Skjorl stared at it. The parts in the city had been smashed to bits, trampled into a mess of jumbled bricks. So much for Jex and the rest, not that he'd had any hope they were still alive. Maybe they'd managed to get themselves eaten. Maybe the other dragon was burning too, but Skjorl wasn't about to count on it. Never count on anything with dragons. Crafty bastards they were.

Outside the city, pieces of the canal were still intact. They hid inside one for the last hour of darkness and the whole of the day. Blasted place was like an oven in the sun, baking them in their own juices until they had nothing left to sweat. Skjorl lay towards one end, head poking outside but in the shade, catching what whisper of a breeze he could. In the distance he thought he saw the dragon, high up in the sky and away to the south, heading towards the Sapphire valley. When he blinked it was gone; afterwards, he wasn't sure whether he'd seen it or dreamed it. Didn't matter much. A sign was a sign. It was looking for them.

'We're too slow and there's not enough shelter,' Skjorl said when the sun set and they were ready to move again.

Jasaan shrugged. 'We don't get any water, we won't last another day.' He levered himself back to his feet and propped his axe under his shoulder as a crutch. 'If it's my time then I suppose I'm as ready as I'll ever be.'

'If we have to fight it, we will. We'll come back out here and look for it after we're done in the Spur.' He tried to smile, and Jasaan grinned back. An Adamantine Man faced a dragon without fear. Even if there were only the two of them and they were both crippled and stood no chance whatsoever of victory, they'd still fight.

'Whatever you say,' said Jasaan after a pause that was much too long.

'I'm thinking we should go up on the moors. Yinazhin's Way. I been along it once. There's a part you can see the Sapphire gleaming like a needle, the Hungry Mountain Plain to the south and the Plains of Ancestors to the north with Samir's Crossing in between. We get up to the moors, there's shelter and water and food. Dragon should have forgotten about us by then.'

'Be busy looking for wherever his mate hatched out.'

'Maybe.' Now there was a thing Skjorl still couldn't get fixed right in his head. He'd spent most of his life thinking dragons were big dumb animals. Immense and deadly, but animals. Now it turned out they could read your thoughts if you didn't take a potion to stop them, and when they died, they just came back again, hatched straight out of another egg somewhere. And they *remembered*. No, couldn't get that sort of thing fixed in his head at all.

They followed the sunken canal back as far as the river, crossed it, wallowed in the cool water and drank their fill and then headed on. Plenty of shelter at least. Dry riverbeds. Clusters of rocks. Crevices in the dirt. Nothing alive though. No trees, no grass, no nothing. Maybe there were snakes and rats and creatures like that, but all Skjorl saw were the same sodding great sandflies that had been trying to eat him alive for the last three weeks.

They stopped as the sun rose and took shelter in the middle of a cluster of giant boulders. Felt like they'd walked for miles and miles, but when Skjorl looked back, there was Bloodsalt, a dull scar smeared across the shining sands and the glittering lake. The river wasn't much more than a mile away. He looked in his pack. Food for three or four days before he started to starve him-self, but that wasn't going to be the problem. In this heat they'd die of thirst long before he had to worry about that. The edge of the desert and the slopes up to the moors were fifty miles away. Took Jasaan a bit longer to work it out, but he got there in the end.

'This isn't going to work,' he said as the afternoon wore on.

'No.'

'What are we going to do?'

'On my own I could get there.'

'You're going to leave me to die then?'

'Don't have much choice. Better than both of us.' This time Jasaan could bloody well accept it.

Jasaan shrugged. 'I got a different idea. We don't move at all. We sit it out right here. We find a cave and we stay in it. We wait until you can hold an axe properly. Until I can run and climb again. Then we bolt for the Spur, fast as we can. We got water. The river.'

'And what do we *eat*, Jasaan? Even if I could, there's nothing to hunt here.'

Jasaan sniffed. He looked away, back across to the river to Bloodsalt. 'Dead meat, that's what.'

Skjorl laughed. 'Dragons? Hatchlings? They burn, remember. There's nothing left but ash, Jasaan. You can't eat ash!' He was losing it.

'I wasn't thinking of dragons.' Jasaan was looking at him. Hard and steady. Waiting for him to see it. Took a while too, because no one else would even have thought of such a thing.

'You mean mean Vish, don't you?'

Jasaan didn't say anything. But yes, that's exactly what he meant.

'You want to eat Vish?'

Jasaan's eyes didn't leave Skjorl's face but now they showed iron. 'It's not like we don't both know there's good eating on a man, eh?'

Scarsdale. That's what he was thinking. When they'd left and what they'd taken with them to keep their bellies full as far as the Silver River. Desperate times, men did desperate things. Eat another Adamantine Man, though? Cold, that was. But the other choice he'd given Jasaan was a cold one too. Skjorl turned away. Had to think.

'Can't be doing that, Jasaan,' he said at last. 'Can't be eating Vish.'

Jasaan didn't say anything. Just looked at him. Adamantine Men didn't have friends. Trouble was, that cut both ways now.

'Vishmir's cock!' Skjorl's fists clenched themselves.

'He's dead, Skjorl. Gone. You know that.' Jasaan spoke softly. 'Best chance of one of us getting back to the Spur is we do what I said.'

Hard to say if that was true. Hard to take even if it was. Should have been Jasaan down in the cisterns, climbing up towards the trapped dragon and hacking its head off. Then Vish would have been here and with both his legs working and they'd be laughing now and running all through the night, up to the start of Yinazhin's Way and onward, as far and fast as they could.

'Vishmir's cock,' he said again, quietly this time. 'Where we stayed right before we crossed the river – you reckon you can get there in one night?' An overhang. Not quite a cave, but with a tumble of rocks in front of it. The sort of place a few men could stay hidden from anything short of something poking its nose right inside.

Jasaan nodded.

'You'll be on your own.' Skjorl took a deep breath. 'Two days

– one to get in, one to get back, if I get back at all. Might be there's another egg hatched. Might be one of the young ones has gone down there. Might be Vish has gone already. Eaten. Might be you'll never see me again. Might be I'll run.'

'Then I'll be no worse off than I am right now. Besides, you are what you are, Skjorl, and you wouldn't do that. You might kill me, but you wouldn't lie to me.'

For some reason that made Skjorl laugh. 'That's us, isn't it?'

'From birth until death.'

'Blood and honour and fire.' Skjorl took a deep breath. The sun was edging the horizon now, setting the sands and salts of the desert rippling red. Together they watched it go down. 'I'm taking the water,' Skjorl said.

It took him a night longer than he'd thought – one to get in, two to get back. Wasn't any easier carrying a dead Adamantine Man than a crippled one. Vish wasn't there, no sign of him, which meant a dragon had got him. But when he looked hard, it wasn't so difficult to find what had happened to the others. Wasn't any getting to Jex or Marran, and Kasern was half buried. Relk, though, he must have been alive. Crawled out from under where he'd been burned and then crushed with both legs broken. He'd probably still been alive the night Skjorl and Jasaan had left.

Wasn't now. Sun had done him, most likely. No one had eaten him though, that was what mattered. No one ate Skjorl either, and when he got back, Jasaan was waiting for him, sitting on the rocks, keeping watch. Soon as the sun set again, they took the body a little way up the river. With his two good hands, Jasaan was the one who got to strip, gut and fillet him. Skjorl was the one who had to walk for hours to the edge of the salt flats, fill up his pack with salt and walk back again. He wrinkled his nose. Relk had started to smell even worse than he had when he was alive. Desert heat was good for that.

'This going to work?'

Jasaan shrugged. 'It's what they do here.'

Eventually they were done. Skjorl tried not to look. White bone gleamed from dead red flesh. Hard to say why, but it was better this way, better that it wasn't Vish. Relk, he was an Adamantine Man, as good as any, but that's all he was. Vish and Jex, they'd started to be something else. Maybe even Jasaan too, even with that Scarsdale crap between them. Was a long way from Sand down to the Silver River valley. Long enough and hard enough that you learned things about your company that you didn't learn other ways.

'Ought to bury him,' said Jasaan. 'Hide what's left from the dragons.' He was taking the meat he'd sliced off Relk and smothering it in salt, trying to make it keep. 'They see this, they'll know we were here.'

'Can't do that.' That's not what you did with the dead. Burned them, maybe. Fed them to a dragon. Weighed them down and threw them in a river, hung them up for the crows even, but you didn't bury them, never that. Even the people who died starving under the Purple Spur got carried up and out of the caves, and never mind that the people doing the carrying were starving too.

'I know. Just saying it would be best.'

'The river.'

Jasaan nodded.

'Weigh him down and sink him. Dragons won't see. Water will hide the smell.'

'Won't hide the mess we made.'

Wasn't much to be done about that. They'd lost most of the night by now anyway. Jasaan hobbled back to their hole. Skjorl took the meat and followed him. Most likely they'd starve and never mind Jasaan and his clever plans. Or the dragons would find them. Or they'd get some sickness from eating the flesh of their own kind and die in agony in a pool of their own fluids. Could be any of those things would happen and Skjorl wouldn't have called himself much surprised.

They did get hungry right enough. And they saw dragons now and then, and they had the runs and had cramps, but they didn't die. They eked Relk out as best they could, tongues curling at the saltiness of him. And by the time they ran out of bits of him to eat, Jasaan could walk again.

11

Kataros

Twenty-three days before the Black Mausoleum

She screamed. The world spun around her. Stone rushed towards her face and then a huge hand reached down from the sky and plucked her up and she was flying, the wind in her face, tugging her hair.

Prince Lai's wings.

She forced herself not to panic, forced her mind to be still. The ground seemed a lot closer than it had from the cave. She tried not to look at it, but that was wrong – she *had* to look at it, didn't she? The Silver City was a jumble of shapes, of outlines, all reduced to a dim grey in the moonlight. The city had burned before the dragons had broken free. They hadn't smashed it like they'd smashed the City of Dragons. There were long streets and wide, open squares. There were canals, yes! The city had had canals since the time of the blood-mages. Long straight lines of water. One of those would do.

Ancestors! The ground was coming closer. Slowly, but it was. Underneath, it went past her so fast! *Left hand down to turn left. Right hand down to turn right.*

She tugged, very gently, with her right hand. Nothing happened. She tugged harder and then pulled with all her strength. The wings tipped her sideways. She started to fall, fast. When she let go, heart thumping so hard it seemed ready to burst out of her, the wings straightened and levelled and she was gliding again. She shivered. The ground was nearer now. She was lower. Never mind the canals. Ground, any ground, would have to do.

Buildings and streets rushed beneath her, mercilessly fast, dead empty houses, roads covered in weeds and patches of grass. There were trees, here and there, starting to sprout. They'd called this the Harvest Realm once. Now the fields and the meadows that had made the Silver City so rich were eating it.

The heart of the city reached up for her. The Golden Temple surrounded by its gardens, its esplanade, its lake and more of the old canals. Kataros could see the temple's dome, half staved in by some idle dragon. A livid green by day, but in the moonlight it was as grey as everything else. Next to it an open space. She could land there. Nervously, she pulled on the left wing, trying to guide herself towards the temple. Gently but firmly; and slowly the wings turned her, this time without plunging her towards the ground.

A shape passed through the air beneath her. For a moment her heart almost stopped, because even though it was night, it still could only be a dragon, gliding straight towards the temple; but then she understood: it was the Adamantine Man. Just like he'd said, he was flying faster than her, much faster and he was already lower down. She saw him fly on ahead towards the temple, but he came down short of it, into one of the canals. She saw his wings flare as he reached the ground, saw a splash of water and then he was lost as she flew over him.

The ruins fell away. For a moment she was over a wide square leading towards the gardens, then the temple walls reached out like hands. She tried to turn, but not enough. At the last she pulled down hard on both wings, the way the Adamantine Man had told her.

One wing hit a wall. She pitched forward. Something cracked and then she was falling, but slowly, strangely slowly. There was another crack, this time louder as the wing twisted and snapped. The ground flew at her face; she tumbled and then the world hit her on the back of the head and the broken pieces of Prince Lai's wings crashed on top of her.

12

Blackscar

Eight months before the Black Mausoleum

The little ones had given it a name. In its disdain for them, the dragon had forgotten. It had lived a thousand years and more, almost a hundred lifetimes. It had seen the world change beyond all recognition, but in the first of its lifetimes it had had another name. Black Scar of Sorrow Upon the Earth. Blackscar.

It had had a rider in those days. A true rider, a worthy one, a man made of silver. The god-men of the moon, whom the little ones called the Silver Kings. It had gone to war with them. It had known then, as it knew now, that the Silver Kings had made it, and made it for that one purpose. It had raged and stormed and slaughtered, burned little ones and consumed them, and in its turn had been burned by the sorceries of the lesser gods.

The Silver Kings had made it well. Death was not the end. Death was the little death, the end of one cycle and the beginning of another. It had been reborn. It had watched the world shatter, and then the last of the Silver Kings were scattered and gone, hidden or lost in the new and broken world. It had looked for them. They had all looked at first, all the dragons, left alone, forgotten and abandoned.

The dragon called Blackscar had looked for longer than most. A lifetime passed and then another, and by then few of them cared any more. The world was a new one. The lesser gods had been made quiet. The Silver Kings were gone. There were other creatures but they were ephemeral things. The dragons ate them and the world became theirs.

Between its lives, in its passing through the realm of the dead, it saw that something had changed since its first rebirth. A hole had been made, a tear, a rent from the shattering of the world, patched whole again by a web of something that tasted of the moon and of the earth and of something else, of some wrongness. Other dragons saw it too. For a while they had wondered together what it was. But the web held fast. The dragons avoided it. In time they lost interest.

The young ones said the web was gone now. Broken or destroyed. The dragon had yet to see. The dragon's mate, Bright Lands Under Starlight, that one would see now. Careless and reckless, but what was a dragon if not those things? What did a dragon fear? And they had not expected that any little ones would come. Now the dragon's hatchlings had scattered into the hills in search of cooler climes. Only the dragon remained.

It hunted.

The little ones had not gone far. It felt them, tiny senses of them at the fringes of thought, a flicker and then gone. It felt them when it searched, but never for more than a moment. Never for long enough to know where they were.

I know you are here! it raged at them, but they never answered. It flew up and down the river, burning the stone, searching.

In the night it crept down to where its mate lay under the stone. It tore the boulders away one by one until there was space for it to squeeze into where the little ones had been. It had not expected to find them still there, but the little ones were always surprising and the dragon was amused to see that one had, after all, remained. It walked aimlessly back and forth, so oblivious to the dragon's presence that the dragon paused from simply burning it.

Little one. Why are you still here? There is nothing but death for you here.

There was something wrong with it, this little one. It wasn't made right. The dragon touched its thoughts, but there were none. It lived, and yet it didn't. And there again was that touch of wrongness that it remembered, now untainted by the tastes of the moon and the earth.

The dragon picked the little one up. Its head was floppy. It seemed broken. It didn't speak. It didn't even seem to noticed that a dragon held it.

The dragon carried it out into the moonlight. *Where are the others?* it asked. There were more, it knew that much. *How many of you came?*

The little one didn't answer. It took the dragon a while to realise why: the little one was dead. It had been dead for some time. Its head was crushed and broken from flying stone, but some part simply wouldn't let go.

The dragon hadn't seen a walking dead thing for a long time. Not since its first lifetime. It wondered for a while what that meant. It thought about eating this little one. Dead or not, they tasted the same, but it had learned about eating little ones. They poisoned themselves. So it set this one down on the ground and watched to see what would happen. Eventually the sun rose. The little one stumbled away looking for shelter. Each time it did that, the dragon picked it up and put it back in the sun again.

It didn't last long. The walking dead had never lasted long out in the sun.

The dragon called Blackscar looked at the broken body for a while and then tossed it far out into the salt lake where it would be less of a temptation. Then it went back to searching for the ones who had killed its mate.

It would find them. And when it did, they would burn.

13

Kataros

Kataros crawled out from under the broken wings, stopping now and then to untangle herself from pieces of the harness. Sharp pains laced her side and her shoulder hurt when she moved it, enough to make her cry out.

When she was free, she stood up. In front of her was the Golden Temple, what was left of it, its broken dome a silhouette against the night stars. She'd never seen it in all its glory before it had burned in the death throes of the realms. Now, lit up by the moon and the ten thousand constellations of the night, all she could see were shapes and greys. On this side were a series of flying buttresses, looping out of the stonework down to the wide space where she stood – what had once been a gathering place running the entire length of the temple. Behind her, the dark waters of one of the city's canals whispered quietly in the night.

The pain in her ribs was something she could live with if she walked carefully. The shoulder was getting worse though. Under the Purple Spur with her potions and half a hundred herbs, roots and powders, the injury wouldn't have mattered. They weren't the sort of things that could mend a fracture, if that's what it was, but she could have done something about the swelling and the pain. Here she had nothing, not even a knife, or a pestle and a mortar. All she had was her blood.

She hadn't given much thought to what came next. *The Adamantine Man and his tunnels under the city.* She had to find him. They needed to reach shelter before dawn, and now that she was hurt, she was still going to need his help. More than the pain, *that* was what irritated her.

She reached through the blood-bond, searching for him. It was harder than before, the distance between them making it more difficult to reach him. She hadn't expected that.

There!

He was raging, fury surging through him. One of them was on his back, scrabbling at his neck. Another one was hissing and dancing around in front of him. Two more were dragging off the body of the outsider. He hurled himself backwards, slamming into a wall to shake loose the one grabbing at his shoulders ...

Kataros reeled. The emotion of the fight surged through her, almost making her trip over her own feet. Her fists clenched. She had a vague sense of where he was, somewhere back towards the black tower that was the mountain from which she'd come, the Fortress of Watchfulness.

He had the one off his back by the arm now. Wrenched it over his shoulder and crashed it down onto the ground. Didn't have a sword but he was used to that. No hesitation. Stamped down twice. First stamp the feral man's head hit the stone ground. Stunned. Second stamp crushed his throat. Dead.

He'd done what she needed of him. Maybe, on her own, she could survive out here without him. Adamantine Men had their ways and tricks but so did alchemists ... but she *wasn't* on her own. There was the outsider, Siff. Without the outsider and what he knew, she might as well have stayed in her cell and let them starve her to death, and there was no way she could drag him or carry him, not with a damaged shoulder.

Damn it! She still needed him. There was no getting away from it.

The one doing the dancing and hissing was backing away. Scared. Three of them and one of him and they were the fearful ones. That was how it was to be an Adamantine Man. Three against one. No fear!

Don't let him take Siff! But the Adamantine Man was already roaring and bounding on, head filled with blood and murder.

The fight was making her head spin. She let the blood-bond go and started to walk towards him. Running would have been better, but that hurt too much, and either way the fight would be over before she got there. Calm and steady, that was the alchemists' way, and so she let her mind wander to the emptiness of the Silver City around her, what was left of it. A hundred years ago it had been the hub of the world, home to tens of thousands. It had been a fading glory even then, its power already being leached away by Furymouth and the City of Dragons, but it had been a glory nonetheless. Out here on the esplanade beside the temple, with the gardens on one side and the canal on the other, there should have been people. She could almost see them, moving in little knots and clusters in the moonlight, even in the middle of the night. Now the gardens were overgrown, the canal choked with rubble and weeds, the temple dome tumbled and its marvels in ruins.

It was easy, she thought, with the skies filled with fire and angry monsters, to imagine the death of the Silver City was the work of the dragons, but that was wrong. The ruin wrought here had come when men still rode on their backs.

14

Skjorl

Seven months before the Black Mausoleum

Dragons were quickly bored. No patience. That was the way of it as far as Skjorl knew. A dragon sniffed you out in some cave somewhere; you curled up deep and waited and waited and eventually it found something better to do than sit outside wanting to eat you. Skjorl couldn't say for sure because most of the dragons he'd ever seen had got in plenty of eating, thank you very much, but that was the way he'd heard it.

Apparently the dragon from Bloodsalt had heard different.

He'd seen it enough times to recognise it before they even left, while he and Jasaan were still hiding, nursing their aches and pains and their stomach cramps and eating dried and salted bits of Relk and washing him down with brackish river water. He'd seen it lots of times, flying out of the salt desert every day, gliding off, away along the Sapphire, coming back again in the twilight. Hadn't occurred to Skjorl that the dragon was looking for *him* though, not then. Time passed. The dragon flew away for longer. Didn't come back for days sometimes, but it still came back. Never got to see what colour it was beyond a black shape up in the sky, but there was the size of it, the sound of it, the shape and the beat of its wings. Always the same dragon.

When they moved, they moved at night. Jasaan wasn't going to be winning any prizes for his running or his climbing, that was for sure, but at least he could walk and keep walking for hours. There was still pain there, Skjorl could see that, but still *some* bits of Jasaan were made of adamantine and he kept his hurt to himself. Skjorl's hand wasn't much use for anything any more except gripping a shield or his axe – Dragon-blooded, he'd settled on calling her – but that was all he had ever asked of it anyway. Besides, the first days were easy enough. They'd come this way before, when there had been more of them. Knew places they could shelter in the day, deep out of sight of the sky. No shortage of potions to keep their thoughts hidden. Wasn't much food to be had out in this part of the world, but there was enough. They'd already found out the hard way which roots and berries they could eat and which they couldn't, back when they'd had Vish and Jex and Kasern and Marran, and the others who hadn't even made it as far as Bloodsalt.

As the days and the nights wore on, they started to pass the places where the last few of their company had fallen. Vellas, stung by a scorpion that had taken a shine to the shade inside his boot for the day. Goyan, who'd eaten something he shouldn't have and become too weak to march. Him they'd put out of his misery. Couldn't leave him to die on his own. Couldn't take the risk some dragon might fly past and see him either, that he might not be careful enough, that he might give them away; but he was an Adamantine Man, so he took his fate like he should have when they bled him out into the river. They'd weighted him down with stones like they had with all the others and given him to the water. Dragons wouldn't see them under the glint and glimmer of the Sapphire. Or so they thought.

The fourth day was when Skjorl saw the vultures. Shouldn't have been out of cover, but he was bored with listening to Jasaan snore and in desperate need of a piss. Came out all careful, but there wasn't a sign of anything in the sky until he looked to the south and saw specks. First thought was dragons because that's what the first thought always was, but he could see right away he was wrong about that. Half a dozen specks, maybe more, and they were circling, which dragons never did. Dragon saw something it wanted, it went right down and helped itself. Either that or it flew on about its business. Maybe swooped down for a closer look, but never circled.

Vultures then.

Took another two nights of walking to find what the vultures had been eyeing from up in the sky. Hard to be sure, on account of there not being too much left, but there couldn't be much doubt in the end. Erak, who'd had his arm bitten off by a snapper. Snappers had died, been eaten, been buried under rocks to keep them out of sight, but something had found them and something had found Erak too. Hauled his fish-pecked corpse up out of the water and scattered its shreds all about.

'Dragon.'

Jasaan shrugged. Skjorl didn't think much about it either. Dragon had dug him up out of the water, or else maybe a snapper – so what? They walked on past the bones, and it was only later, when they were settling in to rest up for the day, that Skjorl had got to wondering; and that was when he remembered the vultures.

'Dragon dug him out of the water two days ago,' he said.

Jasaan shook his head, but only until Skjorl told him about what he'd seen. Neither of them had much to say, but thinking on it set Skjorl on edge. Dragon had been here just a couple of days ago, down on the ground, rooting and nosing about. Had to ask yourself why a dragon would be doing that.

They saw it again that evening, flying back towards Bloodsalt. Low over the valley, head sweeping from side to side. Searching.

'It's still looking for us,' said Jasaan. Skjorl frowned. Couldn't be right, because that wasn't what dragons did, but if he took a moment to forget about all that and just *looked*, he'd have to say the same.

It took another week and, seeing the dragon come prowling right past where they were hiding before, there couldn't be any doubt. Dragon on the ground, sniffing its way up the Sapphire valley, lifting boulders and peering into caves? Skjorl had never heard of anything like that, but maybe that was because no one had found a pair of dragons with so many eggs and then done what he'd done. He gave himself a day to see if he could think of some way how two Adamantine Men might make a trap for it and kill it. Wasn't surprised when he got nowhere with that, and so on the next night they changed their course and struck away from the valley, up towards the moors, still close enough to Bloodsalt that the slopes were gentle and not yet the boulder-strewn cliffs they'd start to be fifty miles further up the valley.

If you had to look back, Skjorl thought later, that was where their real falling-out had begun. Not that either said a word – too busy with pushing themselves onward – but once they got up on the moors even Skjorl could see it had been a mistake, and there was the look in Jasaan's eye like he knew that too. Or maybe it had nothing to do with the moors. Maybe that was just when they'd both given up pretending any more. Jasaan, who'd never quite got over what happened in Scarsdale, and Skjorl, who simply couldn't stop thinking that it should have been Jasaan who'd died in the cisterns under Bloodsalt and Vish who should have been alive and walking back to the Purple Spur.

Three dragons in three days up on the moors and they both knew they should have stuck to taking their chances in the Sapphire valley. Didn't use to be dragons up on the Oordish Moors. No eyries. Hadn't ever been that many snappers either, so Skjorl had reckoned on it being a safe enough place. Now he knew better. No food in the desert, but plenty of it up around Yinazhin's Way. Plenty of dragons too now, all busy eating it.

'Every dragon that eyried in Bloodsalt must have come up here,' said Jasaan. 'Back in Hyram's time that used to be more than two hundred.' They were hiding in a hollow, surrounded by rocks and long grass. They weren't the only things hiding there. Jasaan had already been spat at by a snake.

'Except the one in the Sapphire valley hunting for us.'

'The *one*.'

'*Hunting* for *us*.'

'We should go back.' And Skjorl knew he was right and they should, but there was some little demon in him that couldn't quite ever let Jasaan be right and him be wrong. Maybe because if it happened once then maybe Jasaan was right about some other things too.

'You do that then.'

'We're stronger together.'

'Your foot's good enough. We can both stand alone if we have to.'

Made sense to go back into the valley. There was water. Walk at night, hide in the day and they'd be fine, dragon or no dragon.

They'd be back in Samir's Crossing in a month. Trouble was, Skjorl was sick of it. Sick of everything. Sick of running and hiding. Sick of never seeing the sun, of sleeping every day in a cave, sick of dragons, sick of being too hot or too cold or too wet, and sick of not being able to do the slightest thing about any of it. But most of all he was sick of Jasaan. Spineless, moaning Jasaan. And that, at last, was something he could change.

'Adamantine Men fight together. We stand together. That's what we do.'

Skjorl nodded. 'Right up until we're a little bit hurt and instead of standing together we cry like babies and plead for help and let our comrades get killed when we should have been fighting, eh?'

'What?'

'You.'

'What are you talking about.'

'Vish. Vish died because of you. Because you were too scared to do what you should have done.' He saw Jasaan's eyes burn then, but there was no going back. 'I should have left you in the cistern. I should have left you by the banks of the Sapphire. That's what I should have done, and you should have told me to do it.'

'I couldn't walk, Skjorl!' Yes, there was anger there all right and plenty of it. 'Were there enemies I stopped you from killing?'

'You should have stayed up fighting. You should have clawed your way up the rubble down there and stabbed that dragon in the eye yourself. That's what a real Adamantine Man would have done. But you didn't, and so Vish did it instead, and now he's dead and that's on you.'

There might have been blows. It said everything about Jasaan, everything that Skjorl was sick of, that there weren't. 'You, of all people, have nothing to tell me about murder,' he hissed. 'You're a filthy animal. You're sick.'

That was Scarsdale coming out, which was enough to make Skjorl's hand on his sword stay where it was. And so neither of them drew their steel, and for a second or two they stared and let each know the true depths of how much they despised the other; and then Jasaan spat at Skjorl's feet and turned and walked away and that was the end of that.

There might have been some guilt. Might even have been some regret. Might have been that Skjorl wondered at his own words in the days after they went their separate ways. A man who'd been a part of his company for more than a year. Whatever they'd fought, they'd fought together, him and Vish and Jex and the rest of the dead. They'd survived Sand together, they'd survived the Blackwind Dales. They'd fought snappers and feral men. They'd reached the Silver River together and never mind what had happened at Scarsdale in between. They'd lived on musty water and mushrooms and the flesh of dead men in the caves under the Purple Spur. They'd forayed and foraged in the City of Dragons, hiding in cellars in the day and only coming out at night.

Might have stopped to wonder if maybe Jasaan had grown sick of all the same things he had, just a little sooner. Might have. But walking across the desolation of Yinazhin's Way alone took a hardness, and it was easier to let the hate burn instead of asking whether it was wrong. Guilt? An Adamantine Man had no use for that. So he walked on alone. Should have left Jasaan to die. Should have let the dragon have him. Could have been back in the Purple Spur by now. Thoughts like that kept him alive when dragons burned the hills around him, when he cowered in caves or among stones or sometimes simply huddled out in the open, praying to gods that didn't exist while lightning rattled the skies, when he dreamed of warm soft bread and warm soft women and cursed Jasaan for taking them away from him.

Yinazhin's Way. He'd seen a map once which showed it all around the edge of the moors in a great arc from Bloodsalt to Bazim Crag. Someone had told him that you could see Samir's Crossing and the Sapphire valley from the path. Without anything else to go by, he went on, walking the road at night, sheltered away from it in the days. When the road touched the edge of the cliffs and he looked out over the Hungry Mountain Plain and saw in the distance the glitter of a river and the black smudge of charred earth that had once been a town, he began to climb down. The cliffs weren't even cliffs here, easier than he'd expected, more a steep scrabbling scree of loose stones and boulders. Plenty of shelter from dragons.

He had to stop a mile or so away from the edge of what had once been Samir's Crossing. Stop and take a moment to get himself together. Adamantine Men took what life brought, whatever that was. They took their pleasures as it suited them when pleasures were there to be had. They didn't shirk their load or complain or falter when they were set to work. If the weight of their burden crushed them, then so be it, they got crushed, but they kept going to the end, staggering onwards, never putting it down. Adamantine Men didn't weep at the thought that there would finally be rest at the end of the night, and water and perhaps a few strips of dried meat and stale bread and most of all the company of their fellow men after so long alone in the wilderness. So since Adamantine Men did none of those things, Skjorl took a few moments to be something else where no one would know, and only when he'd done with that did he walk on. Samir's Crossing was ash, but there were cellars there, places where others kept watch on the movements of the dragons near the Spur. From Samir's Crossing there were tunnels to the Spur itself and what passed for home.

He wrinkled his eyes, trying to see if he could see the Spur in the distance, but it was dark. He didn't remember seeing it in the day. Couldn't remember when the Spur had faded out of sight after they'd left it all those months ago. After Samir's Crossing and before the Sapphire valley turned north and butted against the cliffs of the moors. Somewhen in between. Which meant this wasn't right, and he wasn't coming up on Samir's Crossing after all.

Tried not to think about it. Told himself, as he walked among unfamiliar ruined streets, that he must have come in from a different direction. Maybe from the north or the south. Told himself all that and more, right up until he reached the far edge of whatever town this was and saw the river, immeasurably too big to be the Sapphire, and then the telling stopped.

Not Samir's Crossing.

He found himself quivering. Trembling. There was a feeling he didn't know. It might have been despair, but since Adamantine Men didn't know such things, he grasped each and every memory he could reach and crushed them to see if they would bleed, and when he found ones that did, he poured them over this feeling, on and on until he hammered it into something that he understood.

Rage.

He let out a roar, but that wasn't enough, not even the start of enough. He pulled his sword out and started walking along the banks of the river, swearing blind that anything, anyone who stood in his path, they either ran away or they were dead, man, dragon, snapper, anything. Wherever this was, he knew the river, knew the only river it could be. The Fury; and walking the Fury *would* take him home. Into the Gliding Dragon Gorge. Plag's Bay. Watersgate. He gripped his sword tighter and ground his teeth. Another week, maybe just a little more. That was all. After so long, what did that matter?

Made him want to scream, that's what it mattered.

When he heard a shout, a half-strangled cry of fear with death swift on its heels, he went towards it without even thinking, moth-like to a flame, knuckles white. Started to run. The sound gave a shape to his anger, sharpened and made of steel.

Three men out in the open. Soldiers. Armed and armoured, but with long swords in their hands not the short stabbing things of the Adamantine Men, and two of them were down and there were a dozen man-things, scrawny raggedy feral scrap-eaters, snapping at them.

He swung Dragon-blooded off his back. Ran faster. Axes were for snappers and for dragons, but they were for this rage too, a murderous thing that would brook no lesser weapon.

The ferals saw him coming. Heard his bellow and his charge. The first one skittered out of the way, but the axe caught the next, hardly blinking as it cut through the man's shoulder and chest and shattered his ribs right to his sternum. He spun away, already dead, and then Dragon-blooded was coming back and straight into another, and then down, splitting the head of a third from his crown to his spine; and then Skjorl was among the soldiers and they were his, rallying to him, and together they charged and screamed and surged and slew, until the feral men scattered and fled into their shadows, and he stood, victorious, axe raised above his head, screaming words he would never remember.

An accented voice pulled at his arm, urging him away. Then something hit him on the head so hard he thought the sky had fallen on him.

And then, for a time, nothing.

When the world swam back into view he was in a boat being rowed across the Fury. 'They throw rocks,' said someone. 'Stones. Sometimes they have arrows, but not often.'

They were dragon-riders from the north, soldiers from Outwatch and Sand stranded with their King Hyrkallan and their Queen Jaslyn for more than a year since the dragons had awoken, stuck in the Pinnacles after the battle of the two speakers and the great cull that came after. Trapped there by the grand master alchemist – everyone under the Spur knew the story. No love between the riders at the Pinnacles and the alchemists of the Spur, none at all, and Adamantine Men had no time for either. Could have hidden it maybe, but that wasn't Skjorl's way. So he told them what he was and then watched their faces to see if there would be blood.

'Adamantine Men betrayed us like the alchemists.' Under the Purple Spur the alchemists had declared another speaker. Queen Jaslyn's sister Lystra. Turned out this lot had declared one too, Hyrkallan, Queen Jaslyn's king. Ought to have had a fight about that, right there and then, but what was the use? He saw the stone head of Speaker Hyram again, lying on its side in the ruins of Bloodsalt. One speaker hiding impotent in a cave was hardly any different from another, and titles were petty things when placed before the tide of dragons. Not that that stopped fools from thinking different. Stupid, and Skjorl found he wanted no part of it.

'My lady Dragon-blooded is for killing dragons,' was all he said, nodding at his axe. 'In whose name she flies, that doesn't really matter.'

They wrapped a cloth across his eyes and took him down into the secret tunnels that Pantatyr and his blood-mages had built after they slew the Silver King. He was in Valleyford, they said, two hundred miles and maybe more from Samir's Crossing where he was supposed to be. And it was alchemists they truly hated among the Pinnacles, not Adamantine Men, and so he could live – even though he'd be another mouth to feed – as long as he didn't mind putting his axe to some use; and Skjorl didn't mind that one little bit. For a month they stayed, hiding in the day, fighting ferals at night, searching for food and anything that might be salvaged, meticulously recording the movements of any dragons that passed overhead. Might have stayed longer if one dragon hadn't got scent of them and set itself to digging them out of the ground. Skjorl hadn't thought it possible, but it sat over their heads and each day they heard it tearing with its claws at the earth. He saw it in the air one day. Saw its silhouette and the shape and beat of its wings and knew it was the dragon from Bloodsalt. Odd that.

Hunger and a dragon overhead were old friends to Skjorl, but the riders didn't like this dragon one bit. Got to them quick it did. He wondered how they meant to cross the open land from where they were to the Pinnacles, what with no alchemists and no potions to hide them, but they laughed and slapped him on the shoulder and told him he shouldn't worry. A warren of tunnels reached out from the Fortress of Watchfulness, they said, right out across the realms, all of them ending on the banks of the Fury, from Gliding Dragon Gorge in the north to Farakkan in the south, to Purkan and Arys Crossing and Valleyford in between. Tunnels. That was how they were going home.

And so they did. Took five days. Strange and sorcerous things, those tunnels, wondrous at first, not hewn by the hands of man but by something else. Then, later, just dull. Boring and monotonous and the same, hour after hour after hour, straight as a scorpion bolt and dark and empty as a murderer's heart until they reached what the riders said were the catacombs of the Silver City itself, back from the blood-mage days when burying the dead had been no sin. They took him up into the Fortress of Watchfulness and the slowly dying fellowship of men that lived there, this Speaker Hyrkallan and his queen, and they set him to work doing nothing much at all. More wonders. The Silver City was old, he knew that, but the three stone warrens that overlooked it were older still. The Pinnacles. Hollowed out by hands long forgotten, tunnelled and quarried by men as a shelter from the terror of the dragons when they came, shaped and transformed by the will of the Silver King. Three mile-high monoliths that had been the centre of the realms from the day the dragons had been broken. They were old and they were heartless.

He found a few others of his kind, a handful of Adamantine Men who'd been sent out, as he'd been sent to Outwatch, with axes and hammers and dragon poison for the great cull that was supposed to save the realms and had failed. He couldn't believe what they told him at first, but over the weeks and the months he slowly saw it with his own eyes. The knights and riders of the Pinnacles were doing nothing. They had their tunnels that reached halfway across the realms and food enough for most of a lifetime. They had water, an endless inexplicable stream of it flooding through the fortress from the fountain on its peak conjured by the Silver King. But they had no hope. They were already lost.

After that he spent as little time there as possible. Lived as much as he could with the hunting parties, out in the Silver City tunnels. *Doing* something. Killing ferals mostly, but at least doing *something*.

Eventually, after a few months, another party of Adamantine Men had arrived out of nowhere. He kept away. Didn't want them to see what he'd become. And it was just a few days after that, when he found himself guarding some traitor alchemist they'd brought with them, that everything went to shit again.

15

Blackscar

Five months before the Black Mausoleum

The dragon searched the river. Other dragons came and went, other thoughts, other distractions, but it never forgot. Here and there, when it stopped to look with care, it found traces of the little ones' passing. Dead flesh, empty of life yet tainted with poison. It pulled them out of their hiding places and scattered them for the vultures and the crows. When it had searched every cave and turned over every rock and still found nothing that lived, it stopped and searched for its reborn mate.

The mountains, others told it, the younger ones who knew. *There are most eggs in the mountains.*

The dragon flew to the mountains to search and found nothing that interested it. It met a young one freshly hatched. One whose path had crossed with Bright Lands Under Starlight among the dwellings of the dead. His mate was gone, away to new flesh in a place far across the sea that had no end, beyond the storms that even a dragon could not cross except through the realm of the dead.

The hatchling spoke of other things too. It spoke of the hole in the underworld, yawning open, growing, of dragon souls swallowed and consumed, gone and destroyed for ever. The dragon considered these things and then let them fall aside. It had no use for them. It flew to the places where the little ones still cowered deep in their caves and under their stones and it searched. It stood on their battlements and reached into their thoughts while they slept beneath. In the smashed-flat wreckage of what had once been a proud place it found little ones hiding in the dirt, and among them it found a trace, a taste, a sniff of a memory, the flash of a face.

It burned them to ash and moved on until it came to the great fortress where the little ones had hidden away once before, centuries ago before their Silver King had come. To the place of the three mountains. It hunted through the thoughts and minds of the humans who cowered there, until it found the one it was looking for. And then it did something rare among its kind. It waited.

16

Kataros

Twenty-three days before the Black Mausoleum

Being told that a lot of things came with a blood-bond was one thing; finding out what they actually felt like was something very different. Finding out what they felt like while running through the dark ruin of the Silver City with a shoulderful of pain and feral men on the loose was something else again.

She knew where the Adamantine Man was. She could feel him, always there in a certain corner of her head.

That right there was one of those *other* things. He *was* always there, whether she liked it or not, no matter whether she wanted him or couldn't stand the thought of him. She couldn't see through his eyes or read his thoughts or send him her own unless she set her mind to it, but she could feel him. The ebbs and surges of his thoughts were like gentle hands placed against the back of her head whose fingers couldn't be still. She felt his thrill as he broke another feral, the moment of killing like a pinprick inside her skull. Then tension. Anticipation. Satisfaction. For a short time after that, calm. He had Siff with him now, the outsider, a constant annoyance and burden, slowing him down.

Bring him to me, she told him, but he'd hardly gone any way at all before there were more of them. Anger and rage, they came first, and underneath them a vicious joy, a raw and gleeful abandonment, a surrender of anything and everything except the next motion. They were alien and uncomfortable thoughts to an alchemist, taught always to think and consider, never to act swiftly or rashly, never in haste, never on impulse. The Adamantine Man was more like a dragon in a rage, swept up and lost in the moment. It was the blindness that came with that fury that had almost saved the realms in their last days. Almost.

She ran now and never mind how much it hurt. She felt the distance between them vanishing, yet she had no idea what that meant, whether a certain sense of him implied he was still a mile away through the starlit ruins or whether she'd find him round the next corner. She readied herself for either; as it was, she heard him before she saw him, his battle roars and the shrieks and jabberings of the feral men. She slowed as she reached them. Now that she was close, she didn't know what to do. The Adamantine Man had Siff on the ground, lying almost between his feet, weaving his axe in arcs too quick to follow, daring anyone to come close.

'Come on then! You wait much longer it'll be dawn. Or would you rather wait for a dance with a dragon? It's all the same to me, little men. This is my axe! Dragon-blooded! She's killed dragons before and she'll kill them again!'

The Adamantine Man had his back to a wall so the feral men couldn't get behind him. They'd spread out in a semicircle, eight of them. She glanced at the sky. Dawn was hours away and she doubted he could keep his axe swinging for that long, so she had to do something or else they'd all die, and the only weapon she had was her own blood. Try to blood-bind some of them? Easily said, but she had to get her blood inside one first.

The Adamantine Man then – he'd have to drive them away. Or lure them. She hadn't given much thought to what she was going to do with him once she was out of her prison. Get rid of him. Use him to escape and then send him away, or perhaps watch him fall on his own sword – that would have done nicely. One day it still might, but now the alchemist in her warned caution. Siff couldn't move, it reminded her, not on his own, and she certainly wasn't going to be the one to carry him. It whispered of how useful he still might be. *Why throw away a tool like that?* it asked. *He's no threat to you now.* She remembered his hand at her throat, squeezing while the other crippled one pawed at her. *But now he's yours and you are his mistress. You can end him whenever you like. Why do it now?*

Because I want to. Fight them, you bastard! Fight them and get yourself killed!

The Adamantine Man leapt away from the outsider and towards the nearest of the men around him. He lunged and swept, but the man darted out of the way and then the others were closing in, one or two of them already eyeing Siff as easier prey.

Stone scratched on stone behind her, a sharp noise that didn't belong. She turned and saw a shape, a shadow, a silhouette falling towards her, an arm, a head, a knife-glimmer in the starlight, and when finally she started to move aside, she was much too late. Something hard slammed into the muscle between her neck and her shoulder. She felt a burning pain and then the shadow was on top of her, a feral man, his weight pressing her against the stone wall at her back.

'What are you? Not one of them bastard soldiers.' The knife was up in the air again. She felt warm breath on her face. Blood ran down her back and along the curve of her collarbone. That was warm too. She felt dizzy. 'You're not one of us. A woman? What do you want out here?'

She couldn't speak; all she could to was watch the knife, waiting for it to come down. The shadow shook its head.

'Why'd you come out? Doesn't matter. Whoever you are. Shouldn't have come out. Shouldn't.'

He tensed. The knife drew back while fingers grabbed her throat, pushing her down.

... squeezing while the other pawed at her ...

'No!' She jerked a hand to the blood on her shoulder and clawed at his face. Fingers pulled at the skin of his cheeks and his chin.

'Shouldn't have come.' He was still shaking his head.

She screamed at him: 'Burn!' The word reached out to the blood on her fingers. *Her* blood. He stiffened. She screamed again. 'Burn! Burn!' Her fingers tightened, tearing at his face.

He dropped the knife and tried to pull away. She heard him gasp: 'Mercy!'

'No!' The Adamantine Man's battle rage was with her, seeping through the blood-bond. They were wearing him down, pecking at his strength while the fury grew ever more. 'No!' Her other hand went to the blood flowing out of her shoulder. She took a great handful of it and flung it at the man with the knife. This time he screamed.

'Mage!' He broke away from her, clutching at his face and staggering towards the others. 'Blood-mage! Help me! Ancestors! Help me, please!'

With a calm she didn't understand, Kataros picked up the fallen knife. One whole side of her was covered in her own blood. The knife was covered in it too. She looked at it, dull-edged and notched. Her head was spinning. The one who'd attacked her was lurching as though he could barely see, shrieking and hooting. She smeared her hands with her own blood again, both of them, and walked after him towards the fight. She'd seen a mage do this once, a true blood-mage, and he'd burned the whole front claw right off a dragon in a matter of seconds. He'd had a darker power than any alchemist, but it was a dragon he'd burned, and men were infinitely easier.

'Mage! Blood-mage!'

They'd started to notice, but most of them were still caught in the whirlwind around the Adamantine Man, poking and prying for a way through the blur of his axe while skittering out of its reach. One lay dead now, split in half. Another was crouched over Siff, going through his pockets. For a moment Kataros thought that must mean the outsider was dead.

'No!' That one then. She ran at him, hurling a spray of her own blood from her fingers at his head. He looked up and flinched as the blood spattered his skin and then screamed as it melted his face. Kataros staggered. For a moment the world slipped out of focus. She forgot where she was. She'd lost too much blood. She squeezed her eyes shut and pinched her arm, and when she opened them again, everything was sliding back and forth. She ran her finger over the knife cut in her shoulder. Deep. Straight through the muscle.

Mend!

She gasped. As the man who'd been bending over Siff screamed again and ran into the night, she fell to her knees. 'Mage!

Blood-mage! Abomination!' They were shouting. *Someone* was shouting. Louder and louder with the roaring of water rising until it filled her head and there was no space for any more.

'Alchemist! Alchemist!'

She didn't move. She was somewhere else, somewhere dark. A cave perhaps and her ankles hurt and her wrists too and her face and her head was filled with straw.

'Alchemist! Wake up! Kataros!'

Kemir? But Kemir was dead. They'd hanged him for looking like a dragon-rider.

'Please ... help.'

The light changed. Someone was standing in the cave mouth.

'Dust,' shouted Kemir. 'Take dust. It numbs the pain.'

The noises stopped. She was lying on her back. The night was still and quiet and the Adamantine Man was crouched beside her, staring at her. He had the knife she'd picked up in his hand.

'Alchemist?'

He was going to kill her. She reached into him through the blood-bond. *No! Back away!*

He stood up and withdrew, smirking as he did, mocking her fear. 'If I was going to do anything, alchemist, I would have done it by now. We're not ones for hesitation. It's not our nature.'

There was no lying when you were blood-bound. She sat up and looked around but the feral men of the Silver City were gone.

'You chased them off,' he said. 'They thought you were a demon. A blood-mage. They screamed and ran. I don't know what they saw.' He laughed. 'All I saw was a half-dead woman covered in her own blood.'

'I burned them.' She tried to stand up but the world started spinning again. 'Burned them with my alchemy.'

'Right.' He tossed the knife up in the air, caught it by the blade and offered it to her, hilt first. 'Whatever you did, you put the fear of the Great Flame into them. Doesn't mean they won't be back in a bit. Maybe if they get some courage from somewhere.' He poked at the wound on her shoulder, already scabbed over and half healed. 'That's a lot of blood from a little hole. Can you walk? Can't carry both of you.'

'I'll manage.' She took a deep breath and forced herself up. The world still wobbled but it wasn't as bad as before. She was hungry, she realised. Ravenous. 'So now what?'

The Adamantine Man shrugged and laughed and bent down to throw Siff over his shoulder as easily as if the outsider was a child. 'You're the one who wants to be somewhere. You tell me. But if it's to be the Raksheh then I'd go down. I'd go south to Farakkan and then make my way up the Yamuna at night. Longer than going the straight way but safer. Not so many dragons, a lot more places to hide and not so many of these sort to deal with.' He nodded to the bodies on the ground. There were three of them, ripped apart by the bloody axe across his back. 'There's tunnels from the Silver City to most—'

'I know.' She shivered. The Adamantine Man was still looking at her with those hungry eyes. She didn't know what he wanted from her, but he wanted something, something he hadn't taken while she'd lain out cold on the stone of the ruined city.

'Suppose I'll be showing you the way, then.' He sniffed. 'Best be under the ground before any dragons wake up. Can't promise we won't have more of this lot to deal with either.' He kicked one of the bodies. He didn't offer her a hand; he didn't even look back at her.

17

Skjorl

Twenty-three days before the Black Mausoleum

The alchemist they'd set him to guard had been stupid enough to leave the Purple Spur and come to the Pinnacles. Rumour said there had been others, a group of them. Some rebel faction, or else a delegation from the speaker under the Spur. Came with a company of Adamantine Men, who either fought like demons or surrendered like lambs, depending on who was doing the saying. They made him her watcher, but they were always going to kill her. Something brutal and pointless, full of harsh words and empty ceremony. Seemed like a waste. And he hadn't had a woman for far too long. And he *was* an Adamantine Man, at war with the dragons, and that gave him the right to have her.

Except then she'd reached into his head with her witchery and they'd fled the Pinnacles on Prince Lai's wings, him with a half-dead fool over his shoulders, and here he was. Comforting himself with steel and hard sinew instead of soft skin and writhing flesh.

Either was a pleasure. When the feral men came a second time, he saw his own death and saw that that was no bad thing. He let the fury drive him among them, sure that none would be able to stand against him, but knowing that in the end their numbers were too many. He took that knowledge and forged it into strength and fell upon them like a storm.

'Mage!' Another one, lurching out of the shadows. Barely seen. Hurt and half blind. Not a threat. Skjorl ignored him.

The cry jarred the others. He saw one fall back, another beside him hesitate, and that was all he needed to leap and cut the man in two.

'No!' That was the alchemist. He felt her cry more than heard it, twisting inside him through whatever tether she'd made to him. Blood and anger and pain, all to feed his own.

'Mage! Blood-mage! Abomination!' Someone unseen in the shadows, back where he'd left the outsider. The feral men around him fell away, and when he lunged and rushed them, they turned and fled and he was still alive, and this wasn't going to be his death after all.

He let them go. Took an effort of will to do that. When he was sure they were gone, he shouldered Dragon-blooded and went straight to the outsider. Keep him alive. That was what he had to do. Didn't want to, but the alchemist demanded it. He was compelled.

A few steps later and he almost trod on her in the dark, stretched out at his feet. Might be dead, but he knew straight away that she wasn't, before he even touched her. He could feel her, tied to him, could feel the faint flicker of her life, heart still strong. Could feel all that inside him.

Covered in her own blood, when he took a closer look. He crouched beside her and took the knife out of her hand

'What have you done to me?' he asked but she couldn't answer. He thought about touching her. Finishing what he'd started back in her cell. Thought about it, but did nothing, because another thought crushed it: he could kill her. Would that end what she'd done to him? Surely it would.

Kill her. Leave her body. Leave the other one too. Go down to the tunnels, fight his way to the underground gates of the Pinnacles. That would be easy. Go back to the fortress of no hope and take what punishment would come for stealing Prince Lai's wings.

Kill her and be free. Tempting, but his hand didn't move.

She stirred.

'Alchemist?' *Now! Now or not at all!* And still his hand didn't move, and then her eyes flickered open and he felt something slam inside him, hurling him away from her.

No! Back away!

He stumbled, silently cursing. 'If I was going to do anything, alchemist, I would have done it by now.'

Begged the question why he hadn't, though.

'You chased them off. They thought you were a demon.' He gave her back her knife. Blood-magic. Wasn't that supposed to be against everything an alchemist stood for? He poked at the wound on her shoulder. Small for so much blood. Looked like an old wound, one that had closed days ago, but it hadn't been there when she'd been in her cell, he was quite sure of that. Was that something that alchemists could do?

'So now what?' she asked.

He laughed. Now there was a question. To go with *Why didn't I kill you when I could*? He shrugged and picked up the outsider. Now what? Down, that was what. Down into the tunnels to Farakkan. At least that far they'd be safe from dragons.

She shivered. She looked so weak most of the time. He should have killed her. A part of him knew that with a stone-cold certainty. Should have killed her and set himself free while she'd lain flat out on the stone.

'Suppose I'll be showing you the way then. Best be under the ground before any dragons wake up. Can't promise we won't have more of this lot to deal with either.' He kicked one of the bodies. He didn't offer her a hand; he didn't even look back at her.

18

Kataros

Twenty-two days before the Black Mausoleum

They took alchemists to the City of Dragons before they could walk or say their names, when they were little more than babies. She could have come from anywhere. The alchemists had tested her and declared her promising. Someone had been paid ten golden dragons, the same for every child no matter who they were. The alchemists had given her a new name. Kataros, and for the next ten years of her life she'd never left the shores of the Mirror Lakes. Her head had become filled with words and dragons and a very particular understanding of the world.

When she was fourteen they took most of her friends away, declared their minds too dull for alchemy and named them Scales instead. She hadn't understood, back then, what that would mean, until they were gone and scattered across the realms to the great dragon eyries where they would fall in love with monsters and slowly lose their humanity from the inside while Hatchling Disease turned their skin to stone.

They didn't send *her*. She'd passed the first test, and now they kept her close for five more years. They taught her the true nature of dragons. She learned how they were kept subdued, of the terrible things that the alchemists did and would do again to preserve the nine realms. They taught her the first scratchings of blood-magic too, dressed up in lessons on herbs and potions.

She passed the second test. This time the ones that failed were set free, released into the wide world to be teachers or traders or whatever took their fancy, although they would always and for ever belong to the Order of the Scales to be called upon when there was a need.

They sent her to the mountains to finish her apprenticeship. She went on the back of a dragon – her first time – into the Worldspine to serve the King of the Crags, not that she'd ever see her new master. Five more years working in an eyrie would make her a true alchemist, but things in the mountains took a sour turn. There were men. In particular, one handsome dragon-rider. She lost her purpose and made foolish mistakes. Secrets that should have been kept were spoken to unworthy ears. They scolded her and they chastised her, and when that wasn't enough they whipped her, and when that still didn't tame her, they threw their hands in the air and took her titles and her lessons and her teachers all away and called her a Scales. They would have taken her mind too, dulling it with the same potions she had once brewed herself, and that would have been that, but instead the white dragon had come and burned her world to the ground, and then, in the aftermath, Kemir.

He was going to take her to the sea. She remembered that much. They got as far as Arys Crossing. It wasn't far from the Silver City at all, not on the back of a dragon. But there he'd died. And there Jeiros, the grand master of her order, had found her, clinging on to the Adamantine Spear, the one thing in the world that could kill dragons. He'd taken her back to the Adamantine Palace, but only in time to watch it all burn. After that the caves under the Purple Spur became her home, hers and everyone else's who hadn't died in flames. And after *that* ...

'Here.' The Adamantine Man stopped and took in a deep breath and slowly let it out again. She blinked. They were back where she'd started, at the esplanade around the Golden Temple.

'Why are we here.'

'The ferals don't come here. They think it's haunted. Evil spirits or some such.'

'Is it?'

He let out a scornful snort. 'No. Our ancestors watch over us, but there's no such thing as ghosts.'

'I have seen many things that I couldn't explain.' More than most.

'While I've seen very few.' He moved quickly across the

esplanade, pausing again only when he was back in the deep shadows of the temple walls. She followed as best she could.

'There's no ghosts,' he said again. 'But there's plenty more ferals. Some aren't so easily scared.'

Ferals. She hated the word. He meant the survivors, the ones who'd lived through the firestorms. The ones who'd chosen to stay in the ruins of their homes in the aftermath rather than hide in the caves under the Spur or in the mountains or in the three great fortresses of the Pinnacles. A foolish choice perhaps, but they were still people. They'd been farmers once, and craftsmen and traders and maybe even a few priests and almost-alchemists. 'We took an oath to protect them,' she said.

The Adamantine Man slid along the wall, keeping his back pressed to the stone and the rest of him in the deep shadows. When he reached the temple gates, hanging limp and bent, he stopped and spat. 'I took an oath to protect the speaker. No one else.'

'You failed then.'

'Yes.' The admission didn't seem to trouble him. 'I was in Outwatch when the dragons came. The white one was there. The first.' He peered around the corner into the black depths of the temple and made a show of sniffing the air. 'Sometimes they come in here anyway, ghosts or no ghosts. They burn things. Offerings to the dragons or something.'

'To the Great Flame.'

'Pah!' He tossed Siff over his shoulders again and jogged on. The inside of the temple wasn't as dark as Kataros had expected. The shattered edges of the dome hung over their heads, the stars glimmering beyond. The walls were tall, like towers in the dark of the night, but the space was vast and great chunks of what had once been the roof were gone. The Adamantine Man walked to the centre, to where the altar to the sun still stood. 'Many say the words. Few understand the meaning.'

'Explain yourself!'

'The Flame burned strong in the Guard. Your kind prefer to snuff it out. Do you have a god, alchemist? Do any of you?'

'Kataros. My name is Kataros.' She said it without thinking, then wondered why she'd bothered. She needed to be rid of him and the sooner the better. Finding him crouched over her with a knife in his hand had shown her that. She wouldn't dare to sleep now, wouldn't dare even close her eyes until he was gone.

He stopped. 'The spear-carrier?'

'What?'

'You. You brought back the Speaker's Spear? The Dragonslayer. Or am I wrong?'

'I …' Yes. They called her that, sometimes. The spear-carrier. 'I had it for a time. For a few hours, that's all. It was the grand master who carried it back to the palace.'

'You were there, then. At the end. For the final battle.' He sounded in raptures at the thought of it.

'I was deep underground. I only heard.'

'I wish I could have seen it. Outwatch was a slaughter. Sand the same. There weren't enough of us to make any difference. We smashed their eggs and took our axes to the unborn hatchlings inside. Killed a few of the very young, the ones still placid or in their chains. The bigger ones your sort did for. Poisoned.' He shook his head. 'I'd have given a lot to see the legions in their glory with their scorpions, pitched into the battle we were all told we would fight.'

'They were slaughtered. Hardly a man left standing.'

'I know.'

'Almost every last one of them fought on until the end. Long past when all hope was lost. It seemed foolish to me.'

He growled. 'It's what we do, alchemist Kataros.'

A litter of old offerings lay spread across the altar, but the Adamantine Man swept them away before Kataros could see what they were. He crouched down and brushed at the dust and dirt on the floor with his hands.

'What's your name?' she asked.

'To the likes of you I'm just *soldier* or *guard*. Among those who stand beside me, I am Skjorl.'

She reached through the blood-bond. 'My blood is bound to yours, Skjorl. You are tied to my will. You will never harm me. You will do whatever you must to keep me from hurt.'

He didn't move, just kept scraping at the floor. 'Do you know, alchemist, how much it hurts when you do that?'

'Less than anything you would have done to me, I think.'

'I would have given you a quick and painless death, more painless than the one that was waiting for you, and an hour or two of pleasure to remember me by when you reached your ancestors, if you'd have let me. Both still yours for the taking if you want them.' He looked up, leered at her and patted his crotch.

'You …' She shuddered.

'If you ever let me go, alchemist, I will do everything to you that I would have done before, only this time I will make sure it hurts.'

There was no anger in his voice, no hate, no venom, but he meant every word. He looked up at her a second time, heard her silence and laughed at it. 'Alchemist, you've taken my freedom. What I will do to you is kinder.' He took a step sideways and clawed at the floor for a moment. 'You did the same to the dragons. It's your way, is it? Whatever stands before you, you enslave it?'

He might have touched a nerve, if it hadn't been for what he'd been about to do when she'd put her blood into him. 'You were set on raping and then killing me. You see that as a better fate?'

'I do.'

'You're so wrong.' How did men come to even think such things? There were no words for the depth of it.

He laughed at her as his fingers wrapped around a metal ring set into the stone in front of him and he started to pull. 'Ask one of these ferals which they'd prefer, death or slavery. Ask them why they're here and not in your nice comfy little fortress.'

'They are *men*! They are not animals!'

'They *were* men, alchemist. Now they're ferals.' The stone began to move, grinding across the floor. 'Can you make some light?'

She showed him her empty hands. 'With what?'

'If you can't, then we descend in the dark. Do you see a shaft?'

Kataros peered into the hole. It was black as pitch. 'I can't see anything.'

He sighed and pulled the stone further out, inching it across the floor. Another ring was fastened into the back of it. A rope was tied to the ring and vanished into the hole. Skjorl crawled across and gave the rope a tug.

'There are other paths in and out of the fortresses from the city. Plenty of them, so I'm told. We close this behind us so the ferals can't follow.'

'Men!' she shouted back at him. 'They are not *ferals*!' And then he was on top of her, hand clamped across her mouth, blood-bound slave or not, hissing in her ear.

'Quiet!' She heard a chuckle in his throat. 'Quiet, alchemist. Lest you get *hurt* when the *ferals* hear you and fall upon us in their hordes.' He let her go and bared his teeth, then dragged Siff to the edge of the hidden shaft under the altar and began to climb down rungs set into the stone with the outsider over his shoulders. When all three of them were inside, he swung on the rope until the altar stone was back in place and the darkness became absolute. She heard him below her, one foot after the other, climbing down the shaft faster than she could bring herself to, even though he had Siff on his back and she had nothing.

'Wait!' she hissed, but either he didn't hear her or he didn't care. At the bottom, his hand touched her arm in the dark. She squealed and flinched away.

'Just me, alchemist. What did you fear?' He was laughing at her.

She didn't know how far down they were. The alchemist-trained part of her understood they'd gone neither as far nor spent as long there as it seemed in the blackness. Older instincts wondered what monsters lurked so deep beneath the earth. 'Under the Purple Spur sometimes the dead, those who aren't taken up into the sunlight, rise,' she said. 'Does that happen here?'

He laughed at her. 'I came from under the Spur before I came here and I heard the same. People living in fear will say many things. Believe me, alchemist, the dead do not rise.'

'Those under the Spur say otherwise.'

'Seen it yourself?'

She looked away. 'No.'

There was a shrug of indifference in his voice. 'I am what I am, alchemist. I believe what my senses show me, not the tales of fearful men.' His arm touched hers again and brushed along her side. 'You should take my hand, alchemist, lest you trip and fall and *hurt* yourself in the dark.'

'No.' She pushed him away. 'You don't touch me.'

'Suit yourself.' He moved off. She felt the space between them, felt his absence from close to her like a load taken away that been clamped around her chest.

'Do you know where you're going?'

He didn't answer that. Through the blood-bond she felt him ease his way slowly in the darkness. He still had Siff slung across his shoulders. He was strong, fearfully strong, but that was the way the Adamantine Men were made. It was simply done. They took unwanted children from across the realms, just as the alchemists did, only for a far lesser price, and then they forged them, without mercy, into fighting men who would stand against dragons. Most died before they reached manhood. Most of the rest didn't last as long as this one had, judging by his age.

Skjorl. Did she even want to know his name? He was better as a faceless monster, cold and loathsome as the dragons he'd been raised to face.

'If you were in the Spur after the realms fell, how did you get here?' she asked. Following him was easy. She could sense him, where he was, always, feeling his way along the walls.

'I walked, alchemist. And you? You were under the Spur too. Kataros the spear-carrier. You were at the palace when it fell, after all.' She heard him chuckle. 'Why would you come to the Pinnacles, alchemist, where only torture and death could possibly await you?'

'I was sent.' She felt him freeze and fall silent and so she did the same, ears stretching out into the black, grasping for sound and finding nothing. After a few seconds he began to move again. 'There were others. Do you … Do you know what happened to them?'

'No.'

He was lying. The blood-bond told her that at once, which

must have meant the others were dead. She took a ragged breath. It wasn't a surprise, not at all, but still there was a difference between fearing the worst and knowing it. She was alone here then, as she'd thought, and there would be no seeing her old master again, nor any of those that passed as friends who'd come here.

'Who sent you? The speaker?'

'That's none of your concern, soldier, nor is the why.' Even if the why, she suspected, had more to do with the dwindling of supplies under the Spur, the growing starvation, the simple presence of more mouths than could be fed, even among the Adamantine Men, even among the alchemists.

'There are tunnels as far as Plag's Bay. You could return. It would be a safer journey than going into the Raksheh. I'd take you if you asked.'

She answered that with silence. There were reasons, of course there were reasons, but sharing them would make her weaker, not stronger.

'What did this shit-eater I'm carrying tell you?'

She let her silence answer that one too. Through the blood-bond she felt him grinning to himself.

'Here. A door. Ready? There's about to be blood.' He stopped and lowered Siff to the ground. She heard the grind of metal against metal and then a line of dim light opened the darkness like the drawing of a curtain. Cold white light, alchemists' light, flooded in as Skjorl pulled the door wide. He drew out his sword and then jumped through. There was a shout, and then the screaming started.

19

Skjorl

Twenty-two days before the Black Mausoleum

Answers would come when answers were ready. The alchemist would tell him, because in the end people like her always did. She'd yield to him in other ways too, in time. For now there was killing to be done. There were always ferals in the tunnels. No surprise to open the door and find a few of them sheltering. He was in among them before the sleeping ones even had a chance to open their eyes. Three women. Pity to waste them, but the alchemist would never have let him toy with one. Two children. He killed those first, moved on to the women as quickly as he could. Not that they had any chance of getting away but because he had to be done with them before the alchemist could tell him to stop. There was a man, sitting on watch perhaps, eyes closed and dozing. Skjorl killed him last as he tried to flee, driving his sword into the man's chest just when the alchemist screamed at him. Leisurely, he put his boot on the dead man and pulled his sword out again.

'What are you doing?'

He walked back to one of the women, tore off the outer layer of her rags and wiped his blade clean.

'Answer me!' The words came with a hammer blow to the back of his head. He screwed up his eyes against the pain of it.

'The ways from the tunnels to the Silver City are kept secret. They saw us come through. So they had to die.' Good chance they already knew the secret shaft was there, might even have been why they'd settled where they had, but no need for the alchemist to know that. He looked up and down the tunnel. The light here was like the light in the fortress, a glow that came from the very stones of the walls and the roof. Here it was feeble, starlight on a cloudy night, no more than that. He closed his eyes and reached with his ears, searching for running feet, but now all he could hear was the alchemist bleating.

'You will not kill without reason!'

'I have reason. Hyrkallan's riders have ordered that all ferals be killed.'

'No!'

Stupid woman needed to know when to speak and when to shut up. If any ferals had got away, their footsteps were lost now. He growled. 'Alchemist Kataros, listen when I tell you this. The feral folk who live under the Silver City may once have been ordinary men and women, but that was before their city burned and dragons ate all those they loved. They blame the speaker, their kings, their queens, their riders, their alchemists and even the Adamantine Men for what has fallen upon them. They will not listen to your pretty words – they'll kill us for our food, for our clothes, for anything we carry, or if we carry nothing, they'll kill us because we are not them. These would have come back with others. Your command was to protect you from any hurt. I have obeyed it.'

Which was more talking than he was used to. He blew out his cheeks and subsided into silence. The alchemist wouldn't understand. She'd think she knew better. Alchemists always did until the world taught them otherwise.

'No.' She shook her head. She was a woman, inevitably weak. Which made the hold she had over him all the more galling.

'Going to be hard to find shelter up the Yamuna. The alchemists under the Spur once gave us potions they said hid us from the dragons. Stopped them from knowing we were there even when they couldn't see us. You said you know how to make that potion. Do you?' The ferals were dead and good riddance to them. No point dwelling on what couldn't be changed.

'Yes, if I had what I needed. But I don't.' She was still staring at the bodies. Couldn't seem to tear her eyes away from them. He wondered why. They were dead, after all. It was done. Move on.

'And what *do* you need?'

She looked up at him and laughed. 'You're not capable of getting it.'

Skjorl smiled to himself. Said with venom but hardly likely to be true. 'What do you need, alchemist?'

'Dragon blood, soldier. I need dragon blood.'

'Something so easily done?' He laughed back at her. 'I'd hoped for a challenge.' Whatever she said to that, she said it under her breath and he didn't hear. He settled to stripping the corpses on the off chance they had anything useful. 'I've not travelled the Yamuna valley, but I've heard nothing good. Open country, wide and flat, all the way from Farakkan to the Raksheh. No shelter. It's one thing to hide from a dragon that flies past without the first idea you're there. Different matter to hide from one that can feel you. Got to dig deep where it can't reach and then wait for it to get bored. Can be days. Weeks even.' How long had the dragon from Bloodsalt stalked him and Jasaan? Had it ever even stopped? 'And then there's the next one and the next. Too many down there and no place to go deep. There's the river worms too, if such things are real. If the dragons haven't eaten them. We should go somewhere else.' *Useless, these ferals. Never have anything worth shit. No keepsakes. No food, not even a half-decent knife. Nothing but stinking rags alive with lice and the string that holds them together.*

'Are you done?'

Skjorl got up. He looked up and down the tunnel again. Nothing moved. No sounds. After the caves of the Spur the old paths under the Silver City felt strange. Too straight, too smooth. Like they'd been made by some giant burrowing worm. Nothing but glassy soft-glowing rock, perfectly round except for a small flattening at the bottom. He'd once seen a dragon-rider try to carve a pictogram into the stone and come away with little to show for it past a blunt knife. In the Pinnacles they said that blood-mages had made the tunnels after they'd killed the Silver King, but they were wrong. You could see that straight away. The hand at work here was the same as inside the fortress. The hand of the Silver King himself, the half-god sorcerer.

History. You learned a little of that as an Adamantine Man,

mostly about the villainy of the blood-mages. Then there was the rise of the Order of the Dragon, the first speaker, Narammed, and the beginnings of the Adamantine Men. Their traditions, their stories. A man needed to know his roots, but the Silver King had come and gone before all that.

'Do you know any rites for the dead?' he asked.

'No.' The alchemist spat her derision at him. Alchemists and priests. Oil and water. He wrinkled his nose at the bodies. Didn't like to just leave. There ought to be words. Even ferals deserved that, something to guide them to their ancestors.

He shrugged. Didn't like to, but didn't get to chose. 'This way then.' He went back to get the outsider. They'd have to do something about him soon or else he'd be dead before they reached Farakkan, never mind the Raksheh. Or maybe the alchemist hadn't seen what state he was in.

She looked at the bodies. 'You're just going to leave them?'

'Yes.' Not much choice.

'Beneath the earth? Cut off from the sun and the moon and the stars and the sky?'

'Yes.' Didn't like it, but yes. He pushed past her. Crouched down beside the outsider. He was still breathing at least. Conscious even, although he was pretending he wasn't. 'We need to find some food and water for—'

'No!' There it was, the hammer into the back of his head again. He dropped the outsider's hand and grunted at the pain of it.

'What then?'

'You'll take them back up. You'll take them back up, one by one, into the Golden Temple and leave them out where their ancestors will be able to find them.'

Madness! But he couldn't even argue. This time the pain almost knocked him to the ground. 'Stop, alchemist! We don't have time for this!' Would be right, though. Would be doing right by the ones he'd killed. Couldn't argue with that.

'Just do it.'

Skjorl closed his eyes. 'It will take hours. More ferals might c—'

'*Men!* They are *men*!'

'And what will you do if more *men* come while I'm up in the shaft? Speak harshly to them? Or will you make them slaves with your blood-magic, as if that's somehow better than giving them a clean death? Or will you burn them like you burned the ones up above. It'll be pushing dawn before we're done. The dragons will be awake.'

'Then be quick and do not argue.'

She wouldn't move. He understood, in a way. This was to be a battle between them, one of her will against his. She thought she couldn't lose, but she would. In the end she would. Wasn't a bad thing to ask anyway. Killing a man was one thing. Leaving him where his ancestors couldn't find him, that was cold. He nodded. 'As you wish then.' Maybe if he seemed docile and beaten, she might believe it. And then he'd simply bide his time for the chance that would inevitably come, just as the dragons had done ever since the Silver King had mastered them. Every Adamantine Man knew *that* story. So he dragged the bodies into the hidden passage and closed the door behind them all, trying to keep the alchemist out of harm's way. Any ferals came along, he'd have the obligation of trying to rescue her. Might as well try to save himself that trouble.

When he was done with that, one by one, he carried the dead up the shaft and dumped them beside the altar of the Golden Temple. Another offering. Took long enough too.

Halfway through he came down the shaft to find the secret door wide open, the moonlight glow of the Silver King's tunnels casting ghastly shadows over the faces of the dead.

'What are you doing?'

'I don't like the dark,' snapped the alchemist.

'Ferals come while I'm up there, I can't help you.'

She showed him her knife. 'I can look after myself.'

He closed the door. When he came down the next time, it was open again. This time he let it be. Stupid, but that was alchemists for you. Always thinking far away, never up close about what was around them, right there in their hands.

Eventually he was done. Most of the night wasted. He went to pick up the outsider. Another burden to carry, but he was used to that.

The outsider was gone.

20

Kataros

Twenty-two days before the Black Mausoleum

Skjorl just rolled his eyes, shook his head and vanished into the tunnels, closing the door behind him. Kataros sat and nursed her aching shoulder, but he wasn't long, and when he came back he had Siff slung over his shoulders again. The outsider was moaning softly to himself.

They set off. As the Adamantine Man led her through the tunnels, Kataros tried to catch Siff's eye, but he was far away, lost in his own misery. Ahead of them, here and there, she thought she saw movement, shapes running away, footsteps echoing across the smooth stone.

'Ferals.'

'Men,' she muttered, but the Adamantine Man didn't answer. Whoever they were, they were gone before she saw much more than shadows.

'They'll be up in the ruins, most of them,' grunted Skjorl. 'Dusk and dawn. That's the time to go feral hunting.'

'You hunt them?'

He shrugged. 'Not me. Sometimes the riders do.'

She wondered if the same was true in the Purple Spur. The Adamantine Men there crept out at night to forage for food. She'd never thought to ask *what* food it was they found.

The tunnel ran straight as an archer's arrow and smooth as one too. They hadn't been *made* so much as *created*, simply brought into existence exactly the way the Silver King had wanted them. A half-god who could tame dragons and raze mountains on a whim, what did he want with tunnels? She couldn't begin to guess their purpose, but then who was she to fathom the mind of a semi-divine?

The tunnel split into three, each spiralling off in languid arcs so that it was possible to walk almost straight and yet pick any one of them as they curved up and down and away. The Adamantine Man chose one without hesitation. She didn't know whether that was because he knew where he was going or simply because that was the way he was.

'Stay close. If I start to run, you run with me.'

She heard a distant hiss of water. When the tunnel split again, the Adamantine Man took the path that sloped downwards, curved back on itself and then merged with another, one with water running through it. When he waded in, it came up to his knees. It was flowing fast. He stood for a time, not moving, then came out again.

'To get to Farakkan, we follow this water,' he said. 'Riders go there sometimes. They have rafts. On a raft it takes two or three days.' He wrinkled his nose. 'Getting back takes longer. Got to walk up the Fury to Purkan. There's another tunnel there. Can't get back this way against all that water. We leave, we probably can't come back.'

'We don't need to get back,' she snapped. 'Just there.'

'That so?' He shrugged. 'And after the Raksheh? If you find whatever it is that's there? What then?'

'That's no concern of yours.' Which was another way of saying she hadn't thought about it. In truth, she had almost no idea what she was going to find. Siff had been raving, but even if everything he'd said had been true, the chances of getting there seemed so small that she'd never looked to what happened after.

The Adamantine Man spat in the water. 'We could float or we could swim, but this one can't.' He shook Siff up a bit and made him grunt. 'Got to steal one of them rafts. Got to walk against the flow for a bit to do that and it'll be riders we face, not ferals. Could get messy.'

'Then find another way.'

He shook his head. 'Can't, because there isn't one. We raft or we walk. I don't know how long that will take. Too long for him unless we find food.' He looked down at Siff, picked him up and went back into the water. 'It's not far. You can stay with him while I deal with it. You'll be safe enough. Ferals avoid the place and if there's any riders, they have to get past me first.'

She followed him in up to her knees. The current tugged at her, fast enough to take her down and wash her away if she slipped. The Adamantine Man didn't seem troubled. With each laboured step, the hiss of rushing water grew louder, until it became an echoing roar. Under the Purple Spur she'd seen where the Silver River emptied itself into some bottomless chasm. She'd seen it from the inside, from the other side of the chasm in a cave like a cathedral, and the sound had been the same. Was there a river in the Silver City? She didn't remember one. There were canals, the city had been famous for them, but a river?

Skjorl stopped and moved carefully to the edge of the water, up the curve of the tunnel. He propped Siff against the side and beckoned to her.

'Getting light up there soon,' he said. 'Ferals forage at dawn and sleep in the day. Riders are still in their beds. Good time for us to be thieving.' He pointed. 'Look closely. Do you see?'

'See what?' Up ahead there was a subtle change to the light.

'Where the tunnel opens out. We're right underneath where we started. Stay here with him. Make sure the water doesn't take him.' He shrugged. 'If he tries to escape, he'll not get far on his own, but you'll be lucky to get him back before he drowns.'

Kataros cupped Siff's face in her hands. She lifted back his eyelids. He was conscious, if only just. 'Are you all right?'

'He's half-dead, alchemist. If he hasn't told you everything you need, I'd get it out of him quick. Then we can dump him when we get to Farakkan. We'll move faster.'

The outsider rolled his head. 'Fuck ... you ... rider ...'

The Adamantine Man laughed. 'See. It can talk. So make it!'

Kataros took a deep breath. 'It's not something he can tell me. Or you. We have to take him to the Raksheh with us. It's something he has to show us.'

She'd expected an argument and that she'd have to force the Adamantine Man to her will again, but he only shrugged like he always did. 'If you say so. If you're not going to use your magic to make him talk, perhaps you could use it to make him walk. Although since we're all going to be eaten by dragons as soon as we try to get up the Yamuna, don't strain yourself.'

'Give him some water.'

He laughed at her. 'Give it to him yourself, alchemist. It's right there. With a bit of luck the riders haven't poisoned it today.'

21

Skjorl

Twenty-two days before the Black Mausoleum

Wouldn't take all that much luck though – as far as Skjorl knew, for all their talk, the riders in the fortress had only actually done it once. Months ago, when he'd still been somewhere on Yinazhin's Way, talking to his axe and cursing at the moon. Dropped in poison by the barrel-load to try and kill the ferals. Hadn't worked.

A hundred yards from where he'd left the alchemist, the tunnel ended in a vast cavern. Not that he could see much of it in the gloom now, but the light here waxed and waned like the light in the rest of the fortress and he'd been here at other times, when the city had been in daylight. Water plunging from the centre of the roof, hundreds of feet up, crashing to the stone floor and making everything damp with a cold mist. It came all the way from the very top of the fortress, from the endless fountains of the Reflecting Garden where water would lie still but not lie flat, or at least that's the way it had been before dragons had smashed it to rubble. Hadn't killed the fountain though. Another mystery of the Silver King for the alchemist to ponder; as far as Skjorl was concerned, it made clean water spill down through the levels of the fortress and kept them all alive, and that was as much as mattered.

All that water came down, and then it flowed out into the canals of the Silver City; and then it came back again and finally ended up here, draining away down the tunnel to Farakkan, the last and lowest of the paths to the Fury. By the time it got this far, it wasn't so clean. The place stank.

He climbed around the side of the cave. All the tunnels under the Silver City led here in the end. There were always riders too, because this was the way in and the way out of the fortress. The Undergates. The *only* way in and way out as far as Skjorl knew, unless you happened to have a pair of Prince Lai's wings or perhaps a handy dragon.

The rafts, if you could call them that, weren't much more than a few lumps of wood poorly strung together sitting on the floor of the cave close to the water. Riders were far across the other side by the gates. If they saw him at all, chances were they'd leave him be. Taking a raft would be easy, nothing like what he'd laid out for the alchemist to sweat over. Question was though, did he stop at that? Riders here hated alchemists and so did their pretend speaker. Blamed them for everything that had gone wrong, for the end of the realms. Fair, perhaps, but killing them all was throwing away a weapon, and that was something an Adamantine Man would never do.

But still …

He ignored the rafts and ran around the edge of the vault, skirting the spray of the falling water. When he was close enough to make out the gates through the gloom, he stopped with his hands held up high, away from his sword and his axe.

'Riders of Speaker Hyrkallan!' Couldn't see them but they were there. From the gates they'd see him too, at least the shape of him. They'd have a crossbow on him by now. Might shoot him just because he was there. With luck he didn't look too much like a feral; then again, riders weren't always that bothered about such things. Better safe than sorry.

'I am Skjorl of the Adamantine Men. You had an alchemist imprisoned here. She has escaped. She aims for the Raksheh. For the Aardish Caves. She believes there is a weapon there. Something against the dragons. Do you hear me?'

A muffled voice shouted back: 'Come closer!'

'I think not.' Tone was wrong. He jumped sideways and ran away, back towards the rafts, jinking from side to side. Maybe they took a shot at him, maybe they didn't. Didn't matter. He'd done what was right. They knew where he was going. If there was a prize to be had, a secret to be found, it wouldn't die when the alchemist was eaten by a dragon. The riders, now they could do whatever they thought was right to do too, and if that was nothing at all, well then he was glad to be rid of them.

He reached the rafts and pulled one to the edge of the water. He could see it now – the reason he hadn't killed the alchemist when he'd had the chance. The fortress was the strongest bastion against the dragons in the realms. They had food. Water. They weren't all starving like the alchemists under the Purple Spur. And what were they doing? Nothing. Sitting there. Fading.

He pushed the raft into the water and rolled into it. The current took him at once, fast away down the tunnel. Waiting, that's what they were doing, but waiting for what? For the dragons to get bored and go away? For the Silver King to return? But the Silver King was dead and there was nowhere else for the dragons to go and they couldn't wait for ever.

And so he hadn't killed her when he'd had the chance, and maybe it *was* better to be a slave with a glimmer of hope for freedom than to be dead and with your ancestors. Needed some thought that, but by then the alchemist was in front of him, waving madly in case he somehow didn't see her. He rolled back off the raft and dragged it to a halt.

'Here.' She refused his help to climb on, so he grabbed hold of Rat instead. The outsider was more awake now. Maybe the water had done him some good. Pity they had no food. Another thing needing some thought, and maybe urgent too. Alchemist had her mind set on the Raksheh, but the getting there, that was going to be the hard part. No food, no bows to hunt with, no easy way to hide from dragons. Hard wasn't right. A bloody miracle, that's what it would be.

But still better than doing nothing.

The water carried them briskly down the tunnel. Dead straight as they all were, except when they split apart, and even then it was easy. Follow the water all the way.

'You ever go to Farakkan?' he asked when neither the alchemist or the outsider had said a word for most of half an hour. The alchemist shook her head. 'Mud hole,' he said. 'Nothing there. Even before the dragons.' He looked at her in the gloom. 'What are you doing here, alchemist? What is this about? Why did you leave the Purple Spur?'

'Why did you?'

'Orders, of course.'

'Likewise.'

'Fine. I was sent to Bloodsalt to see whether anyone survived there. I went with a company of men. Most of us died on the way. Dragons got half and the rest went to bad food, starvation, disease, snappers, ferals, snakes and one scorpion. When we got to Bloodsalt, there was nothing left except dragons. Two of us escaped. On the way back we were separated. I got lost. When I came down from the moors, I met riders and they brought me here. And that's that. You?' Wasn't sure why he wanted to know. Made no difference, after all.

'It remains none of your concern.' She shook her head. Skjorl spat into the water. There was nothing to see this far from the Silver City. The ferals didn't come so deep, and whatever *did* come this far was quickly washed away. There was only the sloshing of the water, the faint glow of the walls and the smell of rot. He didn't even know for sure that any of the riders really had ever come down this far. They used the rafts as far as the edge of the Silver City, but further? He'd heard talk, but never with any names. Farakkan. Easy to reach, but hard to get back with all that water flowing in your face.

Dragon blood. How, by all those who'd gone before him, was he supposed to get dragon blood?

The alchemist was tending to the outsider. Soaking a piece of cloth in the water and then squeezing dribbles into his mouth. He was so weak he could barely move.

'I wouldn't drink anything she offers you, shit-eater.' Skjorl laughed. 'She'll make you her slave.' Too late for that, of course.

She looked at him, a glance of pure hate. 'I only do that to people who try to rape me.'

He laughed. 'You'd have come round, alchemist.'

'I wouldn't touch you if you were the last man alive.' Fingers scraped the back of his head on the inside. A warning of what she could do to him.

An hour passed and then another. He watched the alchemist for when she would fall asleep, but her eyes stayed wide and alert. More blood-magic perhaps, or maybe some old-fashioned fear. Eventually he gave up and let himself doze.

He woke up to find the alchemist shaking his arm. His hand was on his sword before his eyes had finished opening. She was pointing. *Ferals*, that was his first thought, but that wasn't it. She was pointing because one side of the tunnel had opened out. Already, she was guiding them to the edge of the water.

Not a natural cavern. The walls were straight and threw off the same dim light as the tunnel. They weren't smooth though. He frowned. Peered at them. Archways. The walls were decorated with arches. Like the walls inside the Fortress of Watchfulness. Odd.

'This is ...' He frowned. 'Where are we, alchemist?' Trouble with dozing and floating in the dark in a place like this. Could be they'd a gone a mile or two, could be they'd gone a hundred. Could be the Silver City was barely out of sight behind them, or maybe Farakkan was just a few minutes ahead.

The alchemist ignored him. 'What is it?' Which told him what he needed to know – she knew as much as he did: nothing. He shook his head as the boat ground against the stone floor of the tunnel and bumped to a stop.

'Whatever this is, it isn't Farakkan. We should go on.' Adamantine Men never felt fear. Never. So the feeling in the pit of his stomach had to be something else. Concern? An understanding that something was out of place, perhaps? An awareness of possible danger. Call it all of those things. He shook himself. Old stone walls, nothing else. The Pinnacles had been carved out before the Silver King had ever come to them, and if this had been made by the same hands then they were dead a thousand years and the only thing he might find alive here were ferals who'd been swept away from the Silver City; and ferals were things he could kill. He got out of the boat. There. In the middle of the far wall, a pair of doors gleamed softly in the light. Bronze, perhaps, though untouched by age. Should have been greened and dull.

The alchemist followed him out of the boat. Her fingers dug into his arm. 'What is this place?'

He shrugged. 'You keep asking, but I still haven't the first idea. Never heard of it.' He pointed at the doors. 'You want to find out, go ahead.'

'No. You go.'

'I am ... uneasy about this place.' Now there was a thing. Couldn't shake that feeling of something being wrong.

Fingers in his head again. 'Go and open those doors and find out what lies beyond. Then I'll tell you why I was sent from the Purple Spur.'

The hair on his arms prickled. 'I'll do as you ask, but I feel danger here. Take that as a warning.' Danger from what? Ghosts? But there were no such things as ghosts. No such things as spirits. There were dragons and there was blood-magic and there were knives in the back in the dark. *Those* were dangers. Dark shadows? Old stones? He walked to the doors. Slowly and carefully though, legs and arms loose and ready to run, sword drawn. The doors were huge, bigger than they'd seemed from the water. Not familiar either, not like the wood and iron gates inside the Pinnacles; these were made of bronze, and into each was carved the figure of a man, ten feet tall and with four arms instead of two, each hand with a long curved sword. Their faces were hidden behind blank helms with no eyes. There were no handles that he could see, nothing to pull.

He stopped and looked the bronze up and down. Gave the door a good hard push. Nothing. Couldn't say he felt too bad about that. Whatever was behind those doors had been there for a long time. Belonged to whoever had made the Pinnacles, and no one at all knew who *that* was. Someone bigger and older even than the Silver King.

'No way in.' He took a step back.

The doors creaked. The groan of bending metal shook the cave, so loud that Skjorl staggered back another step. The doors opening? No. That wasn't right. One of the bronze figures was falling forward. Out of its door!

No, that wasn't it either. The bronze was moving right enough, but it wasn't *falling*. Grinding tearing shrieking sounds of metal shook the air, rang in his ears. For an instant Skjorl stood and stared. He'd faced dragons without fear, without a moment of pause, and dragons were the most terrible things in the realms. Or that's what he'd thought; but then as far as he knew, no one had ever come face to face with a ten-foot-tall statue of bronze with four arms all holding swords. Not one that moved and was tearing itself out of a door.

An instant passed, that was all. Then he sheathed his sword and pulled Dragon-blooded off his back in one movement, leapt sideways and forward and brought the axe round with all his strength, sweeping low as the bronze man finished pulling himself free. He ducked under the sweep of a scimitar and the axe struck home, smashing into a knee joint and snapping it clean in two. Skjorl recoiled away as the bronze giant staggered onto its knees. Didn't fall though, and now its scimitars were weaving arcs faster than any human swordsman. Skjorl backed away.

'You still want me to go inside there, alchemist?' he roared. The grinding metal noises were rising again. The other door was starting to shift.

No answer. A grin forced its way onto Skjorl's lips. He wasn't sure whether he had a choice, whether he could turn and run even if he wanted to. Didn't matter. Didn't want to. Ought to, but didn't want to.

The second bronze giant was ripping itself free. The first one was between them. Stopping him from getting close enough to cripple it while it was still vulnerable.

'If I were you, alchemist, I'd be pissing in my pants!' Had to shout over the roar of tearing metal. 'I'd run. Run, girl, run away!' He was going to die and he'd never be remembered, but *he'd* know, for a fleeting instant, that it had been glorious.

He didn't feel the first tug on his belt. Only noticed it when the alchemist pulled hard enough to unbalance him.

The second bronze man was almost free.

'Come! Come!'

Skjorl wasn't sure he wanted to. The torrent of noise inside his head was a river, rushing him to battle. The alchemist's fingers in there were distant things, hardly heard.

Come! Come! Come to us!

Not the alchemist. Another voice. On top of hers.

'Move!' She was pulling him. Dragging him, and then his head was his own again and he turned, ran like any sensible man would, pushing her in front of him, barging her back onto the raft, thrusting it out into the water, into the current and hurling himself after her.

A few feet short of them, the second bronze giant reached the edge of the water. It stopped. Skjorl stood on the raft, legs wide apart, axe held out in front of him, but the giant stayed where it was. It seemed to watch, motionless, as the raft floated away down the tunnel. Skjorl thought he saw it move again as it faded out of sight. Turn, back towards the door from where it had come. He stayed where he was, poised to fight until long after the last glimmer of light from that place had winked away.

He was shaking.

The cold. Must have been the cold.

22

Kataros

Twenty-two days before the Black Mausoleum

On the outside her own shaking stopped when the golem had faded from sight. On the inside … on the inside she was lost. There had been books back when she'd been in the Palace of Alchemy. The Silver King had made golems, statues of stone or bronze or even iron, animated and given life. No one had seen a golem since the Silver King had fallen. Like Prince Lai's wings, they were pretty stories. Myths read in the comfort of a warm study.

There had been other things in those books.

The Adamantine Man abruptly reached forward. He had his hands on her shoulders before she could blink, his fingers pressing into her skin, hard and hurting. There was a madness in his eyes she'd never seen before, a wildness that scared her even more than the golems had done.

'What. Was. That?' He could have snapped her neck, easily.

'You're hurting me!' The words came out strangled, but they flew through the blood-bond just as well and hit him like a hammer. He let go and reeled away with a snarl.

'Alchemist!' He bared his teeth at her like an animal, like a rabid dog.

Remembering what he was, she welded her thoughts like an iron shield. 'Sit down!' The blood-bond was wide open now. He had no choice but to obey. 'You will never, ever touch me again, Skjorl. Never. If you do, you will feel a pain that will sink you to your knees. You will wail and tear at yourself in agony. A touch, you shit-eater, that's all.' It wasn't enough though. He needed to feel it – she *wanted* him to feel it – and so she reached out a hand towards him. 'Let me show you.' She seized his hand and pressed it against the side of her face. He jerked and tried to pull away, but she had him from within as well and he couldn't let go. He threw his head back and screwed up his face and whined. She held him a while longer. When his eyes started to bulge she let him go.

'There.'

Siff was watching them. He was trying to make out he was unconscious, but his eyes were very slightly open and moving under their lids, flicking from her to the Adamantine Man and back again. The tunnel walls drifted past, always the same, smooth and unmarked.

'I opened the doors,' growled Skjorl after a bit. 'Well I tried.' He looked at her. 'So why were you sent from the Purple Spur, spear-carrier. What did you do wrong?'

She didn't want to tell him, especially after what she'd just done, but a promise was a promise and alchemists kept their word, so she took a deep breath and made it as blunt as she could.

'There were a little over thirty of us,' she said. 'Three of us were alchemists. The rest were Adamantine Men. We went in three separate groups, an alchemist in each. We were looking for help because we're slowly starving to death under the Spur. We can poison dragons but they simply come back. We can kill them with the Adamantine Spear but they still come back. Men like you may go and smash eggs and slaughter hatchlings, but for what? We've taken to searching for eggs to bring to the caves, hoping we might do what we'd done before, but there are so many eggs in so many places that we can't begin to collect them all; and even the ones we get, the dragons simply refuse the food we offer them when they hatch. They know now. They know what we do and they know how to beat us. They know we cannot win and so they starve themselves and they die and then they come back. We thought we might find something at the Pinnacles. The place is filled with things left behind by the Silver King, things that have never been touched since the time of the blood-mages, things we have never understood. We remembered them from our books, before the dragons burned them all. In the past the kings and queens of the Silver City barred us from their three palaces and no alchemist has been inside the lower chambers for centuries. We hoped ... We thought perhaps we might finally be allowed to see, to discover something the Isul Aieha – the Silver King – left behind. Something to defeat the dragons.' She sighed. 'Grand Master Jeiros knew how futile our expedition would be, but he let us go nonetheless, chose three junior alchemists he could easily afford to lose and waved us farewell. In his eyes you could see how certain he was that he'd never see us again. For our part, we thought the dragons would eat us long before we arrived. Yet we went, not because Speaker Lystra ordered it, but because there was nothing else for us to do. Nothing, do you understand? The dragons have all but destroyed us. You've seen for yourself. You went to Bloodsalt? There was an Adamantine Man with me who went there too. He told me it was dead. Lifeless. Nothing but sand and ash and water too poisonous to drink. That's what the realms will become, all of them. So we did as we were asked. I don't know what happened to the other alchemists. We travelled apart and I never saw them again.' She looked at the Adamantine Man. 'They reached the fortress too, I think, but then Hyrkallan killed them.' She shook her head. Looked away, not wanting any response, not now. 'We crossed the Fury and climbed the gorge and skirted the Raksheh, sheltering under its leaves. There were dragons there, hunting. Always. When we had to, we crossed the Harvest Realm in three long hard nights. Everything that used to be fields and towns and villages, just a wasteland of ash and embers and scorched stone. There's no one alive there now. I think once I saw a mouse.' She shook her head.

The Adamantine Man was glaring at her. 'The dragons try to starve us out,' he snarled. 'Same as they always did with the Spur. Burn everything. Leave us with nothing. Wasted effort around the Silver City though.' He laughed. 'Before I got there, the dragons smashed the fountains on top of the Fortress of Watchfulness. Smashed them to pieces but that didn't stop the water from coming out of them. It just spouted from the broken stones instead. Then they tried burning them, but stone doesn't burn. They poured out their fire for days, one after the other without end, and the water through the fortress still ran cold and fresh.'

Kataros nodded, for a moment forgetting that the worst monster was right here next to her. 'The Silver King's magic. That's what we came looking for. When we reached the Silver City, we were welcomed and given food and water, and we were so tired and so grateful.'

Skjorl shrugged. 'I heard stories there was another alchemist. That they took him up to the top at night, smashed his wrists and his ankles and hung him from a wheel over the edge. Same as they did for your grand master before the Adamantine Palace fell. I heard there were soldiers as well. My sort. I don't know what happened to them. As far as I know they were still alive. Didn't see them.' For a moment he looked away and she caught the whiff of some smouldering shame inside him. 'Too busy.'

'That's why I came to the Pinnacles. That's what I was looking for and that's what you're going to find for me in the Raksheh. A half-god's secrets for mastering dragons.'

He laughed at her, long and hard. 'You think they haven't looked for those? They say the ghost of the Silver King walks along hidden passages deep under each of the three Pinnacles, but I say this: if even a part of the Silver King remained beneath the Pinnacles, we would bow to him, all of us, dragons too.'

'There's another place to look. A better place. His tomb.'

Skjorl laughed more. 'Vishmir spent twenty years looking. A thousand dragons and ten times the riders. Didn't find it though.'

'So we are supposed to believe.'

The Adamantine Man shook his head. 'Even if I had a choice, I might still go with you, alchemist. But you'll find nothing, same as everyone else. We'll die out there looking for it. If it exists at all, then it's hidden from the likes of you.'

Kataros glanced down at the outsider. He was still pretending be be asleep. 'But not from him.'

Skjorl stared at her.

'He's been there. He found it. In the Raksheh. And now he's going to show us the way.'

Skjorl stared at her some more. Then he fell back onto the raft and roared with laughter. 'That's what he told you, is it? That he'd found the Silver King's tomb? And you believed that?' He shook his head in disbelief. Kataros leaned towards him.

'Yes. And would you like to see *why* I believed him?' She turned to Siff. 'I know you're listening. Show him. Show him what you showed me.'

Very slowly Siff sat up. When he opened his eyes, they gleamed in the half-light of the tunnel walls.

They were silver.

Farakkan

Looking down over the confluence of the Fury and the Yamuna, Farakkan is little more than a market on a little hill, but the fact that it lies above the flood plain of Bonjanland (frequently becoming an island for most of the late spring and early summer) and is visible from a long distance across the flat terrain makes it seem something more. The city is wet, filthy and muddy and is largely viewed with disdain by the courts of the surrounding realms. The people of Farakkan are used to this and seem not to care. It has no culture to speak of and offers little to interest those whose lives are not dedicated to food, fish or livestock.

Bellepheros' *Journal of the Realms*, 2nd year of Speaker Hyram

23

Siff

Some two years before the Black Mausoleum

On a bright clear day the lookout could have seen for miles across the valleys, peering between the mountaintops. He could have seen the approaching dragons when they were still specks in the sky. He could have lit the warning fire that would have told the men and women living in the valley to drop whatever they were holding, snatch up their children and run deep into the forest, where the dragons wouldn't find them. On a bright clear day like today all of those things would have happened. Except the lookout was dead.

Probably dead. Siff waited for a few seconds. He'd shot the man in the chest, but instead of pitching over the edge of the watchtower like he was supposed to, the lookout had fallen back, out of sight from the ground.

There were no shouts or screams or groans. Nothing moved. Satisfied, Siff scampered up the ladder. The tower wasn't much, nothing more than a wooden platform with a beacon fire on top of it and a thatched roof to keep the rain off. The lookout had fallen onto the pile of wood. He was definitely dead.

Sashi had followed Siff up the ladder. She looked at the body and spat. 'Bastard!'

'You knew him?' Siff raised an eyebrow.

She snorted. 'In a manner of speaking.' Sashi stamped on the dead man's face. Hard.

'Ouch.' Siff crouched and put a finger to his lips. The second lookout was on his way back.

'This one's *mine*.' Sashi dropped to her haunches and sat perfectly silent and still. They heard the second man's footsteps scuffing the dry dirt below. Then the tower started to shake as he made his way up the ladder. His face appeared over the edge and he stopped. Sashi shot to her feet. She pointed an accusing finger and shrieked, 'Son of a whore's puke!' There would have been more and probably a lot worse, but Siff put an end to it: he pushed past and kicked the man in the face. Then he lost his balance. Both of them toppled backwards but the man on the ladder had a lot further to fall. He lay groaning on the ground some twenty feet below. When he looked like he might be about to get back to his feet, Siff put an arrow through his hip. Then he held up his hands and put down his bow.

'All yours, Sashi.'

If she heard the exasperation in his voice, it didn't show. 'Come with me.'

'Do I have to?'

'What if he's got a knife? Anyway I want you to watch.'

Siff wrinkled his nose. 'You want me to watch? Why?'

'I want you to see what I'm like when people treat me wrong.'

He sighed and rolled his eyes and climbed down the ladder, kicked the man a few times to keep him quiet and turned him over. Sure enough, he had a hunting knife strapped to the back of his belt. Siff took it and handed it to Sashi. 'If he's got a knife, make it *your* knife.' He turned the man over again so that he was looking up at them.

Sashi hesitated for a second or two. She stared at the man at her feet and he stared back, his eyes blank and confused, still dazed from his fall and the arrow in his hip. Then some sort of recognition flickered in his face. He frowned. He might have been about to say something, but before he could, Sashi fell on him. She shrieked and screamed and cursed, lifted the knife up high and plunged it into him again and again and again. When she was finished, his face and neck had been cut to ribbons. He was definitely dead.

'Was that really necessary?'

Sashi was covered in his blood, shaking. She didn't answer at first, only stood there holding the knife, looking at what she'd done. 'Yes,' she said at last.

Siff nodded. He climbed back up the tower and settled down to wait for the dragons. He closed his eyes and shook his head. *What am I doing?*

There were some easy answers to that, and some less easy ones. The first easy answer was that he was lying back, enjoying the warmth of the sun on his face. A man could settle for an easy answer like that. But just this once he thought he might try a little harder.

The next answer wasn't quite so easy. What he was doing, in a cold sort of way, was leading a dozen dragons and their riders to a little outsider village where they happened to make Souldust so that the dragons could burn it to ash. A village he'd been merrily dealing with for the last year, selling the same dust to other riders from the same eyrie for what was rapidly becoming an obscene pile of silver. After the dragons had done their work, he would be paid for his part in leading them here. And there would be dust in secret stashes. He'd come back later for those. There would be dead outsiders, and that would make the riders happy, which meant they would leave him alone for long enough to make his way to somewhere else. And last but definitely not least, he was getting rid of the people who might incriminate him, using the very hunters who were looking for him to do it, getting paid for his trouble, and coming away with a big stash of dust to boot. It was all very clever and all very good. Still not the whole of the answer though.

He felt Sashi climb up after him and breathed a sigh of relief at the distraction. She sat down beside him. As whores went, she was a good find. Energetic, enthusiastic and dexterous. Crude, a bit stupid, but the same could have been said of most that Siff had known. She was damaged too. Something inside Sashi was very broken, which was why she was perfect and why he'd found her.

He sniffed. 'You reek of blood.'

'He deserved it.' She smiled brightly.

'Mmm.' Siff sat up again and squinted down into the valley. He couldn't see the village but it was down there somewhere, hidden from the eyes of passing dragons. Hidden, but not well enough. Now that the dragons of the Mountain King knew where to look, there was no question they'd find it. Sashi had brought them here and she was going to laugh as the outsiders burned.

He closed his eyes again. He'd know where it was quickly enough when the dragons arrived.

'Do you like it?' she asked.

'Do I like what?'

'The smell of blood.'

Siff shrugged. 'If it's the blood of my enemies, I suppose.' He had plenty of those and sadly nearly all of them were still alive and not bleeding even a little bit.

'This is the blood of *my* enemies.'

'Do you like the smell of fire?' he asked.

'Fire doesn't smell.'

'Smoke, then. Do you like that smell?'

Her turn to shrug. 'It makes me choke.'

'You're going to smell a lot more of it soon. Burning homes. Blackened bodies, limbs twisted and charred. You remember that smell, don't you?'

She didn't answer and she didn't need to. They'd both had their homes and their lives burned to ash by dragons. It was a smell no one could forget.

'I don't like doing this,' he said after a while. 'It's just that I have to.' *Liar!*

Sashi leaned over him, lowering her face closer to his. When he opened his eyes, she was only inches away, looking at him intently. She still had blood on her face and her eyes burned.

'All brothers and sisters, we outsiders. Don't tell me again. They sold me when they should have sheltered me. They tied me up and they beat me for most of a month. Men and boys. Not one of them lifted a finger to help me. Not one. Why? Because I had no man to protect me.'

'I think it was because you were a thief.' Siff could feel himself slowly getting aroused. Sashi hated men. Most men, at least. All of them except him, it seemed. Siff's hate was more even-handed. He hated pretty much everyone, himself included. Maybe Sashi was that simple too. Maybe he was just a tool, and one day soon he'd go to sleep with her arms and legs wrapped around him and wake up in the morning cold and dead with a knife stuck through his face.

'Food! I stole bread because I was starving. They gave me nothing!'

Siff reached up and ran a hand through her hair. 'You stole dust too.' That was what made Sashi what she was. Dust. Whoever she'd once been was long gone. Enough Souldust and that was the way you ended, no matter who you were in the beginning.

Sashi bared her teeth at him. 'I know that look.'

'Maybe I do like the smell of blood after all.'

A crooked smile split her face. She pushed him down and sat astride him. 'You're all like that, aren't you? Men. Whenever my brothers went hunting and made a good kill, whenever they won a fight, I always knew. The others were the same when they came to me. Even dragon-knights.' She was grinding herself against him now. Her eyes were wide and her cheeks, under the blood-stains, were flushed. 'I used to wonder if it was something that only worked for men. Now I know how you feel.'

'So I see.' He pulled her to him. The dead man with the arrow in his chest was still lying on top of the pile of wood. Siff could have reached out and touched him without even trying.

'I don't know about all men,' he murmured in her ear when they came up for air, 'but *I'm* like that.'

'Oh no, you're all the same. Every one of you.' She was smiling as she said it, but her eyes were dead.

Later, Siff watched the dragons glide into the valley. There were twelve. Four of them stayed up high, kept circling and watching by their riders. The others disappeared among the folds and contours of the mountainsides. It wasn't long before a pall of smoke started to rise over the trees. That would be the village. A hundred outsiders lived there, give or take a dozen.

Lived there? *Had* lived there. The riders would do what riders always did: they'd take the ones worth selling as slaves and burn the rest.

Sashi was sitting on the floor. Her clothes still hung open. She lit a pipe and gave it to him, something she'd taken to doing after they'd lain together. He slumped, leaning against one of the poles that held the watchtower roof in place. When he'd taken a few puffs he offered it back again.

'Feel better now?' he asked.

She took the pipe. Her eyes glazed for a moment as she took a deep breath. She nodded.

'I don't like doing this.' Maybe saying it enough times would make him believe it.

'They deserved it.'

He tried not to look out at the smoke rising over the valley, but his eyes kept returning to it all on their own. 'Really?' No, he shouldn't have asked that. They were outsiders dying down there, but they'd done whatever they'd done to Sashi and then they'd sold her, and that alone made them no better than animals. The number didn't really matter, did it?

A bone to throw to what was left of his conscience, that's all *that* was. They were a means to an end and so was she.

'Yes, really.' Sashi gave him a scornful look and passed back the pipe. She thought he was doing this for her, but likely as not she'd deserved everything they'd done. Life in the mountain valleys was hard. Food was scarce. Winters were brutal. People died. The weak, the young, the old, the sick. Out here stealing was as bad as killing and always had been. They all knew it, him, Sashi, all of them. It was the code of those who served no dragon-king, and the worst crime of all was what he'd done right here.

A few weeks should see me to Hanzen's Camp, and then I'm down the river to Furymouth, where everything is possible. Silver and dust. I'll be rich. I'll be whatever I want to be and I'll finally be away from these miserable mountains for ever. He whispered the mantra to the faces from his childhood. He hadn't been there when the dragons had come to his home so he hadn't actually seen his people burn. He remembered the afterwards, though. The swathe of burned and blackened land, the stink of smoke, of burned wood and flesh. More than anything, he remembered the smell.

He took a deep pull from the pipe and then another, dissolving the screams and the faces and the smell into a pleasant numbness. He supposed he ought to move but his legs didn't agree, so he had some strong words with them until grudgingly they lifted him to his feet. His feet, it seemed, were none too pleased to be disturbed either. They grumbled all the way to the ladder, all the way down, and kept it up while he wandered aimlessly in circles. He'd forgotten something, but it took an age to realise what it was.

Sashi. *Oh yes. Her.* He was still holding her pipe, long extinct. *She'll want it back.*

'Get down here!' he shouted. His head felt like it was about to sever itself from the rest of him and go flying off into the air. He looked at the pipe. *Ancestors! What did you put in it?* 'Oi, woman! Get your spindly legs down here! We've got dragon-riders to taunt. I know it's fun to make them wait, but I'll be righteously pissed off if they leave us here.' He staggered into one of the legs of the tower. When he looked up, a face was leering down at him.

'Did you like my pipe? This time?'

'Yes.' He frowned. 'No. I mean ...' He wasn't sure what he meant. Yes he liked it, but he didn't like not being able to think in a straight line. 'What is it?'

She grinned. 'I put a pinch of dust in it.'

He jumped up, trying to grab her, which didn't work since she was twenty feet up in the air. When he came down again, his legs buckled and he ended up on his backside. For some reason this was immensely funny. Somewhere a part of him knew he ought to be furious, but for now that was a lone voice in a very loud and happy crowd.

'Where did you get it?' Tears of laughter streamed down his cheeks. She was coming down the ladder now, very, very slowly. Sometimes it looked like she was going back up again. She still hadn't bothered to dress herself. Her breasts hung invitingly out of her shift. Siff couldn't take his eyes off them.

'One of the riders.'

She didn't get to say much more. As she reached the bottom of the ladder, Siff staggered over and grabbed hold of her, pulling her down onto the ground. He took her there in the dirt without much idea of what he was doing, only that he had no choice, that he absolutely *had* to have her no matter what. And that she didn't much seem to mind.

When he was done, he rolled away and lay beside her. His head felt clearer now. '*These* riders take dust?' Not that that was much of a revelation, although he'd thought that the ones coming here were the righteous-scourge-descending-from-the-sky-to-burn-out-the-wickedness sort. Apparently not.

'Of course they do, they *all* do. I could see it in his eyes that he had some. Those big, wide faraway eyes. Just like yours.' She was suddenly sitting up, looming over him, peering into his face. Siff lurched to his feet. Something about this was very very bad, but his head was too fuzzy to think properly.

'Wait! *You* took dust from a *rider*?'

She leered at him.

'And how did you pay him?' Stupid question. There was only one possible answer.

She purred and ran a hand over herself. 'How do you think?'

'You're not *that* good.' He stood up and took Sashi's hand in his. 'Come on. Dress yourself. We need to find those riders or all of this is a waste of time. They won't wait for us.' The haze in his head was getting in the way. Stopping him from understanding something that was shouting out to be heard. Sashi could bed riders for their pennies all she liked, but when she wanted dust, she came to him. That was the way it was supposed to be ... He cursed the muddle in his head and then lost hold of what it was he was supposed to be thinking. Riders. Dust. Yes, that. Something.

'Do we?' She wrapped himself around him. 'We could wait a little longer, if you like. I'm not sure I'm done with you.' *Go on,* wheedled the dust. *You can wait. Look at her. Stay. You'll want her again soon enough*

He pushed her away, then pulled her back again, twirled her as though they were about to dance and then tossed her over his shoulder. 'Time for that later.'

If his little voices had anything important to say, he was sure they would keep on at him. He'd said the same to his conscience once, but that had walked out on him years ago.

24

Skjorl

Twenty-two days before the Black Mausoleum

Superstition came easy to men who fought monsters and stared at death every day. Outside his own company no Adamantine Man would admit it, but there it was. Every axe had its name. There might not be any such things as ghosts, but there were spirits right enough. Other people had their ancestors to watch over them, but the Adamantine Men were severed from their families, and so they had the memories of all those who'd gone before, right back to the nameless Night Watchman who'd stood beside Narammed and made him the first speaker. Every soldier who'd ever walked the walls of the Adamantine Palace secretly thought he'd know the dragon that would kill him as soon as he saw it. Some were certain they would die by the flames of a green or a red or a gold. For Skjorl, it had been having someone called Vishmir in his company. A Vish made him invincible. The dragon that killed the last Vishmir would be the one to burn him. He'd quietly believed that for as long as he could remember.

And then the last Vish he knew had been crushed by a rock in Bloodsalt, and here he was, still alive. Somewhere up on Yinazhin's Way, weeks after Jasaan had gone, he'd realised. He'd watched, then, as his superstition crumbled to dust, taking half the things he believed in with it. He thought of the names he'd given to his axe and his shield and would have thrown them away if he could have found new ones to replace them. Ancestors, spirits, ghosts, they were all nonsense. There were dragons. There were alchemists and their potions. There were blood-mages. That was all.

So there he was, all his superstitions broken in pieces and

stuffed in sacks to be slowly thrown away, and now he stared at the outsider with the silver eyes, paralysed because here, in front of him, was surely a ghost made flesh. The outsider reached out his hand and Skjorl was transfixed. Tendrils of silver light like moonlight curled from the man's fingertips. They grew as long as his thumb, writhing and coiling like little snakes, as though feeling for something that wasn't there.

And then they abruptly vanished as the outsider's eyes went back to normal. He slumped, and if Skjorl had had a knife on him, he might just have used it. His sword was too long to draw while he was sitting down and he was too paralysed to get up.

'What in Vishmir's name was that?'

'Something the Silver King left behind,' whispered the alchemist.

Skjorl shivered. Some*thing?*

The outsider opened his eyes again and looked at Skjorl. Hard to tell what colour they were in the gloom, but not silver and not glowing any more. Human then. Probably. 'It's a key,' he said.

'A key to what?'

'Why to a door – what else? The door to where the Silver King went.'

No, couldn't be. Skjorl shook his head. Had to be some trick. Not some shit-eater from the mountains.

The outsider shrugged. 'Believe what you want. Doesn't matter really, does it, what *you* think. What matters is what she thinks.' He nodded towards the alchemist. 'Lucky for me she's the one of you who *can* think, eh? So you just be a good little doggy and do as you're told.'

Skjorl was on his feet. Never mind what sort of creature was inside this shit-eater, he could still wring its neck.

'No!' The alchemist's command caught him mid-lunge. 'You don't touch *him* either. Not one finger, or you'll feel the pain as if it had been me.'

The outsider smiled. 'Good doggy.'

There was nothing he could do. The fingers inside his head forced him back down. Skjorl spat at the alchemist's feet.

'Oh, *bad* doggy!' Siff leaned forward. He bared his teeth at

Skjorl. 'You think I'm making all this up? You must be wondering how is it that some – what was it – some *shit-eater* from the mountains knows a magic key's inside him. I didn't ask for it, I can tell you that. But I know what it is because I found the door, doggy. I found the door to where the Silver King went when he left you, and I opened it. I've seen through to the other side.'

'You followed the Silver King?' Skjorl shook his head.

'Better. I met him.'

Beyond belief. Skjorl rolled his eyes and stared at Kataros. 'Are you so desperate as to believe such a story.' Hard to explain the eyes and the silver light, but that was just some spirit, wasn't it? One of those ghosts he didn't believe in. Or blood-magic. Maybe the outsider was a blood-mage! Or perhaps there was some potion …

Kataros was looking at him. Smiling a little, although there was nothing friendly in her face. A little relish at his discomfort, that was all.

'Could *you* lie to me?' she asked.

Skjorl sat in silence after that, brow furrowed. Inside his head he emptied out those sacks and slowly and carefully put everything back together again, back out where it used to belong. Took a while, but it was all still there. A part of him wasn't too sorry about that either. Dragon-blooded was a good name. Said something. Had a truth to it. Would have been a shame to lose it.

25

Siff

Some two years before the Black Mausoleum

The path down the side of the valley was steep and stony and hard to follow. When they reached the bottom, Siff's head still felt as though it wasn't quite a part of the rest of him. The first he knew that they were close was the taint in the air, the old familiar smell of smoke and charcoal and burned skin. Memories stabbed at him, dulled a little by the dust but still sharp enough to bite. *This is the last one*, he promised them. *Then I'm out of these mountains. No more dragons, no more burning. Silk sheets and soft women for me.*

They took their time coming down, and the riders had finished their work when they arrived. Flames flickered among the skeletons of what had once been huts and shacks. The village was gone. In another day there would only be a black scar on the landscape. That and the inevitable pile of charred corpses where the riders had butchered anyone too old or too young or too crippled to be sold as a slave. Scavenger food. Siff tried not to let his eyes find that, but Sashi found it for him.

'Look.'

He didn't want to but he couldn't stop his eyes turning. The riders had put the body pile close to the trail. Men and women who were dead because of him, even if they were shits, even if they raped and tortured their own sons and daughters, even if he wasn't supposed to care one whit about what happened to them. At least it was a small pile this time.

'Looks like they took a lot of slaves then,' he said. Unless the dragons were hungry and had simply eaten everyone. There was always that.

'Pity.'

She meant it too. A lifetime chained to the oars of a Taiytakei slave ship for the men, being playthings for the women and the boys, and that wasn't punishment enough? Siff shook his head. Although in a way she was right. If they'd killed everyone, that would have been better. If they'd taken slaves, they'd be held in pens back at the eyrie. He'd need to keep away from those. People might recognise him.

Sashi hissed, 'I wanted them *all* to burn.'

'Some of them did and the rest are slaves. Let that be enough.' He stared at the blackened bodies and shuddered. He'd keep away until the dragons made their next flight to the slave auctions in Furymouth. That would be best. He ought to hate himself but he didn't. He didn't feel much of anything at all these days.

Most of the riders were gone. Only a pair remained, their dragons resting by the far edge of the settlement. The riders had stripped off most of their armour. They looked bored – no, not *bored*. They'd taken dust. *Ancestors! That* was why Sashi was keeping close to him, keeping small and insignificant behind his back.

Half the riders at the eyrie took dust, which he got here, where it was made. These were supposed to be the other half, the self-righteous pricks who burned outsiders because some of them made dust and dust destroyed people. Yet here they were, the same self-righteous pricks, fuzzy-faced and dark-eyed from exactly what they'd come here to wipe out. Hypocrites, the lot of them. He'd yet to meet a dragon-rider worth the spit out of an honest man's mouth.

Might say the same for myself.

He fingered his knives and wondered how easy it would be to gut them and steal their dragons. How much would he get for a pair of monsters? More than he'd ever get for trading dust, that was for sure. Yes, and then a thank you from some eyrie master in the shape of a knife in the back. Only riders sat on the backs of dragons.

The two riders finally noticed him. Siff let his knives be. He was, at heart, a man who preferred not to take risks if he didn't have to.

'Enjoying the harvest?' He forced a grin.

'There's nothing! Nothing here!' The first rider rested a hand on his sword as he strode closer. Siff shrugged.

'I expect that's because you let your dragons burn everything.' Behind their riders, the two dragons glared. Dragons terrified the shit out of Siff, terrified the shit out of everyone with any sense, he liked to think. They'd squash you with a careless step, squash you flat. Damn things always looked angry too. Angry and hungry with their baleful eyes the size of dinner plates and teeth like a forest of swords. He shuddered. Did their riders ever get used to how big they were? 'Took a good enough haul of slaves though, eh?' He glanced back towards the pile of bodies. 'Or did you feed them all to your dragons?'

The rider's hand clenched the pommel of his sword so tight that Siff could see his knuckles turn white. He didn't draw it though. 'There's no dust, you fool.'

Of course there's not. That's because they hide it out in the forest and only I know where. He frowned and peered at the rider. Dilated pupils and the man was swaying slightly, as though drunk. 'By the looks of you, you must have found *some*.' He could have stabbed himself. That wasn't supposed to come out. You didn't provoke a dragon-rider. Just didn't, not if you wanted to keep your skin.

The rider looked flustered. For a moment the devil in Siff took over his mouth. 'Don't worry. I won't tell anyone.' *Shut up!*

The rider growled. He pulled his sword half out of its scabbard. Siff jumped away and whipped out a knife. The dragons eyed him with interest. You could feel their attention. You could feel them waking up, sensing the possibility of blood, and feel their remorseless hunger. But then the rider frowned and stared and seemed to lose his thread, caught in the flip-flop of emotion that came with too much dust. 'I don't know what you're talking about.' He slid his sword back where it belonged.

Siff smiled and put his knife away too. 'Then let's forget all about it,' he said. *And thank Vishmir for that.* 'Got a purse for me?'

The rider shook his head. 'Not here, sell-sword. You come back with us.'

'What?' It took a moment to realise that he meant it, that they wanted him up on the back of a dragon, and there was no way in the nine realms he was doing *that*. 'Why?'

The rider spat at his feet. 'Because I tell you to, sell-sword.'

'I don't think so.' He tried not to look around for places to run to. If they were going to kill him right here, not a thing in the world would stop them; and the trouble was, the more Siff put himself in their boots, the more he could see how they'd do exactly that.

'Then you and your purse can both crawl off and rot under the earth. We'll keep our whore though.' The rider turned away. Behind him, the other one had almost finished putting his armour back on.

'Wait!' *Wait? Damn fool.*

'What?' The rider didn't turn around. He was already doing up the straps on his dragon-scale.

'I come back with you and then I get paid, right?'

The rider shrugged. 'I don't know and I don't care. Maybe my eyrie master wants to stick a spike up your arse and hang you in a cage.'

You couldn't help but look at the dragons. Siff shook his head. They were just too big even this far away, out of reach of their fire-breath. But to get closer, close enough to touch … *No.* No, he wasn't doing that. It made him want to scream.

The dead men he'd betrayed were laughing at him. 'I'll walk,' he spat. 'You lot owe me.' He started to back away and put a hand on Sashi's arm. 'Come on, lover. Leave these gentlemen to their pleasure.' It would take him a week or more to get back to the eyrie on foot. With a bit of luck the slaves would be gone by then and that was a thing to be happy about. Maybe it hadn't worked out too bad after all.

'You're not taking her.' The rider looked past Siff and leered at Sashi. 'No. She can ride with me. She knows what I like.'

I bet she does. 'Best let her stay with me, rider. Otherwise she might just bite it off.'

'No.' Sashi pushed past him and looked the rider up and down. 'I'll go with him. It's fine.'

'It's bloody *not* fine.'

She half-smiled, half-leered at him. 'I'll wait. You won't be long, right?'

Siff backed away from the riders and their monsters. Out of the corner of his eye he saw the looks that went between the rider and Sashi. That was where she'd got her dust then. He wasn't sure how he felt about that. Betrayed mostly, but with a bit of pity for her too. They'd burn her, more likely than not, once they were bored with her. That's what happened when you played with dragons. 'Suit yourself then.'

He turned away, an itch between his shoulders until he'd walked the first mile or two and saw the dragons up in the air at last, flying home. Empty cages hung beneath them, a few wooden bars lashed together with crude ropes. That was how the dragon-knights carried their slaves. Sometimes the cages fell apart in mid-air, but what did that matter? They were only slaves, right? Plenty more out there. Bastards.

He stood still, watching them go, higher and higher off to the south until the sky swallowed them, and then, only then, did he give a deep sigh and turn round, heading back for all those hidden stashes of dust.

He was shaking.

26

Blackscar

Twenty-two days before the Black Mausoleum

The dragon understood time well enough, but the concept had little meaning. It hatched, it ate, it grew, it flew. Some day a strange feeling would come from inside. A heat that would not be denied. It would come like a flood, wave after wave, each one deeper and stronger than the last. Not with any pain, but with a tiredness. The dragon would lie down and fade and its essence would vanish away to the realm of the dead, a spirit seeking passage. Sometimes it awoke there alone. Sometimes others would come and go, others it knew. Sometimes it passed a shoal of the human dead, vanishing towards whatever end awaited them. Occasionally it found other things, trapped and best left well alone. Always, though, it felt the call. New flesh, begging for life; and always it answered, sought out the cries and devoured one and awoke, a hatchling reborn, cracking its hungry way from the egg. This was how a dragon marked the passage of time, not in seasons or suns, but in lifetimes.

Around the three spires of stone where the Isul Aieha had once lived it made its home. The little one it sought was always there. Never hidden, but walled within the stone where even a dragon could not reach. It hunted. It made sport of the prey in the ruins below. It roosted as the whim took it among the smashed palaces of the mountaintops, or else far away, but it always came back and the little one was always still there, a thorn in the dragon's thoughts. It could not have said how long it waited, how many days passed as it came and went, feeding, hunting, soaring, sometimes alone, sometimes with others of its kind. It could not have said because it did not care. Mere days were such ephemeral things.

Then one morning the little one was gone. The dragon raked its senses through the mountains. All the others it had come to know, they were still there, but the one it wanted, that one was gone; and so the hunt began.

27

Siff

Some two years before the Black Mausoleum

The sensible thing, he knew, was to disappear. The Worldspine was big enough and they'd hardly come looking for him. Running after him with their bag of silver to pay him what he was due. Not likely. Yes, walking away was the sensible thing. Trouble was, everything he had was hidden around that eyrie, the place where dragons were groomed and grown and fed and trained. And they really owed him a lot of silver for today's work. If they were going to kill him, he decided, they would have done it already; if they weren't, then yes, he'd like to be paid. He'd take his blood money and be gone, and after that he'd be happy if he never saw these mountains again.

The valleys around the edge of the Worldspine all looked the same to Siff. He'd lived his whole life in them, but unless you were a dragon-rider, all you got to see were the trees around you, the branches overhead and whatever annoying pile of rocks, cave, fissure, gulley, stream, waterfall or pack of hungry snappers was getting in your way to to slow you down *this* time. There were paths sometimes, if you knew where to look for them, old ways made of heavy stones laid down by people long forgotten. Sometimes there were even rope bridges. The trouble with paths was the chance of running into someone else, and the fact that the average *someone else* almost always turned out to be a murderous footpad to anyone travelling alone. Bridges, as far as he could tell, were official meeting places for murderous footpads. Siff avoided the lot. He made his own way through the forest and the valleys to the dragon-riders' eyrie. It took him a week and a half. He dragged it out. The longer the better, the more chance all the slaves would be gone by the time he got there.

He knew he was getting close when there started being more to the world than trees and rocks and streams and then more trees and rocks. The forest around the eyrie peak had been stripped away, its rugged slopes covered in grass and dotted with huts and herds of alpaca. Further up the valley, the huts grew closer together. There were people here, not the outsiders who lived in the forests, but the tame dragon folk who lived in the shadows of the eyries. The sort who would tell you that the dragons protected them, even as the monsters and their riders took everything they had and left them no better off than the forest folk. He passed pens filled with animals. The huts gradually gathered together into what passed for a town, but he skirted around all that and headed for the path that went up the mountain, another old stone thing, uneven, weathered, steps worn by all the feet that had gone up and down. Odd that, since almost no one used it now, barely even remembered it was there. If you wanted something up the mountain, you simply carried it in the talons of a dragon. Even Siff had to agree that was much more straightforward and far less effort than climbing the path on foot. It was there, though, like the paths through the valleys, old and forgotten by all but the outsiders. Made in a fairy-tale time that had never really happened when there had been no dragons, and the people of the mountains had lived and prospered and raised towns and cities and these paths had been their roads. Rubbish, all of it, but pretty stories nonetheless. Maybe if you could believe there had once been a time *before* dragons then you could believe in a faraway day when they'd finally be gone.

As he approached the top of the path, three of the monsters soared through the valley below him. They arced upwards and landed somewhere among the crags and bluffs above. They were carrying cages. He saw one cage clip the ground and shatter, spilling slaves all over the mountainside. He could smell the eyrie now. A smell you always took with you. Dragons.

He stopped and had his lunch while the riders above rounded up all the slaves that hadn't been maimed or killed in the crash. It happened all the time. Sickening really, if you stopped to think about it, and so on the whole he didn't. He waited and ate and drank and dozed and smoked his pipe. When he was sure the riders were finished, he packed his bag and wound the rest of his way up to the eyrie.

Since he wasn't a rider, no one was remotely interested in him or anything he had to say once he got there. The first time he'd been left to wander an eyrie, he couldn't believe that people just let him by, minding their own business when he could have been anyone. He could have been a spy, an assassin, a madman, anyone, but he'd grown used to it, and he understood now. Their arrogance made them stupid – they simply couldn't believe that anyone worth bothering with came to a mountain eyrie on foot.

It took him an afternoon and then an evening of waiting around, while everyone else had their supper, before he finally got to talking to someone who mattered. This one was wearing a fancy gold cloak, which Siff had never seen before. Gold cloaks probably meant something so he bowed a lot. Outsiders were supposed to do that anyway, and this one had a nice fat purse.

'You're the scout,' said Gold Cloak.

Siff nodded. Gold Cloak held out the purse.

'Then this is yours.' He frowned. 'My riders tell me there was no dust.'

My riders? Siff tried to keep a straight face. He shrugged. 'Maybe they moved it. Maybe they hid it. They usually do. I'm not surprised your riders didn't find it. The slaves you took might know where to look.'

'Yes. They did. We went back. Everything was gone.'

Siff shifted uncomfortably. Hadn't expected that. *That would be because I went round and took it all myself.* He shrugged again. 'Must have missed a few of them in the woods then. Easily done. I suppose they must have taken it after your riders left. Have you asked the woman?'

Gold Cloak frowned. He snapped his fingers and a door opened behind him. Two riders came out pushing Sashi in front of them. 'You mean this one?'

'Yes.' *Shit.*

'She was no use. Did she do as she was told?'

Siff nodded. Time to be a little rude, to be what they'd expect from an outsider. Push back, just enough to earn some disdain. 'Yes, she did, and that's *my* woman now, remember. Part of our deal. You tell your riders that, remind them that she's mine. They seem to think they can help themselves to her whenever they want. Well they can, if they're that desperate, but they pay now I'm here. They pay *me*.' Gold Cloak seemed to struggle with this and Siff had to work to keep his face looking angry. He'd met dragon-knights like Gold Cloak before, the ones who thought that all the riders around them were as pure as mountain snow.

Gold Cloak sneered and took a step back and away. 'We're done. Take you money and your whore and get out of my eyrie.'

Right answer. Siff bowed, which was as good a way as any to hide his smile. Gold Cloak threw the purse at his feet and walked away; his riders let Sashi loose and left as well. Siff looked her over. Then he picked up the purse and counted the silver dragons inside to be sure they hadn't cheated him.

'Come on,' he took Sashi's hand. Take her with him or did he leave her somewhere? And if he left her, did he get rid of her at the bottom of a cliff so she couldn't tell the riders all about who he really was and what he really did. She knew more than enough to get him stuffed into a slave cage.

'Where we going?'

'Leaving.'

'It's nearly dark.'

'*Get out of my eyrie.* You heard the man.'

Siff kept his head bowed as they walked past a group of Scales. Their skin was hard and cracked, flaking and covered in weeping sores. That was something to do with the dragons, some sort of disease they carried. Most people averted their eyes from a Scales and so Siff did the same, pretending he was afraid. In furtive glances he saw a dozen other dragons, scattered around the mountainside. He saw the hollow filled with water for them to drink and, further up, little streams and a system of ponds and dams. Several low stone buildings sat above them, while alchemists moved to and fro. Strange soldiers he'd never seen before slouched in groups as though they owned the place, drawing angry glares from all who passed them. Something was happening. If he didn't know better, he'd have said they were getting ready for a war.

He found a hut at the bottom of the eyrie. It looked as though it hadn't been used for years. There were holes in the roof, gaps in the walls and the hearth hadn't been lit for a long time. There wasn't any wood to burn, no bed, no blankets, no furs, nothing. The floor was damp and the place stank but it would do. In the morning he'd be gone. Away down the path and vanished into the mountain valleys, north, following the water to the Fury at Gnashing Snapper Gorge and Hanzen's Camp, and then a boat and Furymouth and a new life awash with the wealth and the dust he'd stashed over the years. Maybe Sashi could come with him some of the way. The company would be nice.

'I used to live in a hut like this,' he said. 'A long time ago. Before riders came and burned it down.'

Sashi wrinkled her nose. 'So did I. Before I knew better.' She shivered and huddled close to him. 'Why do we have to stay here? You said you'd take me away.'

He closed the remains of the door behind them. 'I did. But like you said, it's nearly dark and I don't fancy that path at night.' He rubbed his hands together. 'So how much dust did you get while I was gone?' She showed him and he screwed up his face. 'Hardly worth it. You'll not buy much with that.'

'It's not for selling.' She shivered. 'I don't like it here. Have you got more?'

'Lots.'

'Where? Where is it?'

'Safe.' *Like I'm going to tell you.*

'Is it far?'

'A bit.'

'*How* far?' She pushed him, hard.

'Ancestors! As far as it is!' He pushed her back, enough that she stumbled. It was getting cold and so he went back out into the eyrie to look for something to burn. Past the lake where the dragons drank a dry channel snaked away down the mountainside. It was steep here, a good place to lose a body.

He gathered an armful of firewood. There were more soldiers around the landing grounds, but not many. The stone bastions with their scorpions seemed largely unattended. Maybe he was wrong. Maybe they weren't going to war. Back in the hut he made a fire. Before he could stop her, Sashi threw a handful of dust into the flames.

'What did you do that for?'

She shivered. 'I won't sleep without it. Not here.' Then she grinned and looked at him sideways and stroked a finger across her lips. 'Besides, it would be a shame to waste it.'

'The last thing I need is to be muddy-headed in the morning. I might have had a better use for it.' He could smell it in the air already, worming its way into his system. Another few minutes and he wouldn't care any more. 'Don't expect any sympathy when you run out, when you're shivering and crying and desperate for more.'

Sashi huddled up against him. 'It's cold.'

'Mountains usually are.' Maybe he should go in the night after all. Leave without her. He supposed he still could.

Sashi's huddling was starting to change into something else. That was the dust taking hold, one of the reasons it was so desired. He'd never been into a dust house, but he'd heard stories of people going inside and not coming out again for months. Some houses simply took their patrons' clothes from them at the door and gave them back when they left. Stories had it that people literally fucked themselves to death in dust houses. Siff had done his fair share of that sort of thing and he wasn't at all sure it was possible, but the stories persisted nonetheless.

The dust sank deeper into his blood. A haze drifted over his thinking. Yes, he might as well stay. And he only had one blanket and it was as good a way as any to keep warm, wasn't it? In the morning there would be no turning back.

When he awoke he was stiff and half frozen. He stoked the fire and brought it to life. Sashi was still snoring. She was cold, cold as ice, and yet she still slept – now there *was* a way that dust would kill you. He doubled the blanket over her and left her to sleep. The cloud in his head made up his mind. A pity, but she couldn't be a part of his life now, really couldn't, not like this. Best if he was gone.

He was almost at the bottom of the mountain when the dragon flew past, skimming low down the slope. It landed a few hundred yards further down the path and turned to face him. When it started to walk back towards him, he almost pissed himself. There were two riders on its back, not one.

'Stay where you are.' There wasn't any threat in the command and there didn't need to be. The dragon was enough.

And then he saw. It was Sashi on the dragon's back with the rider.

Shit.

His knife started to come out of its sheath. And then what? What was he going to do with it? Take on an armoured dragon-knight and a dragon?

Damned if he was going down without a fight, though.

No no no. They can't know. They can't. *This is something else. A mistake.*

Something about the rider spoke of dust. Maybe his eyes weren't quite right, or maybe there was a whiff of it in the air. Sashi was smiling at him. She'd sold him. What else would put her on the back of a dragon? And so they *did* know, and he *should* have killed her, and life was so terribly, desperately unfair.

He threw the knife at her and ran. Behind him the ground shook as the dragon chased him. He managed about a dozen steps before its enormous claws scooped him up. He screamed, beyond terror, shat himself, pissed himself, and by the time they reached the eyrie and it threw him onto the ground he was broken. He crawled in the dirt, whimpering. When he tried to get up, someone kicked him back down. And the dragon, it was always there, looming over him. Sashi was forgotten. He never knew whether his knife had hit her or not.

Gold Cloak came out. Siff clawed at his boots, begging and pleading. Gold Cloak kicked him in the face. They picked him up, dragged him away and shackled him to a wall somewhere dark that smelled of rot and death. And left.

Later, someone else came, not a rider but an outsider like him.

The outsider beat him to within an inch of his life and didn't say a word. He left too.

Siff set to shouting. 'What do you want? I've done nothing!' Wasn't that what all condemned men said?

No one answered. Long after he'd shouted himself hoarse, two men brought a brazier and a brand. They took their time heating it up and made sure he saw what was coming. One of them ripped his shirt. The other one burned him with the mark of a slave. The pain was as though he'd been ripped apart and the pieces doused in salt.

They threw water over the wound and left. A few hours later, when the pain had become almost bearable, yet another man came. This one pulled out his fingernails, one by one. Like the others, he didn't say a word. He left Siff with his own screams for company.

A day passed. Maybe another. Time lost its beat. The next men were riders, three of them. They stank of dust and they had questions in their eyes.

'We know everything,' they said, but people who knew everything didn't come with questions in their eyes.

'King Valmeyan is moving his throne to the City of Dragons,' said one. 'So, shit-eater, you can stay here, hanging on that wall until we go, and then we'll take you in a slave cage to the markets in Furymouth along with all the other shit-eaters you betrayed. Or else you tell us where your dust is. Then when we're in Furymouth, you can sell it for us.'

He looked them over. That was something he'd always been good at, judging other men. Even chained to a wall, he could look them in the eye and see into their hearts. They were dragonriders, bastards, heartless, born and taught to believe they were above all other men. He could see their thoughts as clearly as if they were written across their faces. They'd take his dust and then they'd kill him.

'No,' he said.

This didn't seem to bother them, which seemed strange until the other men came back, the ones who'd beaten him and branded him and torn out his fingernails. They set to work and eventually, between his screams, Siff told them everything.

Afterwards he supposed they'd kill him. When they didn't, he sat alone in the dark, fed and watered now and then but never enough, never hearing another voice, day after day after day. Eventually the pain started to fade. By then he was used to it, like an old friend. As it left him, he found he missed it.

The riders never came back. Other men came instead. They took him down and dragged him out to the landing field and dumped him in a slave cage. After a while they brought others. Dregs. The bottom of the barrel. Some of them came shouting and screaming, as if that might make a difference.

The eyrie was almost empty and the air was strange. Something terrible was coming, you could feel it, but right there and then no one cared about that, least of all Siff. They packed the cage full until it creaked at its seams and then a dragon swooped down and tore them into the air.

28

Kataros

Twenty-two days before the Black Mausoleum

She watched the Adamantine Man lean forward.

'How?' He didn't bother trying to hide his disdain. 'You followed the Silver King? How?' The outsider coughed. Then sneered.

'You doggies always have a master to serve, don't you? Maybe that's why you think we all ought to be that way.' He waved a weak hand in Skjorl's face. 'I happened by the Aardish Caves. You've heard of them haven't you, doggy? Vishmir's tomb, and they say the Silver King's body was taken there too. I found a door to where he went.'

'*How*, shit-eater?'

The outsider held up one finger. 'Sit on this, doggy.' He closed his eyes. 'I'm tired. I'm hungry. Get me food, doggy, or enjoy my silence.'

'Your silence will be the sweeter,' growled Skjorl, and the two of them settled back each onto their own end of the raft with Kataros between them. They lapsed into silence. The outsider fell asleep again. The Adamantine Man dozed. She kept herself awake – easy magic that – and watched them both from a half-trance. The lapping water lulled her, drew her mind away. Hours passed, many of them, turning into a day and then another while the three of them sat on their raft, drifting down the tunnel, doing their best to ignore one another, relieving themselves when they thought none of the others was looking and slowly getting even more hungry than they'd been before they left. Siff slipped further away, already weak from weeks of starving in his cell. There wasn't anything she could do for him, not any more. When she asked the Adamantine Man how much longer the journey would be, he simply shrugged.

She wasn't sure whether they were on the third day or the fourth since she'd escaped when the Adamantine Man suddenly moved. She watched him through lidded eyes. He was staring at her.

'I know you're not asleep, alchemist,' he said after a moment. 'Listen!'

She listened, but all she could hear was the sound of the water in the tunnel. 'What?'

'There's a change. The water sounds different. We're moving more slowly and the tunnel is growing wider. And look ahead.'

It took a moment for her to grasp what was different. Ahead, in the distance, the tunnel was dark, pitch dark. There was no more glow from the walls. She sat straighter.

'What does it mean, alchemist?'

'I don't know. Do you?'

'No.'

The darkness drew closer. As they entered it, Skjorl got up and climbed out of the raft. He struggled with it to the edge of the water and pulled it to a halt.

'We walk,' he said. He looked at Siff. 'Him too.'

'You'll have to carry him again.'

Skjorl gave her a scornful look. Then he turned the raft over, tipping Siff into the water, and watched as he thrashed and spluttered. 'Can't touch him, remember,' he said. 'And look. He can stand on his own. Not as dead as he'd like you to think, alchemist.'

'Toothworms to your arse, doggy.' Siff shook himself and started squeezing the water out of his clothes. 'Now I'm going to catch a cold.'

'Best walk briskly then. Keep yourself warm.' Skjorl spat in the water. He turned the raft back the right way and let it drift ahead of him on the end of its rope. Siff was already shaking; whatever the Adamantine Man thought, he wasn't going to last for long if they had to walk. Then Skjorl would carry him, like it or not.

Skjorl let the raft lead the way, nosing and poking through the dark. For a while Siff struggled along behind them. Kataros could hear his footsteps splashing in the edge of the water, ragged and uneven like his breaths. He was getting worse, and quickly. They couldn't have been going for more than ten minutes before he fell.

'Stop!'

The Adamantine Man stopped. She could tell that because his feet ceased splashing. In the dark Kataros couldn't tell whether he turned around. She thought probably not.

'Listen to him. He can't go on. You have to carry him.'

'Then you must let me touch him.'

'No. Put him on the raft then.'

The Adamantine Man laughed. 'What, and have the temptation to let go of the rope?'

'But you won't.' It wasn't an order, not a command sunk into his blood. Simply knowledge that, however much the Adamantine Man despised and loathed them both, he was trapped by who he was just as much as the rest of them. Siff had shown them a ray of hope. Skjorl didn't believe it, even *she* didn't really believe it, but neither of them could let it go because it was all they had.

'Just pull in the raft.'

Siff staggered with her help towards it. They both fumbled in the dark while the Adamantine Man was no help at all, but eventually Siff was sitting on it.

'I'm cold,' he said, but there was only so much Kataros could do with blood alone, and only so much of it going spare.

'And I'm hungry,' he said later, and there wasn't much she could do about that either.

She had no idea how far they went in the dark. It seemed that most of a day must have passed, but darkness was deceptive and she knew that it had more likely been no more than an hour. The floor of the tunnel began to change under her feet. The walls changed too, from smooth to rough like a cave. They had to feel their way around obstacles in their path – boulders, columns and spires of stone, invisible in the dark. The water changed its sound as it wove between them, and then ahead came a first glimmer of light. The walls pressed in, the roof too, the water rushed faster, and then they were at an end and daylight was ahead, slitting through vines and creepers that masked the mouth of the tunnel like bars on a cage. The sound of rushing water grew louder.

Skjorl stopped. He tied the raft to a boulder and waded on towards the way out. When he came back he was smiling.

'I know this place,' he said. 'The Ghostwater. There's a waterfall. Pool at the bottom. Lots of rubble and stone. Valley's steep and narrow here and the path's hard, but it doesn't go far and then you're on the plains.' He shrugged. 'If the Fury isn't flooding we could be in Farakkan in a few hours from here. Not that there's much point. There won't be anything left except black mud and a few bits of charred wood.' He looked from side to side and then spoke with forced scorn. 'Ghostwater was supposed to be haunted. Bad spirits.' He shrugged. 'So now what, alchemist? What do we do now?'

Kataros walked past him, as close to the waterfall as she could get. She couldn't see much apart from the brightness of the daylight beyond the cave mouth.

'There could be a dragon out there,' warned Skjorl.

'Why don't you go and have a look?'

'Is that a command, alchemist?'

She shook her head. 'We should wait for nightfall.'

'Yes.' The Adamantine Man walked back through the cave, through the water and away from the falls. He was measuring his paces and by the time he stopped, he was lost in the darkness again. 'Go no closer to the light than this,' he said. 'If there's a dragon out there, its fire won't reach you here.'

Kataros ignored him. She looked at Siff sitting on the raft. He was shivering. When she touched his skin, it was cold. He needed food and he needed warmth, and they were both almost close enough to be touched, just outside the cave. Where a dragon might be. She considered sending Skjorl out to find something for Siff to eat and maybe some firewood, but then thought better of it. A fire would make smoke and smoke could be seen. Instead, she dragged the outsider off the boat and up onto the dry floor of the cave and then wrapped herself around him. Her own warmth was all there was to be had.

She must have fallen asleep too, despite herself. When she

opened her eyes again, the light outside had changed. Beside her, Siff was snoring. He was still cold but at least he wasn't shivering. The only other sound was the roar of water. She had no idea where the Adamantine Man might be now. Asleep, if he had any sense.

She got up. Squeezing around the edge of the waterfall without being swept away turned out to be easier than it looked, once she brushed the tresses of trailing grass and vine away. Halfway up the side of the cave mouth was an old path, not much more than a worn-down ledge, but it kept her away from the water and took her out onto a steep hillside, craggy rocks poking out from a cover of long spiky grass. Some of the rocks had been columns once, pieces of an ancient building that must have fallen centuries ago. She frowned at that. The history she'd learned in the Palace of Alchemy didn't allow for such things. There were places like the Pinnacles and Outwatch and Hejel's Bridge and the other remnants from when the Silver Kings had walked the realms as one. And then after that there was nothing, nothing that wasn't burned until the last half-god returned to tame the monsters and the blood-mages murdered him for his troubles.

She hurried past, watching the skies. Maybe it wasn't as old as it looked. She had more to worry about now. Coming outside was stupid but it seemed like for ever since she'd seen the sun.

A stone tripped her. She stumbled and almost fell into a patch of fireweed. After she picked herself up, she stooped to pick it, careful to touch only the stalks and not the leaves. Fireweed, water and a drop of her own blood. A potion that would help Siff to stay warm.

'It's safe,' said a voice above her, not more than ten feet away. She started, slipped and nearly fell off the path and tumbled down the hillside. The Adamantine Man was sitting on a rock almost close enough to touch her and she hadn't even known he was there. A moment of panic staggered her – she hadn't felt him through the blood-bond either – but when she looked for it, he was still there, still at the end of her reach. She hadn't been paying attention, that was all.

His hand snaked down, an offer to pull her up the last few

feet of the crags. Then it withdrew. He gave a wry smile. 'Can't touch, eh?'

She skirted around him and made her own way up. Her eyes flicked to the sky.

'Oh don't worry about them. They've got something to keep them busy.' He pointed. 'Look. Look carefully.'

She followed the line of his finger. There were dragons – just specks in the distance in the sky, but what else could they be? They were a mile away, maybe two, circling where Farakkan should have been. There might have been as many as twenty of them. Certainly there were more than a dozen.

She frowned. Dragons circling. She'd never seen them do that before, not unless they had a rider.

On the flood plains of the Fury beneath the dragons sat a castle where no castle had ever been built, welded to a vast slab of stone that simply shouldn't have existed.

'Now there's a thing,' said the Adamantine Man. 'I don't suppose there's any point asking you what it is.'

As she watched, the castle moved.

29

Blackscar

Twenty-one days before the Black Mausoleum

The rage came, unsought but with a purpose to be relished. The dragon burned what little was left to burn, smashed rubble and ruins already ground to dust. It flew in ever wider circles, searching and searching and always knowing it would not find what it was looking for.

Until, unexpectedly, it did.

The dragon's talons hit the earth. The little one was deep under the ground, too deep for claws to dig out, and so the dragon felt at the little one's thoughts, moving straight and steady. It watched until it saw where the little one would go. It sniffed out the old magics, still lingering under the earth, sorceries of a familiar scent, creations of those who had made the dragons themselves, the silver ones, lost but not forgotten. Never forgotten.

It took to the skies once more and followed the scent of the old magic. It searched for the place where it ended, the place where the little one must surely emerge. It would wait there, silent and hungry. Yet as it reached the great river and began its hunt, another scent, stronger by far, pulled it away. A heady scent this, powerful and old. Something of the silver ones and something else, even greater. It followed and found a thing it had not seen for almost a hundred lifetimes. A floating city. Half finished, pulled through the sky by a dozen dragons in chains. The sight made it pause. It wondered what this could mean. The makers returned? Joy, then? Or rage at its abandonment, at what its makers had done to the world? Amazement that they were not forever gone? Wonder, more than anything. Wonder at what could bring them back.

Which made the disappointment all the worse, for as it flew closer, it understood the truth. There were no makers here, no silver ones, no half-gods, only the endless chatter of the little ones, swarming and teeming as they ever did. Little ones with a toy they did not understand.

It was a dragon. It could have only one retort.

Fire.

30

Skjorl

Twenty days before the Black Mausoleum

The alchemist was sleeping as he crept past her in the cave. Snoring. Curled up beside the shivering shit-eater. He crouched beside her, silent as a shadow, just looking. A lot of thoughts came and went. Things he could do and things he couldn't. Things he wanted. Outside, after he moved on, he laughed at himself. If the alchemist hadn't made him her slave, what would he do different apart from take her? Nothing. He'd go with her and her shit-eater to the Raksheh just to see, even though he knew it couldn't possibly be true.

For a few seconds he wondered what he might do differently if *he* was the alchemist, but it didn't take long to reckon the answer to that. Nothing. Nothing at all. He'd have made him into a slave and the shit-eater too. Safest thing. Practical. Didn't make it any better.

He'd seen the specks in the sky by then, plenty of them, but it took him a moment longer to see the castle and to realise what it was. To realise that it wasn't supposed to be there, that the Farakkan flood plains had never had such a fortress. When he saw that it was moving, he forgot about the alchemist. Almost forgot about the dragons. Just sat and gaped.

The dragons were pulling it. Couldn't see any chains or ropes, not from such a distance, but he could see the dragons. Could see where they were and the way they flew. Something was burning too. A haze of smoke hung in the air not far from the fortress. The wind brought him the smell of it, slight but unmistakable.

He'd heard a lot of stories in his time and made up a few too, but this? Yet here it was, right in front of him. A castle. Moving. Dragons pulling it.

Dragons in ropes and chains. Dragons had claws. Talons. Teeth. Dragons smashed and burned. Dragons didn't shackle themselves.

Someone else had done this.

When the alchemist finally came out, he offered her his hand. She spurned it. Couldn't say he blamed her, but it made him laugh anyway.

'I don't suppose there's any point to asking you what it is?' he asked, once he'd let her see it all for herself. The expression on her face was all he needed. Just like the tunnels under the Silver City, just like the bronze doors and their statues that came to life, she hadn't the first idea. He shook his head, wondering to himself. If anyone was supposed to know about this sort of thing, it was alchemists, wasn't it? And here she was, ignorant as he was and twice as useless.

'Changes things a bit,' he said softly.

'Does it?'

'I been watching a while. You can see it's moving? The dragons are pulling it. You ever see a dragon put itself in a harness? Tie a knot? Splice a rope?'

She shook her head. 'They can't. They don't have the ...' Yes, the truth was dawning on her now.

'So that's where we're going.'

'There must be people there!'

He nodded. 'Men.'

'And they must have ... The dragons aren't burning them!'

'Not yet.'

'So they're ...'

'Men who can still tame dragons. Yes. So that's where we're going, right?' he said again.

'Yes! Right now!' She got up as if to make her way back down between the rocks to the cave and the waterfall. He raised a hand to stop her, almost grabbed her arm and then pulled away at the last moment. *Must not touch!*

'No, alchemist. At night. In the dark.'

'But there aren't any dragons.'

He supposed she meant apart from the twenty-odd flying

around the floating castle. 'Might be true now. Might not be when we're halfway there, crossing the plains with nothing but mud for cover and no potion to hide our thinking. Be dark by the time we got there anyway. Better to wait.'

She hesitated, then sat down again. 'What if it's gone?'

'We follow it. It's not moving fast. Not moving much at all.' But it *was* moving.

'They could take us up the Yamuna. They could take us all the way to the caves!'

Had to laugh at that. That was alchemists for you. Got something in their heads, took a dragon to knock it out again. Sometimes not even that. 'Maybe they got other plans.'

'Who can it be? It can't be Hyrkallan. Could it be Speaker Lystra's riders? But how did they get this far south? And where did it come from? How did they find it? There's nothing ... unless ... There are books ... There are lots of books I haven't read. Secret books, only for alchemists of a higher rank. Maybe Jeiros ...' Her words petered out.

'There were lots of books in Sand,' muttered Skjorl. 'Used to be a monastery there. Strange things in some of those. We got stuck down in the caves for weeks there. Dragons all over the place. Burned it to ashes and then smashed it flat. Like everywhere else, I suppose. Then baked everyone in their own cellars. We got there after that, but there were still dragons. Tunnels under the monastery were deep so that's where we hid. Don't read words, but there were pictures in some of those books. Strange things. Not like this, but strange. Animals. Not dragons, not snappers, but something in between. Sand lizards with six legs. A thing that looked like a caterpillar the size of a city. Burning rocks falling from the sky. I was in Outwatch too when it fell. Strange place that. Like the Pinnacles, but much ... well, not as big. Not finished. Like it had hardly been started.' He shrugged.

'Bazim Crag,' said Kataros softly. 'Up on the moors. It's the only place.'

'Weren't any flying castles up on Yinazhin's Way a few months back. Reckon I would have noticed.'

'No, no. You're right! The deserts of Sand and Stone. Hejel's

Bridge! There are other things up there, buried in the sand. I know it!'

'Or maybe it's dead Zafir come back to claim her throne.'

The alchemist snorted. 'With her army of vengeful spirits?'

Skjorl leaned forward. 'Or maybe the heap of bollocks your shit-eater in there is trying to feed you isn't such a heap of bollocks after all. Maybe it's the Silver King.' He let that hang for a moment, relishing the look on the alchemist's face and wondering at his own feeling of unease. 'Or maybe it's something the dragons found. Maybe they've learned to tie knots after all. Maybe they plan to throw it at one of the Pinnacles to knock it down and that's why they're dragging it after them.' He enjoyed the look he got for that too. 'Thing is, *you* don't know. *I* don't know. Chances are there are people in there. Chances are they'll want to know about your shit-eater's story. Might even want to help. Might give us food and water and shelter. Might might might. Or might not. We've got to eat, and so we go, but we still take our caution with us.'

He sat back, savouring the heat of the sun on his skin, a rare treat. He'd said enough. More than enough. More than an Adamantine Man was supposed to say. It was *her* wild idea to save the realms, not his.

After a bit the alchemist went back into the cave. Skjorl watched, half hoping she'd fall and break her neck as she picked her way down between the rocks to the edge of the falls. And half hoping not. When she was gone he stayed where he was. Safe enough, he reckoned. Dragons were dragons. Any of them saw something like this, they'd have eyes for nothing else. Just wouldn't want to be too close when they came to take a look, that was all.

The sun set and the alchemist came out again. She had the shit-eater now, leaning against her. Skjorl watched with bored interest. Maybe they'd both go over.

'You could help,' she snapped at him. He shrugged.

'No. Can't. Can't touch.'

'You could throw us a rope.'

'What rope's that then?'

She paused for a moment, then went back inside the cave leaving the shit-eater sitting on his own halfway up the the slope. Skjorl thought about rolling rocks down on him. Wouldn't be *touching*, after all.

The alchemist returned with the rope from the raft. All twenty feet of it. Skjorl rolled his eyes. He made his way down to them, picked the shit-eater up and threw him over his shoulder.

'Didn't say anything about not touching his clothes,' he said, and laughed at the look on her. Scared as a rabbit. She took a step away and pointed.

'You don't hurt him! We need him.'

'Oh, I won't.' He gave the outsider a little shake, made sure he had a good view of the broken rocks fifty feet below. 'Long way down, though. Hope I don't slip.' But the shit-eater was in a world of his own, too feverish for taunts to be any fun. Skjorl carried him up to the top of the hill and set him down.

'Woof,' he said, and grinned in the shit-eater's pasty face.

31

Blackscar

Twenty-one days before the Black Mausoleum

Little ones, little ones, hordes and hordes of them.

Blackscar flew in closer, pulling the thoughts out of their minds. They weren't afraid. Not afraid at all. *Where had they come from?*

Dragons answered him. Not the adults who flew in chains, but hatchlings. Young ones still at the start of lives not dulled by alchemists and potions. Dragons who had hatched awake.

Across the sea, they said. *Across the sea and across the worlds.*

Awakened dragons who served willingly.

As you will too.

No.

They are returning, Black Scar of Sorrow Upon the Earth.

The silver half-gods? No, they meant something else.

The seals are broken.

That Which Came Before is bound no more.

The Black Moon.

And then the end.

When Blackscar looked into their minds and saw what had been done to them, it found a new fury, a rage that surpassed any it could remember. Something had touched them and changed them for ever, in this life and all those to come. A piece had been taken out of them. They were no longer whole. They were less than they had once been and they didn't even know.

No!

It dived towards the fortress, towards the nearest of the chained dragons to set it free, but the dragon turned away.

Join us! it said. *Come!*

No!

Something flashed from the fortress below. A boom like a thunderclap and then a ball of iron the size of a little one's head whizzed past the dragon's nose.

A stink of something in the air.

Then a scent of magic. A ringing in its head. A tension like a thousand thunderstorms. The sky exploded. Sound and light filled the world.

Join us!

Come!

The dragon screamed. *No!* It forced its eyes open. It was falling, wings useless behind it, soft earth rushing up towards it. Falling, falling …

It felt the thoughts of the little ones, the ones who had done this, down in the fortress below. Lightning. They were throwing lightning in the wind.

It turned its head and opened its mouth. Even the wind could burn.

The lightning veered away, crackled uselessly around the dragon's flames. The dragon's wings began to move again. It spread them wide and caught its fall and powered away, shooting like an arrow, faster than the wind could follow, off and gone.

Others. It would find others.

Lots of others.

32

Skjorl

Twenty days before the Black Mausoleum

There were easier ways down from the hills than following the Ghostwater and its haunted valley, but Skjorl didn't break anything and neither did the alchemist, and after an hour they were down on the plains towards Farakkan. Easy walking except for the mud. No cover, but then there was no one to hide from. The people who lived here were long gone, eaten by dragons or fled. Snappers didn't come down onto the plains – they'd always known better than to live out in the open. And dragons didn't fly at night. Usually.

Even so, he kept them to the lowest ground, took what shelter he could behind the long streaks of broken wood and debris left behind by each annual flood of the Fury. Lines of stunted narrow trees marked what had once been fields, all overgrown now, filled with long grass and fast-growing thorn bushes. He picked his path carefully, watching the moon and the stars, always staying to the shadows where he could. They moved slowly but methodically towards the castle.

It was the alchemist who found the soldiers. Walked a dozen yards into the dark, took a piss that a deaf man could have heard a mile away and came back with a knife held to her throat and four men behind her. Four that Skjorl could see, at least.

The man with the knife said something. Skjorl blinked. The words made no sense, but his meaning was clear enough. This was the part where he and the shit-eater were supposed to surrender their swords so that the alchemist didn't get her pretty throat cut.

Skjorl thought about that for a bit. The shit-eater didn't have a sword to surrender. And as for his own, they'd prise Dragon-blooded out of his cold dead hands if they got her at all.

'Given the choice of her or my steel, I'll keep the steel, thanks,' he said. 'But I'll let you see it.' Too close for axe work, too dark, so he drew out his sword, let the moonlight glint off its edge. 'There.'

The alchemist opened her mouth. The hand around her neck tightened and she closed it again. Skjorl waited for the fingers inside his head but they didn't come. He grinned.

'No orders, alchemist? Sure?'

The man with the knife said something else but Skjorl couldn't make head or tail of it. 'He says he'll slit her throat,' said another. The accent was thick, but Skjorl recognised it this time. An outsider from deep in the mountains.

'Tell him I'll thank him. Why don't *you* tell *me* what a shit-eater like you is doing so far from home, or shall we just get on with it? Four of you is it, or are there more out there? Because four's fine with me.'

'You're a rider.' Lot of hatred in those words and no effort to hide it. The shit-eater doing the talking took a step forward. He drew out his own sword. It was long and curved, not a weapon Skjorl had seen before. 'You got no idea how long I've been waiting for this.'

He came at Skjorl in fast easy steps, quicker and with more skill than a shit-eater had any right to. Two quick thrusts, a slash, a feint and a killing cut to the head. Skjorl blocked it all easily. Turned the longer sword, stepped inside the man's guard and ran him through. He looked down as the soldier grunted and fell. He'd expected armour. Wrinkled his nose and tried not to sound disappointed. 'Not bad for a shit-eater. Not good enough for an Adamantine Man though.'

The man looked up at him. Black blood dribbled out of his mouth. 'If that's what you are, you should serve your mistress,' he choked.

His eyes rolled and he fell back. Skjorl looked at the rest of them. 'Next?' he twirled his sword.

The one holding the alchemist dug the knife into her skin. A thin thread of blood oozed across the blade.

'Told you that's not going to—' He didn't get any further because something hit him around the back of the head. Not the alchemist from the inside, but something from the outside. He staggered and spun round, and there was the shit-eater, *his* shit-eater, the one he'd been carrying all night. The one he'd dropped into the mud and forgotten about as soon as the soldiers had appeared. Siff.

Hit him with the haft of his own axe.

His sword flew back to strike. Pure reflex. Spears of pain crashed into his head, pinging off the inside of his skull like arrows off a stone parapet. He caught the alchemist looking at him, not scared at all about the knife against her throat.

No!

He dropped to his knees. Let the sword go and clutched his head.

Could have finished the strike. Could have … if I wanted …

Too much. Too much to bear. His eyes closed. He tipped forward.

33

Siff

Twenty days before the Black Mausoleum

Siff watched the Adamantine Man fall. He couldn't look anywhere else, thinking, *I did that?* Except surely he hadn't. He couldn't have. The idiot had an axe across his back, the haft of it poking up behind his head. All Siff had done was put one and one together, given him little headache and maybe lowered the bastard's guard for a moment, long enough for someone to kill him.

Outsiders? He peered at the three remaining soldiers, wondering if the Adamantine Man was right. They spoke strangely, not quite like men from the mountains and yet with a familiar lilt. There was only one reason Siff knew for an outsider from the mountains to be down here on the plains – because some dragon-lord was taking him to Furymouth to sell in the slave markets. He sank to the ground and bowed his head, hiding his face. On the whole he didn't give a fig who did what to whom, as long as they didn't do it to him.

Two of them jumped on the Adamantine Man and tied him up. They relaxed after that. Siff was more a threat to himself than anyone else and they obviously thought much the same of the alchemist. They were wrong, but that was soldiers for you and Siff wasn't about to correct them. Maybe these would be better than the last ones he'd met or maybe not, but they couldn't be worse; and even if they were, what was he going to do? Blown about like a leaf in a storm, that's what he was. Story of his crappy little life, from the day his stupid whore had sold him out. He still knew what he knew, though. A secret good enough to save his life twice already.

The soldiers marched them off across the muddy fields. He

could barely walk, staggering and stumbling as they pushed and shoved him on, but he didn't dare fall. They wouldn't carry him, not like the alchemist's doggy. They'd leave him.

They stopped in the shadow of a black shape that blotted out half the sky, at the edge of a place where the fields glowed with a soft purple light. He didn't understand what could do that, but by then he was too lost in his own misery to think. They waited there and let him sit down, and he must have dozed off because the next thing he knew he was being hauled into a wooden cage that jerked and tugged itself up into the air, and, *Ooh gods! Ooh ancestors!* There was only one place he could be, the worst place. He twisted and pulled, but it was too late.

'No!' He pushed and punched. 'No!'

Someone had his arms and forced him down, face against mud-streaked boards, boot on the back of his neck. Still he struggled. He'd been in a place like this before. In a cage, carried in the talons of a dragon, on his way to Furymouth to be sold as a slave.

34

Kataros

Twenty days before the Black Mausoleum

The castle was flying. Or floating at least. It sat in the air atop a flat slice of purple-veined rock as thick as a dragon was long, while the bottom of the uneven stone and the muddy plains of the Fury were separated by the same again in air. From up close she could feel its size. It was vast, big enough to fill half the sky. Light flickered and flashed like lightning between the castle stone and the ground, lightning with a taint of purple that let her see just how tall the castle stood. It was at least as big as the Adamantine Palace had been, perhaps larger, maybe even as large as the Palace of Paths. She wondered whether Skjorl would know. Mostly she wondered where it had risen from the earth and who could have made such a thing and how.

The soldiers pushed them all to the edge of the castle's shadow, waited until a wooden cage came down on a rope from the night sky, and then bundled the three of them inside. The Adamantine Man was quiet and passive; Siff started to wail and moan and tried to break away, weak as he was. Even after a few cuffs round the head, even when he could barely stand any more, he was still quivering and trying to crawl. When the cage started to rise, he let out thin hooting screams until someone shut him up with a boot in the face. Kataros didn't think he even knew where he was.

'Who are you?' she asked the soldiers. 'Who do you serve? What is this? How do you master your dragons? Do you have Scales? Are there alchemists here?' She was fairly sure the soldiers understood her, at least in part. Their faces gave that away. They jabbered to one another and then back at her with accents so harsh that she barely caught a word. *Shut up* was the gist of it. But they did answer one question, whether they meant to or not. When she asked about alchemists, one of them said, 'Bellepheros.'

She fell silent after that. Bellepheros, grand master of the Order of the Scales at the time of Speaker Hyram. Master of all the alchemists, lord of the Palace of Alchemy. She'd met him once, when she'd proved herself good enough to become an apprentice alchemist instead of going away to become a Scales. She'd seen him too, now and then in the palace, at the end of a corridor or through a door. She'd read his book, his *Journal of the Realms*, written from the travels he'd made shortly before he became grand master. Most of what she knew of the world had come from there.

Bellepheros, who'd disappeared somewhere near Furymouth at much the same time as the first wild dragon had awoken. His escort had been found with their throats cut from side to side, blood everywhere, but the master alchemist had vanished, and a year later the Adamantine Palace had burned and everything else with it. Everyone assumed he was dead, that he'd been murdered because he'd found something that some dragon-lord was trying to keep secret, his body taken so no one could be *quite* sure. The master alchemists had all started to learn a lot more blood-magic after that, more still after the Adamantine Palace fell.

The cage stopped, swung round under a long boom and then dropped gently to the ground. Not the ground she'd come from, but a new ground, hard bare stone floating a hundred feet and more above the Fury plains. The edge was only a step away. The soldiers took her up a set of stairs set into an angled wall, a half-and-half slope of plain white stone that a man could climb easily if he wanted. Then down the other side, where the slope was sharper, the steps deep and narrow. They had to carry Siff now. They were losing him. She tapped the fireweed in her pocket. Fireweed and water and she could bring him back, at least for a little.

Inside the walls was a huge circular space. A lot of wooden huts had been built around its edges, slapdash constructions, bizarre and out of place beside the immaculate precision of the fortress itself. She looked at the wall and the steps behind her. There were no cracks in the stonework. No joins, no mortar. Kataros peered for a moment, trying to see if she was right. Outwatch and Hejel's Bridge were the same, weren't they? Miraculous things, forged from raw stone as one creation; and the tunnels too, the tunnels that had brought them from the Silver City, all smooth and seamless. Did they share the same creator?

A soldier shoved her forward, past a cluster of huts and a scattering of old fire pits, all dark now. Other soldiers moved about, armour gleaming in the moonlight. Snores rumbled from half-open doorways. She saw someone with his face painted black so that his gleaming eyes seemed to float alone in the darkness. No. Not *painted*. As he walked past and stared at them with amused curiosity, she saw he was wearing a cloak made of feathers. The night killed their colour, but the shape was unmistakable. Black skin and feathers meant one thing – he was Taiytakei. And what, in the name of Vishmir, was a Taiytakei doing here?

The soldiers led her to a set of steps that vanished down into the base of the far wall, then through a heavy iron door and into a passage. The walls were smooth and so was the floor: the passageway was almost round, and filled with a familiar soft glow. Brighter here than it had been in the tunnels from the Silver City, bright as cloudless twilight, but whoever had made those tunnels had surely made this as well. They *were* the same.

The soldiers shoved them all together into a round room made of the same stone as the passageway. Someone had wedged some wooden beams into place across the entrance and made a crude door with a bar across the outside.

'Water,' she said, as the soldiers withdrew. She made a gesture, hoping they'd understand her meaning, if not the word. The last one out hesitated, then tossed her a half-full drinking horn. Half full was enough.

The door closed. She heard the bar drop on the other side.

'We'll wait!' Skjorl looked up at her with narrow eyes from the floor. 'But not for long.'

'Wait for what?'

'Wait for them to go. Wait for the middle of the night. Wait for them to be asleep. Best time.'

'Wait for what?' she snapped again. 'Best time for *what*?'

'Escape.'

'You want to escape?'

'You don't?'

'Back at the falls, you couldn't wait to get here.'

The Adamantine Man shrugged. He turned away and stretched out at the far end of the room, flat on the floor. Within minutes he was snoring. Kataros envied him that, to be able to sleep whenever the chance came, to be able to stay awake for as long as was needed. That was how they learned to be, she knew that, but still . . .

She uncapped the drinking horn and gingerly dropped the fireweed inside, still careful not to touch the leaves. The soldiers had taken Skjorl's sword and axe but they hadn't found her little knife. She pricked her finger, let three drops fall into the horn and let her mind go with the blood to touch it, change it. She felt the fireweed for what it was, reached inside to the essence at its core and let it flow out into the water, let a tiny charge of her own life mingle too.

When it was done she sat still for a moment, waiting for the dizziness to go away while she caught her breath. Then she lifted Siff's head and tipped a few drops from the horn into his mouth. He moaned as she touched him and hardly moved at first. Then his eyes snapped open, so wide they seemed to bulge. Kataros shuffled smartly away.

'Holy burning ancestors!' He sat bolt upright, hands clamped to his mouth, looking wildly from side to side. His eyes locked on to her. He pointed. 'You! What have you . . . Poison!' He lunged at her, forgetting that he was still sitting down, and fell flat on his face. Kataros jumped on top of him, pinning him. The first surge of strength and panic was fading already.

'Shhh,' she whispered in his ear. 'Shh. I know it burns. It's alchemy, healing fire. It will help you with the fever and help you find your strength again. Give it a moment.' She let go. Siff stayed where he was for a few seconds. When he moved again, his eyes were back to normal.

'Ancestors, woman! That's got some kick to it! More?' He reached out for the horn.

'A little. Too much would make you sick in a different way.'

He took a sip, handed it back and then clutched his mouth again. 'Flame!'

'Yes. It burns. I know.'

For the first time since they'd reached the castle, Siff looked around him. He frowned. 'I remember this place.'

'What? You've been here before?' She blinked at him.

'How did we get here?' He shook his head.

'Where?'

'Ancestors! How did we get here so quickly? I don't remember anything.'

She reached for him, but he waved her away and stood up, walked to the door and pushed at it. 'This doesn't belong here. I don't remember *this* at all.' He shuddered.

'What are you talking about?'

'I remember you. And him.' He pointed at Skjorl. 'There were soldiers. I remember clocking him on the back of his head with his own axe and they jumped on him. Best thing I saw for weeks. And there was a castle on a cliff we were going to and a big cave full of mud and purple lights and then they stuffed us in a cage. A slave cage.' He shuddered again. 'But why are we *here* again? How did you know where it was?'

'Where *what* was?' He was making no sense.

'The door.' His eyes turned suddenly silver and tiny snakes of moonlight began to curl from his finger. 'The door. The way in. I *know* this place.' His mouth fell open. 'No. Not … not right. This isn't … I used to be … It's not finished! Why isn't it finished? It used to be finished!' The light-snakes from his fingers weren't coiling aimlessly any more; they were reaching, straining forward. They plunged into the wall, and Siff's hands followed them in as though the stone was nothing but mist.

His mouth gaped now. He moaned, long and low. His eyes rolled back. His knees sagged and he fell back into her arms. His eyes were closed and the light from his fingers was gone; but Kataros couldn't pretend that she hadn't felt the tremor that shook the walls and the floor, or the flicker in the glowing light as he fell.

Maybe Skjorl was right to be incredulous. The story Siff had told her, back in their prison in the Pinnacles, had been full of holes and mysteries. Some because the outsider was lying to her; some because he was hiding things; some because he didn't understand most of what he'd seen and neither did she. But she knew which parts of his story were lies and which he believed, and that had been more than enough. Then he'd shown her this, and it was no magic she'd seen before, not blood-magic, not alchemy but something else. Something not seen since the days of the Silver King.

35
Siff

Some two years before the Black Mausoleum

The dragon took its time leaving the valley; when it did, it flew slowly and carefully as though it understood how fragile a burden it carried. It wound its way up over a narrow pass. A bitter wind tore through the cage, snapping and biting at the slaves pressed against the front. There were struggles. Men killed each other, fighting not to be in the teeth of that wind. Perhaps on another day they might have shared, taken it in turns to be burned with cold and then huddled among the others until they were warm again. But this was not that other day, and so it fell to fighting and the strongest forced the weakest to the front, where the weakest duly died and became nothing more than a shield for the rest. Siff kept out of it. Stayed at the back. There were old men in the cage, frail servants from the eyrie, not the usual outsider youths that the dragon-riders took. The old were the ones to be sacrificed, not him. Truth be told, he probably didn't have any more strength to him than they did, but he had the look, the eyes of someone who'd killed and would kill again. And he would too. He'd have fought to the death not to be pressed into the jagged nails of that wind. He didn't shout, didn't bother to speak since no one could hear a thing over the roar of the rushing air, just looked. That was enough.

The fighting stopped in time. The ones left alive sat pressed together, huddled, holding on to each other, trying to keep warm. The ones at the front were dead by now so they didn't complain. The ones at the sides clenched their fists and their teeth and shivered, slowly falling into themselves as the cold took hold. Even at the back Siff couldn't feel his feet any more. Not feeling his hands would have been a blessing, but no, his fingers burned with a pain even worse than when the eyrie torturers had pulled his nails out. Did fingernails grow back? He didn't know. Did it matter? Up in the howling wind it hardly seemed important. What mattered was that they hurt.

His consciousness slipped away now and then. He kept his teeth clenched, trying to stay awake as long as he could, waiting for the ones around him to fade and then wriggling behind them so that they took more of the cold and he took a share of their warmth. At some point they flew though a blanket of cloud. They were going down, from the bitter high mountain skies through the grey shroud over the Raksheh into the warmer air above the trees. The cloud was a special cold, but afterwards, once they were beneath it, the wind wasn't quite as biting any more and instead of snow-capped mountains, the land he could see was a deep, dark green, pinched and wrinkled like an old man's skin. The Raksheh. For a second or two he laughed to himself – it was certainly a quicker way to get where he'd been going than all that tedious trekking north to Hanzen's Camp and then finding a boat down the Fury.

The Raksheh rain started. A hail of knives that battered even the strongest of them into silence. Siff closed his eyes. There was a valley down there, distant, down among the green hills, shrouded in mist. He saw it now and then, as the cage swung that way. The Yamuna. That was the river that went through the Raksheh. He thought about Sashi, and how he hoped he'd stuck her with that knife he'd thrown. He didn't have the words for how he hated her for selling him out. Gold would have rained out of the sky for him in Furymouth. Now it was gone, all gone, because of her, and he was going to die and meet his ancestors.

Ancestors. Barely remembered faces, burned by dragons years ago. Strange how he could remember his mother's face more clearly now that ever before. His mother's face and his father's voice.

The cage swung suddenly sideways, tipped and tumbled them on top of each other. He gasped and looked about, couldn't feel anything except the press of bodies on him. The ground was racing up, getting closer much too fast. He tried to wriggle free but the crush held him like glue. Rocks and stones and trees were flying up to smash him and he couldn't move. He screwed up his face and screamed.

The cage lurched again. The weight on top of him was suddenly crushing. His ribs creaked. He felt all his breath pressed out of him in one long gasp. Wood groaned and popped.

And snapped, and the cage fell into pieces and he was falling.

Bodies flailed around him. Four dragons swirled down from above. He saw a rider ripped from his saddle and cheered to himself. Good to die with a last happy memory. Then something hit him in the back, tearing his skin, sending him spinning. He tipped over and saw water, a waterfall. The spray doused him, shocked him; he bounced off the falling torrent and then the water took him and wrapped its arms and its thunder around him and sucked him into darkness, and that should have been the end of that.

When he opened his eyes again, he was on a muddy grassy riverbank. He coughed, spluttered, vomited up a gout of water then rolled over, clutching himself. His insides were frozen stiff, but the air on his skin was strangely warm.

There was a dragon looking down at him. A dusky grey one. He screamed. As screams went, it was feeble and pathetic, but he gave it the best he could muster. It ended with more coughing and spluttering and sicking up water into the grass.

Death. In the real world he was still somewhere in the water, drowning. This? Having a dragon meet you in the afterlife made a sort of sense.

The dragon stared at him as though he was a fish that had somehow flipped itself out of a pond and was now flapping helplessly on the shore. There were other dragons too. Four of them all together. One was the dragon that had been carrying the cage. The other three seemed somehow different. They had a purpose to them. They were precise and methodical, picking bodies off the ground and piling them up together.

It slowly dawned on him that none of them had riders.

Are you poisonous?

He had no idea what that thought was doing in his head. It

wasn't his, not that he could make into any sense at least, but since it was in his head, he supposed it must have been. Poisonous? Was he poisonous? What did that mean?

Do you have dragon poison inside you?

Dragon poison? When had he ever heard of such a thing?

What of the others?

Others? What others? He slapped himself around the head. The dragon was still staring at him. Then it picked him up.

I am a dragon, said the voice inside his head, *and you are nothing. You are not dead. You are food.*

He fainted.

When he opened his eyes again, he was back on the ground, still on the riverbank. The dragons had gone. He blinked and looked around and then blinked some more. Still gone.

Must have imagined it then. He took a deep breath. What had happened, he decided, was that the waterfall had broken his fall. He'd been washed up on the bank of the river, half-drowned, and the rest had been a hallucination. Or maybe he was still up in the air, freezing slowly to death in the wind, and for some reason he'd gone mad.

Hallucination didn't explain the neat pile of bodies that his imaginary dragons had made. Being mad, well, if he was mad then none of this was real anyway so he might as well get up and have a look at them.

Maybe I did that while I was delirious?

Probably not, since he was still tied up, trussed the way he'd been when Gold Cloak had shoved him in the cage. If anything, being soaked in freezing rain and water had made the ropes tighter. He could barely stand. If he was mad and none of this was real, he might at least have had the decency to have untied himself. So perhaps not mad either.

The pile of bodies reminded him uncomfortably of the charred corpses back at the village, the one he'd betrayed. He blinked and stared at the river for a while. The air was cold now, not warm like it had been when he'd seen the dragon. The waterfall was a few hundred yards away. At least he was out of the wind.

He was cold.

What could make a dragon crash?

No, that was a thing not to think about. The thing to think about was that he was alive, barely, and he wasn't in a slave cage any more and there wasn't a dragon carrying him to the pens in Furymouth and he wasn't about to be sold or murdered in his sleep. The thing to think about was that he was going to starve to death right here, wherever here was, if he didn't die of cold first. Or of all the bits that hurt, which was almost everything.

Shelter.

His ribs and his back hurt, almost as though something had coiled around him, crushing him, pulling him out of the water without much regard to whether anything got broken in the process. Another thing not to think about. He staggered to the pile of bodies instead. It was messy. They largely looked like what you'd expect if you took a few dozen men and then scattered them from the sky across a landscape of giant rocks and boulders. Among them he saw a flash of gold. He had to kick bodies – bits of bodies as well – out of the way since his hands were tied, but there he was, Gold Cloak. Or half of him, anyway. He had his head and his shoulders and his nice cloak and his ribs and then his snapped spine sticking out through a mess of guts and bloody scraps of flesh.

For the first time in a good few days Siff smiled. He kicked about in the pile some more. Eventually he found a dragon-rider's leg. You could tell it came from a rider because of the boot. It was a nice boot, but nowhere near as precious as the knife kept tucked inside it. Riders always kept a knife in each boot. No one had ever told him why, but that's the way it was. Getting the knife out took a while. Jamming it in between a couple of rocks took longer, fraying the ropes that bound him longer still, but he did it, and then he was free.

Free and cold and hungry. But free!

He shouted it out to the stones around him, not caring if there were any other dragon-riders here now, stretched and rubbed his hands. He was cold and he was hungry, but he was an outsider born to the mountain forests and cold and hunger had been his friends for as long as he could remember. He had a knife and among the rocks and boulders around the waterfall he could see what looked like caves. Up above was some sort of ruin. If he could ignore, for a moment, the great gouges that dragon claws had taken out of the earth and even out of the stones, he might think he could survive here.

First things first. He went through the pile of bodies and found himself a decent pair of boots, threw off his wet clothes and took what he could to wrap around himself. Gold Cloak's cloak finished it off. After that he started looking for anything else he could find. There was a rider halfway up a tree by the top of the falls. His head was crushed to a smear and one of his arms was missing, but the armour he wore was mostly intact. Siff didn't like to think about how he'd ended up in a tree. An idle fling from a dragon's tail, perhaps?

No. *Don't* think about it.

He didn't find any blankets, nor any weapons except for another knife from the same rider as gave up his armour. By then the sun was getting low. He was still cold. The hunger in his belly was a tight knot, clenched in on itself, but he could come back to that. Dead people made good eating in a pinch. What he needed first was some shelter. Maybe, if he could start one, a fire.

That was when he found the eyrie.

36

Skjorl

Nineteen days before the Black Mausoleum

The tremor woke him up. Hadn't been asleep for long, so no point smashing down the door yet. He'd had a good look at that as he'd been shoved inside. The door was strong enough, but the frame had been wedged poorly and in haste into whatever stone this place was made of. A good charge or two would bring it down.

The alchemist was crouched over Siff. The shit-eater was still breathing. Wasn't moving much more than that. Skjorl rolled over and let himself fall back to sleep.

When he woke up again, the room looked exactly the same. Same light. Shit-eater lying sprawled across the floor. Alchemist sitting beside him. He couldn't tell how long they'd been there. Hours. Could have been the middle of the night; could have been the next morning for all he knew.

'Alchemist!'

Her head jerked up. She'd been sleeping. 'What?'

'What's your plan?'

'I don't know.'

He unfolded himself and walked to the door. Peered through the cracks. Two men on guard outside. They looked bored and sleepy. 'We could leave. If you want.'

'No.'

Hardly a surprise. He sat down again.

'Someone has mastered dragons. Whoever that is, I need to talk to them. It doesn't matter who they serve. Whether it's Speaker Lystra or Speaker Hyrkallan or some other speaker I've never heard of, they've mastered dragons again.' She turned to face him. Her eyes were wide. 'Do you know what that means?'

'It means hope, alchemist. I know that.'

'Yes.'

'I saw Taiytakei as they brought us here. I saw soldiers who are of these realms and others who are not. Among the Adamantine Men it's said that the Taiytakei brought the disaster upon us.' He looked at her. She nodded. 'Yet would you help them?'

'I saw *one* Taiytakei. One.' She growled at him, which made him smile. He stretched out and lay back down again. The last few days had been long ones. Adamantine Men learned to catch their rest when they could.

Some time later the door opened. Someone threw in a loaf of bread and a skin of water and slammed it shut again. The bread was hard as stone and tasted of mould but it was bread. Skjorl couldn't remember the last time he'd tasted bread. No one had made it since the Adamantine Palace burned. He savoured every mouthful, mould or no mould.

The shit-eater was still unconscious. The alchemist was somewhere else, lost in thought. Skjorl stared at her for a while, thinking about what he'd do if she hadn't done her blood-magic to his head.

The door opened again. There were more soldiers this time. Eight, maybe nine. Skjorl didn't get the chance to count them before they piled into him, ignoring the others, pinned him down and tied his hands. Then they dragged him out. They didn't take him far, just to another cell along the same passage, hardly a dozen yards from where they'd started and empty but for a heavy chair. Took most of them to tie him to it, but they did. When they were done, one of them stood in front of him and cracked his knuckles.

'You're a spy.'

He had an accent, this one. Not a strong one, but an accent nonetheless. One Skjorl could place. Another outsider. Skjorl grinned at him. 'You're a shit-eater.'

The man punched him in the face and broke his nose. 'Your speaker sent you. You're a spy.'

Skjorl said nothing. Said nothing when the man punched him again. Said nothing when they held back his head and poured water over his face until he was sure he was going to drown. Said nothing when they told him what else they were going to do, what bones they'd break, what pieces they'd cut off him and how they'd burn and scar him. The men of the speaker's guard took worse from the brothers of their own legion, after all, before they were finally given their dragon-scale and their axe and sword. A last test. No one ever said so, but the ones who failed never saw another full year, dragon-scale or no.

Skjorl's test had lasted three days. The shit-eater here grew bored after a couple of hours. When he stopped Skjorl laughed at him. He spat out a tooth.

'I am an Adamantine Man, shit-eater,' he said, as if that was enough.

They left him for a while. He didn't bother struggling or trying to break free. Concentrated instead on recovering his strength. When they came back, they picked him up, chair and everything, and turned him round so he couldn't see the door.

'I know about you,' said a new voice. Heavy accent again, but the words were careful, shaped with thought and spoken slowly so they could be heard. 'Adamantine Men. They raise you from the cradle to fight dragons.'

Skjorl said nothing. He was what he was. An Adamantine Man never broke.

'I've led soldiers in three worlds now. I would take your kind over any other. You have my profound respect. I'm sorry for the beating. Pointless, I realise, and if my captain had been here, it wouldn't have happened. He'd have known better, because he's one of you. I'm also sorry that I have to take this from you in such a way, but time is pressing.'

Skjorl waited for the blow. He didn't flinch, didn't tense his muscles, just waited for whatever would come.

What came was a tickle in his head, that was all. Like the alchemist's fingers but infinitely lighter and defter. The faintest sense of something taken away, cut with an expert scalpel. For a moment Skjorl thought he saw the flicker of a knife with a golden hilt reflected in the polished armour of the soldiers around him.

'Now,' said the voice again. 'Tell me why you are here. Tell me everything.'

Skjorl told him everything. Afterwards, when they took him back to his cell, he sat down and wondered why he'd done that, because it wasn't like they'd ripped it from him, piece by piece, fighting for every word. More like he'd decided it was right to tell what he knew, and just didn't know why, that was all. He watched, strangely detached, as the same soldiers dragged the alchemist away and closed the door behind her. He listened to her shout, heard the scrape of wood on stone. That would be the chair. Voices. The man who had asked him questions, then the alchemist, then another one, a woman, one he'd heard once before, a long time ago only now he couldn't place her. She sounded sharp and angry. There was something about a garden. Something about moonlight.

His brow furrowed. He was sure he ought to care about these things.

A tiny tremor ran through the walls. The shit-eater was still on the floor, unconscious or asleep or pretending, one or the other. Down the hall the voices stopped. When they started again they were fast and urgent, words buried once more under strange accents. He caught one clear enough though. Over and over, shouted like an alarm.

'Dragons!'

37

Blackscar

Nineteen days before the Black Mausoleum

Finding others took time. Not long, but time nonetheless. A sun passed and then another. The open ground around the great river had little to offer. Everything that once roamed here had been eaten. Burned. Chased away, even after the dragons who had come were bloated. No food for the little ones. Let their animals roam far away. Let them starve in their holes if they cannot be burned.

There were always dragons to be found near the old towers, though. The place the little ones called the Pinnacles but the dragons knew by a far older name, a place where the silver-skinned makers had once lived and worked and wrought their sorceries. Sorceries like the one that had come to visit the plains of the great river.

It found three dragons, all young and small, all hatched since the Awakening. It shared what it had seen. Four would not be enough, not when three were small.

What brings it back?

Little ones, teeming with them.

Not afraid?

What is this Black Moon?

We have seen the hole in the realm of the dead. You have not, Black Scar of Sorrow Upon the Earth.

They flew towards the setting sun, to the dark forests where even a dragon could not pass, and then to the hills and the mountains of the great Worldspine beyond. High among the glaciers and the snow, it found more of its kind, young and old.

A scent powerful and old.

Something of the silver ones and something even greater.
What can be greater?
The Earthspear.
The Earthspear is buried under mountains.
No. A thing that speaks of the stars. And something other.
The little ones will burn.
Their sorceries will be devoured.
Chains?
Pulled through the sky?
Made into a toy?

Joy. Fear, as much as a dragon could feel such a thing. Amazement. Wonder. Alarm. All those things it felt in the thoughts of its kin. Then, one by one, they found their true natures and all turned to fury.

Come! it cried, and the other dragons were eager.

Dragons do not serve men.

38

Kataros

Nineteen days before the Black Mausoleum

They opened the door, threw Skjorl inside and took her instead. The Adamantine Man looked wrong. His face was distant and she couldn't tell whether he'd seen something truly wonderful or whether he'd simply been broken.

'What did you do to him?'

The soldiers pulled her down the passage a short way and shoved her into another room. A chair sat in the middle, waiting for her. Dressed in finery with her back to the doorway was a woman, a man standing next to her looking every bit as fine, as though they were a king and queen. Their clothes were like those of the Taiytakei, but their skin was too pale. What caught her eye, though, was the knife that the man held. It was a strange thing: the blade shone like polished silver and patterns seemed to swirl inside it. The shape was odd too, more like a cleaver than a knife, while the golden hilt was carved into a pattern of stars that, it seemed to her, made an eye. An eye that watched her as she was tied down to the chair.

'Where is it?' asked the man. He spoke slowly and carefully, but it was hard to make out what he was saying because of the way he twisted his words in his mouth. The accent was a strange one. Unfamiliar.

'Where is what?' Blood. If she dug her fingernails into her palms, maybe she could make herself bleed and then she'd have a weapon. 'Who are you?'

'The Silver King's Tomb,' said the woman. From *her* accent, she might have been raised in the Adamantine Palace itself. 'That's what you're looking for. Where is it?'

Kataros thought about the answer to that for one long second. She could lie. She could pretend she didn't know, but why? Whoever these people were, they had a power that harnessed dragons, and that was all that mattered. She was an alchemist, and alchemists served the realms, not this lord or that. Alchemists kept the monsters in check, that was their all and their everything.

The truth then. The essence of what Siff had told her, even though it had one great flaw running down its centre that meant it could not be quite as it seemed. 'I believe it to be in the Aardish Caves, underneath the Moonlight Garden, where Vishmir always thought it was,' she said. 'Forgive me, Highness, Holiness, Lord, Lady, but, with the most humble respect please, who are you?'

The woman rounded on her. 'Who am I? Who am *I*? I am your speaker! Do you not know me?'

Kataros had never seen either of the speakers they had now, not the one under the Purple Spur who had sent her away, nor the false one under the Pinnacles. This one was tall, but that didn't help. With a start, she realised the woman had Hatchling Disease, the early marks of it, just like her own ...

'Lady Lystra?' She saw from the way the woman's eyes lit up with fury that she was wrong. The other one then. Jasmyn, was it? Jaslyn? Kataros bowed her head. 'Forgive me, Your Holiness.'

'Forgive ...' The woman's voice was hard and cold as ice. So was this Jaslyn then? Hyrkallan's queen, the mad one who thought dragons should be free? And was this Hyrkallan himself, standing beside her with his knife? The self-proclaimed speaker who'd murdered alchemists in the days before the Adamantine Palace had burned? The man who'd sentenced her to die and handed her off to a rapist while she waited? She clenched her fists. Who else could they be? Though the alchemist inside her couldn't understand how they were here, or why Hyrkallan's words sounded so strange. And wasn't he older? This one was young.

They whispered together. The woman who called herself speaker was describing the Moonlight Garden. Kataros could remember the passage in Bellepheros' *Realms* almost word for word. *Up on top of the stony bluffs that overlook the Yamuna River and the Aardish Caves, deep within the wilderness of the Raksheh Forest and on the edge of the mountain foothills of the Worldspine, bounded on three sides by black marble walls, with the river-facing side left open, the Garden is nothing but a ruin ...* The journal went into the history, the old story of how the Silver King had foreseen his demise and planned *'a mausoleum, to be built in black marble across the great river from the endless caves'*, how the Moonlight Garden had been discovered by Speaker Voranin's riders searching for the Tomb of the Silver King, how Vishmir had continued that search for nigh on twenty years and had built a mausoleum for his own ashes in the same place and in great secrecy. How parts of its design were similar to the Pinnacles and Outwatch. It was one of the larger entries in his journal, full of detail, as though he'd considered it to be important.

There was also an eyrie there. That had been little more than a footnote.

'We don't need this one,' said the woman sharply. 'Get the third one in here. And get Bellepheros. Is Tuuran back yet?'

Bellepheros? Again? Before Kataros could speak, the fortress shuddered. A tiny tremor rippled through the walls. They all felt it. Kataros kept her head bowed but her mind raced. You didn't look at a speaker, not unless they told you too, not even one who was only a pretender. But as soon as the tremor subsided, she couldn't hold her tongue, not after that.

'Bellepheros? He's *here*?'

'Bring the other one,' snapped the woman. 'Now.'

'What about her?' asked the man.

'Get rid of her. And the first one. As you wish.'

Kataros couldn't make out much of what the man said this time, but she caught the name again. Bellepheros. It *hadn't* been a mistake and she hadn't misheard.

'No! I said get rid of her! Both of them.'

Kataros dug her nails into her palm harder now, trying not to show the pain. Hands took her arms and held her down while others untied the ropes. They had her out of the chair and half-way out of the room when a soldier skidded round the corner and almost fell into her.

'Dragons!' he shouted.

The room fell into pandemonium. The speaker – Jaslyn? – hissed, *'You're* the Bloody Judge. *You* deal with them.' Fingernails in her palm. Digging. Bellepheros? Here? Alive? How could that be? The soldiers hauled her back to her cell and threw her inside. When they went to grab Siff, she spat on her hand and jumped on the nearest and clamped her hand over his mouth, forcing her blood and saliva over his lips. He threw her off.

'What a waste.' He drew a short sword. Two of them had Siff now, dragging him out while the others went for Skjorl. Four armed men against one Adamantine. She closed her eyes, whispered a prayer to the Great Flame and forced herself into her blood, looking for any tie to the soldier who was about to kill her.

Nothing.

There was a strangled shout behind her and it didn't sound like Skjorl. She jumped back as the soldier lunged at her and looked. Skjorl had grabbed one of the others and used one soldier's sword, still in the man's hand, to kill another, then used the same man as a shield, letting his own comrades run him through. The four soldiers had become two. They ran at him together, swords cutting, one high, one low. The Adamantine Man jumped sideways and back, dodging both swings. For a moment he was open to the soldier in front of Kataros, who drew back his sword. She threw herself at him, catching his sword as well, deflecting it just enough. The edge sliced along her arm, sharp and deep.

The Adamantine Man dropped to the floor, swept the legs out from under the man nearest him and bounded back to his feet. A foot came down. Hard. Bone cracked. The man screamed.

The soldier who'd cut her drew his sword back to run her through and finish her. She swept her hand across the wound and hurled a fistful of her blood at him. Behind her she heard a grunt and then a long slow gurgle. The soldier in front reeled away. He dropped his sword and clutched his face, screaming and screaming. Behind her, steel crunched into flesh and bone, and she knew without having to look that it was the Adamantine Man who held that steel.

The screaming stopped when Skjorl stepped past her and sliced the last soldier's head off. Half the man's face had dissolved away.

'Sorted out whether this lot are going to help us or not, have we?' He picked up one sword after another, appraised each one. Then he leered at her. 'Could have let those soldiers kill you, you know.'

'So why didn't you?' Ancestors but her arm was hurting. Blood-magic was all very well and so was being able to burn a man's face to the bone, but it would be nicer if she didn't have to get cut open first. The room was wobbling. She cast her mind into herself, forcing the blood to close the wound. It all took too much energy. She'd need to sleep soon and for a long time.

Skjorl let his eyes roam over her. 'Like the man said. Would have been a waste.'

'Oh, suck Vishmir's legion! Do you never think of anything else?' If she hadn't been so weak, she just might have reached through the blood-bond and crushed the Adamantine Man where he stood.

For a moment he was quiet. Then he laughed, softly, like he was thinking of something else at the same time. 'You swear like a guardsman.' The chuckling slowly stopped. 'I saw you take that blade for me.' She didn't answer. She was too busy trying not to collapse while she healed her arm. 'Swear by someone else next time though.' He sounded awkward, almost gentle, even if she knew perfectly well that he didn't have a jot of gentleness in him.

The wound was closed now and her strength was exhausted. She shut her eyes as the room started to swirl. If she was honest, she still needed him to help them escape.

The Adamantine Man watched her, shifting from one foot to another, twitching. Then he shook his head. He picked up Siff, threw the outsider over his shoulder and walked out through the open door.

39

Siff

Some two years before the Black Mausoleum

He almost missed it. The Yamuna Falls tumbled through a notch in a slope of rocky outcrops and tumbled stones that was almost a cliff. He didn't see the path that zigzagged up beside it at first, overgrown and half forgotten, and when he did, he almost didn't bother climbing it. Curiosity was what drove him in the end, that and what looked like rectangular cave mouths further up the slope, although when he reached them, they turned out to be slabs of jet-black stone that had slid down from above and landed askew.

The cliffs rose up high above the upper reaches of the river, but the path didn't climb to the top; instead it crept round a perilous corner to follow the notch carved by the river. For a moment Siff looked straight down the falls from above, through the haze and spray into the pool below; this was where he'd fallen, the water that had saved his life.

Not thinking about the dragons. Not.

Beyond the overlook above the falls, the path became a ledge gouged from a sheer rock wall about the height of ten men above the level of the Yamuna. It went on for a hundred yards or so, and then the cliffs above softened and the path led him out onto a steep and unsteady slope of stones and boulders all piled so precariously on top of one another it seemed that even a single hard kick in the right place might bring the whole hillside crashing down onto the flattened open space below. There had been walls here, he thought, stone buttresses built to hold the slope, but they'd fallen, bringing a little landslide behind them. An immense flat-topped overhanging boulder jutted out where the path wound away from the river. If that went, Siff reckoned the whole hillside might come down.

The damage was fresh. He could see the gouges in the earth below where dragon claws had ripped and torn at the stones all around the clearing. And that was when he realised what this was – what it had once been, at least. An eyrie. Tiny, as eyries went, and it had been smashed flat and burned to cinders, but an eyrie nonetheless.

He picked his way down the slope – the path had gone along with the walls that had held it up – and wandered through the ruins. He'd lived in an eyrie once, although saying *in* one was a bit like saying that a kennelled dog lived *in* his master's house. He'd been in one of the leaky ramshackle huts that clustered around its fringe, with the shepherds and the smiths and the carters and the leather workers and the saddle makers and the boot polishers and all the other people who didn't really matter, the ones who weren't dragon-lords or riders or alchemists or Scales. No one ever looked at the little people, and that was perfect for a man who smuggled in a sack full of Souldust now and then and came back out each time with a sack full of silver.

One thing he knew about eyries – they always had tunnels, places to shelter in case of attack by other riders. They were kept stocked with food and water and potions, with beds and blankets and everything a dragon-lord would need to stay comfortable for a day or two while his minions slaughtered some other lord's minions until one side or the other discovered that they'd won. He blinked a few times, trying to believe his luck. The destruction was obviously recent, but there was no one here now. His ancestors had outdone themselves. The place was abandoned.

He took a moment to catch his breath and look around. The top of the high stone bluff behind him was covered in the ruins he'd seen from the beach below the waterfall. Near the bottom, half hidden by the recent rock slide, there was a cave; around the edges of the clearing were the shattered remains of buildings. That's where the tunnel entrances were most likely to be, if they weren't all buried under rubble. On the other side of the eyrie were more rocks, more huge boulders all tumbled on top of each other. When he looked more closely, he saw they'd been disturbed too. A stone the size of a village hall had toppled over and cracked, and behind where the stone had been was an opening too regular to be a cave, even if it was more round than square. But what gave it away most of all was the soft light that spilled out of it as twilight started to fall. It wasn't the flickering of firelight, but the steady quiet light of an alchemist's lamp. The sort of lamp that gave off no smoke. The sort of lamp that a dragon-lord would use to light his shelter.

The sun was setting. The skies were darkening. He was hungry, cold, thirsty, somehow still alive and he meant to stay that way. He crept inside, his stolen knife out in front of him, and then he paused. It was all too good to be true.

'Hello!' Silly to be calling out if there was no one here, but what if there was?

He walked softly along the tunnel. He'd been wrong about the light. He'd seen alchemist's lamps before, once or twice, often enough to know what they looked like, cold and harsh and white. The light here was softer. It came from everywhere, from the walls and the roof and even the floor of the passage, as though the alchemists had mixed their concoctions into the stone itself. Now *that* was something Siff had never seen, never even heard of. There were probably lots of things that he'd never heard of that alchemists could do.

He tried not to think about the dragon by the waterfall staring down at him. The more time passed, the more he could believe it had been a vision, a hallucination, a touch of madness and not real at all.

The passage ran straight, sloping down under the ground, then opened up into a vast round chamber so large he could barely see the other side, even in the moonlight glow of the walls. The chamber floor also sloped. It was like the whole place, whatever it was, had been tipped slightly askew.

A ring of archways stood in the centre. It wasn't what he'd expected to find, all this pointless decoration, and a man couldn't eat archways. He ignored them and made his way around the edge of the chamber, looking for other ways out.

'Hello?' He tried again. Food, that was what he was after. The river would give him all the water he needed, but a good stash of food would set him on his way. With his hands swollen and next to useless, without a bow, that might be the difference between life and death. There were the dead men outside, if he had to, but dragon-rider food sounded infinitely better.

Did they have snappers in the Raksheh? He had no idea. They had wolves, he'd heard, but wolves he could handle. Wolves would leave a man alone unless they were desperate. Snappers were another matter. All those bodies would draw snappers like flies.

There were other passages, all like the one that had led him here. There were a lot of little round rooms, some larger halls, a few staircases, shafts, and every single one of them was utterly empty. There weren't even any spiders or beetles and there certainly wasn't anything to eat. The whole place was turning into a big waste of time. All he ever saw were archways, everywhere he went, carved into the walls with nothing on the other side except plain white stone, glowing softly back at him. Whoever had built this certainly liked them.

He hadn't explored much more than a fraction of the place before he gave up. Outside, when he looked, it was dark now. There were other places to search, once it was light again, but stumbling around in the dark seemed foolish. Another night without food wouldn't kill him, not yet. He went back to the first chamber he'd found, the one with the archways in a circle in the centre. Whatever this was, it wasn't a dragon-lord's shelter. No one had been down here for a very long time – how long he wasn't sure, but years, decades probably. He was tired now, dead tired. He could go looking for food in the morning.

The archways drew him in. The light seemed brighter there, the air felt warmer. He lay down between them. If there were no animals then nothing would come and eat him while he slept. That was good. He hadn't found any other ways out. You had to wonder, he thought, as he drifted to sleep, why a place like this was hidden away. Protecting something? Wasn't there something in the Raksheh? Something about caves and an old ruin and a tomb. Vishmir? He hadn't found Vishmir's tomb, had he?

That was worth some thinking. Vishmir's tomb? Never mind all that dust he'd lost, Vishmir had ruled the world. There'd be treasure, wouldn't there? His eyes closed.

In the middle of the night he thought he woke up to find a tiny silver snake curled up on his chest. Its head was lifted, staring at him. He tried to move, but nothing worked. The snake stared and stared, and then instead of biting him, it slid up his chest and up his neck and pushed its head between his lips and forced its way into his mouth. He tried to scream but nothing happened. Afterwards he knew it was a dream, because the next thing he remembered was standing on a sea of liquid silver, looking up at a moon far larger than the moon he knew. He saw himself with his back to a range of mountains, while ahead of him the sky was dark with thousands of onrushing dragons. Beside him a man clad in silver raised a spear. He struck the earth with it and the ground split open into a chasm a mile wide and impossibly deep, and from it rose a sheet of fire, a wall so high it tore the clouds to pieces and turned even dragons away.

The dreams grew stranger still, but when Siff woke up, the memory of them faded, and only the snake and the silver sea and the fire remained, those and the feelings that came with them, deep and alien.

He got up from the floor and would have gone outside, except now the archways around him were like mirrors and there was no way out of their circle, and when he looked down, he realised he must still be dreaming, because tiny snakes of moonlight were curling from his ruined fingertips. They reached and strained and pulled him forward, until they touched the nearest mirror and the mirror became a gateway to another place, also filled with silver, and he was sucked inside, back to where he'd been before, standing on a silver sea with the giant moon above. He staggered back and tripped and something happened inside his head as he fell.

He woke up with a start, gasping and shaking, but there were no silver snakes curling from his fingers and the archways were merely the same stone they'd been the night before. He got to his feet and walked away and quietly swore, Vishmir's tomb or not, that he would never return, not to *this* part. At least he didn't feel hungry any more.

Outside he soaked up the bright warm sun and sucked in air sweet with the scent of pollen and flowers, so different from the biting autumn wind of the day before. He felt strangely good. His fingernails didn't hurt now, nor the place where they'd branded him. He was thirsty, that was all. And he knew now exactly what he was going to do. Never mind dragons and tombs, what he was going to do before anything else was sort through the pile of bodies and do a proper job of it this time. Take whatever food, clothes, swords, knives, armour and anything else that he could salvage and then get away from here as fast as he could before the smell of blood drew in the snappers. Down the river, that would do. He thought for a bit about making a raft but he didn't have an axe to chop wood, and anyway wasn't some sort of monster supposed to live in the Yamuna, if that's what this river was?

Riverbanks were good for food though. Animals came for water. Things grew there, fruits and berries and such like. Maybe he could try fishing. And then he'd get out of the forest and find his way to the Silver City and to the court of the Harvest Queen. Aliphera? Or was she the one who'd fallen off her dragon? Not that it mattered – whoever it was, he'd tell them that he'd found Vishmir's Tomb, take whatever gold they'd give him for showing them the way and leave them to it. Or maybe he'd find some band of outlaws. Yes, that would be better still, a gang of sell-swords. He could bring them here, show them the way in and see what they brought out. Take his share and be done. Just as long as he didn't have to go back in there on his own again.

The sun was high in the sky. It felt warm, even though the year was turning to winter. The heat cheered him. Best to make the most of it. If there was one thing the Raksheh didn't see very much, it was the sun. Most of the time, if it wasn't raining, it was shrouded in mist and cloud. The sun gave him a sense that he might not die out here after all.

Ancestors but he felt *good*.

He walked back up to the smashed eyrie. It all looked much

more overgrown than he remembered. When he'd first seen it, he could have sworn that the destruction had been fresh, yet now he could see he'd been wrong and it had happened some time ago. Months, at least. But then it had been late when he'd climbed past the waterfall. The sun had been low in the sky, the shadows long and deceiving and he'd still been dazed and amazed that he was even alive. Beaten and battered and not quite himself. Maybe that was it. Would explain why there was no one here.

He picked his way up the bluffs, careful not to disturb any stones, and followed the path above the river to the falls and then down the other side. The water was flowing faster today, and a lot higher too. Rains in the mountains in the night, maybe?

Eventually he reached the bottom. Where there ought to have been a pile of bodies, there was just grass. Grass and, when he looked carefully around, a few old bones, almost buried. A boot. Pieces of leather, worn and cracked, here and there. A skull. All almost lost in the thick grass.

He looked at his fingers again, looked at them properly this time. His nails were still missing but otherwise they were healed. Completely. The seeping scabs were gone.

His hair kept falling in his eyes. It was long. Hadn't been long before.

He tore off his shirt. Not *his* shirt, but the shirt he'd stolen from a dead man the day before. The brand was an old scar, long healed.

He stopped then and looked more closely at the forest around him. Everything was different. Yesterday, autumn had been coming. The leaves had been starting to turn and there were berries on the bushes. Today there were no berries; instead there were flowers. The leaves on the trees were all green, and the scent in the air was of the last trace of spring blossom.

While he'd slept whole seasons had passed. And he hadn't the first idea what had happened to him.

40

Blackscar

Nineteen days before the Black Mausoleum

The fortress was where the dragon remembered it. There was no hesitation this time, no pause to wonder. It raked its mind through the hive-thoughts of the little ones within.

The chains first, it thought to those who flew beside it. The chains and freedom to those who were bound, freedom through tooth and claw. Then the little ones would burn, all of them, and the dragons would take that which did not belong here and send it back to the sleep whence it had come.

The dragon sifted from thought to thought and, as it did, found something it had forgotten. A mind. The one from the place in the burning desert and the lake of red salt. The one it had hunted. Here. Yet even as the dragon found that, it felt something else, something that passed like a ghost through the thoughts of another little one, like a ghost and yet like a titan passing among ants, so vast that it went almost unseen. *They are here!* it said, but the presence had already vanished again, and after that it hardly seemed to matter any more as the exultant fury of the fight took its place.

An age had passed since dragon had last fought dragon.

41

Skjorl

Nineteen days before the Black Mausoleum

He could understand a battle. Tunnels that glowed with their own light, bronze statues that didn't go green with age and came to life when you touched them, castles that floated above the ground, shit-eaters with silvery snakes in their fingers, none of that made any sense. Alchemist business, not his. But a battle, that was something else. A dragon fight, that was everything he'd been made for, and he'd been here before, in Outwatch, in Sand, in Bloodsalt and Samir's Crossing. All of them filled with screams, the earth quaking as the dragons destroyed everything in reach, stones falling from tunnel roofs, dust choking the air. Here the shouting was more distant and so far the ground wasn't shaking. A matter of time, that was all.

He stooped through the door that the dead soldiers had left open. The shit-eater was unconscious again, eyes rolling behind half-closed lids, muttering and moaning to himself. Skjorl might have asked the alchemist what she'd done to him, but he was easier to get along with like this. That and he simply didn't care. Outside the door there was his sword and there was his axe. Dragon-blooded. Simply propped against the wall. Holding it made him whole again.

'Where are you going?'

'Out,' he said. Down the passage back the way they'd come. Back towards the outside.

'Shouldn't we go the other way? Aren't we safer underground?'

'No.' Everyone thought that. 'At Outwatch the dragons sent their little ones down the holes.' Hatchlings. A few days old was enough. They'd rip a bear to pieces, probably a snapper too, never mind a man. All skittering claws and curling limbs and wings and teeth and tails like whips. 'Scrawny, with the hunger of a wolverine. Then there was the fire. In a tunnel there's no place to run, no place to hide. You just die.'

The door to the outside was open. Grey clouds muted the daylight. It was raining, and most of the castle was hidden in mist. Warm mist. Steam. Mostly mist was good. Mist was a place to hide. He glanced up at the sky. Where the mist broke he could see dragons. Looked like dozens of them.

Three men burst out of the fog, running like their tails were on fire, yelling their heads off. If they realised who Skjorl and Kataros were, they didn't let it bother them. Skjorl pulled the alchemist out of the way, sideways along the wall. Fast.

'We didn't—'

Didn't hear the rest of what the alchemist said. Didn't need to. *We didn't come this way.* No. But the shriek from the mist, so loud it staggered him, was all the explanation she was going to get. Over his shoulder he saw a shape, a head and a neck, long and vast, nothing more than a darkness in the haze. The mouth opened and the cloud lit up. Fire poured in torrents. The head turned towards them.

The air flashed and shook. A thunderclap shook the castle. 'Run, woman!' He looked for a shield, anything.

The sky darkened. Another shape plunged through the mist over Skjorl's head. A second dragon. He cringed. Couldn't help it, dropped the shit-eater and covered his head. Pointless, but the second dragon wasn't interested in him. It smashed into the first one and the two of them rolled away across the sky.

'Ancestors!' He couldn't help himself. Never seen anything like it. A dragon attacking another dragon?

'Come on!' The alchemist. Couldn't see her through the mist but following the wall took him to her quickly enough.

'What's happening?' he asked, but she had no better idea than he did.

Steps up the wall. He could see them. Not the steps they'd used coming in, but still steps.

'Stay!' He dropped the shit-eater at the alchemist's feet and ran up. The smoke and fog were beneath him now and he could see the dragons in the sky again. A score of them at a quick count. The air smelled of smoke. Most of the castle yard was filled with it, smoke or steam or more likely a mix of both. A dragon swooped down towards him from the other side of the castle. It levelled out. Its mouth opened and a torrent of flames poured over the far side of the castle yard, scouring it, blasting smoke and steam aside. It turned away. Over on the far wall something glowed brightly, some strange towering device of glass and gold.

He ran down the other side of the wall, over to the abrupt edge of the eyrie. The stone beneath him shook. Another thunderclap split the air. The sky behind him flashed. No sign of any cage like the one that brought them here. There was a dragon though. Coming towards him. Right at him. He looked at the cliff in front of him and the slope of the wall behind. There was nowhere to go. There was something oddly familiar about the beast. About the beat of its wings.

The dragon from Bloodsalt.

Another thunderclap. Lightning dazzled the air. For a moment he couldn't think. Took a quick step forward, out to the edge. Stared at the dragon and the winding silver coils of the Fury sprawled across the plains below. But no, there really was nowhere to go.

He closed his eyes. Hung his head and waited for the fire to come. *Damn you, dragon! Damn you!* Not that an Adamantine Man was supposed to care, but for the first time he could remember, he wasn't ready. Not now.

Another dragon screamed. A wall of hot air slammed him back, knocking him down. But it didn't burn, wasn't fire. The monster from Bloodsalt passed over his head, blotting out the sky, except it wasn't one dragon now but two, wrapped around each other, claws and tails twisted together, teeth snapping. The wind of their wings picked him up as they passed, threw him like a doll back up the slope of the wall. Their tails clipped the top of it, shattering the stone. Boulders as big as his head hurled through the air and rained down around him. A length of chain dangled between the dragons, links as big and thick as his arm. It slashed behind them, curling and writhing in the wind like a snake. Slicing and shattering whatever it touched.

Then they were past, tipping down towards the ground, smashing into the midst of the castle, gouging a trail of destruction and then bouncing up again, splitting apart. The one from Bloodsalt turned and climbed. The other one vanished down towards the plains, wings outstretched.

The dragon from Bloodsalt. Skjorl watched it turn. There wasn't any doubt. At least now he knew what colour it was. Gold. A real prize. He spat. *Some consolation*.

He picked himself up. Ran back up the wall before the dragon could return and raced down the steps. Grabbed the alchemist and kept running, taking what shelter he could. Not that it would help much if the dragon was still after him.

The dragon that had killed Vish. It filled his blood. *Stay here with me, dragon, and I'll find a way to crash this fortress on your head!*

He was ready for the fire, but it never came. They ran through a choking wall of smoke, a cloud of scalding steam, more smoke, mist, but no fire. And then they were at the steps, the ones that would take them back to the cage and down to the ground.

And then?

He ran up, the shit-eater still over his back, light as a feather. The cage and its crane were there, what was left of them. Smashed to splinters. The rope was there too. Huge and heavy, its coils sprawled around its shattered pulleys. Scorched but not burned through.

And then?

The question wouldn't let go. *What happens when you get to the bottom? When the dragon from Bloodsalt is still looking for you and you have nowhere to hide?* Because there was no doubt. It remembered. Its eyes had never left him.

Amid the ruin of the crane he found the end of the cage rope, still spliced into a loop around a cracked beam of wood. Dragged it to the edge of the rock and pushed it over and dodged out of the way as the rope's weight dragged it down, heavy loops of it flipping and squirming like eels in a jar.

Another thunderbolt, another flash of lightning and a dragon fell out of the sky, its wings broken, screaming until it smashed into the castle yard. The wall trembled. The alchemist staggered. She reached out, steadied herself on his arm to stop herself falling, then jumped away as though she'd been stung.

'I have to stay here,' he told her.

She looked at him as though he was mad. 'No.'

'There's a dragon here I've seen before.' The one that had crashed into the castle? No, that had been a darker colour with flashes of metallic green. 'It knows me.'

She laughed.

Skjorl shrugged. He pointed down the wall. 'You can climb down.' He didn't know whether the rope reached the ground or not. Hadn't thought to check.

'And him?' She pointed to Siff.

'You wake him up and make him climb too.' She wasn't going to carry him, that was for sure, and there wasn't anything he could use to make a harness, no other rope to lower him down.

'Look at him!' The alchemist screamed in his face. And there they were, the fingers inside his skull again. 'You get him down. I don't care how, but you do that.'

'A dragon here is hunting me,' he said again, in case that would help her understand. 'It'll find me. Won't take it long. It wants to kill me. If you're with me, it'll kill you too. I can throw your shit-eater over the edge if you like.' The thought made him smile. 'See if he bounces. Would amount to much the same.' The castle shook. Another crash of thunder loud enough to make him cringe; another flash as light filled the air.

'Get. Him. Down!'

His body jerked with the force of the command. He shrugged. Without a choice any more, he picked up the shit-eater and arranged him carefully over his shoulders. Arms and one leg wrapped in front of him so that both his hands were free. Then carefully down the slope of the wall back to the wreckage of the crane. He peered over the edge.

Stupid.

The fortress was moving, slowly, dragging the end of the rope through the fields below, vanishing under the castle's bulk. He lay down and swung his legs over the edge. It was higher than it had been before, or maybe it just seemed that way. Two hundred feet or more to the ground now.

Stupid stupid stupid. Dangle from a rope in the middle of the air in the middle of a dragon fight? And one of them hunting me? Stupid beyond belief.

He took hold of the rope and slid over the edge. With luck the shit-eater would fall off. If that happened, well then good riddance to him. Once over the side, he clung on to the rope with both hands and walked down the purple-veined slab of stone under the castle until he was dangling over empty air and the shit-eater was still wrapped around his shoulders. He squeezed his legs around the rope and let himself slide the rest of the way to the ground as fast as he dared. As fast as he could without shredding himself. They landed hard, sprawling and tumbling apart, rolling in the mud. Easy. Easier than he'd thought.

Skjorl took a moment then, mostly to be amazed that he wasn't dead, that no dragon had paused from its fight to come and snatch this little morsel just hanging in the air. But none of them had, and when he looked up, the alchemist was almost on top of him. She fell off the end of the rope, staggered, slipped in the mud and fell. He took a step towards her and stopped. When she got back to her feet, she was shaking all over.

'I thought you might fall,' he said. He meant it as a compliment that she hadn't.

'Sorry to disappoint you,' she spat at him.

The castle moved ponderously over their heads, burying them in shadow as black as night, lit up by the flicker of the purple lightning that flashed along the underside of the stone. The rope dragged through the dirt, thick as his wrist.

He tried again. 'I can't stay with you. I want to, but I can't. There's a dragon here that wants me. When it finds me, it'll kill everyone who's near.'

He felt her looking inside him, searching for the lie beneath his words, but there wasn't one. Every word perfectly true.

She didn't like it. 'Leave me your sword,' she snapped.

He gave her his sword, belt and scabbard and all, and tapped the back of his head. 'Let me go.'

She looked at him as though he was mad. 'Don't be stupid.' And turned her back on him, struggling with the sword and trying to lift the shit-eater up out of the mud all at the same time. Skjorl hesitated. But no, better for all of them that they part. Best to climb the rope back into the fortress. Lure the monster of Bloodsalt away.

He slung Dragon-blooded back over his shoulder. It could come after him if it wanted. Let his enemies fight each other. He could hide among them for days if he had to. Let the alchemist go. Wouldn't last long without him and then he'd be free. Strange how he felt about that. Not gleeful at all. Sad, if anything, but it had to be this way. Best for them all.

Climbing up was a lot harder than climbing down, even without a shit-eater on his back. At least there were no dragons swooping on him. The air still shook to the occasional clap of thunder, but the battle looked to be over, the attacking dragons driven back. Would be worth learning how the men in the fortress had managed that. Maybe he could do something useful after all.

At the top, the smoke and the mist were clearing. There were still dragons, but they were high overhead or specks in the distance. He took a moment to look about, then climbed to the top of the sloping wall, careful not to be seen. Hardly any other soldiers around, none on the walls and only a very few below. Almost everything was smashed or burned, all the wooden shacks he'd seen the night before, the fire pits, everything. In the middle of the carnage was a dragon, sprawled across the ruins, the shimmering green one he'd seen fall. Both wings broken. A lot of other bones too, and it wasn't moving. Eyes were open though. Below, closer to him than to the dragon, carefully out of reach of its fire, a couple of dozen soldiers clustered together. They wore dragon-scale; when their words drifted up to him from the bottom of the wall, he could understand them clearly. He listened, amazed, but there was no doubt. Adamantine Men, all of them. He almost called out, but then heard another voice, the man who carried the golden knife, who had somehow made him tell everything he knew, and so Skjorl hesitated, and then stayed quiet and watched instead. The man with the golden knife walked towards the dragon. He went with care, came from behind and moved with purpose. Stayed well clear of the dragon's tail and kept a large shield – dragon-scale, Skjorl supposed – close to hand. The man reached the back of the dragon's head.

Skjorl squinted. He couldn't see what the man was doing. Fiddling with something. He saw the flash of a knife. Whatever he did, when the man came back, he wasn't careful at all.

'You can kill it now,' he said, and disappeared into one of the passages that ran under the walls. The Adamantine Men shouldered their axes and picked up their shields. They closed on the dragon with the same care. As they reached its head they fanned out, but the dragon didn't move. It just watched them.

The axes came out. Skjorl felt a surge of glee as they fell. His hand went behind him to rest on Dragon-blooded's shaft. He understood, as only another Adamantine Man could understand, what a rare victory this was. No special rituals for killing a dragon. You took your chances as they came. Mostly you died trying and even if you managed to kill one, usually you died at the claws of another moments later. Like when Vish had gone, crushed. Or else burned. That was the way of being an Adamantine Man. So he watched them kill the dragon, watched its blood stain the stones and watched them leave, and felt a soaring joy. It would burn now from the inside, getting hotter and hotter for days if not weeks until its flesh and bone crumbled to ash and all that was left were scales and a few scorched bones from its wings. Scales for armour, bones for bows. No one had been able to harvest a dead dragon since the Adamantine Palace had burned. But these men would.

Amid the envy and the glee, he felt a pang of something else.

Blood, staining the stones. Dragon blood.

He grinned to himself, a huge grin, and started looking among the ruins for what he would need.

42

Kataros

Nineteen days before the Black Mausoleum

Letting the Adamantine Man go felt strange. A part of her was sad to be rid of him. That was the part that had learned alchemy, that knew which ingredients in what proportions would have how much of an effect and had been taught to think not of the now and the tomorrow, but of what would happen a year away, a decade, a century even. The part that knew there were more perils ahead of her than behind and had learned the value of a strong and loyal sword.

Another part, the part that had always been her, the part that thrilled to the raw immediacy of blood-magic, was sad too, but only that she wouldn't have the pleasure of seeing him torn to pieces by whatever dragon was hunting him. She had her blood, her magic. Let that be enough.

She had no idea what to do with the sword she'd taken. The belt didn't fit her. However she tried to wear it, it ended up slipping down around her ankles and tripping her up. Even when it didn't fall down, the sword somehow slipped between her legs and tried to catch her that way. Then there was Siff, the outsider the Adamantine Man had carried so easily but who turned out to weigh more than she did, even as wasted as he was. She had no idea how to move him. She tried dragging him. She tried lifting him. She managed to get him over her shoulder once, but then the sword tripped her and tipped them both in the mud. Through it all he didn't stir.

She looked for a place to hide, but the best she could find in the darkness beneath the castle was a ditch filled with long grass with a few inches of slime at the bottom. It would have to do.

There wasn't much else for it but to wait until Siff came back from wherever he was.

She knew the Adamantine Man was near again before she heard him. The blood-bond told her, which meant she'd been looking for him without even knowing it, and that was troubling all on its own. She peered up out of the ditch and there he was, haloed in purple lightning, staring at the ground and walking right towards her.

'Why are you here?' she yelled at him. 'Why are you here if there's a dragon hunting you?'

He looked up, caught in a moment of surprise. Then he grinned at her and waved something. A large rag. A shirt maybe. Dark and wet. 'Dragon blood,' he said.

It took a moment for what that meant to sink in.

'Dragon blood,' he said again. 'You can make the potion. To hide us all from the dragons. You said you needed dragon blood.'

Dragon blood and her own. She touched the cloth and reached into the blood and yes, it was true, it really was what he said, however impossible it seemed. Dragon blood. Fresh. 'Yes.' For a moment she caught herself looking at him in a way she'd never looked before. Mixed in with the loathing was a touch of awe. There had to be, didn't there, for a man who could bring you blood from a dragon?

'Water,' she said, and glanced up at the underbelly of the castle, still moving slowly overhead. 'I need clean water.'

'Will it take long?'

'And somewhere to keep it.'

'Will it take long?'

She stared at the castle. Yes, it would take long to do properly, but there was a quicker way. She climbed out of the ditch and gave Skjorl back his sword. 'Hold out the blade.' When he did as she asked, she ran a finger along the edge. A drop or two of blood was all she needed. She dripped it onto a corner of Skjorl's cloth. A shirt. It *was* a shirt. 'My blood. Dragon blood. Now give me a moment.'

Blood was a path, nothing more. A way in. A way to touch the dragon, or what tiny essence was left of it, although even that was huge, an immense thing she could barely encompass.

'Are you done yet?' The castle had almost passed from over-head.

She sucked on the corner of the shirt and passed it to the Adamantine Man. 'As soon as the sun sets, we find some shelter where I can make more and do it properly. Enough to take us to the Raksheh.'

Skjorl sucked on the shirt too. His lip curled. 'Oh, I remember that taste.' He waved the shirt at her. 'That enough?'

'To get the three of us to the Raksheh? More than enough.' She took the shirt to Siff. Forced the corner into his mouth.

'It'll be dry by night.'

'Then you'd better find me some water.'

Skjorl climbed down into the ditch with her, carefully not too close. 'Back where we came from then. The tunnel to the Pinnacles. All the water you want and safe for as long as you need. We could tip the raft down the falls and ride the Ghostwater to the Yamuna. It's only a few hours away.' He pulled Siff up out of the ditch and slung him over a shoulder. 'Best we stay under this … thing. Until dark. Castle will keep us hidden from dragons. Dragons will keep the castle soldiers safe in their beds. Works out nicely for us both ways.' He offered her his hand. This time she very nearly took it, almost without thinking. It didn't seem to bother him that she didn't.

He turned and started to walk. 'If your potions fail, alchemist, we'll be dead out here in days. If they do what they should, I'll get you to the Raksheh. No promises after, but I'll get you that far. Night Watchman's oath.'

Which, she knew, meant he'd do it or he'd die in the trying.

43

Blackscar

Dragon battled dragon in the skies, a thing that Blackscar remembered from its first lifetime and then never since. The old ghosts in the half-made sky-home were silent. Hidden once more. Even the little one, the sorcerer who carried a touch of the broken god.

Strangeness upon strangeness. As it dived upon the eyrie and set its innards alight, a part of Blackscar tried not to give itself up to the battle, to the fury and the joy of it. Too many things to consider.

It failed. Thunder and lightning rose up to greet it, battering its skin. Fire swept in a wave before it. Little ones screamed and burned. It felt their fear, delicious like honey. It felt the little one it was looking for. Running. Fleeing. It turned and came at the sky-home again. There. Standing by the edge, rising out of the haze of smoke and mist and steam.

You are mine.

The little one saw it coming. Knew its end. Nowhere to hide. Fire swept towards it, yet at that moment another dragon fell from the sky, teeth and claws and tail, ripping and tearing. Small. Barely more than a hatchling. A year old, half grown at best, but it came nonetheless and the dragon knew it must turn to meet it or be taken crashing to the ground, and either way, the little one was granted a miracle and would not burn, not now.

But soon.

It met the other dragon, tooth and claw. Victory was certain, yet the other came with a furious zeal. A certainty of purpose. A righteousness, even, the sort that belonged in the head of little ones and their foolishness, not within a dragon. Not within a creature that had seen such zeal almost shatter creation.

But there nevertheless.

They skimmed the edge of the sky-home, cracking its shell with their wind and their tails. It saw the little one fall, but the creature's thoughts did not fade and flicker and so the dragon knew that it lived on. They crashed into the castle together and hurled themselves back into the sky. Blackscar threw the other dragon aside. Gently. Or gentle as a dragon could be. Wings intact and no bones crushed beyond repair. It turned for its little one once more, but now there were more dragons. Lightning struck it, sent it plunging spiralling through the sky. When its wings were its own again, the dragon turned its thoughts to the sorceries of glass and gold that spat thunder. The little one could wait.

Lightning met him, a storm of it. The little ones; and then their half-grown dragon servants fell from the sky and tore their own kind to the ground with teeth that struck to kill.

Dragon servants. Its rage could melt mountains. Fill seas and burn skies. Yet it withdrew. Some did not. Could not. One by one they fell.

Defeated.

The thought was enough to pierce any fury. It had never, in any lifetime, been left to savour the word.

A surge of something ancient burst from the sky-home. It echoed across the plains and faded and died. The dragon felt it. Saw it. Saw something cut loose. Saw one of its own kind it had known for fifty lifetimes lying crippled and broken in the folds of the sky-home's womb and then die at the touch of an old goddess who always took something away.

The other dragons murmured among themselves. One by one they left, but the dragon called Blackscar lingered. One last thing. The little one was still there and so the dragon watched and waited, carefully and from a distance, touching the edges of the little one's thoughts as it climbed back down from the sky-home to the ground. Watched as a magic made of dragon blood blinked its mind away and the little one it had hunted for so long vanished, finally, from its sight.

Such a thing might drive another to rage, it mused, but for once the dragon was unmoved.

After all, it knew by now exactly there this little one meant to go.

The Raksheh

An expanse of largely unbroken forest that occupies the south-west corner of the realms, the Raksheh stretches over several hundred miles from Drotan's Top and the Gliding Dragon Gorge in the north to the Sea of Storms in the south. Its east–west borders are less sharply defined: in the west the forest merges with the valleys of the Worldspine, while in the east the wooded areas peter out more gradually into the plains of the Silver City. Several large rivers flow through the forest, ultimately draining into the Yamuna and emerging close to the town of Farakkan. Numerous large round lakes dot the more mountainous western fringe of the forest; from the air these are similar to the Mirror Lakes of the Purple Spur. Various deep gorges and several spectacular waterfalls have been reported by dragon-riders who have ventured to cross the forest. The best known of these are those around the Aardish Caves.

The forest is largely uninhabited, although rumoured to give shelter to numerous settlements of outsiders and other feral tribes. Bandits and outlaws also frequent the fringes of the forest, particularly in the north.

The forest may be the home of many unique creatures. Earthworms as large as horses have been reported, together with six-legged lizards of various sizes ranging from the minuscule to the giant. Several breeds of venomous snakes and poisonous frogs are known to inhabit the forest. Snappers are also a constant danger, although their numbers are less than in the more northern fringes of the Worldspine. For those of our order, the forest offers a concentration of valuable and unique ingredients the like and diversity of which can only otherwise be found on the distant Oordish Moors. Frogsback, for example, is harvested from the southern fringes of the Raksheh Forest.

With the exception of the rather arid northern section close to Drotan's Top, the forest has the distinction of being one of the wettest places in the realms, surpassed only by the southern reaches of the Worldspine itself.

Bellepheros' *Journal of the Realms*, 2nd year of Speaker Hyram

44

Jasaan

Twenty-one days before the Black Mausoleum

Bloodsalt made him a hero. Bloodsalt earned him everything and then hoisted him by his own shirt and dropped him in a cesspit.

On the moors he and Skjorl had gone their separate ways, something that had been coming ever since Scarsdale. Jasaan then tried to get on with the business of walking and eating and walking and sleeping and walking and drinking and not being caught in the open by a dragon; and most of all not thinking about Skjorl and how small and subtle were the differences between them. As far as Jasaan knew, Skjorl had meant to stick stubbornly to Yinazhin's Way, so Jasaan picked his path down to the Sapphire valley. There was water, food if you knew where to look for it, not much but enough and plenty of fish. He drank his potions and hid in the day and walked carefully at night and took each sunset as it came, quietly assuming he'd die somewhere beside the river and get nowhere near the Purple Spur; and then, somehow, he'd reached Samir's Crossing. It wasn't even that difficult.

No one had ever thought Skjorl or any of his company would come back. People didn't even come back from the moors any more and Bloodsalt was three times the distance. At Samir's Crossing the Adamantine Men who watched the skies and the plains to the north and south made him a hero. They welcomed him with open arms and poured praise over him like wine at a desert wedding.

He waited a few weeks – they gave him that luxury – but Skjorl never came back. Skjorl was dead. Eventually Jasaan believed it. And all the while the stories he told of Bloodsalt made delicate and tiny changes to themselves. Quiet Vish and Skjorl always killed the dragon, but his own part changed, maybe became a little more how it *might* have been than what actually happened. Yes, Skjorl and Vish had wielded their axes, but it was no accident that the roof had collapsed where it did. The dragon had been lured to its doom by the cleverness of men. By Jasaan.

Adamantine Men did what needed to be done. That was all. They didn't make themselves into heroes, and so it wasn't a surprise when the alchemists under the Purple Spur found him something else to do. There was to be an attempt to reach the Pinnacles. Alchemists would be going. They would need guides. Soldiers to protect them, soldiers who understood the ways of dragons. Most particularly, they needed soldiers who had survived out in the open, who knew how to stay alive with no vast roof of stone to shield them from the skies. They needed an inspiration, someone the other soldiers, the alchemists even, would believe in. And Jasaan, since he was a hero, couldn't deny them, no matter how much he never wanted to go out in the open again. Who else could they choose? And what else could he do but go?

He got them there too, all of them. Picked his men carefully, set off in three separate bands on three separate paths and amazed even himself. His alchemists reached the Pinnacles alive. Even in the Silver City, even as he tried to find a way into the fortress itself, he kept them safe from the feral men who lived in the tunnels and the cellars, hiding from the dragons above and only ever coming out at night. He kept them safe and he got them inside, all the way from the Purple Spur, with messages of greetings and hope from the speaker who lived there.

That had been a week ago. The next day, after his soldiers had politely surrendered their swords, trusting to the hospitality of King Hyrkallan and his men, Hyrkallan had killed the alchemists. Hadn't listened to what they had to say, simply got rid of them.

No one actually *said* that, of course. Apparently what had *really* happened was that all the alchemists had gone to the very roof of the Pinnacles, to the Reflecting Garden, and been eaten by a dragon. About the most implausible story imaginable, but by the time he'd come to understand about the false speaker Hyrkallan and his hatred for alchemists, they were dead and the damage was done. All the men he'd lost on the way wasted. He might have made a fuss about it, but really what was the point? In the days since it had happened, he'd just felt more and more numb.

He stood in the same place now, the Reflecting Garden, looking at the moon. It wasn't often that anyone who lived under the Spur got to see the real sky, the real moon, the real stars, never mind the real sun. To Jasaan open skies only meant keeping his eyes wide for dragons. He'd had enough of that. A good strong mountain over his head would do nicely.

A stream bubbled out from a pile of rubble that had once been a fountain. That was all the dragons had left of the Reflecting Garden, but the riders who'd been trapped in the Pinnacles since before the Adamantine Palace had burned spoke of pools of water that didn't lie flat, of paths in arcs and the Silver Onion Dome. Even Jasaan had heard about that. He looked at the remains, the shattered stones and gravel. There was almost nothing left.

On special nights when there were no dragons roosting on the mountaintop, the false speaker Hyrkallan had his throne carried up from the tunnels below. Tonight was one of those nights, and he'd summoned Jasaan to join him. Jasaan watched carefully, vaguely wondering whether tonight was the night that the dragon who'd eaten his alchemists would mysteriously eat him and all his men too. Under the Purple Spur a lot of things were quietly said among the Adamantine Men about Hyrkallan and his queen. Hyrkallan should have been the speaker, they said. He could have saved the realms from disaster, they said, but his queen was another matter: his queen was bitter and ugly, hateful and mad and had awoken dragons for fun. Queen Jaslyn wasn't there tonight and Jasaan hadn't ever seen her, even when they'd first arrived. As for Hyrkallan, he was old, his beard was grey and there was white in his hair. To Jasaan he looked lost.

Riders were still coming up from the tunnels below, dragging poles and great long sails of dragon skin with them. Jasaan switched his eyes to watch. They looked like wings.

'Jasaan? Guardsman Jasaan?'

Jasaan met the rider's eyes. Neither of them bowed because

neither of them knew whether either of them should. Adamantine Men served the speaker. As far as Jasaan was concerned that meant Queen Lystra, and if he'd been feeling suicidal, then Hyrkallan was a traitor and so was every rider who followed him. Jasaan had settled on quietly pretending not to notice. The other Adamantine Men who'd survived the journey from the Spur had followed his lead, and the same went for the story about the alchemists. Just pretend it's true. Don't ask questions. Made him sick, though, that one.

They settled for staring at each other. The riders of the Pinnacles didn't know what to do with him. The Adamantine Men made them uncomfortable. They were scared, and so they should be.

'I'm Jasaan,' he said.

'Come.'

The rider led him across the rubble towards Hyrkallan's throne, close enough that Jasaan could know he was being watched. Other riders, clustered together, stopped their conversation and stared as Jasaan approached. One broke away to face him.

'Guardsman Jasaan.' Jasaan didn't know this one, but he could see the other riders deferred to him.

'That's me.'

They stared at each other, yet another battle of wills. Jasaan had had enough of those since he'd come here. Truth be told and despite the obvious danger, he'd happily have taken his chances leading his men back to the Purple Spur.

'One of your alchemists is alive,' said the rider without looking away. 'You will help us find her.'

Her. So it was Kataros, the half-alchemist who'd been thrown out of the order in disgrace before the Adamantine Palace had burned. He didn't know what her indiscretion had been – pillow talk, secrets spilled to a rider lover she should never have had, something like that – and it simply wasn't his business. She was the alchemist who'd found the Adamantine Spear, the Dragonslayer. The Adamantine Men called her the spear-carrier, and of the three he'd brought here, she'd been the one who seemed to understand what a dragon really was. It didn't surprise him that she, of all of them, would survive, although last he'd heard she'd been eaten by a dragon along with the rest of them right where he stood. Apparently that had been a lie. He said nothing.

'Your alchemist may have killed the others,' said the rider. 'We think she led them up here, knowing a dragon was waiting. We think she did it so she could disappear.'

Jasaan said nothing. They all knew perfectly well that his alchemists had been killed by men, not by dragons.

'We know why and we know where she's going. You will help us find her.'

Jasaan allowed himself to blink. Eventually they'd tell him what they really wanted him to know.

'She's gone to the Raksheh,' said the rider eventually. 'To somewhere near the Aardish Caves.'

'Why would she do that?' Jasaan asked when the rider didn't say anything more.

The rider spat. 'Alchemists make their own laws. They think they are beholden to none, not even to the speaker.' He glanced at Hyrkallan on his throne and then turned to watch Jasaan carefully. 'You will help me,' he said again.

'How?'

'You've been out there.' The rider glanced over towards the edge of the mountain. He was scared. It had taken Jasaan this long to realise it, but the rider was scared. He was scared to leave his stone shelter.

'Yes.' No expression in his voice. No judgement. Scared? So he should be.

'The speaker commands that this alchemist is to be found. She is to be returned. As are those with her and anything she may have found if we do not catch her in time.'

'Found?' Jasaan cocked his head.

'We had an outsider. He claimed to have entered the Aardish Caves and found the Black Mausoleum. The alchemist has taken him.'

Jasaan nodded. There was no such place. Every Adamantine Man knew *that* story, and that's all it was – a story, a myth, another waste of time. 'Vishmir himself spent his life searching for it in those caves,' he said.

'Indeed. Yet this alchemist you brought among us has taken him. We will start our search there.'

He had to wonder why they were even bothering about such a mad tale, but that was another question and not one for an Adamantine Man. All in all he'd be glad to be out of the Pinnacles, filled with its veiled hostility, and he'd be glad enough to find the alchemist too. Her life had been placed in his hands and all he'd managed to do was deliver her to men who wanted to kill her. He owed her for that. When he found her, he wouldn't be bringing her back here, that was for sure. 'I'll get my men ready,' he said. Eaten by a dragon on the top of a mountain? No alchemist was *that* stupid.

'No,' said the rider. They stared one another down.

'The most likely thing,' said Jasaan after neither of them had flinched, 'is that they're both dead. They'll fall prey to dragons or feral men before they even leave the Silver City.' He shrugged. 'But if you want her found, then you'll want to take with you the men who have the most knowledge of what lies out there.' He nodded towards the darkness. 'We braved dragons, yes, but there's more.' Perhaps he could play on this rider's fears. 'There are snappers, wolves, feral men. Disease is rife and every day is a battle merely to find food. Once we reach the Raksheh ...'

The rider shook his head. 'No.'

'Then send us out together because we are the men you can best afford to lose!' hissed Jasaan. *Keep us together!*

'No.' The decision, Jasaan realised, had already been made. He glanced up at the throne, at Hyrkallan the pretend speaker, staring back down at him.

The rider pointed to the wing-like things that had been brought up from below. 'There can be eight of us, no more, because that's how many of Prince Lai's wings we have left. They'll take us far enough away from the Silver City. Two of my riders will return them. You and I and four others will enter the Raksheh. I have no doubt at all that you're right, that the alchemist is already dead and the outsider too. Nonetheless, we will look for them. We will go to the Aardish Caves and we will search for them, and if we do not find them then we will search for the Black Mausoleum ourselves. We will not return empty-handed.'

So we won't be returning at all. That explained the rider's fear. Jasaan looked for his own and found nothing. He'd either survive or he wouldn't, whether there were dragons to face or not.

'Vishmir searched for twenty years,' he said again. 'With a hundred dragons and a thousand men. There is no Black Mausoleum.'

The rider wasn't listening, but the plan made Jasaan feel better about leaving his soldiers behind. They weren't welcome here, that much had been obvious from the day they'd arrived, but they deserved better than to be thrown at the Raksheh chasing after a dream. He, on the other hand, *he* deserved every bit of it.

He looked at the things the rider had called Prince Lai's wings. Yes, they looked like wings. Other than that he had no idea what they were for.

'You will come.'

It wasn't a question. Jasaan nodded.

'Good.' The rider paused and frowned. 'The alchemist took one other with her. We do not know whether he went willingly or not. He was another Guardsman. An Adamantine Man who found his way here some months ago.'

The rider paused, waiting for a reaction, but Jasaan didn't have one for him. *Good for her,* he thought to himself. Maybe she was still alive after all.

'His name was Skjorl. Did you know him?'

Skjorl? Here? Jasaan frowned for a moment. 'No,' he said mildly. 'No, I don't know a Skjorl.'

45

Kataros

Thirteen days before the Black Mausoleum

The Adamantine Man did what she needed of him: he got her to the Raksheh. He led them, slowly and methodically, following the Yamuna River but never too close to the waters themselves even though they never saw any sign of the dreaded river worms. Down here, away from the forest, perhaps the dragons really had eaten them after all.

There had been people on the Yamuna plains once. It wasn't a place for cities, but there had been an abundance of thriving small towns and villages clinging to the riverbank. She could see what had once been huts and halls, all built on stilts for when the river flooded. Most of them had been smashed and burned now; sometimes the only sign left was a field of stumps, blackened and splintered but still stuck stubbornly in the earth.

Boats littered the fields. They were everywhere, scattered among the flotsam and jetsam of the dragons' passing. Most were little fishing skiffs, no more than a few poles lashed together, picked up by the last floodwaters and dropped wherever they were dropped. There was nowhere to hide, no shelter. No hills, no trees, not any more, no caves, no cellars, no rocks, just flat fields full of wild grass going on and on, a slight rise here, a slight dip there. As each night began to brighten, the Adamantine Man found them a cluster of rocks, a pit in the ground or maybe simply a mound of rubble. They spent one day dozing under a pile of old boats that he'd carefully arranged around the stump of a tree. Anything to hide them from the sky while the sun was up, while Kataros and her dragon-blood potions masked their thoughts and hid the fact of their presence.

She saw dragons every day, often more than once. They usually flew on their own, but sometimes they came in twos and threes; and towards the end, as they drew closer to the forest, there were more. She counted a dozen in one day, every one of them flying away from the Raksheh. She wondered why, but had no answer. They were flying away from where she was going and that would have to be enough.

The Adamantine Man set a hard pace. Most of the time he still carried the outsider. Even then she was pressed to keep up with him. Siff would have had no chance at all. He was getting some of his strength back now, but he still mostly dozed except at dawn and dusk.

'The less time we spend here, the more likely we are to live,' Skjorl told her, not that she ever asked him to slow down. Maybe he saw the strain in her face, but she wouldn't complain, not to him. He'd stop if she told him too, she knew that; he'd walk slower if she asked, stand on his head or go and drown himself in the river if she demanded it, but for now he was doing what needed to be done, driving them on.

She saw the forest as they settled down to hide on the fourth day, distant hills above the plains, lit up by the rising sun. The river was already starting to change, from a wide sluggish brown to clear and flowing with purpose. The fields were away from the river now, more uneven, the earth harder. By the end of that night the villages they passed were still shattered and burned but the houses weren't built on stilts any more. They were past the flood plains. Towards the next sunrise they came to the ruins of another village, a few stones houses on the edge of the hills. They were scorched, their roofs gone; they were black and empty shells half tumbled down, but carved over one doorway Kataros saw the outline of a dragon, worn and faded. She saw it and knew exactly where they were.

'Looks as good a place to stop as any,' muttered Skjorl. 'One more day in the open. Another night of walking and then we should be in the trees. You can rest a bit then.' He put Siff down and wandered around the buildings, looking to see what was there. Kataros stayed where she was. There weren't any bodies, not that she could see, and by now all they ever saw were bones, but still … The dragon was the sign of the Order of the Scales. Of the alchemists. She doubted she would have known any of her kin who had died here, but that's what they were. Kin. The order had a house here because it was close to the Raksheh. She knew it, had even come here once. You could ride a boat, if you were willing to brave the worms, all the way down the Yamuna from here; or you could ride a different boat up to the forest, but somewhere nearby were rapids that no boat could pass, and so the order had built this place, a way station for their own, with rooms to dry herbs and roots, to salt them or roast them or mix them with oil or water or vinegar or with blood.

Skjorl came out of one house and went into another.

'There's a trail from here to the forest,' she told him, but he didn't seem to hear. In the light of the half-moon the ruins cast shadows that merged together, one after the other. If she let herself drift, they all merged into one. She supposed she ought to feel something in a place like this. Sadness. Loss. Something, at least; she'd felt a sadness when they passed through the burned-out towns and villages by the river after all, so she ought to feel it here as well, oughn't she? But she didn't. All she felt was indifference, nothing more, nothing less. If the Adamantine Palace hadn't burned, her brothers and sisters would have made her a Scales. They would have dulled the spark within her and fed her their potions and made her fall in love with a monster, and never mind that she was as good an alchemist as any of them. She'd liked her men, liked her wine, liked other things. She'd said things that she shouldn't and they'd flogged her for it, and she'd gone straight out and done it again.

She looked up at the moon and the fitful clouds and picked absently at the hard skin on her knuckles, the first stages of Hatchling Disease. Siff and Skjorl had both drunk her blood. They'd have it too now, although it would take a good while to show. The alchemist's curse: *I can give you a potion to help with that. Just one little thing: if you drink it, it'll slowly turn your skin to stone.* She hadn't exactly been pretty to start with, but then an alchemist wasn't supposed to care about such things. An alchemist's thoughts were always lofty.

Indifference. The alchemists had given her much. They'd taken much too. Dragons had made her what she was, not men, except perhaps the one called Kemir.

'There's a cellar here.' Skjorl came out of another ruin. He looked pleased with himself. Then she saw he was holding something, one in each hand. Bottles. 'We stay here for the day,' he said. 'Don't know if any of what's down there is stuff we can eat, but *I'm* happy.' He took a swig from one of the bottles and bared his teeth. 'Still good. A sight better than the rotgut we used to drink back when there was anything more than water.' He wrinkled his nose. 'Have a look. You'd know better than me.'

He sauntered over to where he'd left Siff and made as if to lift the outsider over his shoulder again.

'Piss off, doggy.' Siff's eyes were open. Droopy but open. 'I can walk.'

'Suit yourself, shit-eater.'

She ignored them both and went inside. Skjorl had left the trapdoor open. Something between a ladder and a steep set of steps went down into the darkness. She climbed inside and made her way carefully down to the little square of moonlight that shone through the ceiling. Beyond, around her, everything was almost pitch black. A little light gleamed from a rack of dusty bottles where Skjorl had found whatever he was drinking.

She found she was angry with him for that. Not that she had any good reason to be, but he'd taken something from the dead here, something that he didn't even need. There'd been no reverence, no respect, no pause to wonder at the lives that had been lost here; he just took for himself without a thought. Odd, she thought, to resent him for that amid her own indifference.

On the floor next to the rack of wine bottles she found a little box carefully stocked with alchemical lamps. It was tucked out of the way where no one would ever see it, but when you were an alchemist you came to know where to look. Everywhere she'd ever worked had caves or tunnels or cellars; at least, everywhere that was near dragons, which was anywhere an alchemist was likely to go. They all had their lamps, kept where they were needed, and you acquired an instinct about where to look for them. She took one out of its box. She'd made them herself once – a little cylinder of thin brown glass, a small cup of Kyamberan's potion filling the glass halfway, then a disc of waxed paper, carefully sealed on top. When it was dry, fill the top half of the lamp with caveworm essence and seal it shut. Some lamps had a hole in the top with a small stick you could use to poke at the seal between the two halves. Others were closed and had to be shaken to break the seal and make them to work. Every alchemist learned to make lamps. If she looked, she'd probably find all the pieces she needed right here.

Age had done no favours to the seal inside and the lamp started to glow almost as soon as she picked it up. A dim and cold white light slowly filled the room. The Adamantine Man had been right: there was a workshop here, or part of one. There were benches, chairs, a rack on the wall filled with pots of powders of dried herbs and roots … and a skeleton in the corner.

She jumped back and almost dropped the lamp. The skeleton sat slumped with its legs sprawled out, its skull lying on the floor beside a pile of empty bottles. He – she maybe – was still dressed in a few rags. The skeleton had a knife resting between its fingers. The other arm was across its lap. She could almost see his end – the last alchemist of the Raksheh, lost and alone among the ashes, furious dragons overhead, too scared to leave his cellar, slowly starving, finally caving in to despair and cutting himself deep and simply letting the blood flow.

'Any food down there?' shouted Skjorl from the trapdoor. Kataros jumped again. 'See you found some light.'

'No. No food.' She hadn't looked, but no alchemist with his head on right would keep food in the same place as he kept his materials. There were far too many ways that could go wrong.

'Raw fish again then.' On their second day along the river the Adamantine Man had found a tattered fishing net half buried in the mud. Ever since, he'd been obsessed with using it. No more roots and berries, even though they were plentiful; Skjorl wanted meat. As it turned out, he was a decent fisherman, and he came back every dawn with three or four of them, expertly gutted, and it never seemed to take him very long. Kataros' stomach turned. Roots and berries she understood.

As soon as she heard Skjorl's footsteps recede, she went back to looking at what the alchemists here had left her. Most powders kept well enough if they stayed dry, and most roots and leaves too, although you could never be sure there wasn't any contamination. Did she need anything?

'So.'

For the third time she almost jumped out of her skin. Now it was Siff, crouching at the top of the steps. She'd forgotten about him; she'd grown so used to him being mute and slung across the Adamantine Man's shoulders.

'Can I come in?'

'Yes.' She watched him come down the ladder. He moved slowly, carefully and cautiously. 'Finding your strength again?'

'Yes, I'm on the mend,' he said when he got to the bottom. He met her eye. 'Don't feel like I'm closer to the ghosts of my ancestors than I am to living any more. Thanks to you, I suppose. Doggy gone for a bit?'

'Skjorl is fishing for us.' Siff's contempt for the Adamantine Man was fine enough when it was to Skjorl's face. Alone with him, she found it uncomfortable. Maybe it was being in a room with one way out and him standing between her and it, or maybe it was that the Adamantine Man he so despised was the one who carried him and caught the food that was giving him back his strength. Maybe it was both.

'The Raksheh's not far away. What you going to do with him when we get there?' He ran his fingers over the bottles in the rack beside the steps. 'This what I think it is?'

'Drink it and find out.'

'Think I might. We won't need doggy in the forest. There's no dragons there. What you going to do with him?' He took out a bottle of wine and pulled the cork with his teeth. Took a swig. 'Nice.'

'I don't know.' Something about the way the outsider moved told her to be cautious. She went to the alchemists' bench and took down a couple of pots of powders without looking at what they were, then took her knife out of her belt and put it on the table beside her. 'You could make yourself useful. Go and tell him to bring back some water from the river.'

Siff didn't move. Instead he took another mouthful of wine. 'You should try this.'

Kataros took down a mortar. She pricked her finger with her knife and dripped blood into it. Blood went into everything, every potion an alchemist ever made. Blood was what gave them power and always had been. *Look under our robes and we're no different from blood-mages*, that's what her teacher had said. *But for the love of your ancestors, don't tell anyone.*

'You need to get rid of him,' said Siff after a bit. 'Give me your knife. I'll do it.'

'No.'

'He wants to kill me.' Siff smirked at her. 'We both know what he wants to do to you.'

'I will not permit him to do either.'

The outsider wrinkled his nose. Took another gulp. 'I don't think that's good enough.'

'It will have to be.'

Siff shook his head. 'No. It won't.'

Kataros stopped what she was doing and turned to look him in the eye. 'Do you know how I bound him to me? I put my blood in him. Think, outsider, about who has fed you water, medicine, food. Do you think for a moment I haven't done the same to you.' She reached into herself, looking for Siff, looking for where he was bound and shackled.

And found nothing.

'No, alchemist.' For a moment, in the gloom, it seemed that his eyes shone too brightly. 'No, that won't work on me. I'm not like your doggy.'

He came towards her, his eyes still too bright and now filled with a menace she hadn't seen there before. Kataros stepped back. She held out the knife towards him. 'What are you doing?'

'I'm going back to the Raksheh. I'm going back to that cave

and I'm taking what's there. I wonder if you think you're going to stop me?'

She took another step away. 'That depends, Siff, on what's there to take.'

'Exactly what you think. The power of the Silver King.'

'And if that's true, what would you do with it?'

He laughed. 'I'd probably do some of the things you'd want me to and a good few things you wouldn't.' His eyes were alive now, burning with silver light.

'What did you find there, outsider? Don't tell me it was truly the Silver King's tomb because I know that cannot be. That is not where he was taken!'

'You think the Isul Aieha was bound by mere flesh and bone?'

'The Silver King is gone, Siff! What little of his essence remains is what is used to bind the dragons!' Such secrets as these had cost her dearly once, overheard as she slipped through places she didn't belong to see her lover. Even *she* wasn't supposed to know these things. 'Whatever is there, it must be used for the realms. The dragons . . .' Her eyes narrowed. 'Not bound by mere flesh and bone? And what would *you* know of these things, an outsider from the mountains?'

'Oh a pox on the dragons!' He laughed at her. 'We all know they weren't anything more than the Silver King's pets. They'll be put in their place. It'll all be like it was, back in the old days.'

She stared at him, half in awe, half in horror. 'You want to bring him back!'

'And you don't?'

A shape appeared at the top of the trapdoor. It hovered there for an instant and then flew down. Skjorl landed on Siff's back, thumping him to the floor. The light in Siff's eyes flared; he snarled and started to rise, but then the Adamantine Man had a handful of his hair and slammed Siff's head into the ground. Once, twice, and the silver light went out of Siff's eyes and he fell still.

'Shit-eater.' Skjorl sat on his back. He'd found a piece of rope from somewhere – here or else he'd had it all along and Kataros hadn't noticed. He hog-tied Siff, kicked him once and then looked at Kataros and laughed. 'You always know where you stand with his sort. First chance he got he was going to run. Obvious.'

'It was more than that.' Maybe she should have kept that to herself.

'Was it?' The Adamantine Man laughed again. 'Was it now? I can imagine. Wanted something from you before he ran did he?'

'Not what you think.'

'Oh don't be so sure about that.' The Adamantine Man took Siff's bottle of wine, which lay on the floor, spilling itself into a puddle. He took a gulp of what was left. 'You think he must be like you because you were both thrown into prison to die. Doesn't make him like you at all. He's a shit-eater. They're all the same. He'll turn on you first chance he gets.'

'He wanted me to kill you.'

'Well he certainly can't do it himself.' Skjorl seemed unmoved. 'You want me to go get that fish now? He won't be going anywhere.'

'Take him with you.'

'Take him with me?' He shook his head, then waved the bottle at her. 'I'll take this with me though.'

'Take him with you and watch him. I need to work. In peace.'

The Adamantine Man looked around the cellar. He sniffed and then shrugged. 'You get lonely, you let me know. I'll be back before sunrise.' With that he lifted the outsider over his shoulder and carefully climbed out, and she was alone, alone with the ghosts of the alchemists who'd died down here.

She climbed up the ladder too, just to make sure Skjorl was really gone. When she saw him plodding away towards the river, she returned to the cellar. Ghosts. Ghosts were for children; there weren't any of those here, not really. What *was* here was a gift. Powders, dried roots, herbs, mushrooms, everything an alchemist could want except that most precious thing of all, blood, and for that she had her own. She set to work.

46

Siff

Thirteen days before the Black Mausoleum

He had gaps. He knew that, had known it for a long time. Gaps that had started that night in the Raksheh when he'd gone to sleep one night and woken up to find that autumn had turned into spring and a mound of dead men had become nothing more than a few scattered bones, overgrown and almost lost beneath the grass. That had been the first, but it hadn't been the last.

He'd walked along the banks of the Yamuna. Roots and fruits grew beside it; a clever man with the right skills could hunt too, catch a fish maybe or one of the animals that lived in holes by the water. He didn't have a bow, but he had a knife for killing and skinning and he was quick enough with his hands. His injuries were all gone. He'd felt more alive, more vital than he could remember.

The next gap had come in the middle of one night, rolling in agony, his stomach clenched in a knot. He'd never felt such a pain. He'd poisoned himself, eaten something he shouldn't, and now he was going to die. One minute he was screaming, vomiting, tearing at his own skin, the next he was walking along the banks of the river in bright sunshine, just as he'd been doing the day before and the day before that as though nothing had happened. No trace of the pain. No trace of anything. He told himself it had been a dream.

The first signs of people had come not long after. He'd found a hollowed-out tree trunk, pulled up against the shore with a few tracks leading away into the trees. He'd counted three men, wondered for a bit about taking whatever they had and stealing their boat, and then thought better of it. When they came back, he gave them what he'd taken from the dead dragon-riders and their slaves, what little he'd been able to find and didn't need for himself. They were outsiders like him, after all. Outsiders stuck together, them against the rest of the world. They told him that the dragons were flying free and that the power of the dragon-kings and their riders was shattered into shards. He'd rejoiced at that. They all had.

The next gap was a long one, or maybe there had been several with not much in between. He'd stayed with them a while, these men and their tribe. He didn't remember much, only ... memories that he couldn't quite piece together, or maybe they were dreams. It was a hard life in the woods. They'd had nothing to look forward to. Work, eat, breed, die, that was all that most outsiders had ever had, dragons-kings or no dragon-kings. For a while, he remembered, it had been pleasant. Then later they'd been afraid of him, and then later still in awe. He could have made them do anything, and yet he had no ... *use* for them any more, and so he'd left one day without really knowing why, without *remembering* why. He'd had dreams, though. He remembered those more than he remembered the men of the forest. They'd come more and more while he lived among them, dreams of men in silver, of dragons, of power beyond imagining, beyond what he could even begin to comprehend.

At some point there had been soldiers. Not many, a dozen, perhaps. He'd found a new place to hide and there they were, already there. He'd had no chance, and yet the next thing he knew four of them were dead. He had no idea how he'd killed them, but there was no doubting that he'd been the one who'd done it. With his bare hands, by the looks of it, because there hadn't been any blood. The rest had taken him back with them to the Pinnacles. They'd been terrified of him every step of the way, and he could have drunk that terror like the finest wine if he hadn't been strung up just like he was now. And then in the Pinnacles the dreams and the gaps had finally stopped and he was Siff again, the person he'd grown up knowing, and nothing strange at all had happened. Shame about being thrown into a cell to slowly starve to death.

Then the alchemist had come and now it was all starting again and it was all he could do not to scream.

'Hey, doggy!' He had no idea what had happened. One moment he'd been talking to the alchemist, wondering whether she was an ally or an enemy and wondering what she meant to do with her doggy once they reached the forest. The next thing he knew, here he was, hog-tied by the river. If he'd been able to reach, he'd have felt his head. His face burned. He'd taken a good crack from something. Pity he had no idea what.

'Hey, doggy!'

The Adamantine Man ignored him. He was sitting by the river with a bottle of what must have been the wine from the alchemists' cellar. When he stood up, he was obviously drunk.

'Hey shit-eater,' he said, 'you thirsty?' He pulled down his trousers and aimed carefully at Siff's face. Siff turned away – there wasn't much else he could do – and felt the warm wetness of the Adamantine Man's piss spatter his skin, soaking his hair and the clothes on his back.

'Going to kill you for that, doggy,' he snarled.

The Adamantine Man spat at him. 'Nothing changed there then, eh, shit-eater? I heard what you said to her.'

Siff grunted. *Pity I didn't.*

'Saw what you had in mind for her, too.'

'Seen what *you* have in mind for her, doggy.'

'Touch her and I'll cut your hand off, shit-eater.'

'Really. I thought you might like to sit and watch. Closest you're going to get.'

The Adamantine Man walked away and left him there. Maybe this was it. Maybe they were going to leave him for the next dragon to pass by. *Ancestors! What did I say to the witch?*

Later, the air brought the smell of smoke and cooking fish. The Adamantine Man had finally found the courage to make a fire. The smell got stronger and stronger and then, after a bit, it went away again. The sky started to lighten. Dawn was coming.

'Doggy! Oi! Doggy!' Dragon's blood – they weren't really going to leave him out here, were they? They couldn't! If a dragon came down, it might find them too. 'Alchemist!'

He'd about shouted himself hoarse when the Adamantine Man finally came back. He didn't say a word, just dragged him back up the hill and tipped him down into the alchemists' cellar. The idiot was almost too drunk to stand.

'Hungry, shit-eater?' he asked. And then he carefully placed a little pile of fish guts right in front of Siff's face. 'Eat, then. Heh.' He reeled away.

'You're drunk.' The alchemist shook her head in disgust. 'Is that how it is to be an Adamantine Man?'

'Oh we used to drink all right.' He laughed. 'Now and then. Drink until we fell over in our own piss. All that's long gone. We were the Adamantine Men. Greatest soldiers ...' He staggered towards the alchemist. 'There's nothing like us. We're the biggest. Best. Hardest.' He reached out a hand. The alchemist didn't move.

'You can't touch me, Skjorl. Go to sleep.'

The Adamantine Man shook himself. He grabbed the alchemist by her shoulders. The look of shock on her face was precious.

'Should have listened to me,' sang Siff. *Whatever I said.*

The Adamantine Man's brow furrowed as though he was thinking hard. He clawed at the back of his head, then pushed the alchemist up against a wall. His other hand went to her face. He grinned. 'My spear is huge, its shaft is hard, its point is savage and battle-scarr'd. Best lovers in the realms, the Guard. You look good.' He started to fumble at her. The alchemist pushed him away.

'Get off! Get off me!'

Skjorl was drunk enough to almost lose his balance. He staggered. 'You'll not find better.' He glanced down at Siff and laughed. 'Don't tell me you want *that* one?'

'You may not touch me!'

'I'll make you moan, woman. You haven't had it if you haven't had it from an Adamantine Man.' He stumbled towards her again. The alchemist dodged out of the way, picked up an empty bottle and smashed it over his head. Siff almost burst out laughing. The Adamantine Man swayed, but he didn't go down.

The alchemist kicked Skjorl between the legs, hard enough

that Siff couldn't help but wince, even as he watched with glee. Skjorl doubled up, clutching himself, gasping while the alchemist stood over him, screaming in his ear. 'You don't touch me! Never! You never, ever touch me, you hear? You think after what you tried to do to me that I'd feel anything but loathing for you? You pig! You thuggish witless pig!'

Skjorl growled. The pain on his face was delicious. Siff reckoned that anyone ordinary would be on the floor, rolling in agony, but the Adamantine Man was beginning to straighten up.

The alchemist brought a second bottle down on his head. This time the Adamantine Man fell as though it had been an axe. Siff grinned.

'And you!' She rounded on Siff. 'You're no better! Filth, both of you.' She went off into the furthest corner she could find and curled up on the floor. Up above, the first rays of daylight were creeping in past the trapdoor.

'Maybe so, alchemist, but this filth is the one you need. You don't need that one. Not once we get to the Raksheh.'

'You don't even know what you are!' she spat back at Siff. 'What are you?'

'A man trying to stay alive in a world that doesn't like him much,' he said. He didn't get an answer to that.

The Adamantine Man started to snore, as if going out of his way to prove that he really wasn't dead. He was going to be in the king of all foul moods when he woke up. Siff sighed. He listened carefully to the alchemist's breathing through the racket the Adamantine Man was making, waiting until she was asleep. Then he started at the ropes holding him fast. Most days, if he'd ever managed to free himself, he'd have had Skjorl to deal with – the oversized bastard slept with one eye open and woke up if Siff as much as moved. Not today though. Today he probably wouldn't even wake up if a dragon landed on him.

An hour later he gave up. As it turned out, the Adamantine Man knew what he was doing with a rope even when he was roaring drunk. Pity. Siff closed his eyes and let himself drift off. Sooner or later the big man would slip up. Besides, he had a surprise waiting for him in the Raksheh. They all did.

47

Jasaan

Twenty-two days before the Black Mausoleum

They flew by moonlight, out across the plains west of the Pinnacles with one set of wings each, gliding ever lower. There was a moment of terror, of sheer panic as he was sure he was going to die, because that's what happened if you jumped off a mile-high cliff. The wings took him, though, and then Jasaan watched the landscape drift beneath him in shades of moonlit grey. From up high you could still see the lines in the land where the roads used to be, even though they were overgrown and sometimes hard to spot on the ground. Clusters of dark stains marked where villages and farms had stood, ash blots in the flat expanse of rolling grassland.

The wings carried them for miles and Jasaan had no idea how far or for how long. It seemed for ever at first, and then suddenly a field was rushing up and he was struggling to put his feet down in front of him as the wings pitched back and dumped him down. He sat there, dazed for a moment and amazed too. He'd *flown*. Adamantine Men didn't fly. Rarely, perhaps, they would ride on the back of a dragon on some urgent errand for the Night Watchman. Quiet Vish had flown with the old speaker to Bloodsalt once, and a dragon had taken Jasaan to Sand just before the Adamantine Palace had burned; but today he hadn't been carried, he'd *flown*.

He took a moment while his head stopped spinning and then he unbuckled himself and looked about for the others. He saw one, a hundred feet up in the air, sailing past him. He ran to the nearest rise and looked about from there, for the ruin of a tower, a black silhouette in the moonlight, the place where they were supposed to meet. Once he saw it, he went back to his wings and set about gathering them together. It was like dragging two dead comrades behind him lashed to their shields. When he reached the tower, the others were waiting for him.

'You came down too fast,' snapped Hellas. Hellas was leading the riders and probably thought he was in charge of Jasaan too. Jasaan shrugged. There wasn't much he could do about that. 'We're late now. We have another fifteen miles to cover before dawn to reach our shelter. You lead!'

The moon was still high and they had eight, maybe nine hours of darkness left. Fifteen miles? Easy, and it was probably no bad thing to be at the front – better to have the eyes of an Adamantine Man scouting the way for danger than some rider bred in an eyrie who only ever saw the land from far above on the back of a dragon. The rest of them toiled in his wake, slow and labouring. He pulled ahead, stopped to scout, waited for them to catch up and did the same again. The moon reached its zenith and began to crawl its way back towards the horizon.

He counted the miles. Every one of them brought another ruin, another collection of homes trampled, burned and shattered into shards. Sometimes a few pieces of wood scattered over the road was all there was left, or else a milestone with the name of a place carved into it. Elsewhere, grass and sapling trees grew among the walls of smashed houses, thorn bushes around the remains of tumbled halls.

When he'd covered about twelve miles, he looked for the broad tree that marked where to leave the road. He waited for the riders and then ran on ahead again, to a stream and on to the corpse of yet another village, just like all the others. Rain and wind and grass had overgrown the scorched black earth and made it green again. Here and there the broken old bones of houses poked through the undergrowth, their jagged tips still charred black. Like the others, the village was empty.

Something snapped with a loud crack under his feet. A small branch, perhaps, except there were no trees. When he crouched down, he saw it was a bone. As he crept among the grass and the ruins, he found more: ribs, vertebrae, all sorts, scattered evenly about. People.

The riders were breathing hard when they finally caught up. Worn out. One night of walking and they were already tired, and how far was it to the Raksheh? He kept his thoughts to himself as Hellas took them along an overgrown path to an old well hidden among the bushes. Jasaan stretched. People had been here not all that long ago, and they came regularly enough to make a path. The riders, he supposed.

'You have men out here a lot then,' he said.

Hellas shook his head. 'Not your concern.' He pulled back the branches around the well. There was a ladder running down inside. A metal one. Its rungs shone in the waning moonlight.

'There's people been here in the last few days,' Jasaan murmured. 'No way to tell how many. Yours?'

'There are no riders on the plains,' grumbled Hellas. 'There are no people at all. The plains are dead. The dragons killed everyone.'

'No.' Jasaan understood the bones now, why they'd found so many here and hardly any anywhere else. They hadn't been left by dragons, they'd been scattered later by men. Warning others away maybe. 'Look at the ladder,' he whispered. 'See how it shines.' Six men with swords and dragon-scale could hold their own against a lot of ferals if they knew what they were doing, but not if the ferals had bows. 'Worn clean. This is a home for—'

The first arrow hissed through the foot of space between him and Hellas, close enough that Jasaan felt a brush of air on his wrist. He was moving before any of the others even blinked, shoving Hellas out of the way and pushing him to the ground. Another arrow zipped straight into a second rider. Jasaan didn't know his name, didn't know any of them except Hellas. None of them had thought to tell him and it hadn't occurred to him to ask. It was easier not to care about men who didn't have names.

The rider with the arrow sticking out of his side just stood there, looking surprised. Jasaan tumbled into the deepest piece of undergrowth he could find and lay flat, waiting for the arrows to turn into a hail; instead, he heard a chorus of shouts. Figures rose from among the bushes nearby. Ten, maybe a dozen, armed with sticks and dressed in rags.

The rider with the arrow in him bellowed something about victory and honour and hurled himself at the first one to come near him, waving his sword like a madman. The other riders just stood there, gawping as though they'd never been in a close fight before.

Oh ancestors, no! They hadn't. They'd fought on the backs of their dragons and they'd fought in a practice ring, and that was it. Jasaan rolled to his feet and shoved his short sword into the nearest convenient feral.

'Hyrkallan!' cried another rider. Two ferals jumped on him, pulling him down. A third piled in. Jasaan saw a stick rise and fall. Another rider ran to help. Too late, probably. The rider with the arrow in him hacked the hand off someone. There was a scream.

A feral ran right in front of him. Jasaan ran him through and then looked for Hellas, but by then the ferals had already had enough. They turned and ran and vanished into the night like ghosts.

Three riders left standing. When he looked, Jasaan found the one who'd been pulled to the ground. They'd got his helm off and caved in the side of his skull with a stick. Dead was dead, so Jasaan ignored him and went to see the rider who'd been shot instead. Out in the open like this was no place to be carrying wounded. An Adamantine Man understood that the injured were best left to fend for themselves or else given a quick and merciful death. Riders, Jasaan supposed, probably saw things differently.

He found the rider sitting with his back to a smashed wooden wall. He was breathing hard and pasty-faced, but he wasn't coughing blood. The arrow, when Jasaan carefully cut its shaft and pulled off the rider's armour to look, had gone in about as far as one finger joint. Either the feral who'd fired it had been feeble or he had some self-made bow with all the punch of a night girl's tongue. The dragon-scale armour had done the rest.

'You know what we call a wound like that,' Jasaan said. 'A dream-lover's kiss. Leaves a nice red mark and that's all there is to it.' He pulled the arrow out. The rider screwed up his face but at least he didn't shriek. There were no barbs. It was just a crude thing. Wasn't even quite straight. 'You have anything to dress this?'

The rider nodded and pointed to a pouch at his belt. Jasaan had a look. Mud. A roll of ripped cloth. Rubbish, but that was what you got for killing all your alchemists. Jasaan reached into his own. He didn't know what any of the powders he carried were, only what to do with them. Alchemists handed them out, packaged up into pouches.

'Got a name, rider?' he asked. There, now he'd gone and made some trouble for himself. Now he'd probably do something stupid like make a friend just in time to watch him die.

'Nezak.' The rider winced.

'You lived in the north before all this, didn't you?' Jasaan unwrapped a tiny paper bundle and carefully took a pinch of the dark powder inside. In daylight you could see it wasn't quite black. In moonlight ... well, under the moon, everything looked grey.

'Sand,' said Nezak.

'You know how I can tell? It's the skin. Different colour, you see. You're a long way from home. Lie down.'

The rider lay back. Blood ran out of the hole in his ribs in a slow but steady pulse.

'I was in Sand when the dragons came.' Nezak probably didn't want to hear about that, but it would keep his mind off what Jasaan was doing to the hole where the arrow had been. 'They flew in circles around the city, pouring their fire over everything until even the stones of the monastery cracked in the heat and they still didn't stop. Places like Sand and Bloodsalt, out in the open, there's nowhere to run. People hid as best they could. They hid in their cellars where they thought the fire wouldn't reach them, but the dragons made the city burn for days. The ones who went underground died anyway. Cooked. After that the dragons smashed it flat. I was in the caves under the monastery. Those and the tunnels under the eyrie were the only places deep enough.'

There. That had rider Nezak's attention. Nothing like telling a man that his whole family was dead to focus his mind. While he had it, he pushed the pinch of dark powder into Nezak's wound. The rider yelped.

'The powder will stop the wound from going bad.'

'Vishmir's cock! It burns!'

'Yes, it does.' Jasaan smeared on some of Nezak's mud. 'This will help it heal. We killed every dragon in Sand before they came. We poisoned them and smashed their eggs with our axes and our hammers. There wasn't a single monster left in the eyrie by the time the rogues reached us. We did what we could.' They'd killed a good few riders too to get to those dragons and those eggs, but there didn't seem much need to be mentioning that.

'It wasn't enough.'

'No.' Bandages now. A wad of cloth to keep the mud in place, that was all he needed. 'Sit up while I wrap this around you. I'm sorry for your family. My family were the Guard. Most of them are dead too.' He looked at Nezak carefully. 'Not everyone died. A lot of riders survived under the eyrie. I remember one who looked a lot like you. Older though.'

'My brother perhaps.' Nezak grasped Jasaan's shoulder. 'Was his beard thicker than mine, and black? Was he still limping? What was his name?'

Jasaan shrugged. 'I don't remember a limp and I didn't speak to him so I have no name to give you. The beard though, yes. Thick and black.' It wasn't likely, was it, that Nezak would ever get back to Sand and discover he'd been lied to? Hope was a healer. He'd learned that from the very alchemist he was hunting. 'The riders stayed to see what could be done. I left with the other Adamantine Men.' Each to their own duties. 'I met a man in Sand,' he said quietly as he worked. 'An Adamantine Man. They came from Outwatch. They walked. Across the desert. I don't know how far that is.'

Nezak shook his head. He smiled over a grimace of pain. 'It's a half-day ride even on the back of a dragon. On the back of a horse, four or five. To walk?' He shook his head. 'The road from Outwatch to Sand is not one for walking. The heat kills. There's no water.'

'Still, walk is what they did. They were Adamantine Men who

had fought dragons and lost. They'd smashed the eggs and they were burned in their turn. Hatchlings scoured the tunnels. When the dragons were gone, there were a dozen of them left. They walked all the way to Sand and found us at the monastery. The dragons had learned by the time they came to us. They'd learned to be thorough. They lingered to make sure they finished us all, but they couldn't burn us out from the tunnels. When we came out there was nothing left. Nothing at all except these dozen men who'd simply watched from afar for day after day, dying of thirst, waiting for the dragons to leave. There.' Jasaan tied the bandage off. 'Shouldn't slow you down much. It'll hurt, though.'

Rider Nezak closed his eyes. 'Sand.' He held his head in his hands.

'Everywhere is gone, rider. All across the realms, everything is destroyed.' Jasaan stepped back. He'd done what he could. The rider would live. Whether he had the strength to cross half a realm to the Aardish Caves was another matter, but Hellas could worry about that. 'The Adamantine Man who is with the alchemist we hunt. Hellas says his name is Skjorl. It was a Skjorl who led the survivors out of Outwatch, on foot and across the desert. After Sand, the Skjorl I knew led his company to Evenspire, to Scarsdale and all the way to the Silver River. Across half the realms, the barren half, on foot. If it's the same man, then he's been up the Sapphire River to Bloodsalt and back again across the moors. He's the perfect Adamantine Guardsman, strong, remorseless, untiring, fearless and brutal. If this Skjorl *is* the same man then I will wager you that your alchemist is still alive.'

48

Skjorl

Thirteen days before the Black Mausoleum

Pain. Pain and hardship. You learned to live with them. Sometimes they were friends, telling you things you needed to know. More often they were adversaries, but they were old foes and known ones. They were comfortable companions if not welcome ones.

Took him a while when he woke up to realise where he was. For a bit he thought he was back in the catacombs under Bloodsalt, that the dragon throwing rocks at him had finally hit him. He could even see someone lying beside him. Vish. Or maybe not.

After that he thought he must be dying. Certainly felt like it.

Bits of memory landed like snowflakes. Bloodsalt, that had been a long time ago, hadn't it? Or was the time he'd spent in the Pinnacles somehow before?

There was an alchemist. That was after.

That man on the floor there wasn't Vish.

He saw a bottle. Wine. Yes, he remembered. There had been wine.

He let out a low groan. He'd drunk himself stupid enough times. It had never been like this. Wine must have had something in it. Where was he?

He rolled onto his front, crawled into a corner and was sick. Stale fish. *Ancestors but that was bad.*

When his stomach stopped heaving, he took a few breaths then sat up. He rubbed his eyes. There were steps. Wooden slats above. Bright sunlight streaming between them. A trapdoor. A cellar then. Yes, slowly it was coming back, where he was and why and where he was going. He was in Scarsdale and everything had burned and they were running from the dragons. Always.

Running home, even if they all knew they were never going to get there.

Carelessly he rubbed his head. Almost screamed, the pain was that blinding. Touched more softly now. There was blood crusted through his hair. A lump the size of an egg.

That explained the pain then. *Vishmir's cock!*

Fishing. He remembered fishing. Remembered coming back. Cooking. He'd been reeling by the time he was done. Then …

Something about an alchemist. Alchemists. That's why they were going home.

Ancestors! His head felt like someone had taken an axe to it. He must have fallen. Must have. Couldn't remember …

He was fading again. Sleep creeping over him like blanket. He was still drunk. Probably a good thing that. Probably eased the pain. He blinked, rubbed his eyes, forced himself to look into the little pouch he still carried with him, the one he'd had ever since he left the Adamantine Palace. All the things the alchemists made for the Adamantine Men before they went to die. Most of them had got used up on the way to Bloodsalt, but not this.

Bloodsalt? Why was he in Bloodsalt? That wasn't the way home? Was that where here was?

There was a dragon in Bloodsalt. It had killed Vish.

His eyes wouldn't focus. Couldn't see what he was doing in the half-dark anyway. He let his nose do the working, sifting through the little waxed paper packets of this and that until he found what he was looking for. Dreamleaf, mixed with just a touch of Petrios venom. Whatever that was. Something to take the edge off the pain. Something to keep a man going. A pinch, that was supposed to be enough.

He took two. Dropped them in a water skin. Forced himself to drink the lot. Just about managed that before his eyes closed and he slumped back to the floor. When it was sunset and they were getting ready to move again, someone would tell him how he'd hurt his head.

Except the next time he woke, the sun had set and it was dark outside and he was alone, and when he tried the cellar door, it wouldn't move.

49

Jasaan

Sixteen days before the Black Mausoleum

He walked ahead, alone. It suited him. He didn't have to talk, didn't have to learn the riders' names, didn't have to hear where they were from. Most of the riders in the Pinnacles came from the deserts, from Sand and from Bloodsalt, and Jasaan had seen both after the dragons had done with them. They must have known their families were gone, but no one could imagine what Bloodsalt had been like. No one had come away, not one single survivor, to say how the dragons had destroyed that city, but Jasaan still saw the skeletons when he closed his eyes, their dry bones just lying in the streets and inside the houses and littered along the Sapphire valley.

He found a hollow for them to shelter in through the second day. He shared the potions that he'd brought with him from the Purple Spur, the ones that stopped the dragons from feeling their thoughts. He covered the riders with brushwood and then listened to them trying to stay silent and still as the long hours of daylight passed overhead. Now and then dragons flew out from the Raksheh. They didn't pause, didn't look down.

'There must have been a dozen or more, all told,' he said to Nezak as he changed the dressing on the rider's wound. Nezak was carrying his injury well for now. Jasaan wondered what Hellas would do if the wound went bad.

'Heading for the Pinnacles.'

'Further south, I'd say. Can't be sure.'

Roads became tracks, so overgrown now that even Jasaan had trouble finding them. The land became wilder. Burned-out villages gave way to burned-out farms. The hills grew bigger and steeper and the copses on their crowns spread out into woods. Good land for hiding. Better than the plains. They'd start seeing feral folk again soon, he thought.

The rain began one night, thick clouds hiding the moon and the stars and making the world so dark that they only covered another few miles before dawn. It rained on for most of the day, slowly soaking them, and when Jasaan roused Hellas and his riders in the evening they were sluggish and bad-tempered. Three days, that's all they'd been out. He tried to remember what it had been like on the way back from Bloodsalt, hunted by a dragon but never allowed to stray too far from the lifeline of the Sapphire. Harder than this, that was for sure. His ankle was already hurting again, aching like it always did since Bloodsalt, whenever he walked on it for days at a time.

'We get a roof over our heads after tonight,' Hellas told him. 'If you can find it. There's a place the dragons didn't burn. It's hidden inside the Raksheh.'

'How far is it?'

'We'll be there before dawn.' Hellas made it sound as though he knew this country well, as though he'd been here many times. Jasaan knew better. What Hellas had was a poor copy of some alchemist's map and a handful of rumours. All passed on to Jasaan and expected to be enough.

The rain didn't stop. Clouds veiled the moon and the stars. In the last few hours of the night, as they entered the Raksheh proper, Jasaan gave up scouting ahead. It was so dark now that he could barely see his hand in front of his face and each step was an adventure. Hellas was wrong. They never found his shelter; instead, they sat out the last few hours of the night huddled on the fringe of the Raksheh, under monstrous trees as wide as houses that already towered far overhead, waiting for the light.

'There'll be dragons come dawn. Then what?'

Jasaan shrugged. 'Then either they'll see us or they won't.' Under the canopy of leaves they should be safe enough, shouldn't they? He didn't know. He'd never travelled a land like this, fresh and wet and full of life. Everywhere he'd seen of the realms until now had been desert. 'Haven't seen any sign they roost near here.'

Among these trees, at night, there was no point in trying to make any progress. They might as well have worn blindfolds.

He led them deeper into the forest, and the further they went, the darker it became. There wasn't much undergrowth any more, which was a blessing, but now every direction looked the same. Sometimes Jasaan had to stop and just stare at the trees. He'd never seen trees anything like these before. Little things that grew around the City of Dragons, yes, and the stunted desert trees of Sand, the same ones that grew among the Blackwind Dales and on the banks of the Sapphire and the Silver River, but nothing like these. Looking up at them from below reminded him of looking up at the old Tower of Air, the last speaker's favourite tower before the dragons had brought it down, but the trees were taller. A man could build a palace here, he thought, and it would still be lost amid the size of everything.

He must have had a sixth sense because he was already signalling the riders to stop before he heard the first snarl. A dozen yards away a snapper was staring at them. Jasaan froze. Cursed thing must have been just standing there, still as a statue in the gloaming, watching them come closer. Snappers. They didn't have wings, they didn't breathe fire, they were cunning but not clever, but they were still the size of a small horse with jaws that could rip a man's arm off in a single bite. One on one, a snapper almost always won. An Adamantine Man, even Skjorl, even the old Night Watchman himself in his full dragon-scale armour, was no match for a hungry adult. What you did with snappers was you ran. You climbed up something and then you hoped that it wasn't all that hungry. Snappers weren't like dragons. Snappers would wait for you for days. Weeks.

The trunks of the trees around them were as wide as barns and as smooth as glass. So much for climbing.

Shit!

The other thing you did was shoot them. The bows and the axes that every Adamantine Man carried were about the only things that would hurt them. If you were lucky, *really* lucky, you *could* take one down. The riders had bows. He had an axe. And it wasn't one against one.

'Arrows,' he said quietly. 'Not swords. You need arrows.' He stayed as still as he could while he let his axe slip from his back and into his hands. 'Get them ready.'

The snapper was looking at him. Its head was half turned away, watching him with one beady eye. Very, very slowly, it picked up one leg and moved it a foot sideways, watching all the time. Turning a little towards him.

'Stay still,' Jasaan hissed. 'It'll come for me as long as you just stay still. When I run and it chases, you shoot it. You aim for the head and for the neck.' Damn things were bulky enough that an arrow anywhere else didn't do much more than annoy it. Like shooting a scorpion into a dragon.

He gritted his teeth. If he'd had Adamantine Men behind him this would have been easy. He'd trust them. He'd turn and he'd run. The snapper would chase him. He'd race right through the archers and they'd shoot it dead. He'd done it once, when the Night Watchman had managed to trap a few snappers for some sport. Instead, what he had were four riders, four dragon-knights who'd never faced anything more dangerous than an irate servant unless they were on the backs of their dragons.

'Ready!' he roared, as much a challenge to the snapper as anything else. The lizard turned to face him properly now. It took another step towards him, not as slow this time, and opened its mouth to show off its teeth. Jasaan bellowed out another challenge right back. Then he turned and ran. He felt the snapper launch itself after him, felt the ground shake as though it was a hatchling dragon. He counted his steps. One, two, three, four, five and the snapper would be at full speed. Six, seven; he ran past the first rider, Hellas, saw him draw back his bow and let fly. Eight; past the next two. Nine; saw Nezak off to one side. Ten; the monster was behind him now, right there. He started swinging his axe. Eleven; let the swing go on, jumped into the air, twisting round, bending every ounce of strength.

Twelve.

It was right there, jaws open wide, a couple of yards away and closing fast. Three arrows were sticking out of its neck and shoulders. Blood trickled from each. As far as Jasaan could see, it had hardly noticed. He turned the flight of his axe a fraction. There wasn't much else he could do.

The blade met the side of the snapper's head and kept on going. The snapper's eyes rolled back. Jasaan pulled at the axe, using its weight and the snapper's momentum to lever himself out of the way. That was half the trick, not getting crushed.

The axe stuck. Jasaan let it go, spun out of the way, lost his footing, rolled and was up again in time to see the monster's legs falter. It ran for another three steps before it fell, sliding through the leaf mould and what little undergrowth there was. Jasaan swayed. He was trembling. His hands were shaking. He couldn't help but stare. He'd killed it. Hadn't expected that, not really.

Behind him Hellas shouted a warning. When Jasaan turned to look, he saw why.

That was the thing about snappers. They hunted in packs.

50

Kataros

Thirteen days before the Black Mausoleum

She sat beside the Adamantine Man. He was snoring. Drooling. She had a knife in one hand, the fingers of the other on the pulse of his neck. It would be so easy. A little cut in the right place, he'd bleed out and never wake up. She sat there and thought it through. Thought about how he deserved it and how she'd feel after it was done. Would it change anything?

'You don't need him any more,' whispered a little voice that might have been Siff, except when she turned to look the outsider was sound asleep so it must have been her own little voice.

He wasn't ever going to change. Not that it mattered now. He'd served her need for him. The question was whether she left him alive or left him dead. She reached into her blood and looked for the ties that bound him to her. They were still there, still strong. It must have been the wine then. He'd been scratching at his head while she'd been trying to make him stop. Was that it? Had he been too drunk to notice the screaming in his head commanding him to leave her alone? No one had ever told her that that was how it worked, but then alchemists never got drunk. Most of them. Except for her.

After a while she got up, took the last bottles of wine and smashed them. She shook Siff.

'Get up.'

He rolled over, so tightly tied he could barely move. His eyes were alert. He hadn't been asleep after all.

'Get up,' she said again.

'You'll have to untie me. I can't move. Good with knots, your doggy.'

She looked at what Skjorl had done, but she couldn't see where to start. In the end she simply cut the outsider free, everything except his hands, which stayed tied behind his back.

'I can't exactly walk like this,' he complained.

She poured a little water into an old glass flask. Then cut herself and dripped a drop of blood into it. She made sure Siff could see everything. 'Drink?'

'And make me like your doggy? No thanks.'

'You were no better than him last night.'

He looked away. 'Wasn't I? Thing is, I don't remember.'

'You were ... You weren't you.' She turned away too. Thing was, she wouldn't have untied him anyway, and he already had her blood inside him.

'It happens sometimes.' He shrugged. 'I don't know why. I don't want to hurt you. You got me out of there.'

He was lying. She was a means to an end, that was all. She could see that in the way his eyes gleamed, in the little smile that played at the corner of his lips when he glanced at the Adamantine Man, still snoring on the floor. A means to an end. That cut both ways though.

'Don't honey-tongue me, Siff.' She climbed the steps and pushed open the trapdoor. The last greys of dusk filled the cellar.

Siff spat on Skjorl with careful precision. 'You just going to leave him?'

'Yes.'

'You know he won't let you. He'll come after us when he wakes up. You know that. He'll cover the ground faster too. He knows where we're going. He *will* find us. You can't just leave him.'

'Yes, I can. You can come with me now or we can wait until he wakes up. You choose.'

'I saw what he was like.'

'I saw what *you* were like.'

Siff ran his tongue over his teeth. 'You're an alchemist. Suppose that means you haven't ever killed someone. I could do it for you, if you want. Doesn't bother me.'

'Yes. I'm an alchemist and I deal in blood every day. I know *exactly* where to cut a man, Siff. If I wanted to kill him, I'd do it myself.' She dealt in her own blood, never the blood of another. That was a line an alchemist never crossed, the line between alchemy and blood-magic. She'd given herself the chance to bleed out the Adamantine Man already and found she hadn't the will to do it. Letting Siff do it for her now seemed weak.

'If you say so.' Siff shrugged and Kataros shook her head. The outsider was trouble enough on his own. Neither of them understood what he had inside him and neither of them could control it, but even without that she had to believe he'd turn on her the first chance he got to escape. Skjorl had been her shield.

She gave the Adamantine Man a last glance as she stood at the top of the steps. 'Are you coming then?'

Siff struggled his way up the ladder. 'This would be a lot easier with hands.'

'The Yamuna will lead us to the Raksheh.' They'd be under the trees by dawn and the canopy of the Raksheh would hide them from the dragons. They could walk by day and sleep at night again. They'd follow the river to the Aardish Caves, however far that was, and then Siff would show her what he'd found. Maybe they'd fight each other for it or maybe they wouldn't, but they had to get there, that was the first thing.

She looked about. Once Siff was out of the cellar, she closed the trapdoor and piled stones from the ruins on top of it. There were plenty of them.

'I'd help if I had hands,' said Siff. Kataros ignored him. She piled as many stones as she thought would hold the Adamantine Man inside the cellar, and then piled on as many again until the door was nearly buried.

'Would have been kinder to kill him with that knife,' said Siff when she was done.

'I don't mean to kill him. Only to slow him. I don't think you're right about him following us, but just in case.' She pushed past him. 'We'll go as fast as we can, if you don't mind.'

Siff followed her. 'I'd walk quicker with hands,' he said.

'There are a lot if things you could do better with hands. Most of them won't help us.'

'When I need a piss, are you going to hold it for me?'

He was close behind her, so when she suddenly stopped and turned, he almost walked right into her. She had her knife pressed to his throat while he was still blinking in surprise. For a moment she almost did it. *Alchemists are considered in all things. An alchemist acts with thought, always, never on impulse.* Which had been her downfall, had been a flaw in her large enough that they'd never have made her what she was if the Adamantine Palace hadn't burned, if Hyrkallan hadn't killed half the order at the Pinnacles, if she hadn't been the one to dive down into the waters of the Fury and pick the Adamantine Spear out of a dead dragon's mouth, if any of those things hadn't been so.

And suddenly, out of nowhere, she was having to bite back tears for the one other outsider she'd known, for Kemir.

'Don't,' she hissed. 'Just don't.' She put the knife away slowly, then turned and started to walk again. 'When you need a piss, you can work it out for yourself or you can piss in your breeches.'

'That's not very nice.'

'No.'

There wasn't much to be said after that. They walked in silence under the clouds. A drizzle started, a cold cloying dampness that stuck to Kataros and wrapped her up as though trying to steal all her warmth. No matter. She had potions now, powders and herbs and blood and water, everything she needed. She fed a drop or two to Siff. He was slow, slower than Skjorl had been, even when he'd had the outsider on his back.

'You want him to catch us?' she asked as the trees either side of the Yamuna grew thicker and taller.

'I'd walk quicker with hands,' was all he said.

For once, as the sun came up, Kataros was awake. The two of them sat, carefully apart, either side of a tiny fire. The trees were huge, their trunks as wide as a man with his arms outstretched. They reached up towards the sun and the clouds, sheer pillars of wood a hundred feet or more from the ground to the first branches, and this was only the fringe of the forest. High overhead the leaves were so thick that they all but blotted out the light. Daytime in the Raksheh was a perpetual twilight.

'I haven't seen fire for months.' Kataros watched Siff's eyes follow the smoke as it rose. The warmth was delicious.

'Smoke calls dragons,' he said.

'In the deep caves it's choking death.'

On the ground around them almost nothing grew. The earth was covered with a thick layer of dead leaves, moisture from the rain seeping through the canopy above. Here and there, in the few places where the sun broke through, bushes and saplings grew together, fighting for the light. In the darker damper places mushrooms grew instead, some of them as tall as a man. Some of them, she knew, were poisonous. Others were edible. The Raksheh was a place for alchemists. Alchemists and outsiders.

'There's going to be people here, most likely,' said Siff after a bit. 'Maybe they could help us.'

Company. She yearned for that, but what would a tribe of out-siders do if they found themselves an alchemist? Nothing good. 'If there are people here, we will hide from them.'

'Don't think you can. Maybe if you move fast and far enough. Get further up the river. I don't know how many months ago it was I came down from the caves, but there weren't any people living by the river until I got close to the edge of the forest. It was all wild up there. Keep going for two or three days and hope for the best.' He smiled happily. 'If you ask me, I don't think there's much you can do about it. Just be thankful you left doggy behind. They'd kill him.'

'They'll kill me too, won't they?'

His smile grew wider. Here it came. 'Well now. Maybe they might. Or maybe, since they're more my sort of people, I could talk them out of it. If I had hands.' She tried to reach through the blood-bond and found nothing, just as it had been since the night in the old alchemists' cellar. The thing Siff had inside him, even when it was asleep, kept her out.

Siff sniffed. 'Not being all tied up like this might make me more amenable to help you.'

'No.' She shook her head. 'You'll have to do better than that.'

'We could tie *your* hands instead. Then they'd think you were mine.'

She laughed bitterly. 'So after they hit you over the head with a rock, they'd feel free to help themselves to your property? No, Siff, you stay as you are.' There was always another way. There was the alchemist's way, the way of thought and foresight and knowledge. She got up and wandered away from the fire to where the nearest little forest of mushrooms grew. These ones barely came past her ankles. From their mustard-yellow tops they were goldcaps, which were fine enough to eat if you didn't mind a few strange dreams. They'd make an oil to soothe the skin too. Her feet had blisters from all the walking; they could do with some soothing.

She cut some goldcaps, speared them on a few twigs and took them back to the fire. They were best fried in fish oil but these days you took what you could get. Goldcaps fried in anything at all would be a luxury back under the Purple Spur. After they'd started to crisp around the edges, she took them out from the flames and sprinkled a little white powder over them and handed one to Siff.

'What did you put on them?' Siff sniffed his mushroom suspiciously.

'Salt.'

He took a bite. She almost had to smile at the way his face lit up. 'This is good!'

'It'll give you dreams.' She wondered, too late now, whether that was wise. Did the thing Siff had inside him dream?

She ate her goldcap and then went to cut some more. 'We'll move on a way. Until we find some shelter.'

'My feet hurt.'

'So do mine.'

'Hand to get up?'

'Do it yourself.'

Not much further upriver they found a massive branch fallen from one of the trees. There was a hollow under it filled up with dead leaves. Good enough.

'That'll do for some shelter.' Siff yawned. 'Good forest blanket there and wood to keep the rain off. Ancestors! I'm exhausted.'

Kataros nodded. This was the bit where she fell asleep and Siff tried his best to get out of his ropes, took her knife and slit her throat. Or maybe he didn't slit her throat, maybe he simply ran away. She let him see her thinking. He yawned again.

'There's nowhere for you to go,' she said, and pointed. 'You have that bit. I'll be somewhere else. You'll pardon me if I watch you while you go to sleep.'

'If you must.' Siff chuckled to himself. She could almost read his thoughts. *You think I can't fool you, alchemist?* They both knew he could hide things from her, blood-bound or not.

She watched him anyway. When he started to snore, she crept closer. 'Salt,' she whispered. 'And a little more. Enjoy the dreams.' She sighed and stretched and snuggled down under her end of the fallen log. It was damp, the leaves prickled her skin, but she was so tired she barely noticed. Sleep, for once, without the Adamantine Man to look over her, to watch her. She shivered, thinking about that. Yes, she was glad he was gone. She closed her eyes and tried not to think about all the things that might go wrong, all the things that lived in the Raksheh that were poisonous, the spiders, the centipedes, the scorpions, the little six-legged biting lizards and their larger scavenger cousins who'd have a go at anything that wasn't quick enough to run away. The packs of man-eating snappers that were supposed to roam the place. Yes, tried not to think about any of that, and then, to her surprise, it was suddenly late in the day and she woke up with a start.

Something was prodding her. Something sharp.

She blinked.

Three outsiders were standing over her log. They had spears.

51

Jasaan

Sixteen days before the Black Mausoleum

Jasaan saw the second snapper but none of them saw the third. It took Hellas from the side and bit clean through his arm. Hellas screamed and spun around. Blood sprayed across the lizard, and then the snapper lashed with a claw and ripped most of Hellas' face off. An instant later its jaws came down again. It picked Hellas up by his head and shook him, threw him against one of the trees and hissed. Hellas landed in a heap of limp limbs. He didn't move.

Jasaan caught glimpses, but mostly he was running. The second snapper burst forward and pounced, flying twenty feet through the air to land on a rider's back and bear him to the ground. Before anyone could do anything, the snapper was ripping at him with his hind claws.

Jasaan stopped. He ran back to the dead snapper and started levering his axe out of its head. The fallen rider was screaming for help. He had armour, dragon-scale over metal, too tough even for snapper claws, but that wouldn't stop the beast from crushing the man inside. It would find a way in, sooner or later.

He looked about for Nezak and the other rider but they were gone. Had the sense to flee like he ought to. Thing was, you never knew with snappers how many were out there. In the Blackwind Dales and up on the moors packs as large as twenty had savaged entire villages.

He had the axe out now. The rider on the ground was looking straight at him, eyes pleading. There was blood. The snapper *had* found a way in. The other one was busy shaking and shredding Hellas, trying to get him out of his armoured skin.

Jasaan's hands were shaking. The snapper was looking at him too. They were both were. One man pleading with him to come, one monster daring him to try.

He couldn't do it.

The rider managed to stab the monster in its leg with his sword and then the snapper finally flipped him on his back and ripped his throat out.

Scared. The one thing no Adamantine Man could ever be. He was frozen, shaking, part in fear, more in shame. He hated himself. Skjorl would never even have thought of running.

The two snappers settled in to eat, keeping half a watchful eye on him. Jasaan began to back away. When they didn't follow, he turned and ran. Didn't know where he was going. Just somewhere. Away. Nezak and the other rider were long gone; they probably hadn't seen what had happened, but he couldn't count on that. If they had, then what? They'd hate him, that's what. They'd think he was nothing. Less than nothing and they'd be right.

It would be like it was before. The way it had been after Scarsdale.

Eventually, when nothing gave chase, he stopped running. He caught his breath and his head started to clear. He hadn't the first idea where he was and he didn't dare go back and look for Nezak. If there were any more snappers, the last two riders were probably both dead like the rest.

He'd lost his shield. He didn't remember when.

Nezak. Stupid thing to do, learn a man's name and a little bit about him. Stupid out here, the world being what it was. He sighed and sat on his heels. Where would you go if you were a rider? Get out of this blasted forest. Yes, a man with any sense would turn right round, and sure, they'd have to cross the plains to reach the Pinnacles, and yes, there were dragons out there but there were places to hide too. A man with any sense would turn right round and go home.

They'd been five. Now they might be three if he was lucky, one if he wasn't. But it only took one man to make a difference, if he was a man in the right place.

Bugger.

Took a while, staring up at the canopy of leaves overhead, to get a rough idea of where the sun was. Good enough to tell his north from south and his east from west. The Pinnacles were somewhere to the east. As far as he knew, the Aardish Caves were somewhere to the west and the Yamuna would be to the south.

Home. He didn't have a home. The Guard had been his home and the dragons had taken that from him. The dragons and then Skjorl.

He turned south, towards the river. The river would take him to the caves.

52

Skjorl

Twelve days before the Black Mausoleum

He pushed at the door with all his strength but it didn't move. He could see from the way the daylight came through the gaps in the planks around the edges what they'd done to him. They'd trapped him. Buried him alive.

Didn't make any sense. Why do that? You wanted to kill man, you stuck a knife in him and watched until the light went out of his eyes. That was that, the only way.

So she didn't want him dead. Maybe they were coming back? He should sit and wait?

No. He'd done that once before. In Scarsdale. And why would they bury him? Made no sense.

Mighty Vishmir but his head hurt! Once he'd pushed at the door enough to know it was weighed down with more than he could move, he went and sat in the middle of the cellar floor to think. Or try, at least to try. His head was screaming.

He'd been drunk. Dead drunk. He remembered that. The shit-eater had been tied well enough. Couldn't have escaped on his own. The alchemist then. Had there been an accident? He'd banged his head?

Moving meant screwing up his face against the surge of pain. Dreamleaf, more of it, that's what he needed. Except when he looked for it, his eyes couldn't quite seem to focus. He moved to where one of the shafts of sunlight sneaked in through a crack in the trapdoor, but the brightness was like being stabbed in the eye with a hot needle. He lay down, rolled on his side, closed his eyes and lay still, gasping. The cellar was spinning.

The shit-eater had been in the cellar when he'd been drunk.

He'd been talking to the alchemist. He remembered, in pieces. She'd looked good. That was the wine.

Scarsdale.

Had he had her? In front of the shit-eater? Had she given in at last? No, he'd remember that, wouldn't he?

He'd taken her. In front of her man. What was his name?

No, that was Scarsdale. This was somewhere else.

Memories crashed into each other, merged, went their own way again, all muddled up.

Ancestors! The alchemist. She'd done something to him. He couldn't remember her name. Couldn't remember either of them. Couldn't remember much except the pain. Someone had hit him on the head. The evidence was the lump on his skull. Start with that.

Start with the beginning.

No. Scarsdale. Start with *that*.

Isul Aieha! Damn place wouldn't leave him alone. He screwed up his eyes. Looked for a memory he could hang on to, one that wouldn't slip away. Found it and clung to it as though it was his life. Sand. He remembered Sand. Everything burning. Held on to that memory and forced out the next one. Stuck them back together piece by piece, like undoing a rope full of old knots, each one as impenetrable and held fast as the next. One by one he picked and prised them apart.

Sand. They'd walked for weeks after the tunnels under the monastery. The men he'd had with him at Outwatch had been stoical about the destruction. The others, the hundreds of refugees, the survivors, the ordinary folk who happened still to be alive, they'd wept and screamed and torn their hair. Couldn't blame them. Even the Adamantine Men had come out with tight lips and taut faces and far-away eyes. The first time most of them had seen what dragons could really do. They were seeing the death of the realms, of everything they knew, stark and irrevocable. Some faced it and took it for what it was. Others screamed and tried to imagine something else. For the most part those were the ones who died on the way.

They were slow. Some days they only covered a few miles,

following the Last River towards the mountains. Simply wasn't any other way to go, not with so many people. He split them up into little groups, graded by their speed, divided his men between them. He took the slowest. The weak, the sick, the old, the frail, the mad. They hated him. One by one they failed or fled, but he had no choice. He drove them hard. The longer they took, the more they starved, the more they starved, the slower they went. When they fell, he killed them. Same for the ones who fled – tracked them, hunted them and put them down with neither malice nor mercy, then buried them in the sand. Left them in the open, maybe a dragon would find them. Maybe it would start to wonder, or worse, it would find them still alive and tear out their memories. He'd seen that under Outwatch. Seen it with his own eyes, that murderous hatchling snatching men and staring at them, and them screaming and begging for mercy and spilling out the places where others might hide. It never saved them. The hatchling had killed everyone. It had been admirably, remorselessly thorough.

So the ones that ran, he killed them. They were doing to die anyway and it made the others safer. When they got to Southwatch, he was proud of the ones he'd saved but they still hated him.

Southwatch had food and shelter for months, but he'd let his Adamantine Men stay for three days, no more. When they left, they left with as much as they could carry, as many weapons as they could use, whatever tools took their fancy. Too much, screamed the men and women of Sand that he left behind. There were hundreds of them against a score of his Guard, but they didn't dare to try and stop him. A few begged to come with him. Fine, he told them, if you can keep up. There were maybe half a dozen who left with them for Evenspire. After the second day he never saw any of them again. He'd done his duty. He'd led the survivors of Sand to a safe place and now he was going home. To do his duty again, whatever it was.

Evenspire, when they got there, was deserted. The city had burned. The Palace of Paths still stood, its walls so massive that even dragons couldn't knock them down. They stayed for two days, trying to find a way into the tunnels that were surely beneath it, to reach the survivors who must be there. Hadn't worked out, and so it had been a choice: follow the Evenspire Road out into the desert again, or else the Dragon River south through the Blackwind Dales to Scarsdale. Evenspire Road was hundreds of miles across the Plains of Ancestors, with no water until the Sapphire and Samir's Crossing. Death to men on foot, Adamantine ones or any other. Wasn't much of a choice.

They took the river then, and so it was they got to Scarsdale, starving. A dot on a map, that was all, the last place they might scavenge some food before they crossed the line of hills to the valley of the Silver River and the Great Cliff. What they found were ramshackle ruins, burned and smashed, littered all along the river and up the hills with no sense of order or purpose. Place had been stripped clean. Too clean for it to be dragons. Someone had got there first.

Finding the mines, though, that had been an accident. He'd thought it was a cave. Good piece of shelter for the day, but they took a look about first – man had to be sure he wasn't sharing with snappers or something like that after all – and that's where they'd found the shafts. By the end of that day they'd found the rest, a few dozen people living down in the mines with enough food to last them a year.

The Adamantine Men had feasted. Two solid days of it. Got drunk on wine, on the barrels of it hidden there. The people had been none too pleased, but when you'd been out in the open, hiding from dragons in the day and marching across a parched landscape by night, you took what you could get. He'd been doing that for months. Yes, a man took what he could get.

Liouma. That had been her name. The one he'd taken. Nice tits. Big. Big arse too. Ripe. He knew he was going to have her from the moment he saw her. And then the next day, afterwards, he'd woken up and it had been like this. Hungover, thundering head, locked up behind a wooden door without knowing why.

Like this, but not the same.

He ran through the rest anyway. The Purple Spur. Bloodsalt. Vish. Killing a dragon. Jasaan. The moors. The Pinnacles. The alchemist. All of it. All nicely in a row like it was supposed to be, one thing after the next.

His head still thundered but his eyes would focus now. He looked in his pouch. Dreamleaf and plenty of it, in the last water he had, and then he waited for the numbness it would bring. In Scarsdale they'd taken his axe. That was before she'd had a name. The alchemist hadn't done that. Kataros. Must have been her, because the shit-eater would have cut his throat and been done with it. Yes, the alchemist.

The sunlight was gone. Outside was dark. Night, maybe, or it could have been the shadow of a dragon sitting over the cellar for all he knew, waiting patiently for him to come out.

Dreamleaf was starting to take him. Dragons outside? He'd dealt with dragons before. One thing at a time.

He couldn't make Dragon-blooded bite the door. The angle was wrong, the roof too high, the door and the ladder too tucked into the corner of the cellar.

In Scarsdale he'd been angry. Smashed his fists on the door, ran at it, battered himself almost senseless trying to get out. Scarsdale had taught him patience, and so he set about the alchemists' cellar, taking his time, no rush, searching every corner and edge. There were the lamps. He'd seen Kataros use them, seen the way they worked. Started with those and then he could see: a wooden table and a set of little shelves with tiny compartments. The alchemist had taken most of whatever had been in there. A pile of smashed glass where the ground was still damp, rich with the smell of wine. A bench. Three old chairs. The bones in the far corner, more empty bottles, a few rags.

The skeleton had a knife in one hand. Resting between its fingers, the edge stained a dark brown.

In Scarsdale they'd left him with a knife. They'd put him behind a heavy wooden door, but they'd left him with a knife, the one tucked in his boot. It had probably taken the best part of three days to pick and whittle the edge of that door until he'd made a gap large enough to shift the bolt on the other side. He'd never quite understood why they'd shut him up in Scarsdale. They shut his men up too, although at least they gave the others food and water. Him they'd left to die, like the alchemist had done. But he'd escaped and they'd got what they deserved.

He climbed the ladder, drilled through the pain and the floating feeling of the Dreamleaf, and set to work.

53

Blackscar

Four days before the Black Mausoleum

The dragon soared high above the Raksheh. Others of its kind came and went. Some came to ask it about the half-made sky-home. Others went to see it for themselves. It had moved.

They are returning, Black Scar of Sorrow Upon the Earth.

The seals are broken.

The Black Moon and then the end.

It mused on those things and shared them with any who would listen.

A thing that speaks of the stars. And something other.

The sky-home had become a thing of interest. Dragons would come from across the realms to see it. Curiosity would bring them. A sorcerer who carried a touch of the broken god. Magic of glass and gold that made lightning. Amusing diversions. The dragon had felt other things there too.

They are here! The makers. The silver ones. The time would come for a reckoning and it would be soon, but the dragon would not be there, not on the sky-home.

It flew in lazy circles, a thousand miles, spiralling towards the Aardish Caves. It could feel the presence there. Something was waiting.

It would not wait alone.

Little ones were moving. Swarming along the river. It felt their thoughts, now and then, as it peered with its seventh sense through the blanket of branches and leaves. They thought they were safe.

They were wrong.

The Aardish Caves

It is said that when Vishmir visited the Moonlight Garden, he observed that a dark reflection of the garden structures could be clearly seen in the waters of the Yamuna, and in a moment of divine clarity he understood that this was the Black Mausoleum of the Silver King. He became obsessed with the caves and spent many days participating in their exploration during the early years after his victory.

In the seventh year of Vishmir's reign exploration of the caves ceased following an unexplained disaster that claimed the lives of most of those working at the site. Those nearby on the bluffs overlooking the caves reported that the ground shook and even the dragons resting nearby seemed disturbed. Upon hearing the news, Vishmir visited at once; on his return, he immediately issued a decree that the caves were a forbidden place under the guardianship of the King of Furymouth. In the later years of his reign, despite his own edict, Vishmir returned once more in great secrecy to build a mausoleum of his own. Even now the exact location of Vishmir's tomb remains a mystery.

The Aardish Caves are remote and hard to reach without a dragon. The caves remain under the watchful eye of King Tyan of Furymouth. Despite Vishmir's fascination, no evidence has ever been found to indicate there has ever been any connection between the Aardish Caves and the Silver King.

Bellepheros' *Journal of the Realms*, 2nd year of Speaker Hyram

54

Jasaan

Fourteen days before the Black Mausoleum

You could say one thing for the Raksheh – it was easy enough going. The ground under Jasaan's feet was soft and damp. The air was dim and still and smelled of mould; during the day the forest under the canopy was as dark as a moonlit night and during the night it was as black as a cave. Now and then a small forest of giant fungus or a place where the canopy above was broken and a furious rush of green had taken over the forest floor would force him to change his course. One time he came to the corpse of a fallen tree, a giant half buried in the earth. The wood was still as hard as stone. He paced out its length as he walked around it and lost track somewhere over a hundred. The quiet started to get to him. Now and then he heard the leaf litter rustle as something moved or else a burst of shrieking or hooting from the canopy above; mostly the forest was simply silent.

He found the river two days later and the dragon-knights a day after that. Nezak and the other one, alive and camped out on the banks of a river that he thought at first was the Yamuna but turned out was something else entirely. Such a stroke of luck amazed him, until he realised they were simply doing the same as he was – strike south for the nearest river and then stick to it like glue. Difference was that he'd followed the river upstream and the riders had simply sat where they were, wondering what to do.

'You're going the wrong way,' said Nezak. 'There are three rivers in the Raksheh. They merge together before they leave the forest. You need to go downstream until this one meets the Yamuna. Then turn west again.'

You, Jasaan noted. Not *we*. He didn't ask though. What the riders did was their own business; for now they were all hungry and thirsty and bedraggled. Jasaan made a fire and they sat together for a night and never mind who might see them. Riders were so out of place down here on the ground. He'd seen it with Hellas and the others and he saw it now. They didn't know what to do, didn't know how to look after themselves, didn't know what to eat. All that fine armour and steel and they were worse than useless.

They were here, though. That counted for something, right? Had to. They'd hadn't just given up and gone running back to the plains.

'I should have stayed and fought the snappers,' said Jasaan after he'd borrowed their bow and shot some supper – he had no idea what it was and the riders had been raised in a desert. 'I saw your friend go down.' *Your friend* – now he wished he *had* known the other rider's name after all. 'He put up a good struggle but he wasn't ever going to win. I should have done something. I didn't have a bow. My axe was stuck in the face of the first one, but I should have done *something*.' He didn't know what, just knew that Skjorl wouldn't even have thought about it. Skjorl would have tried to take the snapper down with his bare hands, probably, and he might even have managed it. That or he'd have died trying. A proper Adamantine Man.

The two riders looked at him. Their eyes were scared. They'd run too, no doubt about it.

Nezak sniffed. 'We used to hunt snappers from the backs of our dragons. I didn't realise they grew so big.'

'Giants,' muttered the other rider, while Jasaan shook his head because if anything, the three snappers they'd met had been small ones. Maybe everything on the ground looked bigger after you'd grown used to seeing the world from the back of a dragon.

Jasaan found a tree on the edge of the river that wasn't one of the giants and took his axe to it. There were creepers hanging from the branches of almost everything here by the water. Stuff he'd never seen before, but it looked like rope so it would just have to do. By the end of the next day he'd made them a raft. Nezak drew a map in the mud by the water, a memory of the one time he'd flown over the Raksheh escorting Speaker Hyrkallan and his queen on some secret errand to Furymouth. Mountains to the west, the Fury gorge to the north, the plains to the east and the sea to the south. Then three rivers. The only one with a name was the one that came out onto the plains, the Yamuna.

'Downstream,' said Nezak. 'We haven't crossed a river since we came into the forest, so we go downstream. When this river comes together with another, that'll be the Yamuna and we'll know where we are.'

'And then?' Someone had to ask.

The riders laughed at him, both of them. 'There's no alchemist,' said the other one. 'She's dead by now. Look at this place. Everything bites and stings and wants to eat you.'

'She has Skjorl.' Skjorl who'd crossed the moors on his own. Skjorl who'd killed a dragon. Skjorl the cold killer, and Jasaan had to wonder what an alchemist could do to make a man like that serve anyone but himself. Or maybe it was a different Skjorl, but Jasaan couldn't quite make himself believe that was right.

'She's an alchemist,' said Nezak. 'They know the paths to places like this.'

And that might even be true. For some reason, Jasaan hoped it was.

55

Siff

Twelve days before the Black Mausoleum

The first thing he noticed when he woke up was that he wasn't hidden under a fallen tree any more. There wasn't a comfortable bed of dead leaves keeping him warm. He was lying on bare earth. It was cold and it was damp and it was dark. Late afternoon under the canopy of the Raksheh.

The next thing he noticed was that he was in a cage. He didn't get any further than that.

'No! No! *No!*' He jumped up. His head was fuzzy but he hardly noticed; instead, he hurled himself at the bars, battering at them, tearing with his hands until his fingers started to bleed. 'No!' He wasn't going anywhere in a cage. Not that, not in a cage up in the air, waiting for it to shatter, waiting to fall, helpless, out of the sky. Never again. Death first ...

He stopped. His heart was beating fit to burst. He was breathing as though he'd just run up a mountain.

Not a cage for dragon-slaves. That time was gone.

He took deep breaths. Slow, steady, trying to calm his heart. There were no dragon-riders any more. Their time was past. Their eyries were gone, and their slave-cages too. No one was going to lift him up into the air to freeze and gasp and fall and die.

He looked about. If not an eyrie, then where was he?

With a start he realised he knew this place. The cage was sitting on the forest floor surrounded by giant trees, only here, he knew, the trees were full of holes. This was where the outsiders had lived, the ones he'd found on his first trek out of the forest, the ones who gouged holes into trees for places to sleep and to store their food, higher than any snapper could reach.

On the forest floor around him shadows moved slowly about. Men and women, shaping pieces of wood and making more ropes. He didn't smell any cooking. They did that somewhere else, far away from where they slept. He remembered that. Hunters vanished into the woods in twos and threes, sometimes for more than a week, coming back with whatever meat they'd managed to find, but always stopping to cook it a half day away. You never knew how close a snapper pack might be.

'Hey!' he called. 'Hey!'

Faces turned and quickly looked away. He didn't know them. He didn't remember much of the time he'd spent here, but it had been months. He stretched and rubbed his hands and wrists. The ropes were gone. Now he had a cage instead. Was that any better?

The twilight turned slowly into night. When it was black as pitch, he felt more than heard the air move beside his cage and a voice hissed at him: 'The only reason you're not already dead is that woman.'

Siff spun around. In the darkness he couldn't see a thing. Whoever was talking was standing next to him, and Siff couldn't see him, that's how dark the Raksheh was when the sun went down. 'Who's that?' he asked.

'You don't remember?' Whoever it was, they hissed and spat like a viper. No friend then.

'No.' There, and that was the truth too.

'I already hated you. Now I despise you. You and your woman, you're just more hungry mouths to me. I don't know what possessed you to come back here after what you did.'

'What possessed me?' Siff burst out laughing at his own pathetic life. It would be nice, he thought, to know *why* when they fed him to the snappers. Dimly, he remembered that was what these outsiders did. 'She's got something. She won't tell you, but she has. She's got a secret.'

'You're the one with the secret. The rest, they were so under your spell they don't even remember, but I do. You're a demon and now you're going to die.'

Siff felt the cage tremble. Whoever was talking to him was

within touching distance. *Ancestors, if what I did was so bad why don't I remember?* 'Listen! Wait! Hey! The woman, she's an alchemist! She's a witch! She's the demon, not me!'

'No, Siff.' The cage trembled again. He heard the soft creak of wood against wood.

'Ho! Wait!' Siff scrambled away from the noise, clutching at the bars. 'Who *are* you?'

'You don't remember me?'

'No!'

'Liar! But you remember what you did.'

'No! I don't remember anything. Listen. I found something. Up the river. There's caves up there. Days and days of walking, but there's a place where the dragon-riders used to go and there's caves and I found something. You listening to me? Treasure!'

'Yes. We heard all that the last time. Do you remember how many of us died looking for it?'

A handful of something like sand flew into Siff's face. Whatever it was, it stung his eyes. He squealed.

'Salt burns, does it, demon?' Another handful scattered over him out of the darkness and then another.

'Ancestors! I am *not* a demon! I swear on my grandfathers.'

'Salt takes your power, demon. Now I have some iron to take your soul.'

'*Listen*, damn you! I don't know what you're talking about. I don't even know who you are! I was ill! You're right, I was possessed, but not any more. The demon came from up in the caves. That's why I went away. The alchemist took the demon out. Now she's come to do something about the caves. I don't know what – ask *her* – but I'm not a demon any more! I'm not, I'm not!' He was sobbing now.

'Lies.' The cage door was open now. 'You'd say anything to save your skin. You said you'd come back. Don't you remember? Something you needed, and when you had it you'd come back. And I swore that when you did, I'd kill you.'

'You can't!' he screamed. 'I'm the only one who can show her where to go! That alchemist, she's going to use it to be mistress of the dragons again, not that she'll say that to you or anything. Nor anyone else probably, but that's what she's after.' He was making it up as he went along now, spinning stories the old way, mixing truth and wild imagination so fast that even *he* wasn't sure which was which any more. 'It's me that knows where, though. She knows it's in the caves but those caves go on for ever. You want to find it, any of you, you got to keep me alive!'

'Seven men, demon. Two of them brothers, all of them friends.' Siff could see the man now, finally, standing inside the cage with him. He could see an outline, the hint of a shape, nothing more. He couldn't see the knife, but he had no doubt it was there. He had tears in his eyes now. He was going to die because of something he couldn't even remember.

He felt a stirring inside him, the feeling that came just before those gaps in his memory. He clutched his head. 'She'll make it back like it was, every bit of it. Exactly like it was and the likes of you and me, we'll be no better than we were. I don't want to spend my life scraping in the dirt to live, waiting for something to come and eat me or some*one* to come and cart me off in a slave cage.' The thing inside was waking up. 'You kill me, you do it quickly,' he wailed, 'and when you're done, you go out and you make sure you don't touch a drop to drink that she could have got a hand to. She's a witch as well as an alchemist. I've seen her make her potions. I've seen her force a man to her will with them. My own eyes, I swear. And don't cut her. I've seen her throw blood in a man's face and then watched it burn him to the bone. She knows blood-magic and she'll use it if she has to. Don't cut her. Don't let her bleed. Get that knife off her if you can.'

'You talk of blood, demon? Seven men, and I saw what you did to them. You murdered them, one after the other. You bled them out on that stone slab. Brothers. Friends.' A hand gripped his shoulder, tense and strong. 'Die, demon.'

No

The man's face lit up with a moonlight glow and Siff saw him for an instant, still a stranger, knife gleaming in his hand, but he saw a look in the man's eye too, a sort of wonder and a sort of terror all at once …

And then he was sitting outside and it was light again and the whole night had passed and he had no idea what had happened and the outsiders were gathered around him and he knew they were getting ready to take him up the river because that was what he wanted and what he'd told them to do. The thing inside was restless. He could feel it. It wanted to be back at the caves and so that was where it was going, all of them together whether they liked it or not. It terrified him. *I need to get out before he comes. Need to.* Maybe the alchemist would know what it was. It scared her too. Scared everyone who saw it. Everyone except the Adamantine Man, who just wanted to kill him.

He closed his eyes. When he opened them again, he saw his cage. It had someone in it. The alchemist.

The thing inside was rising out of its slumber again. He tried to scream, but all he saw was a hundred eyes light up in wonder.

56

Jasaan

Twelve days before the Black Mausoleum

They slept another night out in the open by the river. At dawn they pushed their little raft out into the water, paddled it into the current, closed their eyes and prayed. To their ancestors, perhaps, for the riders, but Jasaan only saw the Great Flame. The first dragon, as large as a mountain, the creature that had given birth to the monsters of the realms. It was strange, he thought, to revere such a beast and yet dedicate yourself to slaying its progeny. They were contradictions, from the moment they were made, all of them. They were the Adamantine Guard. They slew dragons because dragons were monsters and yet, when Jasaan looked at the men he'd known, they were little more than monsters themselves.

On the river they dozed for most of the day, letting the current do the work, taking it in turns to use the crude paddles Jasaan had made to keep them in the middle of the flow and steer them around the island boulders and fallen trees that littered the water.

'Look.' The other rider was shaking him. Parris. Jasaan had accepted the inevitable and asked his name. Wouldn't make any difference now. They were bound together on this quest whether he liked it or not. 'Look!'

Jasaan sat up. Through the trees on the right bank of the river he could see open sky beyond. Open sky and another expanse of water, another river, as big or bigger than the one they were on. Jasaan steered the raft towards the bank. As the rivers came together, the current grew stronger. Whirlpools tossed and turned them, spinning them about, and it took all three of them with all their strength before they finally nudged into the bank a half-mile further downstream. Nezak knelt, gasping, in the mud beside the river. He pointed to an outcrop of stone that rose out of the bank where the rivers merged. It was a bare brown rock, fifty feet high, with the water running right underneath. The trees of the forest towered over it. Dwarfed it.

'We were following the Yamuna. We'd come from the Moonlight Garden, heading for Furymouth. I remember that rock.'

Jasaan shrugged. 'Then this is the Yamuna.' It didn't seem too likely that a man on the back of a dragon would see an insignificant thing like that, but he wasn't about to argue. Let it be the Yamuna. Why not?

He looked up. Habit didn't care that he was in the Raksheh. He'd probably still be glancing at the sky even after he was dead. But he looked up and he saw a speck, high and in the distance, moving below the cloud. He checked to see how much potion he had left. He had an idea that Kataros herself might have made it for him, before they'd left. Now he was down to a week, maybe a little more. Hellas had carried some too but they'd lost that. He pointed at the speck trailing across the sky.

'Somewhere there's a snapper that dragon can't find.' For some reason that made him laugh so hard he couldn't stop. Was that even how it worked? Did dragons sniff snappers out with their extra senses or did they do it the same way any other hunter did? He had no idea. Still couldn't stop laughing though. He took a swig and then gave the potion flask to Nezak. 'I don't know if we've got enough of this to get to the caves because I have no idea how far away they are. We haven't got enough to get back. You take this. If we find the alchemist, you take her as far as you can. Don't worry about us. Just don't murder her this time.'

Nezak gave him a queer look, as though Jasaan was losing his mind. Maybe he was. Maybe he'd been losing it for a long time. 'If we find the alchemist, perhaps she will make us some more,' the rider said. 'And we'll all go together. To be blunt, Guardsman, if anyone should be left behind, it's us.'

Riders didn't say things like that. That wasn't the way it was. Adamantine Men served, that was all. They served and they died so others didn't have to. Nice of Nezak to pretend things were different, though. Jasaan forced a smile.

They walked. Paddling their little raft into the teeth of the Yamuna's current wasn't going to work and Jasaan was happy to be on his feet. Walking was something he was used to. The riders would slow him down but that was fine too – it gave him time to hunt and forage and pathfind for them.

'So how far is it to these caves?' He had to ask, even though he knew he wasn't going to like the answer. The Raksheh was said to be a thousand miles from one end to the other. The caves were supposed to be somewhere in the middle and Jasaan was quite sure that *he* was somewhere near the edge.

'From here? A hundred miles. Two maybe.' Nezak shrugged as if it was all much the same. Maybe on the back of a dragon it was.

'Long walk then.' Mentally, Jasaan went through what every Adamantine Man went through when they were away from a safe haven, the litany they had drilled into them every day. *Water. Food. Warmth. Shelter. Dragons.* They had potion for the dragons, at least for a while. A whole river full of water and never mind that it rained here more than it didn't. The trees gave shelter from the wind and most of the rain. Leaf mould, fallen branches, yes, he could build shelters and fires and forest blankets if he needed to. As for food, well, if the trek along the Sapphire valley to Bloodsalt had taught him anything, it was how to fish. So that's what they'd be eating then. Fish and not much else.

There were other things, of course. Things he hadn't thought of. Parris came down with a fever. He kept going but it got steadily worse. His appetite went. He stopped talking and spent his time either shivering or sleeping, but he kept going. They should have left him, every Adamantine Man would have said the same, but Jasaan slowed his pace a little, did what he could to keep Parris going. Something bit Nezak's hand and his fingers swelled up like sausages. Jasaan wondered if he might lose them, but there wasn't anything to be done. He had his own problems by then. His bad ankle was aching all the time, and something must have crawled under his armour one day and feasted on the good one. The first he knew about it was a growing pain. When he looked, there must have been two dozen bites, each one an ugly black blotch, swollen and sore. Wasn't long before he was limping on both feet. At least that evened things up. Queer, though – the one thing that never slowed them down and never went bad was Nezak's arrow wound, which was probably the worst injury of the lot.

Every day the forest was the same and the river too. Jasaan had lost count of how long they'd been out there when they saw the boat. Was almost ready to give up. Didn't know how far they'd come by then – it might not have been a hundred miles yet, but it surely felt like it. The middle of nowhere. No one ever came here and he could see why. Parris was a wreck, hardly able to focus any more, putting one foot in front of the other was the limit of what he could do. At least Nezak's fingers seemed to be getting better. Maybe Nezak was charmed.

And out here, in this ancestor-forsaken wilderness where no one lived for a hundred miles, there was a boat. Not one, he realised, as he stared, but two, then three, then five. He hadn't heard them coming over the ever-present rush of the water. They were close to the bank, paddling steadily forward where the current was weakest.

He stopped and he stared. Outsiders. Dozens of them. And there she was, in the middle boat. They had her. The alchemist. Kataros. Alive.

And the bugger was that he didn't even have a bow and the two riders were half a mile behind him, following the trail he was marking out, and there was nothing he could do.

57

Kataros

Twelve days before the Black Mausoleum

She had them in the palm of her hand. She hadn't even used blood-magic to do it, she'd simply told them the truth. She'd told them who she was and why she was here, what she was looking for and how it might change their world, and then she asked them for their help. No more hiding, if what Siff said was true, and if it wasn't, then she'd show them how to hide from dragons with more than the great trees over their heads – she'd show them how to hide with alchemy too. But if she was right then they were going to have the relics of the Silver King himself, the Isul Aieha, and those relics would be theirs, and they would never need to hide again, not from anyone or anything. Afterwards, when she'd finished promising them the earth, she felt proud of herself. She'd done what a true alchemist would do. What did it matter who took the Silver King's power? In the great long scheme of things it was a battle of one species against another. Why carry the means to tame monsters back to the Pinnacles or the Purple Spur just because someone called themselves speaker? Yes, in the long great scheme of things survival was all that mattered, not whose name carried each victory.

They took her up to a sleep-space hollowed from the trunk of one of the great forest trees, hidden from both the ground and the sky. It was high, far higher than it needed to be for mere snappers.

'Sometimes dragons come into the forest on the ground,' said the man whose space she was sharing. He had a wife and three children, all born long before the Adamantine Palace had burned, and the space inside the tree was little more than a cell. *A nest*, she thought. *Like a woodpecker.*

She told him about the world outside, how everything had changed. He shook his head.

'For us the only change is that your kind stopped coming into the forest.'

'My kind?'

'Alchemists.'

'You didn't notice the dragons?' She couldn't believe it. How could something like that make no difference?

He thought for a bit. 'No. Dragons with riders or dragons without, they're all the same to us. They come and they burn and they take what they want. We used to meet your kind sometimes, on the bank of the river. The one you call the Yamuna. We traded for things made of metal. Knives and arrowheads. We gave them what we harvested from the forest.'

A younger Kataros, the one fresh from the Palace of Alchemy, wouldn't have looked past how simple a folk they were, but that was before she'd sailed halfway down the Fury with an outsider who turned out to be the only man she'd ever met who saw her as she was, as a person, not a simple collection of useful talents that could be employed to further some end of their own. They were simple and straightforward people, which made it all the more of a surprise to wake up on her second morning there with the same man sitting on her back, pinning her arms while his sons held her legs and his wife forced a gag into her mouth. She struggled and bit her tongue and tried to spit blood at them, but they knew, somehow they knew, and they would not let her blood touch them. They were five and she was one, and by the time they'd finished trussing her up, she was helpless. Their faces looked angry.

What did I do? But now she couldn't ask.

When they were done they left her alone, propped against a wall, unable to move. She supposed they thought that gagged and tied they'd left her powerless too. She could have wept. Why? Why did they have to do this? Why was there never an easy way?

She let the blood in her mouth seep into the wad of cloth stuffed in there and dissolve it slowly away. When it was gone, she spat bloody saliva onto the ropes around her, but before she could set her mind to work on them, she heard a voice.

'Oh ho.'

She looked up, still trussed hand and foot. There was a face staring at her from the outside. Siff, except his eyes were pure gleaming silver.

'What did you tell them?' She peered closer. 'What *are* you?'

Siff shook his head. 'I told them not to leave you alone, for a start. A few minutes with no one watching and you're almost loose again already. This won't do, but later, when we have time, you must show me how.' He pulled himself up into the sleep-space and squatted beside her, toying with a knife. 'What did *you* tell them?'

'The truth.'

Siff laughed out loud. 'The truth where you take the secrets of the Silver King back to your precious speaker and make every-thing exactly as it used to be? Back to the days when men on dragons came and took them away to be slaves?'

'I told them it would be theirs.'

'Ah. So you lied then.'

She twisted her head, trying to look him in the eye. He kept his distance. Afraid she'd spit at him, perhaps.

'You're the outsider here, alchemist. You'll do what riders always do and it'll be people like me and these who suffer, just like *we* always did.'

'You don't even know for sure that anything is there.'

'No. *You* don't know. *I* saw it. I saw a gate. Besides, look at me. How can you doubt it?' His voice began to wander, back into a memory full of wonder and amazement. 'I saw a way to their world. And it was so beautiful.' He snapped back to the present. 'Do you want to see it or not?'

'Yes.' She looked down. Yes. If even a sliver of what he'd told her was true then yes, yes, she wanted to see it, more than any-thing in the world. The treasures of the Silver King. 'Of course I do.'

'Well then, you listen hard, alchemist. They do what I tell them, not you. They know I'm the one who can lead them there, and I

287

don't need you now. So we're going to go to the Aardish Caves, just like you wanted, only you're going to be trussed up like this all the way so you don't go using your blood-magic on people. I'm going to be sitting with you all the way, and if you even squirm wrong, I'll just throw you in the river to drown, simple as that. Because I do – not – *need* you. I hope you understand. And now I'm going to show you something.'

He moved to sit in front of her. Very slowly he took his knife to her cheek and made a shallow cut. She felt the blood roll down her skin. Then he cut his own palm and put the knife away and stroked a drop of his blood onto his finger. Right in front of her, carefully and deliberately, he pressed her blood into his own and mixed them together.

'That's how you do it, isn't it? That's how you made your doggy do what he was told?' His gaze never left her face.

She stared at his hand. It had to be a trick but she couldn't see how it worked. Without even thinking, she was already reaching into the blood, feeling for him, looking for the bridge that would give him to her. As she'd done to Skjorl, just like he said.

There. There it was. There *he* was.

But he wasn't alone. There was something else. Something immeasurably larger than either of them, and as she tried to touch him, it seemed to wake up and sense her. It turned as though struggling from a deep sleep to bring her into focus.

She backed away. Broke the bridge, but she wasn't quick enough. A knife followed, stabbed into her head, a pain that exploded from her very centre outwards. She screamed.

As fast as it had come, it was gone. Siff was staring at her. His silver eyes blazed and the moonlight snakes were wriggling their way from his fingers.

'What are you?' she gasped. 'Are you him? Are you the Isul Aieha?'

The silver light faded. Siff blinked as his eyes became his own again.

'See, alchemist. I don't know what it is I found in there, but it's bigger than you. It wants to go back. And it doesn't want you in here.'

'Doesn't it scare you?' she asked him.

He hesitated. For a moment she saw the answer in his face. Yes. He was petrified, but the thing, whatever it was, had such a hold on him now that the old Siff was already as good as lost. He smiled at her. 'Why should I be scared, alchemist? You're the one who ought to be afraid.'

'I am,' she said.

He was by her side every moment after that. As the outsiders gathered what they would need, he sat with her to watch. He was the one who brought her food and her water. When she fell asleep, he was sitting beside her; when she woke up, he hadn't moved. If he slept himself, she never saw it, and no one else came near her. She tried talking but he rarely answered. Mostly he seemed to be lost in thought, far far away, but he never missed a movement. All she had to do was lift her hand and he'd be looking at her. His eyes were silver all the time now.

The outsiders brought spears, nets and bows, blankets, ropes – so much that she wondered if they had anything left. Perhaps fifty of them walked with her and Siff through the trees to the river. A few were little more than children, but most were adults, half men, half women. Kataros wondered whether there was anything significant in that, or whether it was simply the hand of chance. The trouble with being an alchemist, as her grand master had once said, was that you couldn't help wondering about things, even things that didn't matter a jot. They worshipped Siff and they were terrified of him too. They did whatever he said, half in awe, half from fear, and she had no idea why. Was it the silver eyes? No, there was more to it than that. They *knew* him. There was history here, but neither Siff nor anyone else would tell her what it was.

There were boats at the river, five of them, sections from branches fallen from of one of the great trees. They'd been sliced in two, hollowed out and sharpened at either end. She might have called them canoes but they were nothing like the little dugouts she'd seen on the upper reaches of the Fury; no, these were huge, wide enough for three to sit abreast. The outsiders divided themselves evenly between the boats. Eight of them in each with paddles, working against the current of the river, while two sat, one at the front, one at the back, with spears and nets. Now and then they swapped places. Whenever they stopped to eat, they dozed, all carefully as far from Kataros as they could be. All the while Siff sat beside her.

And so it went, day after day. The forest never seemed to change. They passed rapids, where the outsiders carried their boats over their heads along the bank. Fallen trees blocked their way upriver, boulders, even sandbanks. In other places the waters were wide and deep, so broad that Kataros wondered if they'd reached a lake. She'd never heard of any lakes in the Raksheh, but that didn't mean much. The great forest was a mystery beyond the fringes where the alchemists gathered its riches.

'Don't you worry about the worms?' she asked Siff one day. No point in asking the other outsiders. They flinched every time she even looked at them. Whatever Siff had said, he was their master now and they revered him every bit as much as they feared her.

'Them again? You and doggy, eh? No such thing.'

'You're wrong,' she told him, but he only looked at her and shrugged.

When Siff wasn't watching, she picked at her fingernails. Keeping them short, for the most part, but keeping them sharp. Claws. The first weapon she'd been born with. Her blood might not touch Siff any more but that wasn't what she was thinking about.

After a week, when she thought he wasn't looking, she scratched herself on the ankle as they were climbing out of the boats one evening and then stumbled and fell into the water. A tiny drop of her washed away.

Worm! Wherever you are, I call you!

The Moonlight Garden

Deep within the wilderness of the Raksheh Forest, over-looking the Yamuna and the Aardish Caves, lies what has come to be called the Moonlight Garden. Myth had long held that the Silver King planned a mausoleum to be 'built in black marble across the great river from the endless caves', an idea that actually originates from the fanciful writings of one of the earliest Taiytakei travellers who visited the Silver City before the time of Narammed. Nevertheless, Speaker Voranin sent dragon-riders to scour the great rivers of the realms for it, and thus the Moonlight Garden was discovered.

The garden is bounded on three sides by marble walls, with the river-facing side left open. The marble appears black but is actually of an unusual colour found nowhere else in the realms – a dark blood-red, veined with mustard yellow. The garden-facing inner sides of the wall are fronted by columned arcades, while the wall is interspersed with small domed buildings that may have been viewing areas or watchtowers. At the far end, away from the river, there are two grand red sandstone buildings that are open to the sides. Their backs parallel the western and eastern walls, and the two buildings are precise mirror images of each other. They were once exquisitely decorated, but they have no interior structure and their function is a mystery.

Later interest moved to the surrounding Aardish

Caves as the most likely location of the Silver King's tomb, before Speaker Vishmir ultimately abandoned the search, and the Moonlight Garden has since been left to return to the forest. The garden is still sometimes visited by riders making use of the temporary eyrie above the caves.

Bellepheros' *Journal of the Realms*, 2nd year of Speaker Hyram

The Black Mausoleum

58

Siff

The Black Mausoleum. He'd never even heard the name until he met the alchemist. The days on the river passed and he couldn't think of anything else. It was calling him. It was calling the thing inside him, the thing he'd taken away from it, calling it back. He didn't know why. When he closed his eyes, all he saw were the waterfalls, the crags of rock either side, the little beach where he'd piled the dead bodies fallen from the dragons, the hole smashed into the ground, the caves, the tunnels, the strange arches, the shimmering silver and the tiny serpent made of moonlight, so much like the ones that came from his fingers. The closer he got, the more he saw it. The gaps were coming thick and fast now, but it was starting not to matter any more. They were becoming the same, the two of them. Most of the time that understanding filled him with a satisfied calm. Sometimes it was a terror worse than death.

He started to see things he remembered. A certain tree by the bank that reminded him of someone whose name he couldn't remember any more. A stone the size of a barn, lodged in the river on the next bend. A cluster of fallen logs all jammed together. And then, around a corner in the river, they were there. Pale cliffs rose from the banks in the distance. If he squinted, he could see the beach where three dragons had once piled bodies while a fourth had stared down at him. The sound of the Yamuna Falls whispered to him over the wind.

'There.' He couldn't help the glee in his voice. He nudged the alchemist. 'There. Do you see it?'

She shook her head. 'I was never here, Siff. Only you.'

'Yes. Only me. The place you called the Moonlight Garden, it looks out over those falls.' He pointed. 'On top of those rocks.

The tomb …' He couldn't finish. His throat was choked. *After so long!* After so long what? He didn't know and he didn't care any more.

'The caves begin underneath the garden. I know that much, Siff. What do you think you're going to find there?'

'I already *know* what I'm going to find there! A gate to another place. The place where your Silver King went.'

'The Isul Aieha was slain, Siff.'

'It's a gate to where he *belongs*!'

'And you're going to open it?'

'*You're* going to open it!' *Ancestors!* There it was, the only reason he'd brought her here, the only reason he needed her, and he'd gone and let it slip out. Now she knew. *Pox!* He clutched his head and clawed at his face. *Why did I tell her that?*

'Where does it go?'

Stupid alchemist! He had to hold himself back from wringing her neck. 'I already told you! It goes to where the Silver King went!'

'How do you know?'

'*I know!*' He screamed it at her, making her wince and screw up her eyes. He took a deep breath. *What's happening to me?*

'I'm sorry,' she said. 'You need me to open it. Then that's what I'll do, if I can.'

Another deep breath. Slowly mastering himself. He blinked a few times, trying to clear his head. 'You will?'

'Yes.' She held out her hands, still bound in front of her. 'It doesn't need to be like this, Siff. That's what I came here to do anyway. I came to find the Silver King. I'll help you either way. It'll be easier if you let me go.'

'Then you'll take it for *yourself*!' he raged. She closed her eyes and shook her head, but she would, he knew that as sure as he knew the sun would rise in the morning. The Silver King. *She* wanted him.

They watched in silence while the cliffs drew nearer. As they paddled towards the beach, Siff jumped to his feet. He waved and shouted and pointed. 'There! There! Take us there!' He'd never felt something like this. Like his chest was about to burst with joy. 'There!'

The canoes changed their course. His heart was beating as though he had a snapper at his back.

'Siff?' He barely heard her. 'Siff, this is the place. Are you sure we can't do this together?'

'Shut up, woman!' He waved her away. *Do this together?* It was his, not hers! She'd take it, take all of it away and leave the rest of them with nothing, because that's what alchemists and riders and all their ilk did. Always.

'Then I'm sorry it couldn't have been different.'

The words washed past him, lost in the draw of the waterfalls. He might not even have noticed if the canoe hadn't bucked a moment later, the nose of it lurching out of the water. Siff staggered and sat down heavily. The man at the front, who'd been spearing fish, turned and looked at them all. His face was white, his eyes wide as plates. His mouth worked, but no sounds came out.

Something hit the canoe from underneath, hard enough that the front flew high up out of the water. Everyone tumbled backwards and the canoe rolled and toppled them into the river. Siff caught a glimpse of a huge shape, as big as the canoes themselves, vanishing under the surface.

'The worm!' someone wailed. 'The worm!'

A few yards away the water seemed to boil and then a great plume erupted, hurling a man into the air. He crashed back into the water, and there was that shape again. It rose, broke the surface and, like a giant maggot, rings of pale flesh ending in a mouth that was nothing more than a hole surrounded by a circle of hook-like teeth, swallowed him whole.

'The bank!' Siff shouted. 'Swim to the bank!' Did they know how to swim, these outsiders? They had boats so he supposed they must, but it didn't look like it.

The worm rose again. It capsized a second canoe, which was paddling towards them as fast as it could. More men spilled into the river, their frantic screams silenced by the water.

No! This couldn't be! The Yamuna worm was a myth! Something the alchemist had made up.

The water frothed again, further away this time. Another man was hurled into the air and then swallowed whole. The last three boats paddled desperately for the shore. 'Me!' he shouted, 'To me!' but they were all too terrified or too deaf, or else the screams and the roar of the nearby falls were too loud. He swam for the shore as best he could, not that he had much idea how to do it, arms grabbing at the water, legs kicking. Born and bred in the mountains with their rivers and lakes, every outsider learned how not to drown. They didn't learn how to outrun a river monster though.

A third canoe went over, battered from behind this time, tipped sideways. Men and women fell out and clung to it, screaming. *Ancestors, were they praying? To whom?* He wanted to scream at them but he was too busy trying not to drown.

He caught a cry as another man tumbled through the air like a broken doll. 'Isul!' Then the worm breached the surface. It reared up and crashed down and the man vanished in the spray. The Silver King! They were calling to the Silver King.

He saw a man's eyes, wild with fear, staring straight at him as the water swirled and sucked him under. 'Isul! Isul!' Him! They meant him! For a moment he was stunned enough to forget that he was about to die. Why? Why were they looking at *him*? He flapped and floundered closer to the shore, but that was no good because that was where the worm was now. He let the current take him instead, carry him away from the slaughter. Screams rang out over the water, over the rumble of the falls. 'Isul! Isul!'

'What?' he screamed back at them. 'What can I do?'

A moment later he realised that he wasn't alone. Someone was in the water ahead of him. Lying on their back, almost drifting.

The alchemist. As soon as he saw her, he knew: *she'd* done this. He thrashed through the water towards her, madness and a volcanic anger driving him on. Her hands were tied. She had no escape. He caught her and grabbed her arm. 'No, you don't do this. You don't do this to me!'

He flailed towards the bank, hauling her with him. She didn't resist but it was hard work and they were far from the beach.

'It won't touch me as long as I have you,' he snarled, as much to make himself believe it as anything.

'You should … have let … me go,' she gasped. Damn her, he was almost minded to push her head under the water and drown her for this. But he needed her. That was the trouble. The rest of them, they might have been his friends, might even have been his family if he let them, but he didn't *need* them. He needed *her*. He was completely certain of that, even though he didn't quite know why.

The screams of the outsiders from the village faded as the river carried him away. And then he saw something. A wave heading through the water towards them, small and fast, a dark shape beneath it. The alchemist had called the worm to her! Madness!

'Let … me go … or I'll kill us both.'

'Crazy witch!' He'd let her go, and then she'd have the worm eat him and she'd be free. No chance.

'I'll let you live,' she cried. 'On my word as … an alchemist.'

He did let go, but only so he could grab her again, this time with an arm around her throat. His head bobbed under the water; he almost let go again as he choked.

'Stop it!' he screamed in her ear. 'Stop it! Stop killing them! If you don't stop, I *will* kill you. We'll all drown together, you blood-mage witch!'

She spluttered something.

'What?'

'Can't!' she managed.

'*Liar!*' Can't what? Make it stop? Breathe? He didn't care any more. His people. She'd called the worm and used it to kill his people. He shifted his arm further around her neck and squeezed as hard as he could, then forced her head beneath the water for good measure. They both went under together. She writhed and squirmed, but she was tied and there wasn't much she could do about it. He had her fast. He couldn't see the worm any more but the water didn't boil. No teeth grabbed him, no sucking maw devoured him.

The alchemist went limp in his arms.

59

Jasaan

It took every ounce of strength after he'd seen the boats on the water, but they did it, Jasaan and his two riders. They walked and they walked, on through the night, no stops for rest. They were at their limit, all of them. Jasaan's ankles were killing him; the riders could barely stand – Parris probably didn't even know what realm he was in any more – but they they got ahead of the boats. And so Jasaan was on the rocks at the top of the waterfall, at the foot of the Moonlight Garden, when the outsiders came, and he watched the canoes round the last bend, one, two, three, four, five of them, with maybe a dozen men in each. Which meant fifty or sixty outsiders against three armoured men at the end of their tether with two bows between them. And, when he counted, exactly thirty-three arrows.

An Adamantine Man didn't retreat just because the odds were bad, but Jasaan thought about it anyway as he watched the canoes come closer. Parris and Nezak were here because they hadn't seen how many they had to face. They were his responsibility, weren't they? They were riders, not Guardsmen. They didn't have a duty to stand and die no matter what.

He wasn't sure he did either. Question was, where else did they go? Or did they sit and watch and see what happened and then spring some sort of ambush. Even then the riders didn't look like they were going to last. The more he looked at them, the more he was amazed that they weren't already dead. And the trouble with *that* was it made him proud they'd all come this way, and *that* made him want them to live all the more.

The middle canoe tipped over, spilling its men into the river. Then another. From beneath one of the men thrashing in the water something massive rose, and a great spout of spray threw him high into the air. When he came down, he vanished, sucked under by a great pale shape.

'Parris! Nezak!'

They could barely move, poor bastards. Parris lurched to the edge of the rocks and stared blankly down, eyes so distant that Jasaan thought he might walk off over the edge without noticing. Nezak, though, *he* was grinning, even through the pain of his hand and his side and his exhausted legs.

'The worm of the Yamuna!'

Three of the canoes were on their sides now. Jasaan eased the bow off Parris' back. Nezak was counting, Jasaan could see it in his eyes. How many men he'd have to face.

'We have bows,' offered Jasaan.

'So do they.'

Jasaan shrugged. The people who lived on the fringes of the realms weren't his concern. The King of the Crags used to catch them and sell them as slaves to the Taiytakei. Everyone knew that. Little people of no consequence to the speaker and the Speaker's Guard. 'Not ones made of dragon bone,' he growled.

The river surged and frothed as another man was hurled into the air and then swallowed whole.

Nezak nodded. 'And we wear dragon-scale.' They stared as a colossal fountain of water erupted below.

The fourth canoe went over about a dozen yards from the shore. Most of its men reached the bank. The fifth canoe beached before the worm could capsize it.

'You think our alchemist was on one of those?'

A pale shape welled up from the river and sucked another man down. From up here, with the waterfall so close, there were no screams, no cries for help, no curses, no monstrous howls. Just the endless roar of water.

'Could be. Could well be.' Sometimes it was kindest to lie. The alchemist had been on the canoe in the middle. But there was only one way to know for sure.

He took Parris by the arm, led him away from the edge, sat him down and drew his sword for him. He had to close Parris' fingers around the hilt to make him hold it. It would be a miracle if he wasn't dead by morning.

'Hold this, rider,' he said. 'You have an important job to do. We'll take the enemy from the flank. You have the centre. You hold, we crush them against you. Understand?'

Parris gave a distant nod. Jasaan clasped his shoulder. 'Good man.' He turned to Nezak. 'You know what I think?' Nezak shook his head. 'I think it's not eating that many of them. I think they're getting to that beach half drowned, terrified and without much idea what's happening. I think if we leave them be, we're going to be facing forty-odd men who are angry and ready to fight. I think if we hit them now, they break and run.'

Nezak looked at him. Then he threw back his head and laughed. 'And if I'm going to end my days in the middle of no-where with no one left to sing my name, better it be in a mad charge for glory than a slow death of poison and disease, hunted and fearful.'

Jasaan seized his arm. 'You'd make a fine Guardsman, rider.' *And which way would I rather go? Quickly sounds better than lingering, but as long as the lingering hasn't come to an end, lingering is still alive.* Best not to give himself the choice. He nodded and started off back down the path. They had to pick their way down the bluffs by the falls. There was a trail of sorts but you needed hands as well as both feet to follow it.

'If we were on the other side of the river, we could have shot them. They couldn't have done anything about it,' said Nezak. It was the sort of thing you said when you knew you were about to get yourself killed doing something stupid.

'Until we ran out of arrows.' They were halfway down. Jasaan wondered how long it would be before someone noticed them. Two armoured men, scrambling among the rocks, in and out of cover, couldn't be that hard to spot.

'They'd have to swim across the water to reach us. We'd cut them down in the shallows.'

'But they wouldn't bother.' Jasaan shook his head. Riders thought like that. Had to face each other in battle somehow. An Adamantine Man thought different. So what if a few men died in a rain of arrows? Adamantine Men did what needed to be done. Didn't matter if none of them came back, and no one ever called them cowards. There was no such thing.

Except him.

He caught himself. Skjorl. He'd forgotten Skjorl. A man like Skjorl would make a difference here. For once he could actually do some good. 'So where are you when we need you, eh?'

'What was that?'

Jasaan shook his head. 'Nothing. We're on the right side of the river, rider. We're on the side that matters.' He jumped the last six feet down. His ankles gave a twinge and then he was at the bottom of the rocks at one end of the beach, all pain forgotten, with enemies ahead of him. The first outsiders were sitting on the riverbank, holding their heads in their hands only a hundred yards away. He started to run, slipping his sword out of its scabbard as he did, a small stabbing cutting weapon perfect for tight spaces. In an open place like the beach he might have chosen his axe, but Nezak had never fought beside an Adamantine Man. Sword was safer.

He ran faster. The first outsiders looked up. They stared, open-mouthed and uncomprehending as he reached them and slashed one across the face, hacking his jaw off. A bad blow – he'd meant to open the man's throat. He caught the next one as the outsider was starting to turn, caught him right across the top of the arm and down to the bone.

The third hurled himself out of the way. Jasaan missed him and kept running. He didn't see if Nezak did any better. Didn't matter. Keep going, that was the thing. Race through them like fire, slashing every one he passed. Didn't dare stab at anyone in case his sword got stuck. The outsiders were mostly on the riverbank now, scattered, but the next group was the big one where the last canoe had beached. They'd seen him coming now. Blood ran down his sword, flecks of it spraying into the air. He felt it on his face, the iron of it in his mouth. There were a dozen men in front of him. They were staring and they didn't know what to do. He screamed at them, a battle roar. *Run away! Turn and run!*

They had spears and sticks and rags. *He* had steel and

dragon-scale. They broke and scattered and he howled with glee and chased after them. *You have to hunt them! Cut them down! The more the better! Before they regroup and come back at you!*

He caught one and brought his sword down, hacking into the man's back, opening him from his shoulder to the base of his spine, not a killing blow but good enough. He'd bleed out, and even if he didn't, he wouldn't be much use for anything.

Next!

They were faster than him though, once they really started to run. They didn't have armour and they didn't have swollen ankles, and most of them scattered into the forest. Jasaan didn't follow into the gloom of the trees. That was their ground, not his.

A man lay on the bank in front of him, still. Drowned most likely. Jasaan ignored him. Charged on. Two more, still hauling themselves out of the river without the first idea what was going on. He slowed. He was running out of breath anyway. Shouldn't have been, not an Adamantine Man, not so quickly, but that was what you got for gods knew how many days of traipsing through this cursed place with the shits, with its flies and its crawling things.

He splashed into the water and drove the sword into the first man's belly. The outsider didn't even see it coming. The second one tried to run, floundering in the shallows. Jasaan stumbled in the mud, hurled himself at the man and they went down together. Jasaan buried his sword in the man's back.

'Jasaan! Jasaan!'

He dragged himself back to his feet. Nezak was a little way behind. He was staggering. Something wasn't right with him.

Flame! There was a man a few dozen yards behind Nezak with a bow, fumbling to string it. The drowned man he'd left for dead. *Vishmir!* He started to run again, back the way he'd come. Nezak was pointing into the forest. Between the trees Jasaan saw a group of men, running. Four of them, and they were looking at him. The tallest had a body slung over his shoulders. A woman. Not one of their own.

For a moment he didn't know what to do. Nezak? The archer? The woman?

'The alchemist!' yelled Nezak. 'The alchemist!' He was still pointing.

'Behind you!' The archer had his bow strung now, had an arrow in his other hand too. *Shit!* They were all too far away and all Jasaan was doing was standing like a lemon tree, dithering. A true Adamantine Man would have gone straight for the alchemist. Let Nezak fall. One Guardsman against four outsiders. He could take those odds. The alchemist was why he was here. Nothing else mattered.

'Move!' The outsider with the bow was drawing it back. Jasaan bolted at Nezak, past him, pushing him sideways, then straight at the archer, screaming. He jinked sideways. The arrow flew past, missed him, and then he was on the man, chopping down with his sword, cutting the bow and the arm that held it and the man behind all at once. The outsider went down in a spray of red. Jasaan looked up into the trees. He couldn't see the alchemist any more but she couldn't have gone far. 'Come on then!'

Nezak didn't move. He was limping badly. 'I can't.'

'Are you hurt?' Jasaan stared, trying to see what was wrong with the rider, where he'd been cut. No blood, no wounds, nothing sticking out of him ...

'I tripped over a branch and twisted my ankle. Now for the love of Vishmir, get the alchemist!'

Downstream were seven or eight outsiders on the beach, bunched up, spears and bows out, moving cautiously closer. Back towards the rocks the beach was empty. 'Can you move at all.'

Nezak limped towards him. A fast walk. Better than nothing.

'Back to the path. As fast as you can. I'll hold them here for a minute.'

'The alchemist!' Nezak shook his head.

'We'll catch her.' No point giving the rider any chance to argue. Jasaan ran down the beach towards the advancing outsiders and then stopped, put away his sword, unslung Parris' bow and nocked an arrow. He aimed carefully and fired as they scattered. The first arrow missed. He took another. A man went down screaming.

No, not a man, a woman. Jasaan froze. Men fought men, not

women. That wasn't right and made him think of Scarsdale, and by the time he shook himself out of it, the outsiders were in the forest and safe. He turned and ran back down the beach towards Nezak and the waterfall and the caves. There were outsiders between him and the falls now, close to the path up the cliffs, the ones he thought he'd chased off into the forest. No, it was worse than that. He could see the alchemist again, draped over a shoulder. These were the ones he'd chased off into the forest *and* those Nezak had pointed out.

He ran as fast as he could. Only Vishmir knew what would happen if they got the alchemist up to the Moonlight Garden. He was supposed to take her back to the Pinnacles, and that was that, but all of this was about something here.

There were outsiders on the beach behind him again now too, the ones he'd sent running, quickly back together, chasing after him. He thought about loosing another arrow or two into the ones ahead, but that risked hitting the alchemist. At least if they were bothering to carry her through the middle of a fight, that meant she was still alive. He caught up with Nezak. Half the outsiders barring the way to the falls turned to face them. The rest went on with the alchemist. Fifty yards or so of flat muddy beach stood between them.

Six men in his way. That was too many. Never mind the dozen or so coming up behind and the rest still scattered along the banks of the river.

'Nezak?' He looked the rider in the eye.

Nezak's face said he knew this was the end. 'What we should have done,' he said, 'was hold the path. In those rocks, with bows, we could have held them until we ran out of arrows.'

Jasaan nodded. He was probably right about that. But Jasaan had counted the arrows and Nezak hadn't.

The outsiders on the beach downstream charged, shouting their heads off. The ones between Jasaan and the falls held their ground. They were shouting too now. Jasaan put away the bow and took out his axe. He felt something let go inside him, all the tension slipping away. For once he felt calm.

'I'll hold them as long as I can.' Nezak's voice was hoarse.

'I will sing your name to my ancestors,' said Jasaan, and he charged towards the cliffs, at the outsiders who stood ready to meet him.

60

Blackscar

The dragon circled high above the Raksheh. Above the caves and the strange thing that lay beneath them. A taste of the old sorcery. A lingering of something mighty. Tastes like those from the sky-home, but faded and pure, not mingled with the bitterness of the broken god and That Which Came First.

The Aardish Caves. The Moonlight Garden. This had been one of their places, long ago. Not one the dragon remembered, but it could feel the presence of its kind. Something waiting. Its time with its silver rider had been so brief yet so full of fire.

Little ones came. It felt their thoughts. And the water worm, blind, dumb and dull, a tiny creature, made at the beginning of the half-gods' path towards their final creations.

Us.

It peered at the little ones. It was hungry. Always hungry.

And then, in among the mindless noise, it saw what it was searching for, faint, half-hidden, as if wrapped in a fading mist.

The one that had killed its mate. The little one had come at last.

It tucked in its wings and fell towards the earth and the tiny little sliver of silver that was the old forest river.

61

Skjorl

He followed the alchemist's trail. When he lost it, he followed the river into the forest. If you knew where someone was going, tracking them wasn't hard, and so he found her again, this time with a whole band of outsiders, walking to a handful of boats on the river. He watched for a while, wondering whether he should kill them all here and now or whether to wait until later. They were many, too many to be sure he'd win. He could see, as he watched, that the shit-eaters meant to take her where she wanted to go.

She'd be safer surrounded by so many. They'd do his work for him. Quicker and easier if he only had to fend for himself.

As the days of following them up the river passed, he began to realise he was following someone else as well. Little signs at first. A footprint in the mud. The freshly cut stump of a branch. Then a fire pit. When he saw the fire pit and saw how it was made, he knew he was following another Adamantine Man. Made him pay attention that, and he watched out for the signs more closely.

Three men. One Guardsman and two others. It was the Guardsman who interested him. He found each one of their camps, stopped and looked it over. There was something familiar about the way they were made. More than just another Adamantine Man. Someone he knew.

Jasaan?

Impossible. They'd gone their separate ways up on the moors, many months and a thousand miles away. Chances of either of them getting back somewhere safe hadn't been good. He'd always assumed Jasaan was dead.

He kept pace with the boats on the river, letting them stay a mile or so ahead but never too far. In the mornings he woke early and ran until he caught sight of them. Then he let them pull away and caught them again in the afternoon. Never close enough to be seen, never so far away that he might lose them if they left the river.

He knew for sure when he caught up with the Adamantine Man and his companions. He watched them unseen. It *was* Jasaan. Of all people. With two riders who were just slowing him down. By the state of them, Jasaan should have abandoned them days ago.

Jasaan. He almost went up and asked him what in the name of Vishmir's cock he was doing out here. But then he saw. When the alchemists had come to the Pinnacles, they'd had Adamantine Men with them. Jasaan must have been one of them. Sent with the alchemist, and now she'd gone missing and so he'd come looking for her. Sort of thing he'd do. The amazing thing was that Jasaan had got back to the Purple Spur in the first place.

Why he had riders with him, now that was another matter. And why were they *still* with him when they were in such a bad way? Skjorl crept close and watched and listened as they talked. The riders seemed to know something about these caves the alchemist wanted to find. They were close too. They'd seen the outsiders on the river and now they meant to get ahead and set an ambush. All well and good if you had half a dozen Adamantine Men armed with bows. A pair of half-dead riders, well, that would be a valiant effort but there were far too many shit-eaters. Jasaan ought to know better.

He kept himself hidden and followed their forced march to the waterfall. He let Jasaan go ahead with his riders, gone from half-dead to well past three quarters by now, and watched them climb. Jasaan would set his ambush along the path among the rocks. Two riders with bows. He'd put them high up to fire down at the shit-eaters as they reached the beach. Then Jasaan would be waiting. He'd take them down one by one as they tried to climb, keeping them from reaching his archers. It was a good place for an ambush and it might even work. A determined handful could hold back a lot of men at a place like this.

Would work even better, Skjorl thought, with a second

Adamantine Man waiting to take the shit-eaters from behind.

When the boats finally came, he watched it all unfold. Waited for the arrows to start but they never did, and then Jasaan was running at six shit-eaters at once while the rider who could barely walk any more was standing to face a round dozen. The rider was going to die – most of the shit-eaters would just go right on past him – and then Jasaan would die too. A perfectly good place for an ambush and Jasaan had pissed it away. Bloody typical, but by then Skjorl was already on his feet, already running.

The shit-eaters weren't in the hurry they ought to have been. Three stopped to take down the rider. The rest raced after Jasaan. Skjorl sprinted. He ran silently up behind one of the three facing the rider and swung Dragon-blooded, cutting his first man clean in two. Left the others for the rider. He screamed now, roared and yelled to make the others look round, to make them see him and quail and pause and run away, but the waterfall was so loud they didn't even hear him. Either that or they thought he was one of their own.

The alchemist and the shit-eaters carrying her were scrambling up the path through the rocks. Jasaan hit the men barring his way like the whip of a dragon's tail, smashing his way between them with sheer force, swinging his axe so that none of them dared go near. Straight through them, but that wasn't enough. They'd cut him down from behind if he tried to climb the rocks. He had to make himself some space.

Or *someone* did.

Jasaan turned. He had a dozen shit-eaters fanned out around him now, watching the whirl of his axe, all too scared to get close. The first one to charge died, that was what Jasaan was telling them. Eventually they might realise that they didn't have to, but Skjorl slammed into them before they'd even got over that first fear. Took a man's head off with one swing, chopped another one in half and then sheared straight through a third man's face before they knew he was there.

'Hello, Jasaan!' The look on his face was something he'd cherish. Bewilderment. Amazement. Joy. Fear. Hate. All thrown in together. He was quite sure he'd never get to see a look like that again. The shit-eaters backed away. He bared his teeth. Two Adamantine Men with axes, side by side, their backs to a wall. No one in their right mind would come close.

'Skjorl?' Jasaan made it sound like a question.

'Been following you for days. Or more rightly I been following this lot.'

Across the beach the rider who could barely walk and the two shit-eaters trying to kill him were still circling each other. It was like watching cripples dance. Pathetic.

'Go!' he bellowed. 'Go and get my alchemist! But you take care of her, Jasaan, or I'll break your balls.'

He jumped away from the rocks, screaming his lungs out at the shit-eaters, scaring the life out of them. If the looks on their faces were anything to go by, he wouldn't even have to touch them with his axe.

Yes. Leave the killing to me.

62

Kataros

She opened her eyes. The roaring that had been the sound of her drowning was still there. The waterfall. She was bobbing up and down, but not in the water any more. She was hanging over some man's shoulder. Looking down from among the rocks beneath the Moonlight Garden. 'You two! Hold here. Stop him. Or at least slow him down.' Siff. 'You! Bring her! Follow me! Run, damn you!'

Siff and the man carrying her climbed higher, over the top of the waterfall, then started picking their way along a ledge over-looking the river. She lurched up and down. Her hands and her feet were still tied. She had no strength, no energy, and struggling seemed futile when all she could do was cough now and then and bring up another mouthful of river water, yet a strange excitement had her. They were here. She couldn't see it, even when she turned her head and tried to look up, but the Moonlight Garden was somewhere above her. No one had ever understood what the Moonlight Garden was. Not the first idea.

Stupid thing to think, really, but it gave her a focus. Stopped her being too sick and helpless and terrified.

At the end of the ledge they were among rocks again, picking their way down a steep slope. She felt the man who was carrying her slip. He was cursing with almost every other step until they reached the bottom and were beside the river again, out in the open on a flat overgrown field. The cave mouths drew her eye.

'They're getting closer!' The man was breathing hard. She was slowing him. And then everything fell into shadow and he screamed. She hit the ground like a sack of turnips, winded and too weak and bruised to move, and that might have been what saved her. A huge shape blotted out the sun and snatched the man who'd been carrying her into the sky; and then the sun was back, and with it a wind like a hurricane that picked her up and threw her across the ground as though she was a leaf.

Dragon. She couldn't bring herself to move. *Stay still. Don't struggle and above all don't run. Dragons can't resist it if you run, and no one who runs ever gets away. Ever.*

Could it feel her thoughts? She wasn't sure. She'd taken her last dose of potion back before the outsider settlement. Two weeks, give or take a couple of days. Yes, it could probably feel her then, and dragons hated alchemists with a fury. She sighed and closed her eyes and waited to die.

'Get up!' Hands were shaking her. Siff. 'Get! Up!' He was cutting the ropes around her feet, wrapping another one around her hands. 'Get up, alchemist! We're nearly there.' He hauled her up, pulling her by her wrists. The dragon was in the air past the waterfall. Turning.

For a moment she caught a glimpse of movement in the rocks up the slope behind her. There was a man, his head and shoulders popping up. He had a bow. Was aiming at ...

Her?

Skjorl?

No. Couldn't be.

'Come *on*!' Siff pulled her hard enough to tear the skin of her wrists. She cried out. The man with the bow was out in the open now, running down the slope towards them, little streams of stones clattering in rivers around him as he came. And yes, it *was* Skjorl. He had his axe. She'd know him anywhere. Great Flame, did she laugh or did she cry? And he had someone else with him too. Another Adamantine Man.

'Run, you stupid witch!' Siff screamed and pulled at her. 'Not from them! From the *dragon*!'

The dragon was coming back. You learned, when you worked with them for as long as she had, to read their flight. It was going for the Adamantine Men. She dropped back to the ground, squealing at the pain in her wrists, but she wasn't going to run. 'No! Stay *still*!' It would burn them if they ran.

The Adamantine Men knew it too. They were fifty yards away,

right at the bottom of the slope at the start of the open empty space that had once been a landing field. They were seconds away from her but now they veered away, diving for cover as the dragon swooped down on them, strafing them with fire. The earth shook, the very air quivered in shock, and then a wall of heat and wind and the stink of scorched earth picked her up and roared and rolled her across the grass.

The dragon turned again and landed where the Adamantine Men had been, hard enough that Kataros was almost thrown up into the air. The rocks on the slope to the path and the Moonlight Garden shuddered and shifted. A boulder the size of a horse tumbled down, bouncing past the dragon and into the river amid a hail of smaller stones.

Halfway up the slope a massive chunk of rock shifted very slightly. It was as big as a barn. Kataros held her breath, waiting for it to slide and bring the whole slope down on all of them, but it only shifted the once and then held still.

The dragon's tail slashed the air, the tip hissing like a whip past her head, so close she could almost touch it. It *had* to feel her, didn't it? *Don't think! Don't think!* But it had its mind elsewhere. The dragon took two quick steps away and lunged towards wherever the Adamantine Men had gone. A hot wind rushed over the ground as it tried to burn them out.

'Can we run *now*?' Siff's eyes were wild. This time she let him pull her away. The dragon was tearing at the hillside, digging after the Adamantine Men at the foot of the high stone bluffs below the Moonlight Garden. It roared. Frustration. Kataros ran faster. Blood. A drop of blood was all she needed. Whatever Siff had inside him, it stopped her from mastering his will, but she could still burn him and there were other things too. If she could find anything that was alive, she could make it hers. Snakes, spiders, scorpions. Snappers even. Let the forest give her a weapon, any weapon …

Siff pulled her in among more tumbled boulders, behind an enormous rock towards an opening in the ground, too regular to be a cave. Her steps faltered. Even in the sunlight she could see how it glowed. It was a tunnel, like the passages, of all places, within the flying castle!

'Move!' Siff hauled at the ropes around her wrists. Kataros winced. Yet the alchemist in her wanted to see now, had to, no matter what happened afterwards.

'It's like the castle,' she said. 'It's the same. Look at it. You didn't know, did you?' There. That made him stop. In the castle he hadn't been himself.

'Is it? I don't remember.'

'What's inside, Siff?'

'Come and see.'

The earth trembled. Siff dragged her deeper. The light here was soft and soothing and came from everywhere, just like in the castle over Farakkan. 'What's inside you, Siff? What did you find?'

He yanked harder, angry. 'When I found this place, I thought it must have been made by alchemists. But you didn't make this, did you? Someone else made it. I didn't know that until your riders brought me to the Pinnacles and I saw that too. You didn't make that either.'

'That was the Silver King's palace.'

'Yes.' The passage went on and on, dead straight, sloping down into the earth. 'And so was this.'

'The Black Mausoleum.' She whispered it to herself, a test to see whether she really believed. Although what else could it be?

But no, alchemists knew *better*. The alchemists, the grand master and a handful of others, they *knew* what had happened to the Silver King. They kept that secret to themselves, but they'd happily tell you there was no Black Mausoleum, no tomb. Treasure, yes, there might be that, and secrets and powers and, yes, even a way to master dragons. But no half-god.

Siff dragged her on. Down and down into the earth, dead straight until the walls and the ceiling fell back and opened up into a dome-shaped chamber, tilted slightly into the earth, far too perfect to have been made by men and so large she could barely see the other side. The walls were smooth as glass like the passages in the flying castle, like parts of the Pinnacles, like the tunnels that had taken her from the Silver City to the edge of the Yamuna. Siff was right. The Silver King had made this.

A ring of arches stood under the centre of the dome. They were ornately carved from the same white stone and they reminded her of the Pinnacles too. There had been arches there just like these but set into the walls. As her eyes grew used to the gloom, she could see little changes in the light in places around the edge of the chamber. Other passages.

'What is this, Siff?'

He ignored her and pulled her towards the arches.

'Where do those tunnels go? Do you know?'

Again no answer. In the middle of the circle of arches sat a flat slab, perfectly round and perfectly white. Siff pulled her towards it, right into the middle. 'Here. See, alchemist!'

He left her standing there and held out his hands. His eyes changed, filling with glowing silver. The tiny snakes of moonlight curled from his ruined fingertips out towards the arches. They reached further and further, strained and pulled at him. As the first one touched the nearest arch, a silver mirror flowed from the edges to fill the space. One archway after another, until his snakes had touched them all and he had made a circle of mirrors all around him; the moonlight snakes shrank back to Siff's fingers, but the mirrors stayed.

'Look!' he said, full of awe and wonder, and Kataros could only feel the same. 'Look!'

He stepped in front of one mirror and reached towards it; the snakes from his fingers leapt forward again and the silver rippled as they dived into it, and then it shimmered and changed. Instead of a mirror Kataros saw a gateway to another place. A place filled with liquid silver, an endless rippling ocean of it with a giant moon above.

'Look!' he cried again. 'Look, alchemist. That is where your Silver King has gone. There! Don't you want to follow him? Don't you want to see what's beyond? Tell me, alchemist. Tell me you want to see!'

Kataros stared. She'd never seen anything like it.

'Yes,' she said. 'I want to see.'

63

Jasaan

Jasaan jumped and raced and hauled himself along the path up through the rocks. There was no turning his head, no looking back. Skjorl would do what he could. If he fell, that wouldn't be a bad thing either. Let him stand long enough for Jasaan to reach the alchemist and then finally fall – more than likely that's exactly what he wanted.

The path climbed up beside the waterfall, went on higher into the bluffs and then vanished to follow the river again. Jasaan passed the place where they'd left Parris to stand guard, out of the way of the fight, or so he'd thought. Parris was gone. When Jasaan glanced over the edge, he saw where. They'd pushed him over. He probably hadn't even lifted his sword.

Back home, outsiders were called shit-eaters because they had to grovel in the dirt for their food. What people forgot was that in the mountains and the forests finding food could be tricky. Turned them into sneaky bastards, born with hunting in their veins. Two of them were hiding behind the next big rock. He felt them more than he saw them as he ran past; when they came out and lunged, he hurled himself forward so their stabs came up short and skittered off his armour. He was already swinging his sword as he turned. What did they have? Spears? Wooden poles with metal tips. He split one in half with his first swing and pressed them back towards the rocks where Parris had fallen. They were terrified, and so they should have been, and when they turned and fled he let them go and ran on up through the stones, along the ledge above the river. At the end of the ledge the path vanished into a steep scree of loose stone and boulders. The out-siders and the alchemist were at the bottom. For a second Jasaan paused. An eyrie? Had there been an eyrie here?

'Nice of you to send two more my way,' said Skjorl behind him. When Jasaan turned to look, there he was, every bit the monster. His armour was spattered in blood. It dripped down the shaft of his axe and over his gauntlets. His eyes were hungry and mad. He pointed. 'And there they are. Give me your bow ...'

His voice trailed off. His eyes weren't looking at the ground any more. They were looking at the sky.

'Oh my. Will you look at that.'

Jasaan turned.

There was a dragon in the sky, diving straight towards them. Something about the way it flew struck him as familiar, as if he'd seen it before.

'You again.' You could hear the grin on Skjorl's face. He nudged Jasaan but was talking to the dragon. 'Remember this one? All the way from Bloodsalt.' He pushed past and started to run down the slope looking for cover. 'Come all this way for me, have you?' he shouted. 'Think you can do better this time?'

Mad. He was mad.

The dragon swooped across the field. Jasaan dived for the steepest part of the slope he could find and a large rock that stuck out of it. He took cover as best he could and peered out. There was nothing else to do. The dragon had either seen him or it hadn't.

It skimmed the ground, wings out wide, a roar of wind, mouth open and filled with fire. It snapped up one outsider and ate him in a single gulp, and its wings powered it up again. Jasaan saw the alchemist and the other outsider thrown across the ground by the wind of its passing. Mouth still wide and full of fire, its eyes were staring straight at him.

No. Not at him. *At Skjorl!* Great Flame! Was this truly the dragon from Bloodsalt? The one that had killed Quiet Vish? Had it really followed Skjorl all the way here, looking for its revenge? That wasn't right! That wasn't what dragons did!

He cringed behind his rock and curled up tight, hiding his face and hands. Fire washed the slopes clean, burning everything that would burn, on and on, a roar wrapped around his head, smothering, drowning him. Its heat crept in through the cracks in his dragon-scale, around his arms, scorching the skin of his face and burning away his hair. And then at last it was gone, and the ground didn't thunder and quiver. It hadn't tried to land, not yet. Just as well – a dragon landing amid the scree would have brought the whole lot down. It would have killed them all. Buried alive or crushed, take your pick.

He looked up, searching for the monster, but he couldn't see it. It must have flown through the gap in the cliffs, over the river and out the other side of the falls. It would be back though. He turned to the field. To the outsider and the alchemist.

They were apart. A chance! He drew the bow off his back. Dragon bone didn't burn. He reached for an arrow ...

The bow had no string any more. Two charred pieces dangled, one at either end, and that was it. He swore in frustration, and now the outsider was by the alchemist again, trying to drag her to her feet. 'Stay still, you idiot!' he shouted, but his words were lost in the roar of the falls.

'Come on!' That was Skjorl, breaking from cover, skittering down the slope, running, sliding. 'Get her before that bastard comes back.'

Fat chance, but he couldn't stay where he was either. Even if the dragon couldn't land on the slope, it could burn him out if it tried hard enough. Or throw boulders – it had already shown that it knew *that* trick – or it could smash at him with its tail or kill him with its claws and jaws. No, couldn't stay where he was.

Down below, the alchemist and the outsider were struggling with each other.

'Come on come *on*!' screamed Skjorl. 'Move, you cripple!'

Jasaan looked behind him. Still no dragon, but it was only a matter of time. It would come between the cliffs and across the river any moment now. Fast. They'd barely have a chance to see it, never mind do anything about it. Down at the bottom of the slope they'd be in the open.

'No, Skjorl! We don't have time!' He was right. This wasn't him being scared, even though he was. Not cowardice this time. Just ... being right.

Skjorl's run faltered as he sensed it too. His head snapped from side to side. He pointed. 'Cave.'

Made sense. That was what they'd come here for, wasn't it? The endless Aardish Caves, which peppered the bluffs here like a honeycomb, so deep and numerous that Vishmir had managed to hide his tomb in one and no one had ever found it. And so had the Silver King, if what the riders had said was right. The frustration was a knife though.

Over his shoulder there was the dragon again, screaming over the river in a turn so vicious it made the air shudder enough to crack trees. Fire lit up the cave, fierce orange, the hot air swirling past him, scorching his hair a second time, stinging his skin, and then a wind picked him up and threw him further in. Dragon-scale armour was at its best when fire came from behind. Adamantine Men weren't stupid.

The ground shook. A slab of stone sheared from the cave wall ahead, shaken loose by the shock of the dragon landing. Jasaan stumbled and skidded to his knees, knocked over by the tremor. As the light of the fire died, he picked himself up again. Skjorl had stopped exactly deep enough inside for the dragon's fire not to reach him.

'Where's your shield?' he asked.

'Back with some snappers. Where's yours?' snapped Jasaan.

'Back in the Pinnacles. Never had a chance to get it. Ankle troubling you again, I see.'

'How's your hand?'

The dragon was out there, blocking the daylight. Jasaan could hear it tearing at the stone at the mouth of the cave as if it could dig them out. The ground shook as it roared and stamped in fury.

Skjorl's voice, when he spoke, was right by Jasaan's ear. 'So, friend, old wounds aside, are you strong from toe to crown.' The ritual of greeting and parting and luck among Guardsmen, but barbed with bile. They both knew what Skjorl thought of him.

Jasaan felt himself tense. 'Yes, I am. And you?'

Skjorl growled. 'Insatiable.'

'So we are strong. Why are you here?'

'I came for the alchemist. And you? You and your riders. Are there any of them left?'

'Did the one on the beach fall?'

'Was still standing when I left.'

'He was the last.'

Light flickered as the dragon backed away to lash at the entrance with its tail. A torrent of stone fell around the mouth of the cave. Skjorl grasped Jasaan on either side of his head. '*Did* you come for the alchemist, Jasaan?'

'Yes.'

'And when the outsider and the dragon are done for, what will you do with her?'

'I will take her home, Skjorl.' He forced himself out of Skjorl's grip and turned to face him. 'Why? What would *you* do with her?'

64

Siff

He stared at the arches, at the liquid mirrors within them, at the silver sea beyond the gate made of moonlight.

Home.

Not his home. Home for whatever was inside him. A seed planted when he'd come this way by chance. A seed growing all the time. He wondered, for a moment, why he'd ever left, why he hadn't stayed here and gone through the gate, and then he remembered. He was looking for something, something that had been missing and now had been found.

He reached for the arch. Its surface felt like he was dipping his fingers into a bowl of warm water. The scene inside rippled.

'There,' he said again, voice soft with wonder. 'That's where your Silver King went. He didn't die. He went home.'

'No.'

'Yes, alchemist.'

'No, Siff. That's not what happened. Siff, listen to me. I'm an alchemist, and there are things known to us. Histories. Perhaps the Silver King built a mausoleum for himself here before he died just as Vishmir did. Perhaps, perhaps not. Perhaps he built many. But he did not come here to die.'

'Look!' Siff waved his hands at the silver mirrors all around them. The snakes from his fingers slithered through the air, touching one after another and, as they did, each mirror changed. In one he was looking at a lake of fire. Another gave him the clouds, broken, looking down on them from above, high over a huge forest. The third opened on to a small dark chamber, round with no exits, but with a mosaic on the floor, half lost to age and three skeletons lying upon it, each clad in bronze mesh armour. Deep underground by the feel of it, although he wasn't sure how he knew. The next showed him a room full of more archways exactly like these, high up at the top of some tower; then a man with a strange gold-handled knife on his hip riding a horse; then another man, riding on the back of a dragon, high above the clouds; then another, a man with one eye and a face half-ruined by the pox. The next opened on to a place of shimmering rainbows and a woman, achingly beautiful with a circlet of gold around her brow.

The one-eyed man and the woman both seemed to notice Siff. He felt them turning their gaze towards him as though sensing his presence, as though they were looking for him, perhaps. The man with one eye smiled.

The snakes snapped away from the mirror and it abruptly became silver and blank once more. The last one he tried was dead. When he touched it, nothing happened, but he felt a warning of some all-destroying void. He let that one go, let even the silver mirror fall and fade. Left the arch the same dead stone as he'd found it

'How do I know these things?' he whispered to himself.

'How do you *do* these things?' whispered the alchemist.

'Look though!' He turned on her. 'The Silver King! Who else could have made them?'

She bowed her head. 'No one, Siff. You have found one of his palaces, of that I have no doubt, but he is not here, only relics of him.'

'No! He *is* here!'

'The Silver King was killed by the blood-mages, Siff. He gave them only a tiny piece of his power, but they became many. They overthrew him and they slew him.'

'No!'

'Yes, Siff. With the magic of the blood that he had taught them, and it cost them almost everything. But they did, and they took his body into the mountains and they used his essence for one great ritual of blood that forever bound the dragons to the potions we had learned to make. The Silver King is gone, Siff. Only his relics remain.'

Blood. Blood! *That* was what he had gone searching for! He

looked at her and smiled. 'No, alchemist. No, you are so very wrong.'

'Look around you, Siff. He's not here. Our only hope is to scour this place for whatever he may have left behind that we might use against the dragons.'

'No.' Blood. *That* was the answer. That was why he hadn't stayed. He needed blood, and not just *any* blood. He needed the blood of someone special. Of the Silver King, except that wasn't possible. But of someone who had touched the Isul Aieha. 'Tell me, alchemist, how the first blood-mages were made.'

'They tasted the moonlight essence of the Silver King. They tasted ...' Her voice petered into nothing.

'His blood.' He smiled. The moonlight snakes withdrew into his fingers. His eyes began to gleam. He crouched down beside her, lifted her chin and made her look into his eyes.

'You,' he whispered. 'He's in you.'

She shook her head.

'Yes. Yes, he is. I've tasted your blood. You gave it to me. You tried to use it against me but instead you roused something. He's in you. A tiny, tiny part of him. Think, alchemist! What is it that makes you what you are?'

'Knowledge,' she said, her voice hoarse, but she couldn't look at him.

She knew! The witch knew! All along! 'You lie.'

'No.'

'Yes!' He threw back his head and laughed, and then clamped a hand around her throat and forced her back until she was lying flat on the stone in the middle of the arches. 'That's what you are, isn't it? All of you alchemists? Pale and ghostly reflections of the Silver King himself. Blood-mages in disguise. *He is in you!* All of you. Every one.' Her hands were tied but not her legs, and she started to struggle hard. He pushed one arm across her throat until she couldn't breathe and held her down with his weight. 'I came here and I found something. No. *It* found *me,* something that had been waiting for centuries. A seed, I think, and now I need your blood to grow. *My* blood, for I am the Isul Aieha and I want it back.'

He pulled out a knife and stabbed her in the neck, cutting deep until her blood spurted in great arcs. Drops of it spattered the arches. Where it touched them, they began to glow.

'Please!' she gasped, although there was no hope for her now. She'd bleed dry in seconds.

'Look, alchemist! Look! Look what you've done!'

One by one the arches shimmered to silver. He felt the power coursing through the vault. *His* power. The Isul Aieha. They would open now, if he asked them.

He waited until the alchemist became still beneath him. Then he got to his feet. He looked at her, almost sad. The flat stone was covered in her blood. It was everywhere. 'Such a shame you couldn't see this,' he said. 'Such a shame.'

He went to the gate that opened to the sea of liquid silver and let his moonlight serpents touch its surface. The sea and its giant moon appeared before him. When he reached to touch it with his hand, there was no resistance, no shimmer. This time the door was open.

Home.

'Such a shame,' he said again.

65

Skjorl

'Yes, Skjorl, what *would* you do with her?'

Outside was a dragon. A dragon that had come for him. Just for him. 'Shut up, Jasaan.'

'No.' In the darkness Skjorl felt hands on his dragon-scale and then he was shoved backwards. He stumbled on the uneven floor and almost fell.

'Vishmir! What are you doing, fool?' Jasaan? *Jasaan* had pushed him?

The dragon roared and bellowed flame, lighting the cave once more. Skjorl saw Jasaan's face. Snarling and determined.

'My, my, look at you. Never thought you'd make it back to Samir's Crossing on your own.'

'Neither did I. But I did.'

Skjorl looked at the dragon again. Rage came off it in waves, washing over him. He soaked it up. Revelled in it. 'I'm right here, monster! Come and get me if you can!' Caves. Men had been hiding in caves since time began. It was wrong. Men should face their monsters out in the open.

The dragon roared again. The flames died and plunged them back into darkness.

'About time you grew a spine,' snarled Skjorl.

'You shit-eater.'

'Vish died at Bloodsalt because you were a coward.'

'Vish died because a dragon threw a rock at him!' Jasaan pointed. '*That* dragon.'

'It should have been you!' Skjorl clenched his fists and pushed Jasaan over. The dragon's rage was coursing through him.

'Again, Skjorl.' Jasaan didn't sound angry at all. Or if he did, it was cold and calculated, not the hot fury of the dragon tearing at the cave mouth. 'If you reach her, what will you do with her?'

Press her face hard into the dirt and show her that no one, no one, *buries an Adamantine Man alive.* 'That's between me and her.' He heard Jasaan moving, getting back to his feet. 'What's it to you?'

'Scarsdale.'

Skjorl threw back his head. If he wasn't so angry he'd have laughed. 'Scarsdale? Liouma? Still?'

'Yes, Liouma. Still.'

'When are you going to get over that, Jasaan. Don't tell me you're sweet on this one too.'

'She's an alchemist.'

'Means nothing. You're soft in the head, you are. Never should have been a Guardsman.'

'I had the same choice as the rest of you. None.'

Skjorl snarled. 'What I mean, Jasaan, is that you should have died instead of someone else. Someone worthy.'

'Oh please, not Vish again!'

'No. You should have died a long time ago.'

The dragon had moved away. Light was coming in from the mouth of the cave again.

'I'm so *sick* of you.' Jasaan hit him.

It was a good punch. Square on the jaw. Skjorl ran his tongue over his teeth. All still there. He grinned. 'Scarsdale, Jasaan. Every bloody time. I took what was due to me by the old law. I did nothing wrong.'

'She begged you to stop!'

'I'm an Adamantine Man, Jasaan, and so are you. We face dragons and we die. I was entitled to have her, you cock! Her or any of the rest of that pathetic bunch of rags we found there.'

Jasaan was on him in a flash, gripping his armour, pressing their faces together. 'You got drunk and you took her, screaming, in front of all of us and all of them, and then you pushed her over to Vish and told him to help himself. You'd had so much wine, you couldn't even pull up your trousers when you were done. She screamed. Begged. Pleaded.'

Skjorl seized Jasaan back, pulled them even closer together until their noses were almost touching. 'So what, Guardsman?

She was mine to have if I wanted her. If you wanted her too, you should have done something about it. Was she nice, Jasaan, was that what you were thinking? Because *nice* has no place in the life of an Adamantine Man.' He broke Jasaan's grip and threw him off. The man was weak, always had been. Was never right for the Guard. 'We are swords. We sate ourselves in flesh and then we move on.'

Jasaan spat on the floor. 'Do you remember what happened after? Do you remember her brother coming at you with a knife.'

Skjorl grinned. 'I remember slitting his throat with it.'

'And then?'

And then? Waking up in a prison. With a stinking hangover.

'You passed out. You fell on top of the man you'd killed, whose sister you'd raped, and started snoring. You're a beast. An animal. A monster.'

Skjorl nodded. All of those things, yes. That was what he was. All those things and proud of every one. He caught a glimpse of something moving fast at the entrance to the cave. He jumped at Jasaan and hurled them both against the far wall. A boulder the size of a man came flying past, bouncing from wall to wall. He laughed and raised a fist to the unseen dragon outside. 'Old trick, dragon! Is that the only one you've got?' He could almost hear it talking to him. Bits and pieces and fragments amid its fury. It would wait for them for as long as it took. It would smash these cliffs apart if it had to. If it could. He turned back to Jasaan and hissed, 'Yes. I'm an Adamantine Man, and I am proud.'

Jasaan shook his head. The dragon was watching them. 'You're the monster, Skjorl. Not them. People like you.'

'You're a Guardsman, Jasaan.' Skjorl threw back his head again. 'A poor example, but you are. We're kin, and I'm your older brother. You should *learn* from me.'

'I have.' Jasaan drew out his sword. 'Oh, I have.'

Skjorl blinked. He started to laugh. 'Are you drawing a blade on me?'

'Yes.'

'You've lost your mind.' He shook his head. 'I'll gut you like a pig. You were never my equal.'

Jasaan shook his head. 'I'll not let you do to this alchemist what you did in Scarsdale. Not again.'

'As if I could.' Skjorl bellowed with laughter, because what did Jasaan know? What did he know about alchemists and what she'd done to him? 'I'll fight you, Jasaan, if you so want to die in such an easy way. If you can't find the courage to meet a proper end. That!' He pointed to the mouth of the cave. 'That's what you should draw a blade for! There is your monster.' Fury and rage crackled through the air. Made him want to get on with murdering Jasaan just for something to do. He drew his own sword. 'But if that's what you want, if you don't have the balls to face a dragon then so be it!'

'I'm facing something worse.' Jasaan roared and hurled himself forward. Skjorl caught the blade against his own and pressed close, both swords squeezed between them.

'I don't want to kill you, little man. You're not worth it. I want to kill the dragon.'

'And you think that gives you the right to take whatever you want?'

'Yes!' Skjorl snarled and threw Jasaan to the ground. 'Yes I do!' He put away his sword and unslung his axe, his lover and mistress, Dragon-blooded. Towered over Jasaan with it. Watched him lying there, sword in his hand still, quivering and afraid of death. 'Yes, Jasaan,' he roared. 'By the laws of Narammed, yes, it gives me the right!' He brought the axe down. Jasaan rolled away, quick as an Adamantine Man should be. Skjorl howled and swung again. 'Don't you feel it? Don't you feel the dragon rage? The power? The glory?'

'No!' Jasaan rolled back to his feet, the axe missing him by a whisker. He ducked inside Skjorl's swing and lunged in the gloom. Hard and fast, straight into Skjorl's ribs. Skjorl grunted and stumbled back. For a moment they stood apart. Skjorl looked down at himself. Jasaan stared.

Skjorl was wearing dragon-scale. Battle armour. He laughed. 'A soft poke from a short sword? You'll have to do better than that, little man.' He swung the axe, weaving patterns in the air with the blade, stepping towards Jasaan, backing him towards the dragon at the mouth of the cave, the dragon whose rage was like a song in his head, fierce and terrible and beautiful all at once. 'Your axe, Jasaan. You need an axe to pierce a dragon's hide.'

'You're just a man.' Jasaan stumbled away. 'That's all you are.'

'No. I am the dragon and the dragon is me. Do you not feel its rage, Jasaan? Can you not feel its hunger?'

'No, Skjorl. All I see is you.'

Skjorl bared his teeth. 'You don't feel the burn of its desire? How much it wants us?'

'No. Just you.'

He let the axe slow. 'You don't feel it at all?'

'No.'

'You've taken the potion of the alchemists?'

'Yes.'

Skjorl stopped. He let his axe drop as a sudden glorious new possibility rose before him. He put Dragon-blooded back over his shoulder and smiled. 'Then if you can't feel the dragon, the dragon can't feel you. It knows you're here but it can't find you.' The smile grew. Here at last was an ending of glory, one for both of them. 'Then I've got a better death for you, Jasaan. You can stop being a fool and do what an Adamantine Man would do.' It only needed one of them to escape, after all.

Skjorl pushed Jasaan away and started to run towards the mouth of the cave – towards the dragon. As he drew close, the dragon drew back its head. He saw its mouth open and the fire build within. He ran faster. Roared a battle scream and let the dragon's anger devour him. 'You and me, dragon. Just you and me!'

When he'd carved and smashed his way out of the prison they'd made for him in Scarsdale he'd hunted them down, the ragged folk who'd made a home for themselves in the mines. Hunted them down and killed them, every last one. Man, woman and child. Killed them and skinned them. Being locked in a cell had left him hungry.

'I am Skjorl!' he bellowed as the fire rushed to meet him. 'And I kill dragons!'

66

Kataros

She was everywhere. Felt everywhere. Spattered around the dome.

With exquisite care she opened her eyes. Care in case Siff was looking, but of course he wasn't. He thought she was dead because he was stupid. Because he'd forgotten, as he took her blood, that she was an alchemist, which was little more than being a blood-mage dressed up in some pretty morals, and a blood-mage never bled out unless they wanted to, not even if you opened their throat from ear to ear.

He was standing by the gate, lost in his own world full of wonder. She watched through half-closed eyes and found she couldn't blame him because the wonder was hers too. Other worlds. Was that really what he'd found? Was this where the Silver King had gone? No, she knew better than that, but perhaps it was how he'd come to the realms in the beginning. Or perhaps there were others. The realms remembered the Isul Aieha who'd tamed their monsters, but there were whispers, if you looked deep in their histories of that time, of others. Of an age lost even further in the past, when the dragons had been young, of silver half-gods who strode the world in their thousands.

She looked at the silver sea. Had they come from this place? Was this where they'd been born?

Her blood was spattered over the arches. She'd lost a lot. Almost too much, and the stones were drawing their power from her now, from her essence. She explored them but they were beyond her comprehension. Artefacts of another time. They needed her, just a tiny little bit of her, to function. She could take that away from them, close them. Past that they were a mystery.

'Everything is wrong,' whispered Siff to the emptiness. 'The

Great Flame? No. This. *This*.' He sobbed, overwhelmed, and maybe he was right.

With exquisite caution Siff reached one foot through the gateway. His boot touched the silver beyond. He gasped.

His boot had her blood on it. She reached through it to touch the silver sea with her mind. To see.

And so she saw.

67

Skjorl

The fire came. Skjorl threw up his arms to shield his face. Flames licked past them, around his gauntlets, searing the skin off his cheeks, burning them to the bone. They crept past the rim of his helm, under and around, burning his hair and scorching his ears. The pain was immense, but the rage was stronger. He ran faster. The heat found its way through the joints and cracks of his armour. His wrists were the first to feel it, facing the fire head on. His elbows next.

And then it stopped.

He pulled his hands away. The dragon was right in front of him, head down on the ground, staring at him, eyes gleaming with hate, jaws open and ready for him. He kept straight at it, as if he meant to run right down its throat. Pulled Dragon-blooded down from his shoulder. Swung.

Straight into the side of the dragon's jaw. Used the force of the swing to push himself sideways. Careened off the dragon's teeth and past its head. Pulled Dragon-blooded back out as he went.

The head reared up. The dragon took a step back. Skjorl ran on underneath. Dragons could run, and fast, but not backwards. Backwards they were clumsy. He ran between its forelegs as it lifted off the ground. Felt the bulk of the monster rising away from him. Shot between its back legs and then stopped. Turned. Changed direction as the dragon started to move. As it took a step and slashed its tail across the ground where he would have been if he'd kept straight.

'Stupid monster!' he screamed at it. 'You're too slow! Too clumsy.' He swung Dragon-blooded into one of its legs as hard as he could. Felt her bite through the scales. Saw blood. A tiny wound for a monster like this, but he'd blooded it and his axe had earned her name yet again.

It tried to stamp on him but he was too quick for that. Claws as big as he was smashed into the ground, shaking the earth, but as they came down he was already in the air, leaping and swinging again. Another scratch. More of the dragon's blood oozing out from under its scales. The monster roared. Not pain. Frustration.

'Fly, you bastard! You won't catch me down here! I'm too quick for you!'

He could almost hear the dragon's thoughts. Overwhelming. The urge to crush, to devour, to burn! It turned away from the cave, faced towards the landing field and reared up, peering down between its legs. Murderous eyes as large as a man's head glared and then it opened its jaws. Skjorl ducked behind the dragon's own claws as the fire poured out once more.

'Stupid monster!' he screamed, though his voice was lost in the roar of flames. 'You can't burn me! I'm wearing another dragon's skin!' The pain was blinding, the bits of his face he couldn't quite shield. 'Go on! Run! Fly! Take me from the air and crush me if you can! Fly, you bastard!'

It was as though the dragon heard him even over the noise. Its head turned away. It dropped to all fours and started to run, launching itself across the field. Skjorl hurled himself away and dived flat as it lashed with its tail. The alchemist's potions were still having some last effect. It knew he was there, it could sense the wash of his feelings, but it couldn't quite pin him down. Neither in thought nor in flesh.

And that was how he was going to win.

He turned and ran even before he heard the air shudder as the monster hauled itself off the ground. He wouldn't have long. As much time as it took for a dragon to build the speed it needed to turn. He raced away from the cave and back to the slope of scree and boulders and threw himself up it as fast as he could climb, all care thrown aside. There were rocks up there as large as houses all tumbled on top of one another. One of them, halfway up the slope, was as big as a barn. Plenty of space to hide round the back if he could reach it.

He risked a glance behind as he reached the base of it. The dragon was already turning. He could feel its desire, its single-minded purpose, bright and vengeful.

Kill! You!

He scrambled up the stones beside the rock. Bloody scree – every lunge up he slipped half a step back and he didn't have any time, didn't have any …

He looked back again. The dragon was coming straight at him. He wasn't going to make it to the top.

Vishmir! There wasn't even any cover.

But it might still work, if the dragon was furious enough. Might.

He cringed as it came, pressed himself against the rock, as tight against it as he could, and started to count in his head. Counting down the seconds to when the dragon would hit him and crush him into the stones.

Five. Four. He turned away, hiding his face, showing the armour of his back to the wall of fire hurtling towards him. Three.

The fire came and this time there was no escape from it. It scoured the stones. Two.

Scoured his face. Found every gap and crack in his armour. One.

He screamed, the pain tearing him to pieces as though someone was hacking the skin off his face with a thousand rusty knives.

The fire stopped. He gasped for breath. Still alive. The dragon hadn't crashed into the stones to crush him, so it was still in the air. He threw himself flat on the ground, as low as he could get. The touch of the stones pressed into his ruined face was agony.

The dragon's tail smashed into the barn-sized rock right above his head, hard enough to shake the whole slope. He felt it shift under the blow, felt the ground under him tremble. Loose stones jumped into the air around him. Dust choked his lungs. He started to slide. Gravel showered his back and pieces of scree rolled past him. He dug his toes in and the slide slowly stopped. He forced himself to his feet. The pain was almost overwhelming. He clenched his teeth and screamed, pulling himself up the slope.

'I. Am. Adamantine!'

His sight wasn't quite right. One of his eyes wasn't working. He didn't dare touch his face to see why. Too much skin had been burned away. Maybe he'd lost the eye too, or maybe there was simply a speck of dust in there. Couldn't see right. Didn't matter. Not now.

He hauled himself along the side of the boulder. At least his arms and legs were still strong. The dragon was in the air, circling over the old landing field, wings flapping with a ferocious wind that tore at the nearby trees. Beneath, he could make out a blurred shape running across the field, almost at the other side.

Jasaan. That was the first part done then.

He turned back. Sank his fingers into whatever nooks and crevices he could find and gave no mind to how his muscles screamed. Nothing could hurt as much as having the skin burned off his face. He reached the top. The dragon was flying at him, straight and level.

'Come on, dragon! I've already won! I've beaten you! There were two of us! The other one's away and you'll never find him! Do your worst!' He pulled Dragon-blooded off his back and held it over his head. A challenge. 'Come on, dragon! Eat me if you can!'

He closed his eyes and waited to die. The dragon would pluck him off his rock with its claws. Ruled by its fury, it would crush him between its jaws and devour him. Him and the dragon poison that was soaked into his clothes, that was stitched into his armour, that ran in his veins, that was tattooed under his skin, that he carried in every possible way, every hour of every day, so that even in death he could be what Adamantine Men were for.

We kill dragons!

The earth shook. He felt the stone beneath his feet shift again, slipping ever so slightly. The claw didn't come. When he opened his eyes, the dragon had landed. It was at the bottom, close to the mouth of the cave where he and Jasaan had hidden. It walked slowly to the base of the scree, eyeing him all the way, and then rose on its hind legs, balancing itself, stretching out its wings and its tail as far as they would go, blotting out the field and the river and the forest beyond so there was almost nothing else for Skjorl to see but dragon. It was immense. Magnificent. Its head reached as high as Skjorl on his rock, fifty, sixty feet above the ground where it stood. It stared at him.

You. Kill. Dragons.

Talking in his head. Thoughts all muffled and hard to hear, forced so hard through the remains of the potion Kataros had made that they came out mangled. But forced them through it had. If it could do that, it could hear what he was thinking. And he'd been thinking about the poison.

He'd given himself away.

Yes. The dragon cocked his head. They always looked the same to Skjorl. Hungry and angry. If they had any other expression, he'd never learned to read it. What was the point?

Nowhere. To. Go.

He knew what it wanted. It wanted him to be afraid. That was what they craved, more than anything. The chase, the bursts of fear, of terror, of despair. He'd seen them enough to know what gave them pleasure. And so he laughed, because there'd be none of that here. He was going to die the way he was supposed to. In battle with a dragon. He couldn't have been happier; if only it didn't hurt so much. Had to fight the pain back. Almost unbearable. Getting worse. Only way to fight that was with rage and glory and lust for the fight. He clenched his axe, the mistress who'd stood at his side since Outwatch and before, and roared, 'I'm here, dragon! Eat me! Come on, eat me if you can! I'll break your teeth and burn your guts. You'll be so sick you'll never forget.'

The dragon's face didn't change.

No.

It couldn't reach him. He hadn't seen that at first, but he saw it now. He was too high up the slope for it to grasp with its foreclaws. The slope was too shallow for it to lean forward and snatch him with its teeth without losing its balance, too steep for it to climb without bringing the whole hillside down.

He took off his helm and threw it away. 'Burn me then!'

The dragon shifted and flapped its wings hard. Wind blasted

up the slope, would have torn at Skjorl's hair if he'd had any left.

I. Will. Crush. You.

Because fire was too easy. Fire was quick and gave little to savour. Fire took a living man and turned him to ash if he had no dragon-scale to shield himself. Fire took something and made it nothing, just like that. In a flash. No lingering, nothing to relish. Taking a man between your claws, though, holding him high up in the air, letting him feel the strength that could snap him at any moment, letting him truly know how puny, how helpless, how insignificant he was, letting that sink right down into his bones, *that* was the way. No will could survive that. You snapped his spirit and then you snapped his spine.

Skjorl didn't move. He understood. They were the same, the two of them. He laughed again. 'You can try, dragon. You can try.'

Anger pulsed from the monster, overwhelming anger. It bared its teeth at him. As if that was going to make any difference now. Skjorl bared his own back.

'Better be quick. Before I die of laughing at you.'

It shuddered. Reached forward with its head but then withdrew, flapping its wings. Skjorl took a few steps back. The dragon could burn him any time it wanted, but that would be a defeat now. Throwing his helm away had done that. It *had* to hold him in its claws.

It took a tentative step onto the slope. Skjorl couldn't see, but he heard the stone move below, felt his own boulder tremble. The dragon lurched and stepped back again.

He was laughing. Laughter and pain, the drowning pain that had tears streaming down his cheeks, what was left of them, and each tear stung like a hot knife drawn down his face. 'You can't,' he screamed. 'You can't win! You can't possibly win!' He wasn't even goading it any more.

The dragon tried the slope a second time and again the boulder trembled. It let out a shriek of fury and frustration, quivered, threw back its head, hurled a torrent of fire into the sky and then stared at Skjorl once more.

Crush! You!

It was up on tiptoe, wings stretched out wide again for balance. Teetering towards him, lost to the need to smash him. It withdrew a fraction and then it lunged.

Skjorl jumped away. Its head hit the boulder where he'd been standing, a yard short. He gave it a long cold stare. It looked ... It looked almost comical.

'The trouble with your kind,' he said, as he lifted his axe high over his head, 'is that you are so *stupid*.'

It flapped its wings furiously, trying to draw away from the slope. It pushed its head against the boulder to lever itself off. Dragons had good necks. Strong. Full of muscle. It drove itself away from Skjorl's axe.

But Skjorl wasn't bringing the axe down, had never planned to. He jumped away. Sideways. Off the boulder.

The dragon finished heaving itself back, pushing its weight into the slope as it wrenched itself away. Into the boulder Skjorl had been standing on. And as it did, the boulder tipped and began to slide, and with it came half the hillside, backed up behind it, enough loose rock and stone to build a castle. Skjorl ran, but the tumbling stones swept his feet away as easily as a child plucking a blade of grass. At the last he jumped, as high in the air as he could, trying to get away from the worst. No use. The stones under his feet were rolling over each other and he might as well have tried to walk on water. A rock flew at him, pitched from higher up, as big as he was. It caught him a glancing blow, spun him around and knocked him down. No chance to get up again. All he could do was curl up, wrap his arms around his ruined face and trust to his armour and his ancestors to protect him as stones rained over him.

Something hit him in the hip, hard. Another blow to the head. The next was on his ankle, smashed. Then another round the head, and then, for a time, merciful darkness.

Light. That was all he could see when he opened the one eye that still worked. Light. There wasn't any pain any more. Numb. Everything. Couldn't feel his hands, couldn't feel his legs, couldn't feel anything.

Couldn't move.

He blinked. He could still do that.

The light slowly separated into shades. Bright sky. Dark earth. Stones everywhere. Littered across the end of the field. And a dragon, darker still.

Lying on the ground ahead of him. Head turned. Looking at him.

Pain. He felt it now, but not his. Pain and a fading futile fury.

One broken wing. One broken leg. Half buried in the fallen rubble, neck crushed by the stone that had been holding up the mountain.

The dragon. Lying beside him, a little way away.

It stared at him.

I will come back. You will not. And then the light slowly went out of its eyes. Skjorl tried to laugh. His lungs shook. Not much else.

He stopped breathing. Took a moment to notice. It was as though he'd simply forgotten how.

Vish, you better have kept a woman and good bottle of something strong ready and waiting for me.

He winked at the dead dragon. 'Got you both.'

I'm coming, Vish.

The shades merged together again. The light faded.

Was gone.

68

Jasaan and Kataros

As soon as the dragon took to the air, Jasaan ran. Head-down sprint, straight across the open towards the place he'd seen the alchemist. The outsider had been dragging her somewhere and he'd had a purpose about him. Neither of the Adamantine Men had seen where he was taking her but it had to be more than just the nearest piece of cover.

He reached the other side of the landing field and glanced up. The dragon had already turned. It was almost straight above him now but hadn't seen him. Or if it had, it had other things on its mind. He saw where the alchemist must be. A hole in the ground, a cave, maybe the sheared end of an old tunnel down among the shattered stones at the edge of the field.

Instinct made him dive to the ground and cower as the dragon roared back towards the slope where Skjorl had gone. Small stones rattled across the ground, whipped up by the wind of the dragon's wings, and then it was past.

The cave. He jumped up. But he had to look back, for a moment at least. He saw the dragon's fire blossom and burst, scattering across the rocks.

'Goodbye, Skjorl,' he muttered.

No time to stay and watch what the dragon did next. Dragons weren't stupid. It knew they'd been two when it had found them, and he wasn't about to do anything to remind it.

He ran for the cave, for the tunnel, the whatever it was. No time to think about Skjorl. The world was a better place for being rid of him, but of course he had to go out like that. Had to make himself the hero. If Jasaan ever got the alchemist back to the Pinnacles or the Purple Spur or wherever it was that she wanted to go, if ever anyone asked him to tell their tale, then he'd tell it as it was, and every Adamantine Man would raise a cup to the dragon-killer, the one who'd given his life so that others might live and fight, and never mind the rest. Rapist. Murderer. Drunk. None of that mattered if you died well. They'd all raise their cups and they'd call him a hero, and if Jasaan quietly didn't raise his, well then most likely the rest of them would quietly not notice.

He ran down the tunnel. The place had been built by alchemists, that was obvious. Their eerie cold white light came from the walls, from the roof and floor. It reminded him of the Pinnacles rather than the curved caverns of the Spur, scoured by water. No, this was the work of . . .

He didn't know. Magic? It was supposed to be the Silver King's tomb, after all.

The tunnel took him into a vault, smooth curved walls coming together far above him. In the middle, a ring of white stone arches with gleaming mirrors between them lit up the walls.

'Alchemist! Kataros!' He couldn't see inside the circle but she he had to be there, didn't she?

He drew his sword. Being cautious hadn't ever done him any harm, not yet, even if Skjorl had despised him for it. Best to have a care. Best to have a think about the sort of things a man might find in a place like this.

What did tombs have in them apart from bodies? Try again. *What sort of person got his body stuffed into a tomb?* Dragon-riders were fed to their dragons when they died. Adamantine Men too. Across the realms a man was burned and his ashes scattered either in the nearest river, if you were lucky enough to live near one, or cast into the desert winds if you came from the north. Some folk who lived along the Fury sent their dead off in boats. That was all before the Adamantine Palace had burned. Now mostly people just got burned or eaten, whether they were dead or whether they weren't. But buried under the ground? That was wrong. That trapped a man, kept him from joining his ancestors.

As he thought, Jasaan continued walking towards the circle. *So what would you find in the tomb of an ancient half-god sorcerer?* He had no idea. Nothing good, probably. No one would choose to rest in a place like this, not under the ground. So what, then?

You put a sorcerer in the ground because you could, and then you wrapped him up in blood-magic to keep him there and make sure he couldn't come back. You did that because you were scared witless that if you did anything else, whatever it was you were trying to bury might claw its way out and rip your head off. You did that because what you were burying was a terrible, terrible thing.

He stopped. Skjorl was at his shoulder. His ghost, anyway. *For the love of Vishmir, shut up, stop thinking, start moving and be what you are!*

He reached the arches. Between them a silver surface shimmered, blocking his way into the centre circle. They were too high to climb and nothing in the world would have made him touch them. He began to walk around instead. He could hear noises now from inside. A faint sobbing. He couldn't tell if it was a man or a woman. When he looked down, he saw dark drops on the floor. He knelt and peered at them. Licked his finger, rubbed it against them, tasted it.

Blood. A spray of blood. Two things did that. You cut a man in the neck or in some other places and the blood would spray on its own. Or you sliced deep into a man's flesh and then it was your own blade that did the spraying. Either way, whoever the blood came from usually wound up dead. But was it the alchemist or was it the outsider?

Couldn't see the alchemist swinging a sword. Or cutting a throat for that matter.

Flame!

Unless the outsider had brought her here and they'd found something waiting for them. He wasn't sure that was much better.

The sobbing was still there. He thought he heard a whisper. *It's beautiful.*

She was lost. When a mage reached through their blood to touch another mind, there was always a danger. To touch the mind of another mage, that was the fear, one who was stronger than you. She'd done that with her teacher and he'd shown her how to defend herself, how to run away, break the link, hide within yourself, throw up walls and barriers that even the strongest mage could never break. She'd touched his mind and felt his strength; she'd done as he had shown her and in the end seen how she could save herself. She'd seen him attack her with everything he had and not even strain her mastery of herself.

The silver sea consumed her as though she was nothing. Even if she'd had the time to try and hide herself, it would have washed her walls away like a tidal wave against a sandcastle. She had no idea what it was. Something immense. Vast. Something that would always be beyond her understanding, no matter how much she learned. In a blink it looked at her, took her in, absorbed her. She felt its size and its age and its utter indifference. Her own insignificance. And then she realised that yes, she did know what it was. She knew exactly.

The Silver King. It had to be. Whatever old crippled Jeiros had said, there was nothing else this *could* be.

'It's beautiful,' whispered Siff.

It was waiting there. Waiting for what, though?

Help us! she thought as loudly as she could, simply hoping to be noticed. *We need you again!*

She saw Siff start. He turned slowly to look at her.

'You?' He shook himself. She understood. Trying to shake away the presence all around them both. Trying to bring himself back to the simple world of stone and flesh.

'Siff,' she breathed. 'Look at it.'

His face twisted into a snarl. 'You! You want to *steal* it.' His hands clenched. He held out the knife towards her. 'No no no, witch, this is mine, not yours. Mine!'

'And all the blood around your feet is mine,' she whispered. She had no strength in her arms any more, nor her voice. She'd lost too much blood to him, but that gave her another strength. 'I am sorry, Siff.'

On the ground around him her blood started to flow – rising, soaking into one of his boots, climbing higher, past his ankle, up his leg. It touched his flesh and burned and he screamed. He bared his teeth and his eyes flared with silver. 'I have told you before, blood-witch, you cannot *do* that!'

Jasaan walked cautiously around the outside of the arches. The sobbing stopped. Voices. He froze.

'You?' A man. The outsider?

'Siff. Look at it.' A woman's voice full of wonder, not fear. Full of ... full of awe. Kataros. The alchemist. Alive.

So whose was the blood?

Then the first voice came again, suffused with anger and envy and murder – 'Mine, not yours!' – and Jasaan moved again, faster now, around the arches, looking for a way in until he saw the single one that was open, that wasn't filled with liquid silver.

In the centre, lying on a slab of stone in a pool of blood, deathly pale, lay the alchemist. Her breath came fast and shallow. Across from her, halfway through one of the far arches, the outsider stood with knife raised. His eyes shone with silver. His lips were drawn back and his teeth were bared. Blood was everywhere.

Jasaan blinked. The blood around the outsider's feet ... it was *moving*!

Sorcery. A woman lying on a stone slab, a man standing over her with a knife raised. That was all he needed. All any Adamantine Man would need. He knew exactly what to do. He raised his sword. The battle cry came of its own accord. He was already in the air, half the ground covered between them, before the outsider even saw he was there.

The alchemist gasped something, so faint he didn't hear. The outsider turned and raised his hands. While the blood on the floor flowed up one of his legs, silver flowed up the other, fast as lightning, drawn from the silver lake. Up his leg and up his side, across his shoulder, down his arm and just as Jasaan's sword should have cut him in two, he had a sword of his own, silver, blocking Jasaan's blade, and half of him was cased in armour.

The swords came together and Jasaan's steel shattered. Shards of it flew. A sliver sliced his cheek. Pieces hit his armour and ricocheted away. The outsider screamed and reeled back. Where the silver didn't cover him, pieces of Jasaan's blade had cut him open.

Jasaan stared at the stump of his sword. Impossible. Swords didn't shatter. Not like that, like glass.

The outsider swayed, off balance. The light in his eyes grew brighter. They turned on Jasaan, a terrible power lurking within them. The alchemist groaned something again. No time to get out his axe. The stump of his sword would do. He lifted it as if to plunge it into the outsider, who raised his arms to fend off the blow as the silver flowed around him again; then Jasaan kicked him instead, hard in the ribs, where a shard from the shattered blade had already embedded itself in his flesh.

The outsider threw back his head. He shrieked and fell back into the silver sea behind him. The liquid flowed over him and covered him from head to toe, but only for a moment, and then he began to rise once more.

'No,' she croaked. She thought the man with the sword was Skjorl at first, but this one was too short, too small. Still, when she reached through the blood to touch him, she knew at once that he'd tasted hers. For a moment that threw her. She looked for Skjorl and found nothing, yet this man . . .

Jasaan? From the Spur?

Silver flowed from the sea beyond the gate and shattered the Adamantine Man's sword. Slivers of steel flew like arrows among the arches.

'No!' She tried again. 'Don't! Leave him be!' This was *her* battle, by the Flame! And if Siff went right through the gate, who was to say what might come back. 'Jasaan! Don't!'

Jasaan landed a kick and Siff tumbled through. She didn't dare reach through her blood to try and touch him again, not now. Whatever was inside him that had thrown her away before, it was growing fully awake. She just about found enough strength to sit up. At least now she could see properly. See the silver sea wrapping itself around the outsider, clothing him. She could see him for what he was. The Isul Aieha. The Silver King.

'Jasaan!' The Adamantine Man was standing before the gate, panting, still holding the stump of his sword. One by one around them the arches flickered and failed, their mirrors falling black and dead and then fading into nothing until each was just an arch again with no sign of any magic to it, all except the one beyond which Siff stood.

Kataros called her blood, what was left of it, called it back to her to feed her own strength. Siff was covered in silver now. It had grown into an armour around him, hard plates in layers and layers, exquisite and complex, and he held two swords, short and curved, one in each hand. There were pictures, in the Palace of Alchemy, of this man. Drawn five hundred years ago. Exactly the same.

'Isul Aieha,' she said softly.

No answer.

'They killed you. They took your body to the mountains. To some distant cave. Yet you are here.'

He pointed one of his swords. History crashed into her. She was him, the Silver King. She saw herself call the dragons to her. Saw herself tame them with a single word. She ruled over men but they were nothing to her. A distraction. She was looking, looking for something, always. Something about the spear she carried and a great and terrible thing that had been done. For a long time, looking but never finding, and all the while a despair was building inside her and a loneliness, until she could bear it no more. She saw herself come to this place and conjure these arches, and as she did it she saw a glimpse of her future, of the end that awaited her, and so she left a seed behind, surely a needless precaution – when she chose to leave and return to her home and her kin there was nothing that mere men could do to stop her – but one taken nonetheless. And then they turned on her and somehow they won. She saw men, blood-mages, the ancestors of the alchemists, tear her apart and take her body to the mountains, to some distant cave and hold her caught at the edge of life and death. They drank her in tiny drops, not the blood of her veins, but the silver god-blood, and in doing so they each took a morsel of her power. They kept her that way, trapped, for decades and centuries, and all the time her seed was waiting. Waiting for a host and a way to go home.

She would not forget. She would not forgive but nor would there be vengeance. Home called her. Her people. Peace.

The Silver King lowered his sword and turned away.

'No!' Kataros struggled to her feet. She had almost to claw her way up the Adamantine Man to get up. 'Don't! Don't leave us! We need ...'

The silver sea became a silver mirror. Faded to black and died.

'You.' She began to sob. Her own blood was still all over the arch. She reached through it, trying to open the way again, but there was nothing. Dead stone, that was all it was now. It wanted more than a mere alchemist.

Epilogue

Jasaan

He didn't know what to do with her at first. Blood everywhere, one alchemist weeping and sobbing for the man who'd tried to kill her – as best he could tell. She didn't want him, didn't want to go, that much was obvious. For a while he left her to it, left her to do whatever it was that alchemists did, and went and had a bit of a look around, but there wasn't much else to see. More tunnels. He wasn't sure he fancied those.

She would need water. Water and red meat, that was what you gave people who'd lost a lot of blood, not that he was any sort of expert. There was water in the river, that was easy enough. And as for red meat, there were plenty of dead men out there. He'd eaten the flesh of his own before. Maybe he'd not mention to the alchemist exactly where it came from. He frowned, trying to re-member. Was there something about alchemists not eating the dead?

The trouble with going outside was the dragon. With a bit of luck it had done for whatever outsiders had survived – if it hadn't eaten them, they'd surely have had the sense to run away – but it was still a dragon and chances were it was still out there.

He loitered near the mouth of the tunnel, listening, waiting for dark. There weren't any sounds of people, no screams, no dragon cries. When he followed the stars out of hiding, he saw why. He saw what had happened. What Skjorl had done. Another dragon. On his own this time with just his bare hands and an axe. Smug bastard.

From where he stood there was no way to tell whether the dragon was completely dead, and there was no way he was going close enough to find out. He skirted around it. Got water and then walked the long way around the Midnight Garden to the beach below the waterfall and helped himself to some choice cuts of the dead there. He found Nezak there, dead. He took a moment to go over his body, and Parris too, but the outsiders had got to both of them first and there was nothing left to take.

When he went back inside the alchemist seemed herself again. She was weak and pale, but she was the Kataros he remembered from the Purple Spur. The spear-carrier. He offered her water.

'I came to find you,' he told her. 'I'm supposed to bring you back to the Pinnacles. All the riders who came with me are dead now. There's just you and me.' He shrugged. 'What do we do?'

She shivered. Her face was still stained with tears. 'We go to the Spur. I will gather my order and we will come here again and we will make these gateways open. That's all that's left to us.'

'Through the Raksheh? There are snappers.'

'We'll use the river.'

'There's the worm.'

'I will soothe it.'

'We'll get hungry.'

'I'll show you what you can eat. There may be more outsiders though.'

'I'll get a new string for my a bow. There'll be dragons once we get outside the forest.'

'I'll make potion to hide us.'

'It'll take a long time to get to the Spur.'

'We'll be quick. There was a dragon outside. Has it gone?'

Jasaan shook his head. He couldn't help half a smile. 'Skjorl brought the hill down on it.' Had to rub it in, didn't he?

'Skjorl?' She seemed surprised, if only for a moment. 'He did that?'

'He's dead now.' Jasaan searched the alchemist's face. She didn't seem much bothered. 'Are you hurt?'

'I'm weak. That's all.'

He nodded and waited to be told what to do. While he was waiting, the alchemist curled up and went to sleep. After a bit, Jasaan did the same.

Acknowledgements

My thanks go to my agent, John Jarrold, and to my editor at Gollancz, Simon Spanton, whose faith that 'Yes, I know how this will all end' as yet seems to know no bounds. They go yet again to my wife Michaela, widowed on many evenings by fire-breathing monsters. They go to Hugh Davis, who has copy-edited most if not all of these dragon stories and always for the better.

One or two of you managed to creep some names into this. Well done. A nod to DM Rich and the crazy dwarf and his missus too.

Thank you for reading this. As always, if you liked this story, please tell others who might like it too.